The Last Flight Home

Ricky Hausler

Federal Service Books—Tampa, FL
ISBN: 979-8-9896126-1-1
eBook ISBN: 979-8-9896126-0-4
Library of Congress Control Number: 2023924369
Title: *The Last Flight Home*
Author: Ricky Hausler
Digital distribution | 2023
Paperback | 2023

Dedication

For those who never made it home. No matter the conflict, nor the side.

Table of Contents

Chapter 1
All Stop

Overwhelming. Bright red. Enormous. That's all John Thomas -JT- Wayne could recall of the monstrosity that had knocked him out into space. Now he lay stricken inside an infirmary ward. He had little to think about except his buddies and the men and women still onboard the *Vissad*. No doubt fighting for their lives. The truth was, they were all already dead—vaporized by a spectacular bombardment of destruction no feral imagination could conceive. No funerals, no honors, no speeches, or charades to commemorate the sacrifice of the Vissad's crew. Just a big black debris cloud and a radiation-littered quadrant, seven klicks across, expanding like a cancer—a cancer that memorialized yet mocked their existence.

But Wayne knew none of that as he lay wide-awake on his white sanitized sheets sifting helplessly through his own memories. His cloudy recollections. What he had of them. He would try to think of ways he could rejoin his brothers-in-arms, but even this was a challenge. His thoughts kept returning to that moment he experienced the tremendous and powerful force from some enemy cruiser. The giant cloud of red matter that jolted him from duty, left him unconscious and blew him into space with shock wave force; nothing he had ever experienced before, nor wanted to again.

The destruction of his vessel was an event long expected by those in the service who believed in luck, or lack thereof, curses, the occult, unexplainable forces and the like. The Vissad was named after Captain Eric Vissad, an Angolan fleet commander who met his end in the third Inter-Stellar War. Long ago this starship on which Wayne would serve earned a reputation as a cursed ship. A ship on which no sailor or Marine wanted to be. She had been christened in a ceremony that injured a port-worker and killed an engineering director. It was a freakish un-mooring accident that none could completely explain.

Despite the multitude of after-the-fact investigations ordered by very high levels of fleet command, the reports all proved inconclusive.

There were many facts and fictions surrounding the ship and its lineage. A dangerous quadrant-wide meteor shower had cancelled her maiden voyage, but by the time the shower would have reached the ship's charted course area, it had mysteriously disappeared. In fact, other ships had shortly thereafter sailed the very same space and each logged smooth journeys without a trace of debris. This was only one of the many peculiarities associated with the Vissad.

The first major battle in which she fought left her not much more than a scrap of space junk—nearly half of the crew was killed or wounded, and more than a hundred were listed missing. Fleet evaluation teams deemed her nearly irreparable. As such, she was put on the docket of junked cruisers to be stripped of classified material, usable hardware, control systems and electronics.

As luck would have it, shortly after her near-destruction, a division sized battle left all fleet power-core resources in limited supply, and the Vissad was sent to the repair docks instead. Some sailors whispered that her power-core was the reason: cursed by the very engineer who was found dead after the un-mooring. The autopsy revealed he had suffered for ten minutes from intense radiation before succumbing. This—just as emergency workers found him outside the core's atomic pulse generator room. One medic recalled the man had whispered a single word during the resuscitation attempts,—*damned*, or *doomed* he thought. But the medic could not tell for sure as the engineer was already dead. Or at least he appeared to be. No heartbeat. No breath at all. There was; moreover, no valid reason he should have been near the atomic generator room. The generators were in good order and one would think the head engineer would have been at the engineering bridge during her initial un-mooring. More disturbing was the lack of explanation for why the room's sealed three-inch thick, depleted uranium lined, polymer-based glass hatch should have failed. But it did.

Whatever the reason for them, the list of eerie events and mishaps aboard the Vissad went on. And so, when she finally met her end, there were some in the fleet who felt relieved that the cursed ship was now a piece of space-history. There was in truth a greater number of souls who were glad the ship was gone than those saddened by her loss. But in a way the Vissad was left to sail on, if only now in Valhalla… the warrior's paradise… haunting her enemies… and perhaps her own crew.

Try as he might, Wayne could not recall anything following the burst of red energy. He knew that orders for 'reverse thrusters' were given. Then 'prepare to embark.' All Marines at the ready. Boarding and attack transport vessels filled. After he launched his platoon, he prepared to re-enter his transport from the tight and extremely narrow oval commander's hatch. Then came the command, 'all thrusters full stop.' The Vissad slowed and before he even entered his craft- the intense short burst of red light, a long cold pelting sensation, followed by the feeling of falling, weightlessness, *was that a new weapon?* Then BLAM! He was suddenly and instantly transported to his current state- bandaged, drugged and immobilized. Quite a predicament for a gung-ho Marine.

Hooah was anything and everything positive; a favorite term military folks used when at a loss for words. It was generally synonymous with "yes," "sounds good," "affirmative," "understood," or "excellent." If hooah was anything positive, then JT was stagnating in the infirmary world of *anti-hooah.* He was now on the fourth level of St. Demetrius' Forward Fleet Hospital, somewhere several parsecs behind the front. Not exactly where a young, motivated, up and coming Federal Marine wanted to be. He was incapacitated. He should be leading his platoon in battle; that is where he was meant, wanted, and needed to be. But at the moment his desires and reality were at odds. Instead of fighting with his men he was wasting time in the infirmary - ugh. Not hooah.

His instincts kept gnawing at him to get out of bed. Depart as fast as he could. Run to the nearest port. Fly off to his ship and get back to the fight. Wherever that was. His thoughts bounced back and forth like a hologram ball between three walls: his incapacitation and how to escape the infirmary, the medicine concoction he was being fed, and the vague recollection of the mysterious red-light blast. Then, the black cloud of lost memory.

This last thought: that blast. It would not leave his mind. It kept leading him back to preceding events. Trying—trying hard—to piece them together. His logic was sound. But all the details were not. The call. The embarkation scramble. Getting his men on the shuttle and off the ship. Outside and into space. The blur.

He couldn't help but wonder how Sergeant Johanas was doing with the men. His second-in-command was more than capable. Johanas was a leader. A career Marine. He would spend forty years soldiering and retire from the service. Of that Wayne was sure. If the young non-commissioned officer lived that long. The way this war was going, nothing was for sure. Johanas would surely get the men into action quickly. They were all well-trained. There was no doubt about that.

JT's was the best platoon in the brigade. Maybe even the division. They were good men and they were excellent Marines. Loyal, duty-bound, motivated. They exuded what it was to be a Federal Marine. Then his thoughts shifted back to the infirmary. It was not healthy to think about that stuff: the fixations over which he had no control. His wandering mind, so it seemed, was not a bad thing: at least he couldn't dwell on the bad for long.

The main object that kept Wayne's mind off of his crewmates was a wonderful synthetic strawberry ice-cream soda like medicine. The doctors kept delivering it to his bedside. He could picture himself: five years old in junior school at lunchtime savoring the flavor of strawberries and ice-cream mixed together with pure carbon-water. It was delicious. This was his favorite treat as a kid, which into adolescence and then adulthood, turned into his favorite dessert. Strawberry ice-cream soda: at least that's what it tasted like to him. Without fail every hour, or so it seemed, another one of these delicious escapes was brought inconspicuously to his bedside. Each time a straw and napkin accompanied the medicine.

Like his last memory, time was a blur. After two,—or maybe it was ten—minutes though, the drink was gone. Every one of them lapped up heartily by the young Marine sergeant. And then, he would return to his quest of trying to remember exactly what happened. *What had happened aboard the strange and only battle-cruiser in the Federal Alliance to see combat in both the last two inter-stellar wars?* Between his thoughts of getting back into the fray and this tasty medicine, he tried to piece together how he landed here. He had clearly been rescued from space during a deadly and intense scrap out on the edge of the Near Universe. But the rescue? No recollection at all.

Try as he might, keeping track of time in the infirmary was a futile battle. He never really fell into a truly deep sleep. Something inside his stomach would wake him every now and then to check on the status of the next strawberry medicine. The ice-cream soda dose as he liked to think. This was just as well; since his body was adapted to sleeping half-awake in short stints. It helped keep him alert and constantly aware of his surroundings. Even while resting. Sort of like a fish. But any Marine he met would agree that Wayne was more of a cunning but rogue shark. He was a puma not an alley-cat. This erratic and very alert method of snoozing by cat-nap kept him in command of the mental edge in combat. Losing the edge was one of a Federal Marines' worst fears. He wouldn't let that happen.

Every now and then a new doctor or doctrette (a physician's assistant or nurse practitioner of the 21st-century era) would come by and check his vital signs. They would jot down a note or two, see if he needed more of the medicine mush he enjoyed, and move on to the next bed. He could go on like this but he didn't want to; it was certainly a comfortable way to pass the time, but just passing time was not in his character.

JT convinced himself he was set to get out of the infirmary. He would have tried harder to leave, but while he thought he was ready, the doctors and doctrettes disagreed. And of course, he was not quite so ready that he didn't still enjoy a visit from a cute one. The few good-looking docs who attended his ward wouldn't make him sit up or take serious note, but he didn't mind the attention. He wished that there were more healers of the fairer sex. More attractive ones at least.

There were more females in the medical corps than previous centuries, especially as doctors and doctrettes. But their stationings were limited this far forward. Here it was more likely to encounter the usual grumpy over-the-hill doctor-officer the Federal Marines seemed so fond of commissioning. Most doctors who came to check up on him just took his vital signs. They made notes, grunted or nodded as if to say something important to themselves then shuffled on their way.

But it was different when a young lady visited him donning a hospital coat, a hint of soft makeup, maybe a touch of lipstick, gentle eyeliner, and most noticeably: a smile. The female doctors and doctrettes had a softer touch even with the cold metallic equipment and sensors draped around their supple necks. Either they cared more, or their natural instinct was more care-giving. The female human or Cybrinthian touch was much warmer and less impersonal than a man's.

Cybrinthians were a race of blueish human-like aliens that had come to the home solar system in search of new planets eons ago. They bred with humans and inter-mixed with them.

Yes, he thought, *women make much better physicians*.

He mused in fleeting reveille that it was too bad these physicians could not serve aboard forward deployed vessels. No doctors or surgeons of either sex served on forward deployed attack ships. There was a long period centuries ago when women could not in any capacity. But times had changed long before JT became a Marine and now human, Cybrinthian, male, female or neuter could serve side by side if their position warranted it. JT wished the Vissad could have had a few cute healers, but it could not. On second thought, maybe that was a good thing.

Morale was a closely linked, yet precariously perched subject as it related to maintaining the combat edge for a Marine. The state of a soldier or Marine's mind was a basketball in play. Its fast movement went up and down no matter what the direction of travel. And the shot clock was always on.

So the healers came and went from the ward. Every once in a while, one would give him a funny glance or look twice at his name. JT had the misfortune of sharing his namesake, John T. Wayne, with the outgoing Chancellor of the Federal Alliance—not a terribly popular character at best. It was also the first and last name of a once famous but now obscure film actor from centuries ago. But few people except ancient historical cinema experts would know that. However, the commonality with the Chancellor was a good topic for small talk. At least with the pretty doctrettes and doctors who periodically came to check on his and the other patients' conditions. To JT those visits were too infrequent.

Chapter 2
JT

Wayne, Jonathan T., his personal security identification (SID) number was 1002-201377-8718. Sergeant Jonathan Thomas Wayne. That's all he knew himself ever to be. He was most often called just JT. Sometimes he was called John or Jonathan, but only by close buddies, family, and those who made it into his personal inner circle. John was short for Johannes, a maternal family name. Jonathan was a paternal family name. John, or J., stood for them both. JT was a name that his childhood friends had used since his mother first marked J. T. Wayne on his clothes and school gear. John Thomas Wayne. But the nickname his little friends used caught on with all, and his family quickly adopted it. Occasionally, military officials and authorities who got to know him or those wishing to joke with him would also use the moniker. To everybody else; however, JT rarely went by John, Jonathan, JT, or any other derivation. Most of the time he was just *Sgt. 1ˢᵗ Class, Sarge,* or *Sergeant Wayne.* In front of his men, his superiors, and others this was always the case. Sarge was a title his friends respected but never would have used while keeping personal company. He wished he still had contact with them. If he hadn't followed suit with his vow to serve the alliance.

Most of his childhood buddies had joined the Marines, other branches of service, or gone off to far away star systems. No one stayed in Angola very long after the war began. That seemed so long ago now. Regardless, he himself would have preferred *JT* or first names with all Marines. But regulations and tradition were what they were. And most were in place for good reason. He was not going to draw attention over something trivial—use of a nickname at that. Sergeant Wayne truly believed in the order and regimented lifestyle he had chosen. He did question the institution from time to time, but he picked his battles carefully. He knew the old maxim touted by a long-dead revolutionary was true: Sir John Mennes had said in Great Britain in 1641 to ridicule his competitor: "'Tis better to fight but run away, and live to fight another day." Or words to that effect as JT recalled. It was wise to recognize and believe in a just cause, but to be able to let it go when an ensuing fight was un-winnable, was wiser.

Being wise in the face of adversity, was what led JT to join the military. It had not been terribly long since JT joined the service. He easily remembered back to those early days as a Marine. In the mess hall one morning, an argument developed quickly into a shoving match between two troops. He didn't recall what the disputed point was, nor was it important. What he did remember was that his squad-mate came to the aid of one of the fighters. JT's buddy, Raffordy, was the man who tried to help the smaller of the two combatants. Raffordy simply tried to break up the scuffle. At a notch under two meters, Raffordy was not a big man himself. But then again, none of them really were big men. Most were 19 or 20. Some were indeed big *boys*, but *men* they were not. Yet. Twenty was legally the minimum age to enter federal service, but since the war, any young man who applied at 19 was accepted, and there were even some 18-year-olds who joined with waivers from authorities so long as the youth's parents agreed to allow it.

Raffordy was 19, he was shy of the two meters, or six and a half feet or so needed for mechanized bot pilot most Marines strived for. He was smaller than either of the two fighters, but nonetheless he stepped in trying to settle the affair before any of the non-coms or non-commissioned officers or warrant officers came along to quell it themselves. Officers meant settlement with less than desirable means or outcomes. Too often that involved some form of public punishment or humiliation. And Raffordy was a good comrade. He helped others no matter what. A team player who wanted the best for his mates; his fellow Marines.

So Raffordy was pulling the bigger Marine off of the smaller one, trying to talk some sense into them both. Meanwhile, in walked the company senior warrant, second in command only to the unit captain. The end result was this: all three men -Raffordy included- received severe punishment. JT was outraged that his friend, who was only trying to help, would be punished at all. And worse, he got the same punishment as the sorry excuses that started the whole affair. As he was only a first-private, JT could do little about it, but that didn't stop him from going straight to the company captain to plead Raffordy's case. It didn't work. So, JT went to the battalion, then brigade sergeant major; both warrant officers. That didn't work either. Then JT sought audiences with the battalion major-captain, then the brigade lieutenant-captain. Neither entertained his complaint. As he requested an audience with the division commander and warrant sergeant major, the general got wind of this outspoken private making a stink about a fight in the mess. It flowed back down the chain of command that First-Private Wayne was to cease his shenanigans at once. If he did not, he too would suffer disciplinary action for inciting unrest, and insubordination.

JT gave up after that, but it always bothered him that the injustice took place. Injustice in JT's mind at least. What his warrant sergeant explained to him was that an example had to be shown to others in the unit. JT disagreed. The company senior warrant sergeant tried to make him understand. The lesson had to be taught to the other 200 Marines that taking justice into their own hands with their peers was never a good idea. No matter what the intention. The right answer would have been to send for a sergeant or officer to break it up. It would have taken only seconds to call outside the mess hall door. The other Marines needed to see the right way to handle that particular situation. They had to learn if they didn't handle it correctly, they would be punished as well. It was a hard lesson and JT only begrudgingly accepted it. This, he learned only after causing a significant stir all the way up to the divisional command.

There were other incidents like that. There were some close calls, but somehow, he survived unscathed from each of them. A few times he walked the line very closely. And when his foot went deep into his mouth, after some pain or embarrassment, it eventually came out. Generally, he was able to quell his own fervor and stubbornness. Sometimes others saw him as malicious. As a trouble maker. But he was really nothing more than a pragmatic idealist living the life of a warrior in a less than ideal universe. His youth and experiences left him tainted… by good things and bad. He liked to focus on those stories of heroes from his former life. Not ones of sadness and tragedy. Tragedy could build strength; joy could bring complacency and weakness—if one let them. JT certainly knew of both. He had lived through each- but some memories were better left repressed. There were not many who tried to see the glass half-full in the Marines. JT was one of those few. The young warrant was surely an anomaly. He was a role model, but an unpredictable one. A bit of a firebrand; though usually positive. He tried not to cause distress. Most of the time at least...

JT was a good Marine; one of the best in his own and his men's estimations. But he was certainly not irreplaceable. Any Marine was expendable should he end up space dust on some remote meteor. He knew his small part of the fight was just that- a small, a very small, in truth- a nearly insignificant part of the war. He was one out of millions involved in this mighty conflict. But some way he knew that his part was to be important. He felt it. He was different from most Marine warrant sergeants or officers. He often preferred to keep to himself, but still he knew how to have fun and make light of a dire situation. He brought humor and good spirits to those around him. When in battle he was focused like a laser aimed right at his enemies. He drew men with him toward that destructive light. He could be ferocious when needed. But he hated that need and in principle he hated the need for his profession.

He had many interests outside of the Marines. He read books, played an ancient instrument, the saxophone, and between missions, he hiked in the wilderness of alien worlds. Unfortunately, since the war began, he had little time for any of that. JT's most unique quality was that he looked for the goodness in people and trusted others unless presented with reasons otherwise. He knew this was a dangerous practice in a line of work like the federal service. But, *this is what it is* his father told him at a young age—*you can't change who you are, just make it work and use it as strength in whatever you do.* JT tried to heed that advice but it was difficult to follow at times as trying as this.

He missed his father. His dad, technically his surrogate father and uncle; Gus, had died when JT was 19. The loss was hard on everyone in JT's family but it allowed JT to move on from any desires he had to remain in Angola or even on any of Jupiter's moons. A year later, JT joined the service, ready for something new, and to get away from his old home and memories that clouded his normally positive and upbeat outlook. This was before the war. JT always had the unshakable feeling that the tragedy that took his surrogate father's life had to do with politics. A corrupt political situation that led to the great conflict of which he was now a part. By now, six years later, the war had reached planets everywhere and it pained him that the fleet couldn't bring it to an abrupt end. And at this moment it pained JT that he was not doing anything either to help end it.

JT was born to Lisa and John William Wayne sometime in late 1478AN. By then it was over five-thousand years since the birth of Christianity's Jesus. 1478AN could be considered 5328AD/CE, or 4749 by Muslims and a few other human religious groups. But, however one measured it, it was the year JT came into being.

An average sized baby, JT showed incredible promise. The boy grasped concepts like counting and conservation of mass before reaching two years old. At four, JT could pull apart electronics and put them back together. As a baby he crawled at two months, made words at three, and walked within a year. Before that first year of his life was even finished though, tragedy struck his family. JT's parents were killed in a traffic accident. There was no noble cause for their deaths. Simply a drunken pilot's inability to keep his craft safely in the lane of a crowded causeway. Head on impact. Quick, painless. Quick for four or five of the six involved. All four occupants in the drunk's craft were killed instantly. JT's parents were not as fortunate. His mother died within 10 minutes of paramedics arriving on the scene. Her last frail words to her husband, "Take care of our son, you know I love..."

His father was critically injured but survived until the ride to the hospital. Medic transport craft were incredibly adept at preserving life. The computer systems onboard monitored everything possible about the patient. Brain activity. Neural impulses throughout all body systems. Individual cell movements. Bone condition. Pain intensity and effects of all treatment on those, and more. Through thin malleable probes inserted directly into veins or arteries, these microcomputers did amazing things. They could slow, divert, or direct blood flow. Influence migration of white blood cells to critical organs. Speed up clotting to a tenth of its normal time, and much more in the hands of a skilled medic. But for his father, all the technology available was to no avail.

For all true purposes John William Wayne died the moment Lisa did. It was when she passed that he too lost the will to live. Any doctrette, physician, or medical expert will attest to this: it is the desire to be alive that allows a near mortally injured person to survive. The dying can overcome near impossible injuries in cases where his or her will overcomes the physical ailments. The moment John William saw his wife breathe her last, he no longer harbored the will of his own to go on. In a slow painful fashion, his life left him. It trickled away little by little until the medics revived him. Then revived him again. Then finally in the transport, even the best care possible could not save him. He passed away grief stricken, without thought of his son, or reasons to live, just his lost lover and his broken heart.

Since JT's real parents died before he knew or would remember them it was only stories and anecdotes of them that he knew. There was a briefly vague vision, maybe two, JT had as an infant of his mother and father looking at him as he played. Then in JT's mind they gazed at him with wonder and joy before rocking and kissing him goodnight. Everything else he knew of them he learned from others. He was quickly adopted by his uncle, Gus, who he knew only as his father from then on and all of his life. Gus Wayne was a wonderful father who reveled in JT's amazing progress. Gus and his wife Sarah put JT in accelerated learning programs and many expected JT to do remarkable and great things.

JT grew into a fairly handsome young man. He stood 2.1 meters, slightly less than seven feet. He could bench press twice his weight. He ran one of the fastest quarter-mile sprints in his secondary school. JT was one of the more popular students with friends and teachers alike. He had a square jaw, prominent upper body that was incredibly toned, dirty blond hair, and a very formal gait. He talked softly but was well spoken. When he spoke, it was commanding: others listened.

In social gatherings JT always chose the back of the room. For a bulky man of above average height, he blended into crowds rather well; he chose to do so as much as possible.

JT had a dark complexion. While a descendant of mostly white skinned humans, he likely had a mix of many other races in his ancestry. His surrogate mother thought his blood had African, Asian, and even maybe a touch of Cybrinthian in it. He had relatives elsewhere other than in Angola and even outside of the Milky Way. He had family on some of the AX planets, and some more distant kin on minor planets of obscure star systems. His lineage hailed from the far reaches of the Near Universe. No one had ever shown him a family tree, but he was sure if someone did it would have included traces of life from many places in the known universes.

JT had varied interests that branched out into all sorts of different areas. He grew up playing sports but found a tremendous amount of solace in music. He spent free time exploring and he ventured out often to places beyond safety for a child. Prior to secondary school his closest friends were a mix of races. But they were all well-behaved. He never had problems with the law or illegal activities unlike many youngsters growing up in rural Angola.

At sixteen he fell in love. Or so he thought. Mariel Farsew was the girl with whom he thought he would spend the rest of his days. Like many young loves, it was not meant to be for they grew apart quickly as teenagers do. By the time he was eighteen; to him she was no longer the shining star she had once been. And to her, JT wasn't the prince she imagined he would have turned out to be. JT became engrossed in competitions, sports, music, the military and other pursuits which diverged from hers. And so, they parted ways, peaceably. He heard news of her from time to time and from mutual friends who moved out of Angola around the same time she did, but that was it. And that was fine. Love was a distraction, for a Federal Marine anyway. *If the force wanted you to have a family, they'd have issued you one!* was a favorite expression of haughty warrant sergeants.

JT's core group of friends remained in contact for as long as his tours of military service would allow. The friends to which he was closest did so all the way until their own ends. Or at least until the ends of their military service, in whatever form that took: happily sometimes. Sometimes in a flag-draped space coffin to much fanfare. Sometimes just an unknown designation often with many family tears and heartache.

Regardless of their various ends and send-offs, these buddies all thought JT would go on to do incredible things with his life. His friends and the adults around him were in agreement with regard to opinions of JT's future. Had there been a "most likely to succeed" award during JT's adolescent and teenage school years, he would have won it again and again.

On the whole, JT had a happy childhood. While young, he certainly was very accomplished. He was playing for his college athletic programs in two different sports and had top marks in most of his subjects. But for all the expectations and high hopes of others, by JT's adulthood, it wouldn't come to pass. When Gus died, all his progress came to an abrupt halt before JT finished college. For the second time in his young life, tragedy struck. When Gus was killed, it was no accident. His surrogate father's death was the result of a horrible hostage incident in Angola when JT was still in school. He was 19, and, of course the death was unexpected. Most troubling though was the way in which the hostage incident was handled by authorities. It was this event among others, never clear to JT, that was intertwined in a complex web of life problems for which he could not quite piece together answers.

This puzzle of disputes generally included Angolans and their allies within the Federal Alliance. By default, it incorporated the vast number of planets and nations that fell under Federation territory. Even those populations which were not overt members of the alliance. They believed they were fighting unchecked aggression which had been unprovoked. On the other side of the issue was a confederacy of planets from the Far Universe whose ideals were completely divergent from those of the Federation. Like most conflicts, its seeds were not planted simply and neatly.

Chapter 3
1503

3850 Anno Domini was the final year of the first Great Inter-Stellar War. This year I-S hostilities between human separatists and the human-Cybrinthian alliance reached their climax. Since the mass exodus of people from Earth in 3850, mankind generally adopted the next year as year 1 of the new age. Most used the new system and referred to counting years as After New Age (AN) or assumed it. Internationally and interplanitarily all races recognized this system. Except for the few deeply religious sects which refused to convert to the new system, most eventually acquiesced and embraced AN.

After that time no life existed anymore on old Earth. However, the planet's rotation around Alpha-Centauri continued as a universally accepted means of time measurement. And so, years of life known by ancient civilizations on Earth continued. Early humankind would not have guessed that its methods of understanding time could continue in such a universal capacity. That a small world's dimensions would be used by life across inexorable distances would have amazed humanity.

It had now been 1503 years since that first war that ended life on Earth. Two other major conflicts had been fought and concluded since then: the 2nd and 3rd Great I-S Wars. The 4th Great Inter-Stellar War was currently underway without a clear end in sight. This confrontation was a mess. A mess which entangled humankind and the near and far universal alien races. Unlike the 1st I-S War though, this struggle had little to do with the differences between humans and Cybrinthians. It was a political and social clash. A clash of technology and ways of life. The differences of 2,000 years prior were now a thing of history and archives. They were not forgotten, but neither were they a dominating force of the present.

Cybrinthians were a race of aliens who sought refuge on Earth after their home world of Cybrinth decayed. It had failed to support life several thousand years prior. Their technology; however, allowed travel across vast amounts of space through a hibernation-freeze process. They had also developed the ability to travel many times light speed. Unfortunately, these advances were lost completely with their landings on Earth. Their craft and the technology which engineered them were purposefully developed in secret and erased from archive memories prior to landings around 3475. No one knew why. Cybrinthian leaders only believed that it had been done in order to avoid disaster. The knowledge was dangerous and it could destroy any race that used it for wrong.

Cybrinthians' biological make up was mildly human-like. Aided by some early genetic engineering, eventually a blending of races flourished. Despite the purposeful erasure of certain Cybrinthian technology, even those achievements which remained were far more advanced than anything on Earth at the time. Scientific and technological accomplishment was the biggest difference between the species. Physically, Cybrinthians stood a foot or so shorter than most humans. Humankind averaged two meters or a bit more than six and a half feet by 3850 with a few inches variance only between the sexes. Cybrinthians were generally stronger, but not wholly or individually more intelligent than humans. They were just more developed as a species. More advanced. More dangerous? Maybe. They possessed a prominent spinal column which looked like a series of small bumps running the vertical length of their backs. Cybrinthians' skin tended to have a dark blue tint, but, like skin tones of humans, it varied to large degrees. They were not an ugly or unattractive race by any human standard. But outside the opaque visor of a space suit, there was no mistaking a human from a Cybrinthian.

The races cohabitated Earth well at first, but eventually they grew apart and factionalized into predominately different nations. The countries ultimately formed alliances with nations of a similar racial makeup. Differences and disagreements over Earth's fledging natural resources reached an incredibly high intensity. Fanatic human separatists who desired deportation of Cybrinthians to Jupiter's moons or Mars became an outspoken minority. This minority agenda grew in popularity as the whole situation grew worse.

Human controlled states eventually launched several nuclear chain warheads against Cybrinthian countries and strongholds on Earth. The Cybrinthian cities were destroyed, but so was the ability for Earth to effectively sustain life. Within weeks, areas hundreds of square miles around the Cybrinthian held cities of Alexandria and Jerusalem were fast becoming barren waste lands. Several other former population centers soon followed suit. Within weeks, global leaders on both sides of the conflict publicly admitted what everyone already knew: life as all had known it could no longer exist on Earth.

The only solution was to shuttle as much of the population as possible to colonies established on Mars, recently terraformed Jupiterian moon Europa, and a handful of more remote planets. At the time, the Martian colonies were thriving but fast approaching capacity. Europa had more space for immediate colonization and quick expansion; but, with the greater distance to travel, the transport systems in place could only shuttle a few thousand people each month. Plus, Jupiter's proximity and gaseous state was still a newly hurdled obstacle. The generational long-term effects upon the various species now living on Europa was a question still due to be answered. Mars became the de facto short-term evacuation world. Jupiterian moon colonies, less developed and farther away, would not become viable major exodus points for centuries.

The government run federal transport systems for the two planets were antiquated and inefficient. So, most of the transporting was done at the time by private corporations. Since the trip to Europa took several months and there was much less demand for anything but cargo, there were few companies making it. Quicker profits could be turned around from Mars-bound voyages.

Despite fewer departures, the transport ships to Jupiter's moon were able to move larger loads than the smaller shuttles built for Mars. Built for massive terraforming, gas condensation and solidification equipment, they had twice the power, four or more times the tonnage as other Mars-bound vessels. Their greater stores and durability for long distance travel were crucial in survival as Earth died. During the

3850 evacuations, these mammoth ships became critical in saving both people and Cybrinthians. As soon as scientists and leaders recognized the irreparable nature of Earth, most of the big transports were immediately re-diverted to Mars.

There was much time lost during the initial set-up of decontamination and holding areas for those affected worst by the radiation. There was fall-out everywhere from detonated munitions of these weapons of massive destruction. Earth's war-scorched cities and sprawling radiated zones were either barren waste lands or fast becoming them. The emergency facilities were quickly overflowed as people continued to die. Mass panic ensued as officials with their own agendas debated the levels of safety required to admit and treat people. Corruption was rampant before the war and now politicians were openly hostile. They ceased working together to maintain order when the planet needed it most. Rioters burned a few of the evacuation sites and decontamination centers. Some even attacked shuttlecraft outbound from Earth. None were destroyed but a few were forced to abort initial take offs.

People tried to tunnel deep underground, but in the end nothing short of escape worked. Ten months after the initial attacks, all air breathing life forms still exposed to Earth's atmosphere were dead. Slightly fewer than 180,000 lives had been safely evacuated from the planet. Before all of the evacuations, the Martian colony had a population of 150,000. There were 2,000 living in the colonies on Europa. And then there were a handful, just a few hundred each, on the three other far-reaching planet colonies. 43 billion humans and 14 billion Cybrinthians had been quickly reduced to a few hundred thousand. A large stadium crowd. The 1st I-S War was the single most destructive event in the history of the Near Universe. It completely destroyed Earth.

Peace followed the first Great I-S War for more than a thousand years. With the war of 3850/1NA an event of the past, Mankind and Cybrinthians tried to rebuild and not make the same mistakes. Cybrinthians intermixed with humans and traces of the two separate races began to disappear. Eventually, space travel improved so that mankind established significant colonies outside of the Milky-Way

Galaxy and immediately surrounding star systems. Technologies lost from the Cybrinthians were rediscovered. Light speed travel became a reality once again. Known as *neo*, or Neon Based Travel, it allowed humans and Cybrinthians to spread across the Milky Way and closer galaxies. A few remote populations on planets outside of the galactic systems were established. Then, they began to develop in isolation. These were primarily the Andromeda experimental worlds, known as AX planets. Periodically, attempts by fanatical groups to re-constitute the old segregations between humans and Cybrinthians developed. But these were failed movements. Then, in 1237AN, two new factions began to develop.

The alliance of Jupiterians and Martians was solidified when the Prime Minister of Angola, the largest country on Europa, was killed. He was assassinated by a foreign AX1 extremist. Unfortunately for the resultant political fall-out, Angola was not only the largest, but also the richest and most developed country on Europa. While really an isolated event, the assassination was magnified by all sorts of media. But it was incorrectly deemed so. Politically motivated? This it was not.

By 1245, there was open aggression between Martians, Jupiterians and inhabitants of AX1 and 2. Next to the Milky-Way, the Andromeda Galaxy encompassed the most developed quadrant in the Near Universe. It consisted of a loose confederation of the planets AX1, 2, 3, and 4. Of the two groups, the Martian-Jupiterian alliance was more developed and organized. It was made up of predominately human ancestral descendants; roughly three fourths human and the remainder Cybrinthian. But countless inhabitants were of mixed decent. The racial makeup looked much like that of the original inhabitants of Earth prior to year 1. The newer faction, the AX planets, was truly a hybrid of races. One could barely tell the difference here between humans and Cybrinthians.

The Andromeda planets were a great distance from the Milky Way. In the early days of neo travel this was significant. Cybrinthian bodies were naturally more adept at long-distance space travel. As such, more made the trip to the AX planets. Though hibernation-freeze technology was lost, Cybrinthians and their descendants could spend much longer periods aboard space shuttles without major health consequences. Their bodies offered easy tolerance to the prolonged rigors of neo: prolonged distance hyper-space faster than light-speed travel. For this fact and others, the AX planets were racially different than most planets in the Milky Way. Their populations were of prevailingly Cybrinthian ancestry and heritage.

Isolated populations develop their own customs and traditions. The AX planets were no exception. They collectively voted along similar lines. This was especially so when alliance issues regarding taxation and spending came before the combined senate. They favored more development from exploration and research. Some said it was their latent nature to search out their home planet quadrant of the Universe. Perhaps it was just that -instinct.

Despite several reasons, the largest cause for discord centered on the tax issue. Planets and nations of predominately Cybrinthian descent disagreed with more human populated ones over the high levels of importation taxes and where that money should be spent. The planetary factions grew more intense and lines were drawn deeper and deeper. The sides diverged more forcefully over not just taxes but where all planetary alliance money was to be spent following the assassination in Angola. A decade later, there was armed conflict. And by 1260, the Ango-Mar-Jupean Pact, a loose confederation of Martian and Jupiterian states, had declared war on the AX-planetary alliance. After six years of military destruction, mainly of the various national fleets, the war finally ended.

This conflict became known as the Second Great Inter-Stellar War. It only truly ended with the complete demise and surrender of Angola. The surrender caused the Ango-Mar-Jupean Pact to fail, but nevertheless, peace ensued. By 1400, traces of old hatreds mostly vanished. To this day scholars consider it a miracle that all nations involved avoided the use of compound nuclear weapons. It mattered little that any manufacture of large scale nuclear weapons was strictly regulated. Despite unchecked manufacture being outlawed by an inter-galactic council, many feared a repeat of the First Great I-S War. Luckily, the 2nd I-S War never reached planetary destruction levels.

Since its end in 1266, over 200 years of peace and prosperity ensued. Nations and planets flourished then recovered from normal economic booms and busts. Alliances were made and galactic expansion continued. The largest alliance was that of a loose federation of solar systems in several galaxies across the Near Universe. It became known as the Federation but it was akin to the old League of Nations upon earth- it had no one overarching authority over its constituent nations and planets. Nor did it have a united military force. This intergalactic organization held ideals which centered around a belief in autonomy and independence of peoples and races.

The Federation states and planets recognized only an intergalactic senate with no supreme leader who held power over other senators, only an administrator – the chancellor, and his staff. It imposed little control over new colonies or planets outside the major participants in the senate. However, it did provide an intergalactic peace force. Akin to federal police sanctioned and financed by the united worlds, this police force was imposing but not overbearing upon those within the Federation. With this new police force and the advent of faster than light speed travel, quickly expanding frontiers of the universe could be patrolled. And they were.

Technological and scientific advancement moved at an incredible pace. *S-neo* (Super Neo(n) based travel) was 1,000 times single light-speed travel. This ability was reached and surpassed. Then a new goal was attained: *ES-neo*, (Extreme Speed Neo(n) based travel) or one billion times single light-speed travel. Great progress was made in the attempt to surpass this achievement as well. Distances once unheard of were traversed. The Near Universe and Far Universe were connected. The feat was a social equivalent which far eclipsed Christopher Columbus connecting old Earth's eastern and western hemispheres. It was a technological and social triumph like nothing else. But as all good things come to an end, this accomplishment too and its accompanying elation did not last indefinitely.

By 1475, war loomed once more and the 3rd Great I-S War would soon be upon the universes. Since the Near Universe and Far Universe had already been joined by ES-neo for all types of travel, this meant that commerce between the two great spaces began to flourish. With commerce though came greed. Old lines between races and nations surfaced once again. It seemed some races tended to control trade and profit more from the commerce associated with growing colonies. The trade rights on and around the border planets became the most heated topic of debate. Debates became more than just talk by the 1470s and eventually angry polarized organizations formed.

In late 1475, an alliance of Near Universe star systems and planets sent negotiating teams of ambassadors to the Far Universe. The teams managed to buy some time for continued talks but little more. The main problem centered on a race of violent imperialists, the Gnoracs (pronounced -nor-ack-). This alien race came from the Far Universe and was quickly encroaching on fringe colonies in the Near Universe. First they boycotted exports from planets along the universal border. Then the Gnoracs set up an unofficial blockade of all port planets. The action began to take its toll on Federation dominated populations in these remote worlds.

Really what the Gnoracs wanted most was proprietary rights on revenue generated from colonization of these worlds and their satellites. But they expressed these desires by economic sanctions, boycotts, and less noble means. Eventually, the sanctions turned to unorganized looting. This was a subtle but effective criminal destruction of Federation based organizations and businesses. They felt that since they were the strongest race in the region, it was perfectly within their purview to impose policy. The Gnoracs were an unchecked and wholly aggressive race which possessed the greatest amount of firepower anywhere in the border regions. Even more than Federation police. Within their own borders this aggression might have gone unnoticed or just flatly ignored. But upon remote Federation nations and federated planets, it did not.

The loose alliance of Near Universe worlds- essentially the Federation, now had a solid cause to unite. The nations made their common cause official in 1476 and reformed the Federation incorporating other allied planets and nations. The new Federation was known as the Universal Alliance of Advanced Federation Planets and Star Systems. It was commonly referred to as the Federal Alliance or just the Federation as the old smaller organization of previous years had been known.

The chief differences between the old and new Federation lay in two areas. One was a stricter intergalactic police system. Federal police exercised arrest and quasi-military power over all planets within the Federation territories. To a degree they even did so with planets that had not officially joined the Federation. The second was a disbandment of the chancellorship and his staff. There were now three chiefs of the senate who did exercise some powers over the combined governments. Each came from one of the three largest quadrants of the Federation. The system worked well and consolidated many of the formerly delegated or unexercised powers. Freedoms were more restricted but under the threat of Gnorac destruction and war, this was readily accepted as a preferable sacrifice.

The Leaders debated ways to combat the problem of increasingly dangerous and deadly Gnorac aggression. There were many competing proposals and many senators disagreed with the particulars they entailed. But one part upon which they agreed was that the current policies of appeasement were not working. The collective non-action was failing and so they began a subtle mobilization of forces. At first these were only political actions and strategic maneuvers to show the Gnoracs they meant business. But eventually the mobilization included entire national and planetary fleets.

After the stalled negotiations a brief period of military build-up occurred. During this time neither side did anything drastic enough to initiate open armed conflict. The Gnoracs knew human and Cybrinthian history. They knew the destruction the two races had brought upon each other in the past. And they knew neither race nor its allies wanted large scale war again. Throughout 1476 and into early 1477, the stalemate continued.

Late 1477. A bad time for peace. Gilney was a small planet in economic demise in a neutral quadrant. It was orbiting an old star on the border between Gnorac controlled territory and the Federation. Gnorac leadership declared the whole planet within the legal jurisdiction of their command. The planet had two major colonial population centers. One was under influence of the Federal Alliance and the other one under the Gnoracs. The planet itself had no native inhabitants. But it was a convenient and lucrative stop on a major route between the two universes.

Since the start of the Gnorac boycotts, both colonies had suffered greatly. The full-scale sanctions made it terminal for some populations on the planet. The Gnorac prime minister declared military control of all towns and people on Gilney. And then he invoked a set of martial laws designed to subdue any unrest. The power seizure was backed up with great martial force. The final straw was the arrival of super-transports with thousands of Gnorac soldiers within days of the declaration.

This cataclysmic event prompted an emergency session of Federation national and planetary representatives. They came from all over the Near Universe. The delegates voted to award immediate wartime powers to their three Chiefs of Senate. The chiefs then declared a state of war against the Gnorac Confederation. This state of bad affairs quickly spiraled into what became known as the Third Inter-Stellar War. It was to become the largest open conflict yet witnessed by human or alien kind from either universe.

Large scale open conflict in space was very impersonal. Warships were constructed of physical elements from different places and times. They comprised many systems and functioned in organizations controlled by live beings, but they were still just objects. The lumbering things of huge destructive and protective power did what they were commanded. Engines and thrusters sent the behemoths in directions ordered by pilots. The great guns and cannons they carried shot a myriad of death-wielding projectiles at whatever their ballistics crews aimed. The computers that served all the intricate systems and functions of the vessel carried out that which they were programmed to do. All in accordance with their operators' commands. Ship captains and commanders directed their crews making instant life or death decisions. They did so with the best available information they had. And the best technology for them to make it so. The ships performed well and reacted instantly in response to those decisions. But it was the crew members that piloted and fought those mammoth creations who felt the sting of those decisions.

The first shots of the 3rd I-S War were launched by vessels around orbit on Gilney. These early salvos were waged between a dozen medium and large sized cruisers. The ships belonged to fleets of several different nations from a few planets on each side. One ship meant thousands or even tens of thousands of lives. Luckily for the reluctant nations involved, not many ships were completely lost in this first battle. Only one large warship was totally destroyed.

For a small planet with a small population like Gilney, that battle changed her forever. A heavy battlecruiser from the Federation crash landed just outside a large Gilnean town. Instantly that metropolitan area was transformed into a triage center. It quickly became a hotel chain for troops, a command base for military leaders, and a staging area for deployments. The colonial town and shortly thereafter the whole planet doubled in size within weeks. By the war's end three years later there was not a spot of available real estate to be seen on Gilney. Even fresh battlegrounds were overturned to make room for more and more troops.

The 3rd I-S War was fought largely in space except for Gilney and two other border planets. These three worlds became a ground zero for carnage. Twenty-five years later, few soldiers or sailors who lived through the first crash landing on Gilney remained on the planet. But the cities remained, scarred, and tattered from the death and chaos. It was the accepted way of things during major planetary land battles.

Following the war these three border planets became breeding grounds for secret and illegal activity. Cargo that needed to disappear found its way to them. Contraband arms and munitions for para-military groups were often and easily stored there. People and beings that needed to escape authorities regularly made their way to these places. Gamblers, crime bosses, assassins, and bounty hunters frequented Gilney in particular, following the 3rd I-S War. They continued to do so through the turn of the 15th century AN. The border planets had possessed great futures as trade centers and resort worlds prior to the war. Following the Gnorac mobilization and Federation's war declaration, the border planets became slums. And sadly, other border planets followed suit. Soon a dozen once promising worlds were immense disappointments. Symbols. They reflected the fallen hopes and dreams that once flocked to colonize their growing outposts of opportunity.

And so, with this negative impact left upon many worlds, the 3rd I-S War ended in 1480. Most hoped and continued to hope into the next century that life-kind would have witnessed the last of mass carnage. Unfortunately, this was not to be true. After 1480, things calmed a bit and strict sanctions were imposed upon the belligerent losing Gnoracs. But even before JT was born in 1478, and the 3rd I-S War not yet over, things were heating up once again. Peace would last through 1497 when Gus died. 1500, still peace. 1503, no longer.

Chapter 4
Aurelle

JT coughed three times and then tapped his call sensor. A nurse, doctrette, possibly a doctor or technical specialist entered his section of the ward. She was young and very pretty. She made her way to him and asked if he was feeling alright.

"How are we feeling today Mr. Wayne?"

"Well I've…" he started. She looked down at her holographic clip board.

"Excuse me, *Sergeant* Wayne,"

"…I've got a splitting headache and…"

"My, my, Sergeant John Wayne." As she smiled at him.

"…Headache and I was wondering if…" he managed,

"…Are you by chance related to Chancellor Wayne?"

"…If I could FINISH my sentence?"

And so JT thought to himself, *This one has got to go to someone else, I'm going to have twice the headache if she sticks around me any longer.* He coughed again, as if to apologize and evoke some sympathy in repentance for his outburst. His head wandered away again distracted by her looks. *But she is pretty. And now she's blushing. Ahhgh.*

"Oh I'm so sorry," she apologized, "I just don't get to meet many Federal Marines, and a sergeant at that."

"Well it's not that great a thing, especially one so degraded like me," he retorted with a hint of a smile that betrayed he had already forgiven her.

She wanted to find out if he was indeed related to the chancellor but sensed that he was not quite in the mood to revisit the question, at least for the moment. She decided to make small talk instead.

"Degraded?" she asked.

Marines often could not turn off their jargon and forgot when speaking with civilians or even other branches of the service. Military non-Marines or sometimes any other live being, they had to translate into non-military, non-Marine speak. In JT's case, simply editing his musings a bit better might have done the trick.

"Means I'm busted, not operating at 100 percent. Not Fully Mission-Capable. Far from FMC." He thought for a moment about what he just said. *What is wrong with me? She can't understand already and so I sputter out even more jar-head banter.* She gave him an amused look that conveyed she was entertained and she understood.

"Come on now, are you a piece of hardware? Sergeant, you're not so *degraded*; I've seen a lot worse than you come in here. Your type always gets patched up, and heads back out in no time," she stated matter-of-factly as she looked at his bed side monitor screen and its scanners' auto-settings.

"I'm sure you have…" he tried to think of something witty and a hint flirtatious to say. But nothing came. *Damn.* He had never been good at this. He pretended to look out the portal near his bed in the ward, but really he just tried to make out her features in its reflection. He had very keen eyesight and could normally see the most distorted and far off images clearly. Even in the near-black background reflection of the small oval he could make out her more than cute features. JT thought, through his groggy hazed over perceptions, "this healer is absolutely gorgeous and I can only see her window reflection. I need to go back to my ship."

He guessed she was not fully human. But it was only a very subtle variation of skin tone and freckle-like marks on the back of her hands and neck that gave it away. Her skin hue was just a tiny bit different from a human's. The tint gave its greatest but faintest clue. A nearly imperceptible hint of aqua-blue. That was all. Someone with poor eyesight might not have even noticed. The tell-tale Cybrinthian freckles also were so faint; even JT hardly saw them.

She was an average height. Muscular build. With long dark reddish auburn colored hair. It swept neatly just above the small of her back. It was banded into a tight hair tail by four or five leather ties which matched her skin color. She wore the standard issue medical suit of light grey-blue replete with pockets and electronic sensors. While on most, the semi-form fitting suit did not flatter; on her it was rather complimentary. It accentuated her curves.

She had not stuffed bulky medical tools and papers into each and every pocket as some physicians did. With other doctors or doctrettes JT wouldn't have taken care to notice, but with this lady he did. He was caught by her eyes, even through the glass's reflection. He tried to figure them out. JT couldn't tell what color they were. Through the portal image it was difficult. But even after he contorted to catch a glimpse straight on, it was impossible. They seemed to change in the light as she moved. They were deep grey one moment, red-orange the next, and yet skin blue-tan the moment she caught his glimpse.

"Don't sound so doubtful there Sergeant Wayne." She paused. JT was watching her intently. She then looked straight back at him as if to convey she was being completely honest. "I promise you I really have seen patients in much worse condition than you leave here good as new," she said as she returned his gaze. He quickly looked down at the floor. *So stupid, caught staring. What would his men say? He'd not live it down for a while if they knew.*

"I, I, didn't mean to sound like that. I just meant that, er, you must see plenty of patients in all kinds of shape and well. Ah, well. I was, well, sure that you were telling the truth." *What was he saying? Was he dreary on medication? Now he couldn't even carry on an intelligent conversation.* This school-boyish dribble was getting him embarrassed quickly. Unless he recovered and stopped stuttering, he was going to blow this friendly encounter. She probably already thought he was just another dumb grunt. He was afraid he was at a loss for words. She looked at him inquisitively.

"I am not in the habit of telling un-truths to patients." She was clearly paying attention to the content of his ill-thought mumbling and stuttering. *Great.* A half-frown, half-smile followed her declaration. The light hit her eyes and they looked dark grey. Stormy. Like clouds on his home planet before a great downpour.

"I'm Doctor Gifford," she stated in an official doctorly sounding tone. "I'll serve as both your doctrette and attending physician as we are not staffed for full fleet support."

"So it says." JT flicked his eyes to her name badge atop her right breast pocket. "I mean, so I see." *Crap.* "And that's impressive they have you on double duty doc." *Crap again.*

She raised an eyebrow and the half-smile departed leaving only the frown. He decided to try and salvage some of this wreck of a conversation as best he could.

"Ok, so I've spent the last ten months aboard a battlecruiser drilling constantly and running missions against the Confederation. I haven't exactly had time to practice my manners," *Ok, this could go either way.* "…much less talk to beautiful women… beautiful healers." He thought that last part might have been over the top. But what did he have to lose at this point?

"And one a whole lot smarter, well-behaved and in better shape than me," he added. Maybe that would make up for the indirect and tacky compliment. She was staring at him quite intently now. *Here goes nothing.*

"And yes, before I say something else that betrays you've got me off-guard, I do mean you ma'am. You're absolutely stunning." She took a small step to the side and shifted her weight slightly.

"And Doctor, that's intimidating...to a Marine anyways." There. He threw it out in the open. His hand was on the table. And he certainly didn't have much. JT wasn't a good poker player anyhow. He was a tarot-war card player. Didn't have a face for poker. Didn't bluff well. Didn't care much either for games of chance in general.

Dr. Gifford thought for a moment about the various patients she had seen in the infirmary. Most were refugees or displaced people affected by the war. St. Demetrius was forward of the safe areas in Federation territory. It was largely free of the I-S conflict. But not so much so that she didn't see soldiers and sailors regularly. She saw them or at least some war-casualties every day. Some fighting men she felt more for than others. The ones she knew would never make it back to their ships or units. The ones she knew would never make it home. Wherever home was for them. She knew she had the honor of seeing many of them amidst taking their last flights. She hoped that would be to their respective homes if possible… she hoped many would be able to take their last flight home from St. Demetrius, but she knew also that it was not the case for most. There was a war ongoing and a war to win.

Many of the military injured in the fighting were seen aboard their own ships for treatment. If they were wounded badly enough to be taken off of their ship then usually it was fatal. If possible, they would be put into hibernation-sleep and sent back to their home worlds. Or at least sent farther to the rear than her infirmary. Most of her patients were non-combatant casualties of the war or regular sailors and soldiers. She didn't see many Marines. So she was interested in this unique opportunity.

She was curious to know what it was like out there aboard a warship. Aboard a ship but knowing that at any moment you could be called upon to embark and descend onto some strange world. A world on which you could have to fight some alien, Gnorac, or other human-Cybrinthian to the death. She wondered if Marines boarded enemy ships still. Did they ever then have to fight hand-to-hand? She wanted to know what it felt like to fire a blaster and take life in an instant. She wanted to know without actually experiencing it. Maybe this was her opportunity.

She felt pity for him here in the ward. She knew he would rather be elsewhere; that was clear. She thought since he was the only one of a small handful of Marines to visit here, he was special. He was probably a veteran of the recent great Federation loss at Quai-14. She knew there was intense fighting and deadly carnage from that battle. If this was the case, he might not have a spaceship or fleet to which he could return. She sensed this might be the case and then felt even sorrier for him.

Dr. Gifford admitted to herself that his apparent nervousness in talking with her was a touch flattering. She decided at that moment that she liked him and would not give him a hard time. He had likely experienced enough difficulty for a lifetime prior to getting here. If she could ease his stopover here just a little, then that was a small courtesy and she would be honored so to do. Then she realized she had been, for a bit, lost in this little day-dream. Quickly she snapped back to reality and remembered his last comment about being intimidated by her.

"Well then, that makes two of us," she replied. The frown had turned back into a half-smile. JT furled his brow in question, cocked his head to a slight angle, and donned an expression of mild confusion. "Two of us who are intimidated," she finished.

JT understood the kind sentiment- knowing it was probably true to some degree. He knew she had been lost in her thoughts for a bit. Lately he was guiltier than he would like to admit of that same thing.

She moved to his other side and touched the hanging inter-venous bottle giving it a little nudge. Then she moved next to him and cupped his forearm bringing the attached needle into her view. As she ran her fingers over the edge of the adhesive holding it in place, he felt goose bumps on his arm.

"You might not have experience with attractive doctors. But I'll tell you another truth…" She leaned in close to his ear. Lowering her voice to a near whisper.

"I don't have much experience with attractive Marines." She leaned back out, returning to a normal tone of voice.

"Especially ones who get flustered and intimidated easily." Back to her doctor-voice. "Clinically this is curious." She declared the observation firmly yet sensitively. It was her normal speaking tone. But the comments were much louder than JT wished they might have been. For the first time in their brief conversation, she smiled fully. She had perfect teeth. Pure ivory. Straight and shiny. Her auburn lips formed a neat crevice upturned on both ends. Now the goose bumps spread to his back and across to his other side.

"Do you have this effect on all of your patients ma'am?" JT half wished he was back on the Vissad. He preferred the comfort of training and the camaraderie of his men to this embarrassment. He was betrayed by his lack of experience in the suave department.

"Just the worth-while ones," she replied. She still held his arm but turned toward the IV drip. "I don't mean to be a drag on this little exchange Sergeant Wayne, but we've got to get your go-juice input adjusted here, and that means I'm going to need to cause you some discomfort." She was preparing a vile-like instrument of some sort as she looked from his eyes to his arm.

"No problem Doctor, pain is only weakness leaving the body," he mused. That was Rayborn's favorite expression. The young specialist was one of his best guys. A real hard charger. Ray had endeared himself to JT within the first week of joining the platoon by taking a leadership role without being asked or appointed. Next to Johanas, if needed, JT would have turned the platoon over to Ray despite the spunky Marine's junior rank.

"I would imagine from what you've been through recently you've seen a lot of weakness departing," she said this through a half smile, framed by concern which also conveyed a sense of pity towards him.

"Don't worry, this won't take very long." She released his arm and picked up the hanging bag off its metal hook. She clamped the tube extension from midway along the line and detached the IV bag laying it on a tray cart she had moved from the wall to alongside his bed. She pulled a very small vile from her right thigh pocket, unscrewed the cap and inserted it into the bottom of the cylindrical vile-like instrument she had already prepared. This made a single device that she inserted easily by screwing into the bottom attachment of the saline solution IV bag. Turning the pair upside down she shook the bag and attachment for a few seconds until all the contents of the vile were inside the bag. Unscrewing the device, she reattached the clamped hose and re-hung it next to JT's bed. Then, facing back to the monitor, Doctor Gifford punched in a sequence of keys on the touch-screen. The device beeped twice and then made a low humming sound.

"We're sanitizing the elements," she said and looked at him for a second, "here's the painful part." The machine made one more beep. A searing knife-like pain shot through his arm and into his entire upper body. He gritted his teeth, clenched his fist on the un-bandaged arm and suppressed a grunt.

"It's ok, most patients yell at this point, I won't think any less of you. I promise." She frowned and gave him the look of a puppy owner watching her prized pooch get an injection.

"Nothing to it. Feels like an insect crawling up my arm. Doesn't hurt a bit… Just a pinch… would hardly have noticed if you hadn't told me…" The machine beeped once more.

"Why I practically don't even know it's hURTINg." His voice

elevated slightly between the first and last syllables. She giggled to herself quietly. *Now there's a tough one.*

"I told you my brave friend that it would hurt a bit." She returned to the monitor.

"You remind me of my father some," she said so faintly as if it was to herself. JT wasn't completely sure she had said it to him at all. But he decided she must have. Doctor Gifford was surely unaware of JT's keen hearing. She must have meant for him to catch it. JT did have excellent hearing–better than most. *Remind her of her father? I wonder where this might go.*

"I do? ... Was he a Marine?"

She hesitated. It appeared she either hadn't said anything meant for him after all, or at least she hadn't intended for him to hear it.

"No, just a good man." Another pause. "He wa... is, sweet. But a bit hard-headed, full of pride, and with three girls, we – well – we put him at a loss for words more often than he would care."

"I heard some hesitation there ma'am. It's not my place so I won't pry, but I hope that things are ok between you." JT's comfort and confidence was beginning to return.

"We are fine. Well, things are what they are and we have gone our ways but accepted our different circumstances and that is it." There was obviously a lot more to the story but he did not let on that he wanted to intrude into her world. It was hardly something appropriate to discuss with a woman he just met. A well-learned and caring healer. Likely part-Cybrinthian. A beautiful young woman who he had known less than fifteen minutes.

"How much longer do you suppose I'm going to need to be laid up in here ma'am?" JT didn't want to linger on the topic of families and parents anyway. If asked, he did not feel at all like explaining any of the details of his own strange upbringing.

"Sergeant, don't tell me you're trying to leave us already? We've only just met." And she made sure the machine completed its purge then beeped a steady low tone. "Ok, are you ready to get plugged in again there young man?" She didn't wait for his response before starting the process. "Besides, if we send you back out there so soon then what will I look forward to when I come to this wing? You're the highlight of my morning.”

"Young man" –jeese she can't be any older than me. If she is then I can't tell. Doctor Gifford appeared to be the youngest physician, male or female, JT had ever met. She was in fact young, but not so much as JT thought. She was indeed part Cybrinthian and had favorable genetics.

“Well since you put it that way… I guess the strawberry stuff isn’t so bad. And if I’ll get to see you more often from here on out, I don’t mind I suppose either.” He relaxed a little more now. JT eased a few inches down in his bed, and donned a barely perceptible smile.

“But please, you can’t blame me for wanting to get back to my unit can you?”

“Oh Sergeant that’s a relief then for me and fortunate for you. I thought you were one of the few survivors of Quai-14.” She stated this as she began to adjust the IV and all its components back to where they had been before she ran the saline purge.

“Well I was at Quai-14, but we weren’t even fully engaged when….” He realized that he didn’t know what had happened. “...I guess… I am sort of in the dark here on things.”

“But, so if you are supposed to rejoin your crew then you must have been on one of the other Quais or a later reinforcement, right?” She turned, “some sort of reserve or support?” She looked genuinely concerned as she continued the questions. “Do you remember exactly where you were?”

“I know we were headed to Quai-14,” he responded. She was now sorry she had brought up the topic but still let her curiosity lead the way.

“How long after that first attack did you get there?”

“I’m not really sure. I don’t even remember getting to the quadrant at all.”

“So you weren’t engaged at the Quai itself, but you were in the area when the battle happened?” she said as if she was piecing together his memory for him.

“How bad was it? Did you pick up many survivors?” She seemed to be done now with the monitor and his arm. His head spun for just a second.

"No, no, I think we were just outside the quadrant embarking onto one of the bigger planets- AX17 I think. *Or was it AX117?* His head was still cloudy. We caught the entire 5th Confed fleet asleep at the helm. They didn't know we had snuck up on them…"

"You were in the initial assault?" She gave him a puzzled look.

"Yeah, well I think I was… sort of. I would be still, but for... Was with my platoon outside the embarkation transport. Boardings underway. We were about to deal the Confed main battle fleet the biggest blow since the start of the war. The entire 5th Fleet was poised in a giant ambush. Then I have a cloudy recollection of a big reddish jolt that must have knocked me off the platform and out cold or something. Then next thing I know I'm here in your fine establishment."

"Oh I'm so sorry, you poor brave man." She bit her tongue and realized she might have said too much. He didn't seem to know anything about it. *How could he not know?* Just after her reaction gave away the pity she felt for him, three realizations dawned on her. They all came at once: 1) he was a survivor of the greatest single fleet disaster for the Federation to date in this war, 2) he had no ship and no crew left to which he could return, and 3) he didn't know any of this himself.

"What are you sorry for? What is it that I'm missing here – what happened at Quai-14?" A sinking feeling. He was lying down but at the same time standing in a great stream; a stream of what he was not yet sure. An undertow of apprehension was swirling around his ankles. The water was rising and doing so quickly. It was muddy water but the closer it got to his eyes the clearer it became. He was afraid this water was clouded by more blood than dirt. He had asked the question but he was scared to hear the answer.

"Sergeant, I'm not sure that I should be the one to tell you this, can you hold on just a….."

"No Doctor Gifford, I need to know right now. I'm not sure how long I've even been here, but I've been awake for at least a day and I'm completely in the blind. What happened on Quai-14 and where is the Vissad? Where are my men?" She hesitated. Her mouth began to open. She looked at him and then looked down the ward. "Tell me...

Please." She wished she had not stopped to check on him. Not smiled at him. Not gotten him to smile back at her. It was too late to leave this brave warrior begging. Too cruel. She could not let him lie there drowning in an agony of unknowns. She sat down in the chair next to his bed, her stormy eyes filling with sympathy.

"Quai-14 was a total loss," she said as gently as possible. "None of the first ships in survived." She started thinking of what she would say next, "I'm sorry; I had no idea you didn't know; I'm so very sorry...."

He sat there for a second or two not saying a thing, thinking a thing, or even processing at all what this healer had just told him. What this meant... he didn't want to fathom. It had to be a mistake. There was no way that a squadron of heavy battlecruisers could have become a *total loss*. That was impossible. But somehow, someway, he knew it was true. *How could a hundred thousand sailors and Marines, sixteen state of the art federal warships, and dozens of support and auxiliary ships – nearly the entire advanced combat arm of the Fifth Fleet. How could it be a total loss?* He continued to stare at nothing for a moment more. A moment that seemed an eternity.

"That is unfortunate." He took a deep breath. "I don't understand how." Another breath and he clenched both fists hard. The arm with the attached IV seared with pain. At least that's what the nerves tried to tell his brain. But he didn't really feel it at all.

"Is there anything I can do for you... anything at all? I'm so sorry. If you like, I could..."

"Those were good boys." He looked up at her. "We had good leaders- we were ready. We caught them totally off guard for a god's sake." And in his mind flashes of the men went by. There was an infinitely fast cascade of scenes. Pictures from long ago in the barracks. Drills aboard the Vissad during stressful battle runs. At ports while throwing raucous parties. Manning the battle stations and training embarkations. Practice attacks and war games. Then their faces: Johanas, Rayborn, Raffordy. They started coming faster. He closed his eyes, took another breath; opened them again. He felt the unwanted cool liquid forming in his left eye. He forced both eyes wide and looked up; moved them around; tried to think of something different. It wasn't working. He was fighting a losing battle with a logical emotional response. *Why was sadness so taboo in his chosen field?*

Doctor Gifford blinked slowly, edged the chair an inch or two to one side, and then gazed at him longer than she had intended.

"So sorry," she managed.

"Could I have some time to think on this... Doctor Gifford?" he spoke very softly but clearly and deliberately.

She touched his hand gently half holding it as she stood up. "Take all the time you need, I'll be around if you want anything..."

Despite knowing she could never have experienced his exact emotions at this moment, JT thought she looked so genuinely empathetic. She exuded empathy and compassionate beauty right then. As if no one else in the universe could have comforted him at that moment. Maybe no one else then and there at that time could have.

"And if you wish, it's Aurelle." *Why had she said that? It was bad practice to get even the slightest bit personal with patients.* She gingerly retracted her hand and turned to leave him alone. The hand she had touched was already relaxed. He now released his other hand from its death grip on itself. JT could not tell if she was still within hearing range, but before she moved completely out of his view, he looked at her a moment through his now glassy eyes.

"Thank you Aurelle."

Chapter 5
War

The 3rd I-S War ended in 1480. During the post war period, the Federation imposed strict punishment on all losing Gnorac nations. Part of those accords included provisions that the Gnoracs would surrender all claims on the border planets. They were also forced to fractionalize the size of their armed forces. Their interplanetary fleets were altogether disbanded. The largest vessels they were allowed to maintain were 1,000-sailor frigates. And those ships could not be armed with anything more powerful than small-bore nuclear cannons. Sub-atomic Gnorac weaponry was outlawed. After the 3rd I-S War, no Gnorac national armed force remained larger than half its pre-war size. Moreover, on all Gnorac warships ES-neo and masked warp ability were disabled. Perhaps the worst result of the sanctions imposed and the most devastating to the Gnoracs had nothing to do with the military directly. Economics. That was the straw that broke the post-war collective Gnorac back. The breaking point came because the revenue from the few taxes they were allowed to collect was not enough to maintain their functions of government. The Gnorac way of life; and ultimately their very existence, was threatened following the 3rd I-S War.

Some historians and social scholars point out that the sanctions and restrictions imposed by the Federation were the very reason the Gnoracs were forced to declare war again. Others say that it is simply in the Gnorac race's nature to fight and conquest. Whatever the truest root causes, by 1497, the seeds of conflict were once again planted.

Just 17 years after the end of the 3rd I-S War, a small group of Gnoracs decided to rectify the war peace accords they considered unjust. This band of terrorist Gnoracs hatched an elaborate plan to destroy the top leadership of the federated nations at a meeting in Angola in 1497.

Every ten years a summit was held in which all Federation planets participated by sending delegates. It was standard tradition that primary heads of state and all major leaders would attend. The event was so widely and positively regarded that even non-Federation planets petitioned to send delegated representatives. And many worlds, even those not part of the alliance or remotely involved in Federation activities, sent some... if allowed, and if afforded by them. There were Olympic-like games, festivals, major broadcasts across the Near Universe, and networking of businessmen, military and political leaders. Tradesmen, entertainers, athletes, scientists and the like all partook. Every profession and type of intelligent life form was involved or wanted to be in some way. The summit lasted slightly more than a week.

Prior to the 3rd I-S War, the Gnoracs had participated in the summit. They were at war with the Federation in 1480 and prohibited from attendance in 1490. 1500 would be the first year for the summit in three decades that saw Gnorac participation.

The inter-galactic summit of 1500 was to be held in Madison, Angola. The meeting in Angola in 1497 was a high-visibility planning conference for the summit which would be held three years later. As the host nation and primary planet representative, the Angolan prime minister would be in attendance. The meeting would run throughout the course of two days.

The terrorists picked this conference in Madison, which was also Angola's capitol city, to take as many political leaders hostage as they could. Since Angola was the largest nation on any of Jupiter's moons and was regarded as somewhat responsible for past conflicts, it was a logical target. After all, the Angolan prime minister's assassination was widely seen as the catalyst for the 2nd I-S War. Also, Angola made up much of the Federation. Perhaps a plurality, and without a doubt, it was the largest single state in the Federation. Though other nations on Jupiter's moons were still ravaged by the last war, Angola had recovered well and was reaping the benefits of many of the sanctions imposed upon the Gnoracs since the 3rd I-S War. If one particular nation could have been picked as a prime objective for an extremist group of Gnoracs to exact their revenge, it was Angola.

To this day, six years after the hostage attempt, scholars and political analysts do not have a definitive theory as to how the terrorists would have carried out their scheme. No one from the group survived the failed action. No connections to any other larger Gnorac organization have yet been made. The Gnorac government officially condemned the act, but most other populations from non-Gnorac states consider it a given that the Gnorac government was heavily involved. If not the direct facilitator, it was at least largely seen as a clandestine party responsible for the incident. Just a backer, or the impetus behind the plot? Did it matter? The universes were at war and with destruction and death all around, it seemed too close; too painful; too subjective, to give an accurate causal analysis just yet.

The terrorists numbered 15 or 16. One of the hostages was thought to have been involved in the plot but this was never proven. After killing the pilot and the few passengers aboard, these 15 Gnorac assailants hid themselves in a city commuter shuttle. They kept it in service traveling along its established route in and around downtown Madison. This was during a normal weekday with heavy commuting traffic and many riders. The streets and low orbit airways were jam-packed. They picked up several passengers at the next few stops. Silencing each by disabling the individuals' transponders and all personal communication devices, the terrorists continued on their city shuttle's ordinary route.

They blocked any telepath's ability to correspond with outside contacts by use of a homemade telepath-detector. It allowed them to identify and immediately kill the few travelers with this ability. They could also broadcast an interference signal of sorts so nearby telepaths outside the shuttle could not mind-port in. They could not even receive anything alarming from those inside the shuttle. Officials recovered pieces of the device but never publicly released details of its workings. Highly classified, telepath related devices were illegal for private use and not readily available outside of intelligence and special operations military units. Eyewitnesses stated that neither of the two telepath victims killed had any chance to make contact and establish a link before they were murdered anyway. The assailants were heavily armed and they easily overpowered any and all threats to them.

Including one Madison police officer who unfortunately boarded a few stops after the initial take-over.

Since travelers were only boarding the craft and none were allowed to leave, eventually the shuttle filled to capacity. After four or five stops the terrorist Gnorac pilot was forced to skip the rest since the shuttle's maximum load was reached. The terrorists had failed to account for their own numbers and the extremely heavy volume of persons traveling due to the planning conference. It was not terribly uncommon for a commuter shuttle to reach maximum occupancy, but it was uncommon for one to reach it and not stop at each designated station. Despite being loaded, people would always get off allowing for at least a few more to get on at each subsequent stop.

As the craft failed to halt or even slow at one, two, then three stops, dispatchers became alarmed as they monitored its progress. There were four stops to go until the Madison conference center's station. With dispatchers alerted to the shuttle's suspicious movement, they tried to contact the pilot. Then, with no response, they remotely shut down the craft's thrusters. The day was overcast so there were heavy shadows and a dark gloom about the atmosphere. That, combined with high winds and blowing gaseous sands, made it probable the terrorists did not see what was about to take place outside their destination. No doubt at least until it was too late. And when their engines shut off and the craft powered down, they themselves began to panic. At this point the situation became desperate for them.

The terrorists knew they had little time to act, and according to one victim's account after the event, they became combative among themselves. Their apparent leader decided they would shoot a third of the civilian hostages to prove their sincerity. And at the order, his minions did just that. They then started dumping the bodies out one by one at small intervals. They kept the ones not killed on board and then made a demand for the shuttle to be reactivated. The demands would increase as soon as authorities agreed to turn on the disabled thrusters. That did not happen. Capitol police had already closed in on the scene immediately after dispatchers alerted them about the situation. They knew a city shuttle ignoring hail attempts while heading towards the conference center as the prime minister was there was an emergency.

Since dispatchers had disabled its thrusters there was also degraded electric power. Undoubtedly with all the bodies onboard and a shutdown or at best, minimally functioning, ventilation system, things heated up figuratively and literally aboard the craft.

Police and special reaction forces surrounded the downed shuttle as negotiators tried one more time to work with the criminals without success. Next a SWAT team was flown in by armored hover vehicle directly over the shuttle. It blew off the shuttle's roof with smart laser munitions. Immediately being fired upon from the now exposed terrorists, the police team killed them all. But not before one set off an ionic detonator inside the rear of the shuttlecraft. 27 of the remaining 36 hostages were killed instantly from the deadly blast. JT's adoptive father Gus was one of them.

The nine survivors were badly wounded and four later died. Of the five who lived, none could really help the authorities determine what the terrorists' ultimate plan was. That is except for one of the five who spoke Gnish- the Gnoracs' native language. He reported overhearing them talk of the conference center and their increasing arguments about the hostages and what to do with them as they neared the center but ran out of space on the shuttle. A small amount of evidence was found in the shuttle wreckage. But this was only diagrams of the center. Nothing was found of outside contacts or any communication with other terrorist cells. So it was officially determined that the group was acting alone. Though to this day, most informed citizens and most police and criminal experts do not think that was the case.

JT and his family mourned his father/uncle's death. This was when JT decided he wanted to join the service. His ties to home were becoming less and less vital for him; so, in 1498, that is what he did. Gus would have been proud. Gus's wife was Sarah. Aunt Sarah; JT saw her as his mother just as his Uncle Gus he knew as his father. Although supportive, she did not want him associated with the military in any way. She sensed that before the next decade there would be war. She was right. But she supported JT's decision just the same. She knew he would be an excellent soldier. She knew he would be an excellent anything.

Racial prejudice and hate after the hostage incident in Angola soon grew and Gnoracs were being increasingly discriminated against. By 1499, relations between Gnoracs and not only the Federation, but most nations and planets of the Near Universe, had deteriorated. Nearly beyond repair. Despite the invitation which was all but a mandate, the Gnoracs boycotted the 1500 summit. They were by now openly defying the treaty and peace accords of the 3rd I-S War. While the summit was underway, the Gnoracs were rearming and planning on mobilizing their interplanetary fleets. By 1501, their private industries were all working towards their war rearmament. By 1502, they had several heavy battle cruisers nearly completed and were working on solidifying an alliance with several Far Universal planets. Not upstanding or overly peaceful ones.

In 1502 the Gnoracs, Dragarthians and Dwarfen races all had similar ambitions to expand their empires and collect money from these expanded and soon to be imposed trade rights. However, the border worlds and several galaxies which did not fall under their control contested the idea of colonization and turned to the Federation for help. But Federation leadership and most of the general populace did not want conflict. People remembered too vividly the war of less than a quarter-century before. This reluctance could have meant the difference. The difference between early cessation of those developing hostilities and the huge conflict now ongoing. At that time the Gnoracs had not finished or launched any of their enormous battle cruisers or heavy reconnaissance cruisers. These would be the harbingers of death. They had become the carriers of a single doomsday-esq weapon that could destroy entire fleets.

So instead of an open condemnation of the developing Confederation's actions, the Federation states sent border and federal police to the regions affected. They did not send military support. Instead of any real force to check aggression, a policy of appeasement was adopted. This meant a loose understanding that the Gnoracs and their allies would be given small concessions in exchange for limited expansion. Several smaller nations in border galaxies were allowed to be colonized and ruled by first Gnoracs and later Dragarthians. In exchange, there was no increased taxation on the colonized and newly controlled countries. Just a recognized superior political authority.

The Dragarthians and Gnoracs agreed to limit their grasp on underprivileged populations within the Far Universe but would not forward this agreement to their Dwarfen cohorts.

If Gnoracs are aggressive then Dwarfs are wholly violent. To show their antagonists that they were not a second-rate component of the newly forming Confederate Alliance, the two major Dwarf races, Pidetlas and Gedabes acted belligerently. In late 1502, last year, they forcefully overtook two planets in the outer rim of the Far Universe. By the new year, these Dwarfen races were not the only ones of their species openly defying the Federation. In January, the rest of the other Dwarfen independent nations joined suit. Then the next month, Dragarthians had breached their end of the bargain with the Federation as well. They declared several planets in the Gilnean system conquered and all commerce rights they took for themselves.

Crucial events followed. Alternatives slim, the Federation senate formed an emergency session and the three chancellors decided to give the Confederation 30 days to relinquish control of the newly conquered states and 60 days to remove their fleets from the border regions or face military action. This political and costly delaying mistake allowed just enough time for the Gnoracs to finish preparations and launch a dozen of their heavy cruisers. It also allowed Gnorac scientists to make invaluable progress on research of their deadly new weapon.

The Confederation pretended to give in to the demands but, in reality, they simply finalized their battle plans and each state fully mobilized its fleet in secret. On the surface of many planets troops were removed only to join their larger units aboard orbiting transports. Ostensibly the transports were to remove the occupation forces, when really they were only staging stations for the larger more permanent invasion forces. The Federation fell for the ruse completely.

At the end of the first 30 days, all seemed well and confederate delegates spoke of peace every day. The supreme leaders stated publicly their relinquishment on any claims previously made and humbled themselves speaking high praises of the nations they not occupied, but simply meant to defend. They were protectors not conquerors. Meanwhile, their militaries built up and then, built up some more. Confederate nations organized their fleets into super fleets and positioned massive amounts of troops around all of the interested worlds. Those which they meant to occupy. Complete occupation was intended easily as soon as the believed time-clock was up.

At the end of 60 days, they asked for an extension of 15 days to remove all troops so that ceremonial relinquishment and new empowerment of their colonies and neighboring states could be accomplished. The confederate states invited Federation troops and ships to participate in the ceremonies. While the fleets were organizing these events, Gnoracs and Dragarthians were finalizing their operational and tactical attack plans. The trap was being set. After another 8 days of more delays, finally a date was set for the ceremonies. 17 April 1503.

Late on the 16th during major transport operations of several Federation fleets to bring their Marines and soldiers to the surface of various border planets,... it happened. The orbiting Gnorac destroyers all opened fire on the unsuspecting federal cruisers and transport ships. Secretly completed Gnorac heavy cruisers journeyed via ES-neo to the intended ambush areas and also opened fire. Simultaneously all available Dwarf and Dragarthian battle cruisers came out of orbit and also S-neo sped to the closest Federation bases that they could reach on short notice. They then pounded them with everything they had. Every piece of available weaponry of every caliber imaginable was brought to bear.

Analysts still do not know how such a surprise attack went undiscovered. Four distinct major races and several minor ones of three species ordinarily not good joint military planners: Gnoracs, Dragarthians, Pidetlas and Gedabes all pulled off one of the greatest feats in recent memory of allied military and political planning. While initially devastating to the forward deployed battle groups around the border planets, luckily the Federation home fleets were not taken by surprise as well. If not for sound military judgment and espionage, they might have been. Certain astute delegates had picked up tips from calculating opportunists intent on profiting by selling military secrets. All indications from double agents and these locally hired spies agreed. The common picture painted was that if hostilities were to break out, then two nearby Federation bases would be targeted first. Specifically, the heavy cruisers at bay by Ganymede 1A and Europa 3 would be attacked by Dragarthian fast attack cruisers the day of the ceremonies. This proved to be partially true.

The heavy cruisers would be targeted. But not the day of the ceremonies. The evening before. However, the base commanders were smarter than to allow their most valuable assets to sit at bay. Indeed, some were deployed to the ceremonies and these did sustain heavy damage or were partially destroyed. But most were away from their bases and battle stations on maneuvers in neighboring star systems. These single decisions by two cautious base commanding admirals staved off complete disaster for the forward units. The bases in question represented a sizable portion of the Federation's forces. They were home to approximately four percent of all Federation troops. But even more important, they were one quarter of the forward deployed forces. Ganymede 1A or Europa 3 was a home base for one out of every two deployed heavy cruisers not directly in the border region. They also were home for one out of every five Angolan Marines. More than 300,000. JT was one. He had Fleet Admiral Bradford Mayson to thank for the admiral's executive decision. Admiral Mayson sent the Vissad to the Jacksonian star system for maneuvers on the 15th of April.

The day after the Confederation attack- what would have been the formal day of de-occupation- was not ceremonial at all. Instead, it was highlighted by a declaration of war. The combined federal senate was backed up by proclamations from all three chancellors together. It voted to declare a state of immediate war between the Federation and the rebelling nations. No constituent nation voted against or even abstained in that unanimous announcement.

That same day, 17 April, the entire forward element of the Federation's primary international fleet was mobilized. The other Federation fleets would be mobilized while en route to their assigned war sectors within 36 hours. Several hundred million men and aliens were now moving to kill each other. Some were already underway. Some had already dealt death. Some were already dead. The Vissad was recalled immediately for full arming and imminent deployment.

Chapter 6
Memory

He is swinging on a playground apparatus. Maybe inside a holodeck. Maybe it is real. JT cannot tell as the memory is so clouded from time. And he could not have been more than nine months to a year or so old. His parents were killed just before JT's first birthday so the vision was unclear at best and meaningless at worst. Useless data filling a tiny crevice in JT's organic long term memory storage banks. Maybe not. He didn't think on it much anyway.

He swings on the rigid structure and sees his young parents gazing lovingly at him. But the gaze is more than that of just any parent's love for his or her child. It is unexplained but warmer and more connected than any normal human feeling or emotions should be for a toddler. Most toddlers forget their feelings and emotions by the next afternoon. JT's were clouded, but still clearly not forgotten 24 years later. His small form feels warm contentedness and pure joy. All of a sudden, the image changes and he is no longer on the playground or holodeck. He is nearing sleep and in his infant bed. Is it a crib? He cannot tell. He is again warm but in different clothes, swaddled and gazing now directly up at his parents. Both of them hover over his face and he feels only true joy. If he is hungry or sad or bound too tightly, he cannot tell. If any need is not met, he has no idea. He is not there as a child. JT is somehow into the experiences of his parents at the same time as he lies there on the verge of sleep. He has rarely discussed this and made no plans throughout his life to recall it for anyone including himself.

Baby JT is not a baby at that moment. He is color transparent and warm and connected to life through his parents and their experiences. He is at maybe a year or less, the same person he is a quarter-century later. Just not yet grown into that form.

And then this is over. It is only some sort of strange lucid dream-like event concocted by a nervous or over-stressed mind. It bears little relevance to anything JT does in his later youth or adult life and so the memory fades. As he grows it becomes more a surreal, as if it did not actually happen. It develops more vagueness than any sort of actual or perceived truly real event. What did JT's parents know anyway? Their family history was murky and full of holes. Gus and Sarah knew only bits and pieces and tended to steer away from dangerous occurrences or anything unexplained. Whatever it means or meant, JT knew then and maybe deep in his psyche he still knew to this day that he was different. His spirit was different. His lineage came from somewhere strange and foreign.

He had something no one else did. He had a connection through his family perhaps that was different than any human or Cybrinth anywhere at any point in known recent history. At least JT believed this. But what was belief versus known factual entities anyway? Did it matter? Could JT tap into an experience that could serve more than himself or his immediate surroundings? He thought about this and thought on it sometimes over and over again. And then JT decided that some things are best not to be thought on too hard.

Chapter 7
Executive Chief

Executive Chief Remouln Kgnauld grabbed the small ensign by the collar and transferred a thought right into the officer that paralyzed the little Gnorac in his seat.

"I said *full* reverse," he bellowed sternly for the entire bridge to hear, "was that in any way unclear to you? Is it unclear to *any* of you?" All crew on the deck, frozen- mind you, zeroed in on him as he proclaimed this rhetorical question. They then returned to their former tasks; mostly monitoring screens and control stations. There was a tremendous amount of disorder on the bridge.

The cruiser's actual commander, Captain Ganjin Majak had left Kgnauld in charge of the giant ship while he explored the surface of planet 104. Planet 104 was a small icy world a few hundred klicks below the orbiting reconnaissance-attack cruiser, *Suclesahe*. The ship was on a simple patrol mission in the vicinity of this small planet which lay on the border of the two universes. Any contact with Federation ships was supposed to have been unlikely. Sure. Now that less than intelligent, intelligence report had proved completely unreliable. False. But whether or not the mistake was simple oversight or purposeful treason, Kgnauld had not yet decided. Time would tell.

Kgnauld had two Federation attack cruisers doing lazy ovals around him taking pot shots at weak points in the Suclesahe's defenses. The initial attack came from behind the planet and was double pronged. One assault vessel came from the far side of the tiny world but it was small and masked by a debris cloud. At the same time, anther larger ship jumped out of a warp hole. A hole that somehow had not been detected by his early warning staff. How did they miss that? It appeared his intelligence team had likewise failed. *What good were they?* The reports they gave were inaccurate and they couldn't even detect a warp hole orbiting around this sad little planet. *Were there treasonous crew members aboard? Would he be executing sailors before returning home? Would he even be returning home?*

"Why are we not pivoting to engage that meteor fodder yet?" he cried towards his chief helmsman and crew.

"Coming about now sir!" shouted a middle-aged very stocky engineer named Jfandel. He was seated commandingly at the number one helm position. "We've completed eight-five degrees of one-six-zero required and marking at nine per second."

"That's more like it! - Fire when inside safe discharge fan." Kgnauld was beginning to think they might yet pull this off. "Target will be fully acquired this time Mr. Ytelfor. Full neutrino wave- I want nothing left of that cruiser... Nothing!"

"Aye sir," echoed nervously both Jfandel and Ytelfor at the same time. They looked at each other. Was he really commanding an engagement with the neutrino without the captain aboard... and without fleet specific guidance? Then a high voice from the rear of the bridge quipped in:

"Shields dropping below twenty percent strength sir, and fast... Recommend diverting some power to them!" the chief defense engineer yelled.

"I don't care if we drain them to nothing, so long as we destroy that cruiser first. And I want it done with the neutrino," retorted the executive chief with a hefty and agitated groan. Jfandel wondered if Kgnauld had repeated clearly this weapon choice a second time in case there was any doubt on the bridge.

"Sir, we're acquiring now." In the background and across other control decks the engagement commands were sounded out with precision. The main and secondary gun crews all knew the drills well. They were a finely tuned machine. One built for killing.

The Suclesahe's mission was mostly intelligence gathering, but all Gnorac ships were heavily armed. And all Gnoracs were killers at heart. And the weapons array at the ship's disposal was impressive. Most universal fleets would have counted themselves lucky to have heavy cruisers armed as well as the Suclesahe.

While he knew his mission was not to seek out fights with enemy cruisers, he was certainly not going to run from one that found him.

But he was also thinking beyond just the developing fight. He was carefully contemplating his options for engaging the second enemy cruiser. Assuming... he would be able to destroy the first right away and have enough left in all departments for the follow-on. And then he was seriously considering purposefully not destroying the second attack cruiser. *Why?* Well, would not letting it fly back home to report the destruction it witnessed send a very clear message to the Federation? *What would Commander Yfoar think of that?* Group Commander Juselb Yfoar, the Suclesahe's higher organization's commanding officer, was known for espousing innovative and unorthodox tactics. This could go over well with him.

"Shields at twelve percent Chief,... Commander," came from the now, tellingly nervous- defense engineer. His brow furled as he wiped sweat from his palms. Kgnauld was a chief. He was *the* ship's highest and only ranking chief. And while the commander was not aboard, Kgnauld *was* the commander. The defense engineer looked up and around briefly to see if any had noticed his hesitation and re-address of title formality. None seemed to note; the tension was too high on the bridge for nuances like that to go overly observed right then.

Kgnauld's focus quickly snapped back to the chaotic bridge. None of the side distractions and formalities, or even the second Federation cruiser for that matter, really bore any importance should he fail to destroy the first cruiser. Communications were loud and overlapping. Then the sounds of the lead gun crew seemed to drown out those of all other sections on the bridge. "Firing systems check, green..." The gun crews on the lower decks were all patched through to the interlink and they too seemed silent. "Target tracking..." Those gun crews were preparing to mimic the lead team on their respective systems. "Target at minimum safe range..." All waited with their breaths held.

"Gunner; Neutrino; Cruiser!" one voice beamed across a corner of the bridge.

"Lazing... and... locked!" responded a second.

"Fire!" shouted the first.

"On the way!" yelled the second immediately. All silence was broken. The station crews were now all back at their respective jobs shouting orders and reports to one another.

"Neutrino pulse on the way now sir," stated Mr. Ytelfor to Kgnauld as loudly but calmly as possible across the bustle of the bridge. The commotion continued as the new and powerful weapon wielded its death. The long pulsating vibration could be felt through the entire bridge. Most of the fore, aft, and upper and lower decks rattled as well.

"Shields down to five percent sir," shouted the squeaky defense engineer's voice from the bridge's rear suite again. Kgnauld nearly missed the report amidst the bustle.

"Lost contact with the first cruiser sir," reported a lanky dark lieutenant named Clurfg who had just walked in from the rear control section. The entrance he used was at the left back of the bridge. It was partially obscured by a short stairwell which led up to the mid-bridge observation platform. His voice took Kgnauld by surprise for a moment as he had not noticed the young officer come in.

"How? Why didn't we throw tractors around them? They were close!" Kgnauld questioned the young officer accusingly.

"Target! Target!" The gunner's mate yelled so loudly that the entire bridge heard him clearly. Any eyes that were not trained on the main monitor windows shifted there instantly. Just seconds ago, there had been a daunting Federation cruiser class 1 attack ship protected by a visible and previously believed impenetrable Federation defense shield. Now there was a listing broken hulk. Then the expectant shock-wave passed ominously across and through the Gnorac ship. A brief shudder followed by a low tremor for several seconds.

That defense shield had been the bane of the Gnoracs' attacks. Amid any battle-driven haste, no Gnorac weapons could seem to effectively penetrate the highly advanced new shield the Federation had added to nearly all its fleet's recent launches. Until now.

"Cease fire. Gunner, continue to laze the vicinity at range!" the lead firing chief ordered his junior, "prepare to re-engage, at my command."

"That shouldn't be necessary—" interjected Ytelfor, "—and we will need the surge power for shields and the other cruiser," he turned towards the executive chief, "Sir, enemy cruiser ablaze, she's breaking apart now. We should divert power to shields." Kgnauld had already turned his attention to the battle-station main monitor windows and was watching with delight as the Federation attack cruiser rolled to one side from her front and bridge. And burned from burst oxygen stores. An uneven split across her main bulk heads was appearing. The fading red glow was still clearly about her everywhere. The scene was a reddish unfolding nightmare for those who experienced it. It was horrific and painfully beautiful at the same time for those Confederation fleet members watching from the safety of their own vessels.

The enemy ship was done for. This portion of the little yet behemoth scrap was likewise done. The Federation cruiser's hull was cracked gaping wide and widening. She was spilling all sorts of internal debris into space and nothing came from any of her thrusters any more at all. Then as she began to turn listlessly, he saw the gash in her side. Already a quarter the length of the hull and expanding. The ship was not only destroyed as a fighting vessel: she was kaput for any sort of salvage or future use. That much was clear. Even if her main weapons systems were working, which they were probably not, she had no shield at all. No power that he could see. And had lost all hull integrity. In less than a minute Kgnauld now estimated she might be split completely in two.

Something on the enemy ship hull's front lower left exploded. A storage hold maybe. Ammunition bay perhaps. Kgnauld wasn't sure. The Confederation hadn't yet obtained full schematics for these new smaller attack cruisers. They needed to get them though. Recording a hologram of this break apart would be useful to his superiors and the intelligence command. These new ships had plagued his fleet badly in the last few weeks and months.

Despite his mission being for reconnaissance and not engagement, this victory would surely be a feather in his cap. He had faced two of these cruisers. They were smaller, but faster and more heavily armed. Except for the Gnoracs' new secret weapon, the neutrino cannon. And this weapon by all official accounts did not exist. Kgnauld knew his crew would be sequestered. Since they had witnessed first-hand the N-cannon's awesome power, they would be prohibited from leaving the Suclesahe. At least until their individual parts in engaging this new secret weapon were declassified. Their personal communications would be strictly monitored. Including his own.

Because of the weapon's top-secret status, it would be documented that Kgnauld had destroyed the enemy attack cruiser with his traditional weapon systems –lasers, pulse beams, and photons. Kgnauld would be accoladed as a master tactician. Those enemy small attack cruisers could out-maneuver him and either one alone could pack a much heftier volume of firepower than the Suclesahe. Throughout the Confederation there had not been any confirmed battle destructions of one yet. Now he would document the first. He would surely get his own command after this engagement was sorted through and the reports complete. Personally, he felt he would probably be identified for a command before even news of this had reached the general populace.

The Federation's class 1 attack cruisers had only come into service as a distinct class of vessel in the past year and they were the latest new fighting starship in the Federation's arsenal. They fought in packs. Two or three usually. They would ES-neo to a location of a reported enemy cruiser or battleship and take it by surprise. Most of the time, if the Federation intelligence was correct, they succeeded. Only one federal attack cruiser to date had been destroyed, but even that was not at the hands of the Confederation. The little attack cruiser, *Valliant*, had destroyed a Confederate battlecruiser and simultaneously incapacitated a starfighter carrier. Incapacitated enough to allow its mate, *Anialage* to finish it off.

During the engagement, the Valliant sustained enough damage to her power core from a physical collision into the enemy battlecruiser to render her S-neo out of order. Her commander elected to scuttle the ship rather than allow it to be captured. Sadly, most of the Valliant's crew was killed by Confederate starfighters after abandoning ship.

Despite the loss of the Valliant, the attack cruiser class was proving its weight in gold for the Federation. Considering there were now over fifty federal attack cruisers in the war and another thirty-five or more being built, they still posed a huge threat to the Gnoracs and all Confederation races.

Chief, acting Commander: Kgnauld, ordered the monitors and screen chief to enlarge the picture of the Federation attack cruiser he had just destroyed. The old Gnorac did as commanded and the entire bridge walls and a good portion of the ceiling seemed to turn into windows. They looked out into space and the foremost windows zoomed to the stricken vessel's hull breach. It was a virtual movement towards the spot being viewed.

It was as if the Suclesahe was instantly transported into the middle of the action. The zoom allowed those watching the monitor to see up close the fruits of their effort. Kgnauld smiled. He thought flippantly for a second, of all the widows and parent-less children he had just made. His musings quickly shifted to the medals he would be awarded for this victory. Then the display shifted and showed a terrible scene of awful red carnage.

The front of the ship began to roll to one side. But the rear, the thrusters, power core and supply holds were not following. The quarter hull gash was ripping further and further down the hull. It was now over half the ship's length and broke through the left side and all top decks just forward of the thrusters and power supply. The remaining connected right side and bulkheads were twisting violently; they were bending and warping... painfully it seemed. If a ship could feel pain. Certainly, its operators could. The gap was now fully broken through the external roof and bottom hull. Only the twisted ship's right gunwale held the bow. Comparatively, the bridge, quarters, main weapons stations, and ammunition holds together with the stern were not likewise held. The thrusters, power core, bays and other storage holds were having their own dance with evil destiny. Their beat synced with no others. Very few escape shuttles were jettisoned. They hadn't had enough time. The debris field grew and the first bodies were tumbling out into open space.

The hull breach finally held no more. The side bulkheads and remaining decks and frame completely gave way. The cruiser's ends slowly tumbled in different directions. Smaller pieces of the large warship floated in various directions in the void between the two massive halves.

He could vaguely make out tiny forms on the large screens. They looked mostly human. Maybe some Cybrinthians among them. Some were writhing and moving frantically. None did so for more than ten or twelve seconds. Deep space was freezing cold and had almost no pressure. It was an icy suffocating vacuum. Void of oxygen, warmth, and pressure, the body was quickly sucked of life. This was the case no matter what life form or race was exposed to it. It was universally true except perhaps for spirits, but to a Gnorac, spirits were hardly life. Most Gnoracs thought of them as a child's myth of some formless conscious-less being.

Though Kgnauld thought they were real, he was sure there weren't any spirits on that cruiser. Humans and Cybrinthians had no relations with spirits. Most Cybrinthians and humans didn't even know what a spirit was. The few who did know of them believed they were an extinct surreal race of the Far Universe. *No, there were no spirits aboard.*

Chief Kgnauld concluded all crew of that vessel would die. Despite the implications for his next actions, he would make sure of it. They had seen firsthand the destructive power of the Confederation's new weapon. Kgnauld knew intelligence was a valuable commodity. In thinking through his options, he changed his mind from his first thoughts and decided that if the neutrino cannon became universally known, it would lessen his chances of being such a hero. Lessen his chances of earning his own command. He did not want to risk that. So, he also then reflected that the other Federation vessel could not be left to flee.

The neutrino must and would remain a secret. He didn't want even its description falling into the Federation's hands. Knowledge of the new weapon would reach the Federation brass eventually – with its awesome destructive power that was inevitable. But Kgnauld wanted to do his part to prolong the knowing as much as possible. At least until his medals and command were awarded. Had he been brash to engage with the N-cannon without clearance? Maybe. But had he not, the Suclesahe would be space dust and he and his crew a blip in the archives to be heroically remembered. Instead, now this Federation class 1 cruiser would be the blip.

He looked back at the monitor. A few small bodies were in space suits. He ordered a magnification of one of the floating dead crew. The screen shot zoomed right up to a lifeless and eerily faceless face.

Human.

"Check a few more," he ordered. The giant monitor window zoomed to two more floating bodies. Each was human. It went to a third. Human as well. Kgnauld and the bridge crew watched the last few dying gasps; body jerks then a blueish-black turning face of the man. He was an officer. Kgnauld had studied human Federation uniforms and recognized the eagle-like collar insignia. Thousands of years after bird-life on earth as they knew it had perished, the human race still used the old insignia on military uniforms. An eagle. That was a high-ranking officer. Second only to the admiral, general officer, and space marshal ranks. It would have been nice to have that man aboard for questioning.

"Zoom back out and scan the crew on your own monitors," he said to the observation section. "I want you to look for any ranking officers inside space suits. Advise me if you find any."

"Yes sir. But sir, inside suits how do we tell their ranks?" asked one of the observation sergeants.

"Must I teach you everything sailor? Look to the shoulders. If you see those bird-like symbols or stars, that is what we want. If you see a triangle with burs throughout, I want to know that as well. Understand?" he asked mockingly.

"Yes sir." The observation chief officer determined the crew looked to be predominately human. There were a few Cybrinthians scattered among them though. Kgnauld turned to the gun crew.

"You there, gunner's mate: I want any enemy in suits not identified by the observation chief to be officers of interest,... destroyed."

They wouldn't last for long. A day or two at most, even if their suits had a full power charge. Unless they were picked up by that other vessel, it was unlikely they would survive. But the executive chief wanted no chances taken. The other ship… He would hunt and destroy that other attack cruiser at all costs. He must, for his own greed and power thirst was at stake.

"Defense chief: get my shields back up and charging," he ordered. "I want us ready to engage again with 100 percent N-cannon in thirty seconds."

"Aye sir," responded a few different voices across the bridge. That order was impossible. Charging the shields alone took more time than thirty seconds. The neutrino itself would also take nearly that long. With the drain on pulse power for the shields, the neutrino could never be charged that quickly. He didn't care. It would only be another reason to blame someone else if they failed.

"Now lieutenant, where were we...?" Kgnauld turned back to the young stocky officer who had earlier delivered the unwelcome news that they had lost track of the other attack cruiser.

Damn, thought Lieutenant Clurfg. He wished the ship's acting commander would have brushed it off after the Federation cruiser's destruction sequence unfolded. No such luck. It was a wishful thought in the first place but he knew he had to deliver the news. No good commander- acting or not –would let that slide by in the heat of battle just because of some other distracting welcome turn of events.

"Sir we were phasing tractor sequence for firing when she slipped us." Clurfg was smart. He was at full attention. Although circumstances allowed easily for a quickly delivered informal report then moving out to let the acting commander be, Clurfg continued, "I have my team ready with primary and secondary tractors as we speak." A hint of sweat formed on his gray-tan forehead. "I did everything that I knew to do by the book, sir. I don't think we could have moved any faster to attach the beams. The boarding party was ordered onto transports by me personally sir. We were that close to taking them. I swear it." It appeared Kgnauld had already turned his attention to something else on the bridge.

The young lieutenant was in truth a bit nervous, but not visibly other than the tiny bead of sweat on his brow. He looked the part of a Gnorac officer in command of his situation. He acted just as he should have despite the tension. It did him credit considering the situation. It was almost as if he had been ready to deal with the stress. This was the most stress a Confederation officer during his first major engagement in deep space far from anything familiar could have been expected to endure. To himself, he seemed nervous, but just a bit. Not really all that much though. And certainly not too much compared to most of the rest of the crew on the bridge.

Kgnauld wheeled about and Clurfg realized it. Although he thought the executive chief was not paying attention to him, the chief, the ship's current commander, had heard everything in the lieutenant's report very well.

"I would expect nothing less," Kgnauld gave him a piercing glance and touched the large Gnorac's forearm. He sent a probe into the lieutenant's thoughts. He was telling the truth, from first impression at least. Kgnauld did not have the luxury to access the lieutenant's deeper consciousness. Had there been more time, he would have liked to have done so. Success from this officer's department would have earned Kgnauld accolades across the entire fleet. If he had been able to destroy one attack cruiser and take another by force- keeping it intact at that, he would certainly have become a celebrity. He might have been given more than just a medal or two and his own ship. A wing or squadron perhaps. Who knew what would have been in store for an acting commander who accomplished such a feat?

It was not too late however. The other ship was still out there somewhere. Perhaps this lieutenant could redeem himself yet. He peered over at the observation crew's monitors. He wasn't sure, but on one of them he swore he could make out the face of a human man through the debris. A bearded older man. The screen picture was too far away to tell the man's rank, but he could see the whole uniform. It was impressive looking. Quite regal by human standards, at least it seemed so to Kgnauld, who had some education on human culture. Maybe that was the cruiser's commander-

If a human commander knew his ship was bound for something important, maybe a diplomatic mission, he might have dressed up in his best. Then once he knew it was over for his ship, he bowed out like a true commander should- not in a space suit- but in his finest dress attire. Kgnauld would like to believe he would do the same thing. Stay on the bridge at the helm of his ship as she went to the great beyond. *What was he thinking?* No one did that anymore. Starfleet chivalry and code of honor conduct were dead. They were each a thing of ancient history. Neither side in this murderous conflict practiced the old rituals anymore. Of that sad lost art most things were gone. Of this, he was certain. Almost.

"Observation chief, show me that man's shoulder insignia,"

Kgnauld ordered to the Gnorac at the monitor which was closest by. The screen zoomed in. There surrounded by the familiar epaulet swirls were two unmistakable gold stars. The monitor operator zoomed out just a bit. The man's bearded but now blue face stared vacantly out but directly into the monitor. *I beat you old man, I beat you good* Kgnauld thought. But then his spine tingled and a terrible feeling of guilt at knowing he had a secret and far superior weapon. He had not outmaneuvered his opponent. He felt oddly about this. Almost as if... as if he had cheated. That; however, was the way of war. A mix of skill, technology, and luck. Sometimes, as in the recent experience, one overpowered the others and tipped the balance in a single engagement. Kgnauld felt the icy piercing glance of the dead enemy captain in his body for just a moment. Then, as quickly as it came on, it was gone.

"Sir, shields charged back up to 40 percent," came the high voice once again.

"Good. Keep them charging and keep me informed. Status on the big gun Mr. Ytelfor?"

"She's ready for at least one, possibly two at one hundred percent neutrino Sir," was the response. Kgnauld had clearly been lost in his thoughts for more than thirty seconds. He relaxed a bit and walked calmly and deliberately back to the captain's chair. It was time for a cool commanding authoritative presence now. There had been so much chaos earlier he thought. He needed to exude calm and collectiveness now. He would bring full order back to the bridge by sheer example.

"Section and damage reports Colonel Sjouft," he remarked towards his junior in command.

"Aye sir. Forward batteries report zero damage, two injured during defensive maneuvers. Guns fully armed and awaiting further orders. Rear and flank upper and lower batteries report same, excepting ammunition and casualties. Two wounded..." The reports continued for a moment as the colonel reported them matter-of-factly to the executive chief.

"Give me the roll up – we haven't got time to go over the details, there's a bandit out there and I want him," Kgnauld cut him off mid-sentence.

"Aye sir. My assessment: we're ready for full frontal engagement now- shields will hold and guns are ready. A rear or side attack in the next few minutes could cripple us if directly at us; or, until shields reach at least a 50 percent charge. We can reach full charge overall for all systems in four minutes. Overall ship crew strength is 98.5 percent full effectives. We can come about in twelve seconds if we need to without degradation. Swinging our bow one-eighty I believe is the best chance we have for defending against a full size cruiser. Damage reports are negligible. If I may sir, the crew wants to finish this fight."

The old fleet officer knew his systems and knew this ship like no other. But he had reached his plateau. He was great at processing information and supporting a commander. But he was not a gutsy-instinctual leader who could make split-second decisions during the heat of battle like Kgnauld or the commanding chief. Colonel Sjouft was not a born leader. He was a perfect third or fourth deputy chief. As he was now acting second-in-command of the vessel, Kgnauld had all that much more resolve to finish this fight quickly and get the commanding chief back aboard his own ship.

"That's exactly what I want colonel," returned the executive chief. "Keep them rolling in like that and we might just make something of you yet."

"Sir- bogey cruiser just reappeared on rear scanners. Closing fast from underneath the planet. She's shooting at us from below!" yelled a monitor operator.

"Bring us about- *now*," shouted Kgnauld in his naturally deep firm commanding voice, "Full reverse boosters. All available shield power divert to front and bottom. Forward batteries go hot as soon as range angle permits. Fire command is red and I delegate all fire control to observation and gun commanders. Man your positions! Make her turn- you killers! Try this again and make it work this time!" Kgnauld felt his cells pulse. He could try and reach out to access the human commander's thoughts aboard the attack cruiser, but it was fairly risky and he would lose situational awareness on the bridge. He decided to let it go and try his hand at the turning maneuver. It didn't work well last time, but the crew was not ready then and they had been unlucky with the unnoticed warp hole.

"Brace for impact," came the words almost simultaneously with the jarring and shaking vibration of the battle cruiser. A terribly loud thunderous echo filled the bridge. Kgnauld held onto the seat arm and ducked as orders, print-outs and other small unattached materials went streaming across the once neat and orderly control room. Alarms sounded. Several computer stations went blank, the bridge doors automatically shut, sealed and locked. The communication node in one corner of the bridge lit up like a fireworks display and then went dark all at once immediately following. But all of the communication port and general notification system speakers remained on and continued to bark loudly. They mixed with a blast of static and ear-piercing whistling. So, this was it. What it felt like to be hit directly by enemy main weapons systems. In all his years as a Confederation fleet officer, he had never experienced it. He didn't particularly care for it now.

"Number two and four main thrusters failing sir. Re-routing power to one and three. Still in full reverse and coming about, but we won't be able to stop the spin..." Chief Jfandel reported from the engineering helm. The vibration and hue of the massive mega-ton propulsion systems wavered and then fell silent on both lower elements. The power core was holding enough to keep the upper two elements alive. The number one and three thrusters were still functioning keeping all control failure from descending upon the Suclesahe. Kgnauld wondered how much longer those engines had.

"Engineering is out of communication sir, I expect they're balancing shield power with thruster power from the oscillations in the ship's magnetic field," added Colonel Sjouft. Then the gigantic ship lurched and began to keel towards her starboard. The remaining thrusters began to wind down. Kgnauld closed his eyes and concentrated on the engineering deck, he focused on the four huge engines. He could now sense and hear through his intuit vision all four engines had begun to falter, not just the number two and four. No, maybe one was still running. It was hard to tell with all the ambient noise.

"Neutrino is in range- commencing laze..." welcome words from the main gun station. The enemy attack ship was back up on the main monitor windows now. She was closing fast and firing everything she had from her forward batteries at the bottom of the Suclesahe. The turn wasn't yet complete and they hadn't diverted enough shield power yet to the bottom of the ship. She listed even more. The bridge lights blinked off and on twice, held for a moment, and then once again. The communication systems buzzed on from engineering and the other major compartments. There was a huge commotion down there. Kgnauld couldn't make out a thing. There was screaming he thought as well. He tried harder to send his orders directly to the minds of the crew in the engineering bay across the entire length of the reconnaissance cruiser. Some were getting through despite the chaos. His unnatural gift was extraordinarily useful during crisis times like this.

"Lazing… Locked!" he heard from the gunner's station.

"Fire!" came the command. Forty-five hundred lives were depending upon that shot. His accolades and future command were depending upon it. Power blinked off and on again across the board in the entire bridge. Things seemed to slow almost to a halt. Voices were streaming but they all faded into one unintelligible blur. His psychic connections with everything were jarred. He could no longer sense the engineering room at all. Nor could he tell if there was anything taking place on the bridge worth commanding. He was not sure if he heard with his ears or if he sensed with his mind the next exchange.

"Fire again then, I said fire again!" he thought he heard from Ytelfor. But maybe it was Sjouft. Were they taking over for the gunnery officer? Was he dead? The bridge was a haze. The sinking feeling filled Kgnauld's head that he might not live to see his medals or his own command. There was now smoke quickly filling the bridge. The ventilation pumps had failed. *He would be a hero alright.* Not the kind he wanted to be. The kind who gets starships or towns named after him. The kind whose medals go to his family members. He heard coughing and thought through the smog he saw sparks or fire coming from most of the control stations.

"On the way!..." came the muffled and distorted cry from the gunner. But the words were too late. There was no great pulse of energy to be felt. The lights all around surged once more and then it went completely dark. Chief acting commander Remouln Kgnauld's connections to every other active consciousness he had tapped into also went dark. He hoped those crew members and his captain now stranded on planet 104 would not be discovered or taken prisoner. But no one aboard the Suclesahe would be able to save them. Maybe the neutrino would get hit in the final death throws and combust with enough force to destroy the entire orbiting mass of ships and debris. He could hope. There might be some lofty and ideal but unlikely scenarios in his last remaining thoughts. Why not? This war had its share of strange surprises and turns of unforeseen events. He hoped one of them could still surface and take out that other Federation cruiser. But Kgnauld would not admit to himself he hoped luck should or could play a role here before the end came for good. He wished he had had enough forethought as his commanding adversary to have donned his dress uniform already. But he would have needed to have done so before commencing operations around planet 104. However, Kgnauld still took comfort knowing that he was the one who had been surprised and still managed a great feat in destroying a Federation attack cruiser protected by impenetrable shields. He may have turned a corner for the unfolding war. The Gnoracs would know soon enough. The neutrino was, thanks to him, confirmed to function as his alliance envisioned. It was now battle tested. It worked.

His last actions included ordering the video hologram recordings of the neutrino-cannon destruction of the enemy cruiser sent to higher fleet command. This would be his last action for his people, for his race, for the Confederation. At least they would know of the weapon's success and his achievement in deploying it against the enemy.

The moment he anticipated… maybe even feared?... but had otherwise known would come, for the last 45 seconds or so, arrived. He stood straight and proud at attention when the bridge broke apart. The Suclesahe was lost forever.

Chapter 8
Spirits

She moved gracefully through the field weaving in and out of the crops without disturbing a single grain. Delle was a beautiful spirit by any standard. She loved to move freely whenever her teachers or master let her so do. Her remarkability in beauty was unique. It was not just her appearance; it was her soul and character. Also, her uniqueness lay mostly in her ability to seamlessly change forms and sense what needed to precipitate that change. She understood much about many things from her surroundings and her world. But the world outside what she knew was not a welcome place. Not for a young teenage spirit. Especially one without any knowledge of distant lands, much less distant worlds or star systems.

Her mother raised her close at hand and shielded her from the harsh reality of the outer worlds. The reality of conflict, of war, suffering and hate. This meant she was innocent and pure but it also meant that she was unprepared. Preparedness was not of concern to her kin. The old ones knew of the cruelty of the outer worlds but the young ones like her did not. They had been protected on purpose. Protected to make them free from hate and prejudice. Free from the injustices which accompanied those hates. It was an idealistic intent but it was hardly possible outside the bubble of her countryside. Her world. Her home. That home, known only to her kind, was called Spiruthean.

The form she chose today was that of a long flowing red and yellow dragoness. A mystical but beautifully manifested creature. Often, she existed in her own natural form leaving it unchanged; but occasionally she tried something unique. Today was one of those days.

Her naturally given form was translucent: bluish and horse-like. She liked her form for it was fast, pretty, imposing and noble. Most of those in her village were also clear land animal-like forms, but some were not. She had a friend who was nearly opaque and resembled a great bird. He was always asking for her help with letters and she was always willing to give it. Willing, that is, so long as he didn't abuse the privilege of her kindness. Faeruthanamereson was his name but everyone called him Faeru or just Fae. Delle and Fae had known one another for a very long time. At least as long as Delle could remember. At least as long as she had undergone any formal education… which on Spriruthean was all that truly mattered for an adolescent or young adult spirit's life. Training with a master and senior mentor was the most crucial aspect of any culture on Spiruthean. All spirits trained and all reached a level of ascendance in their lives and their craft of greatness unfathomable to outsiders. A spirit did not speak to any outside his or her immediate family until she or he could form complete sentences and understand basic concepts of logic and justice. A spirit did not transform to an alternate form until she could do it successfully in her mind hundreds of times. She did not experience allowed friendship until she could love. On Spiruthean it was an accepted axiom that one should not walk until he knew how to fly. Learning to fly was mandatory for all.

Delle was always in motion. It was easy on Spiruthean. Nothing remained still. Even at rest, the wind seemed to move everything. The gaseous dream-like world was not one like any other in the universes. It existed in real space. But only in a place that could be accessed by those gifted enough to understand how to get there. Entire mini-fleets of reconnaissance vessels had passed directly adjacent to it and never picked up a single anomaly or detection of the world's presence. It was not large. Maybe no more than a dwarf moon. Spirit forms and a few mencas were its only inhabitants. They passed between other realms and those of the universes without much effort. At least these passings were regularities for a spirit once he was properly trained in so doing. Proper training meant years with mentors and elders in the nuances of how to drill and how to learn safely and efficiently… most importantly how to remain undetected by outsiders.

She moved in and out of the plants and sensed Faeru's presence without even trying. Spirits sensed everything intuitively. They spoke out loud but truly they didn't need to do so. They could communicate simply through senses. Not really thoughts, just understanding each other. Faeru was moving carefully along the edge of the field but inside the woods. It seemed that his master had let him have some time to himself today as well. What a welcome surprise Delle thought.

Fae was traveling along his familiar path home but he was moving so much faster than normal. Delle would not be able to catch him if he continued the way he was going. She turned to head in his direction and tried to eye where his path would intersect hers. She would not be able to reach that point in time either. So, she decided to reach out with her senses. She was good at that. Her mind would catch him well before her form could.

She broadcast her presence towards him. *Fae… Faeruthan,* she projected. He was not tuned to accept anything. *My goodness,* she thought. Spirits did not usually tune out their surroundings. Fae appeared to be doing just that at the moment. Delle decided to leave him alone. It seemed Fae had something very important going on. Something he needed to rush for. Delle left him to his task. She would see him again soon, she was sure. She always did.

Just then, both of these young spirits were forced to endure a brief but stressful moment. A huge piece of something burst through their atmosphere somewhere many miles ahead. It was enormous. Like a giant old-wood. Maybe bigger. Delle could see it and its fiery entrail as it cut through space above the planet's atmosphere. It then burst through the upper, mid, and lower atmospheric layers of Spiruthean with violent bursts of erupting flame. It kept on a straight trajectory but arced ever so slightly towards the great woods to their east. It fell with a thunderous succession of crashes and popping explosions through the old forest. After ground contact she could no longer see it but she sensed it easily. She could still hear its destruction and aftermath. There was no doubt for her that every other spirit in the area, maybe most of those on this side of Spiruthean, would hear it too. Certainly, Fae did. *Maybe that was why he was running?* Did Fae see or sense this before her? Delle was young and not as advanced in some training areas but she was normally excellent at foreseeing major events. Surely, major calamities. If that is what this was. She would undoubtedly one day be very good at foretelling. Today she had thus far sensed nothing about a fiery mechanical looking giant object crashing down into her world. She hurried along as fast as she could and then evoked that she was faster in winged stag form. She morphed, took flight, and sped home at twice the pace she had been able to maintain previously. She was quite beautiful in full flight. Beautiful but nearly imperceptible to any and all around her except the most astute and in-tuned spirits.

Chapter 9
Surprise

Faeruthan hurried through the forest. He was not even floating. He was running since he was an incredibly fast sprinter. He couldn't wait to get back to his home and share the news with his family. He had completed his last day of the exams and knew he passed with the highest marks allowable. He was smart, but did not imagine he would do that well. The headmaster was tough and the exams were nothing to underestimate.

Fae's longtime friend, Gammin, worked for the headmaster's apprentice and did odd jobs to help whenever needed. Gammin was not a student but learned as much or more than most of those who attended the academy. As the parchment came in today, he was asked to help sort and mark completion levels for each of the students in the school's log. It was from Gammin that Fae learned he had finished all lessons at the very top of his class. All the other students would find out tomorrow, but he knew today and was bursting with excitement. His class was not large, only twelve students, but it was still a great honor to finish best among his peers. This graduation meant that he would not only continue on to senior status, but that he would have first choice with whom he wanted to apprentice. His mentors at home and outside school would be so proud. He envisioned sharing the news and glowed a bit inside. He was not always a proud spirit but today would be an exception.

Senior status also meant that he would finally be allowed to study the combat magic of the ancients. This instruction was reserved only for the older classes and only those in the classes who had passed the exams with high marks. Those who had shown the greatest aptitude and dedication would be allowed to learn the most secret and highly guarded combat magic. That magic which was only known in the original texts. This surely would mean him.

It was one thing to learn combative magic. Any spirit could do that given the right amount of tutelage, control, and practice. But it took something more to do so from ancient books written in long-dead languages. As a tiny boy Fae showed a tremendous interest in his heritage and the traditions of his people. Now that he was near full spirit manhood, he would realize that ambition.

This news was something to celebrate indeed. He would give thanks to the spirit-god by praise and making his family proud. He was already thinking of the preparation and training he could do during his month-long break in studies. Fae hurried less quickly now but maintained his stride on land. He normally took his time floating when going home. He loved to take in the sights and sounds of the woods. He would concentrate on the symphony of nature as he glided. Ordinarily he would hear the small insects and winds at the high end of his senses the easiest. The creaking and swaying of trees and larger animals he sensed, but not quite as easily. They were in the middle and lower ends of his sensual spectrum. Then there was the underlying pulsation of all the animal and plant life in harmony at the very bottom. He could harmonize with this just as well as any spirit when his focus required it. But today he heard little but the rush of air by his pointed furry ears.

Faeruthan's form was something humans of old would have called a cheetah. Except Fae was nearly clear. When he ran, other spirits would sense him before they would see him.

A tree creaked loudly and Fae felt its presence around him. He knew he was being rude to ignore the aura and keep running. The old tree-spirit probably wanted nothing more than to know why he was in such a hurry. But Fae didn't recognize that particular aura and so he kept moving. He wanted to be home quickly to share the news. He also wanted to convince his siblings that they should talk their parents into taking them all to do something fun in celebration. He knew he wouldn't have to do a lot of convincing, but it would be more fun to reach them first and formulate their plan together. With a little luck, tomorrow they might go gliding, swimming, or maybe even condor-riding. Once home he would see what the chances of that looked like.

As he ran, he could tell that he was not as quick as he had been some months prior. He thought he should have been able to cover the ten spirit leagues faster. A league was approximately 3-1/4 human miles; only half-way home and he was a little winded already. It was probably because he had neglected his movements over the last month. This was understandable. It was due to his end-of-year testing and studies preparation. He thought about it and realized it had been at least two months since he sprinted ten leagues. More than sixty days since he really pushed himself hard in training. That was the problem. He used to run to school and back at full speed at least once a week: twenty leagues round trip would take him forty-five minutes. But now he wasn't sure he could even break an hour. How quickly the spirit body slowed when it was not continually pushed. Fae made a quick vow to fix that before his vacation was done. Fae could have changed form and flown to speed up the trip but he always made a habit of staying to ground. It was good exercise and it was safer and a more secretive means of travel. A spirit in flight was always more at risk of interception or being seen. Although this was not much of a concern or problem on Spiruthean. But Fae liked to maintain all aspects of his training and clandestine movement was an important one. A spirit had to know when and if he or she was being followed or observed.

Something caught Fae's eye in the distance. It was by the edge of a clearing he would pass to the east. He passed the spot every day when he was attending classes and never gave it much thought. This clearing looked natural enough- a simple area of the woods that did not wish to boast any trees. There was no particular reason for Fae to go there; but he had visited it a few times before. Just a simple trip to explore the land around and in between his home, the village center, and his school grounds. This was a long time ago though and he couldn't recall exactly why he had gone. From what he recalled; it was nothing more than a rocky area roughly a kilometer across without any forest cover. A stony clearing. What Fae noticed now was more colorful than just a grassy area or some rock clusters. It looked like a collection of something more than that. He sensed something out of place.

Fae slowed to a halt and peered in the direction of the clearing. He focused on the color-filled area he first noticed while running. He saw some movement. Then he felt the same presence of the tree who reached out to him a league before. He relaxed his breathing for a second and concentrated, opening his mind up to the life around him. *He's asking me something.* The tree-spirit was a very old one and from its aura he could feel it had much knowledge and experience. He was reluctantly able to quell his own thoughts and hear the tree now. He heard but was not truly listening. Between his school success, his physical exertion, and the unexpected glow from the clearing he was having a hard time concentrating. He needed to focus more to communicate with this old spirit. It was on the periphery of his sensory range. He sat and calmed himself. He counted. Counting helped clear the mind. He made it to ten then breathed slowly. Now he listened and understood more clearly.

It asked him to explain why he was racing so fast through the woods. It had some information of interest for the boy. Fae answered in thought that he was heading home after finishing all of his year's studies and that he had done well; he wanted to get going again. The last part of the thought Fae didn't intend to pass along. But he sent something like it—fairly muddled anyway. Whatever the tree understood, it appeared Fae had alluded to wanting to go. The tree's response was that he should wait a bit before leaving. He should not be in such a rush for there were few true emergencies requiring such exertion. He would gain more from slowing. As he normally did on other days he passed through the woods. *How does he know I go by here regularly?* wondered Fae, though he was careful not to pass that part along to the old spirit. Fae thought up an apology, sent it and then asked as politely as he could: why should he stay longer?

The old tree told him there was a group of horsemen in the clearing looking for a family that lived around this area. Perhaps he could take a moment to help them. Their quest seemed important. The tree had been observing and listening to the horsemen since they arrived. All of their actions and discussion indicated they were not a threat. They also had no idea that either Fae or the tree was observing them. Fae thought for a few moments. This would prolong his time getting home. But it would not do any harm if the tree was right. And if their quest was important then Fae could count it a good deed. He had never seen horsemen in this part of the land. People were not native to

Spiruthean. Nor were horses. Outsiders only came here by the invite of spirits or by some great space-time mistake or official envoy sanctioned by outside great councils and leaders. Those influential entities and spirits about whom Fae never thought much. He admitted to himself he was a little curious.

But what if the tree was wrong? If the horsemen turned out to be dangerous then he had a long way to go for help. But then he thought back to his earlier sense of the tree's age and experience. And the trees of these lands were usually old souls who helped others and were good-natured. Fae decided he had little to fear. He remained cautious though since this tree was new to him. He did not know why he had never sensed it before while passing along his beaten path. Then of course Fae was still only a school aged boy. He didn't always notice the things he should.

Alone in the woods with this unknown group before him, Fae became a bit uneasy. He decided he would investigate by moving closer, but would not give away his presence just yet. Besides, men were not good at sensing and Fae was a clear form. He was hard to see and; moreover, he was very fast. He could easily outrun any of the fastest horses visiting the land.

Fae was good at stealth when he wanted or needed to be. He stepped off the wooded path behind a group of trees which lay in the direction of the clearing. He did not change forms although he considered it. He was not so good at shifting forms since he was clear and consequently, rarely needed to hide. He knew it was good practice to blend into surroundings but nonetheless he was not adept at the custom. The two suns of his world were behind him and so he used the shadows created to his advantage. He threw almost no shadow himself and with the suns at his back he moved silently among the trees' shadows. It was impossible for the men to see him. He moved like a ghost closer and closer to the clearing. He made no noise whatsoever.

Since the horsemen were being observed by the trees unbeknownst to them, Fae deduced that they were not adept at sensing spirits. And they certainly did not have any elves with them for the old tree would have known that. An elf or a trained man would be able to sense his aura when he moved too close. But these men did not.

Whsssshhh- a slight rustle of leaves. The breeze passed by. He moved effortlessly to within a hundred steps of the men. There were four in the group. All dismounted. Wait… they were not all men after all. Two men, two women. With keen eyesight he could now make out the small details of these travelers. They were not men as he knew them. He thought they were human. But Fae had never seen a human before with his own eyes. All he knew was that they looked similar to spirit men in a spirit's true and chosen base form. But humans were shorter, had more hair and wore much more apparel. But generally, they looked kind of like the spirit-men he knew in certain forms. They were dressed elegantly by any standard. Fae held in place and slowly, silently, alertly he knelt next to a thick tree. He was within an easy throw's distance of the group. With some effort, he was within a whisper's distance as well. These *humans* would never be able to tell, but for Fae, he could hear their breathing.

The men were dressed like soldiers of some kind. One woman looked to be a servant. The other was either a high-ranking warrior or some kind of noble. Her garments were flowing and lavish. She was tall and had long red hair. She had a broad sword kept in an ornate scabbard. She wore a hefty torso armor piece and a long cape. The top of her blouse and sleeves were adorned with silk jewels. Her leggings were decorated as well. She had a helmet but it was cradled in her left arm. She was giving directions to the others who were huddled about her. They nodded from time to time. All seemed intent on her words.

The two men were dressed in form fitting hard metal armor. It looked very heavy and despite being highly polished, Fae could tell it had seen battle. Both men had shields slung about their hips. They had swords and a few other pieces of weaponry attached to their belts and saddles. They had no capes or ornate garments like the lady. But their horses did have colorful banners attached behind each saddle, which were also very well made. The banners draped upon the horses' hind quarters just aft of the saddles. Fae did not understand their markings.

One man wore a fully enclosed helmet and the other had one with him but it was on the ground next to his right foot. He had a cropped beard and was drinking from a small canteen that was slung over his shoulder. The second lady was listening to the first speak, but she stayed a few feet back. She had no hard armor, but did have a short sword and chain-mail over her torso. She had a pack of some sort slung on her back and had two pouches about her side. She seemed to be keeping a watch on the four horses which were grazing just behind the group next to some bushes in the clearing. They were not tethered but neither did they seem to be paying attention to anything other than the grass they were chewing. They were curious animals to Fae.

He quieted his thoughts again and listened very intently to the group's discussion. He did not want to come to any conclusions until he had heard a bit of their conversation. He was listening but was also conscious that every second gone by was time lost from his original quest. He still wanted to return home quickly and spread news of his school success to his family.

"What say you Valcor? You have stayed quiet during our journey," the lady said to the bearded man who was looking around the clearing. He turned to her.

"I do not presume to know what is thy true desire my lady. Dost thou wish for us to make our presence known and seek assistance if we cannot find the boy? If so, I should be hesitant, but would certainly do thy bidding. I should say, I would not hesitate, but merely I would beseech thee to take caution lest we fail by making ourselves and our quest known too soon." The bearded man spoke clearly and deliberately. He kept his attention on the lady but still watched over the clearing's perimeter with his peripherals.

"I know you would do your duty and my asking no matter how grave the task my friend, I simply ask your opinion for I have learned well to value it," she responded directly. She turned to the other man. "What are your thoughts on the subject Farhale?"

"A agree with Sir Valcor my lady. We would each follow you to execute your grandest and smallest of desires, but that I might add and be so bold as to think my own opinion be also valued by you. I say frankly, might we give it a bit more of a go without arousing any of those who call this place home. After all, the more who suspect such an important spirit among them, the more attention we draw, and the worse off we could be for finding him," the man stated plainly. He accented the proclamation by bowing his head in deference to her. Not very well anyways, as the unwieldy helmet allowed only so much movement. Then he looked up and began to remove it.

"My lady," the second woman broke in, "I beg pardon, but if I may, we have provisions for at least two more days, and that is not counting what we could, if staying here, we hunted." She looked to both of the men as if to be supporting their opinions. "We could continue candidly for a while more without anyone being the wiser for our intentions… and we have three message birds left for use." Fae knew of message birds, but no one he knew still used the ancient custom for communicating. Spirits simply sent their thoughts from a concentration chamber which could multiply their broadcast distance five-hundred-fold or more. The lady spoke to them all now.

"Well that is of note, but it does not change the fact we all know to be true," she looked them each in the eye and took a very serious imploring tone, "we are running out of time." She paused to let that sink in. They all knew it already. "If we do not find the boy or his family soon and convince them to share his bloodline knowledge with our elders, then our race will wither and perish from this world." The group stood silently. Of course, they knew the boy was the key to their survival. His blood and its secrets could help save the dying race. It had long been foretold a young spirit would save them.

Fae wondered what they could have meant. No humans or any non-spirits lived on Spiruthean. Nor had they ever existed here to his knowledge. Was this group some unknown or hidden faction from far away? Could they have stumbled upon Spiruthean by accident and not realized that they were where they were? Fae did not know, but he began to sense that the tree was right and perhaps this was something important. Something not to be brushed off without a bit more attention from his newly discovered top-of-the-class intuitive mind.

One of the horses made a snorting sound. The second woman snapped her fingers and made a clicking noise with her tongue. She held her palm face upwards towards the animal. It stomped twice and then took a few steps forward and sideways towards her. It then shook its head up and down then placed its nose upon her palm and sniffed.

"There girl, that's fine, you just stay quiet. We don't know if your kind is prevalent in these woods and we'd rather not find out by accident," said the woman gently. The horse seemed to understand her. Fae reached out his thoughts and could sense the horse was in a state of total submission to her. It understood the request and willingly obeyed. Fae did not know that men had such ability with animals. He thought only spirits and elves could communicate so well with other species. But now he guessed that spirits may not have been the only native or at least the only currently inhabiting race of his world. At least they were not the only ones which appeared able to communicate with other less advanced species. *So humans could do it too; or whatever this species was could.* His respect for the race of humans increased a notch. But he wasn't exactly sure these were indeed the "mankind" known as humans he had read about. At least he was not certain they were humans from his school book learning and what he knew or understood of them from his studies. They were clearly of a closely related species. He would find out when he got back home. Someone would know.

The leading lady surveyed them. She placed her helmet on the ground next to her and drank from her water skin. She placed the cap back on and declared, "Fine then, we will not seek assistance. But that is only for the next two days. When we must use the wood for nourishment, we will go to the spirit people of these lands and make our case be known. We cannot let our own pride be our downfall while those whose lives depend on us suffer." There was no room to debate the point. She agreed to acquiesce to their wishes. At least she did to a point. But she established a clear limit and there would be no more discussion. They understood.

"Yes my lady."

"Your desires are our commands Lady Shera," the man called Valcor declared.

"Yes Madam," the second woman said together with the others. Lady Shera then beckoned towards one of the horses. It began to walk towards her. The creature looked regal as it approached her. It seemed to just understand her need, and it heeded that.

"We will travel west another few leagues and see if we can find any more well-worn trails. If we do, we shall spread ourselves out and look for signs of spirit people who might know stories of the miracle boy." The lady took her horse's reigns and gently patted his muzzle. The beautiful beast nuzzled her hand gently.

Fae was curious. He had stumbled upon something important, that was sure. Rarely did men ever come into the land of Flarhom, much less the woods around his village. Rarely as far as he knew, did they even enter his world. He knew he had to do something.

The way Fae saw it, he had three choices. And one of them was ill-advised. He could quietly extricate himself and tell his family or someone from the nearest house. Or he could make his presence known and offer to help these people. Finally, he could continue back home and ignore everything he had just witnessed. The last option was out of the question. The first was probably the best. Or at least it would have been best if asking the adults and elders. But then the second option was the most intriguing. He could tell that the group was desperate for help in finding this "miracle boy." It seemed that their pride, or at least the lady's pride, was preventing them from asking for help. Fae's good nature and his boyish desire for adventure inclined him against caution. He would help them out rightly. But first he wanted to find out a little more.

Deciding to consult his new acquaintance, Faeruthan reached out to contact the tree spirit again. It was still there willing to talk. Fae sent a request for advice in his most respectful and politely imploring tone. The tree responded that it sensed the man-group would willingly accept any help he could provide. They would not cause harm to him or anyone who harbored no ill-intent. Moreover, they would offer protection, and the indebtedness of their people for those who helped them find the boy. The tree did not elaborate more though Fae wished it could have.

The tree seemed to know that their race was in peril; that they were not seeking help out of malice or fear but for their livelihood and survival. Their quest was bizarre in this world. Men were inherently distrusting and looked down upon other races. They fought one another and they were inclined to quarrel with other species just as much. The tree knew they must be unnaturally desperate to seek out help from foreigners, much less spirits. The tree knew nothing of man's prophesy or what specifically they thought this miracle boy might bring to them, but it did know they would be grateful for Faeruthan's help. Somehow the tree knew Fae could help them more than anyone else. It supported Fae's inclination to reveal himself and offer assistance of himself and possibly his family or village or others as the case warranted. Fae trusted the creatures of the forest, especially trees. Even if he had not previously known this particular tree, he trusted it. He and his teachers had never gone wrong by putting faith in creatures and spirits of the woods. Now these men were here in the woods needing his or someone's help. Fae had no idea how they came to be here, where they truly had arrived from, or where they were heading. Nor did he have any idea why they were searching for this miracle child of which they spoke. That didn't matter. Fae felt at peace with his decision. He would help.

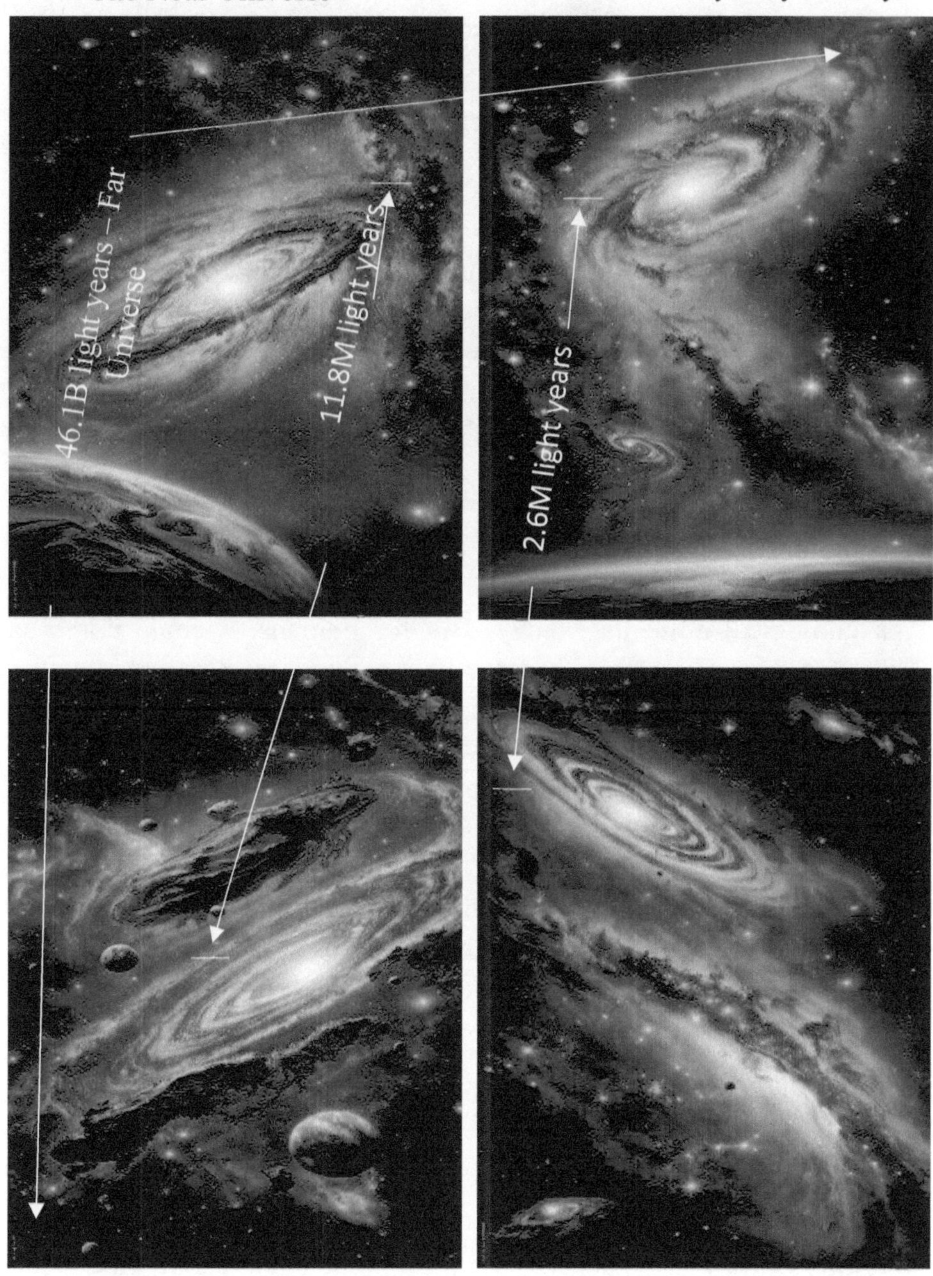
-The Near Universe-
Kiklios Galaxios - Milky Way Galaxy
46.1B light years – Far Universe
11.8M light years
2.6M light years
Messier 82 - Cigar Galaxy
Messier 31 – Andromeda Galaxy

Chapter 10
Discussion

The edges of the machine's rails felt cool to the touch. His bare back lay on the hard metallic surface while high frequency light and radio waves passed over his torso. JT had been inside a tagnometer before. But not three times in as many days. This was also his first time in one while there was something real of concern. He felt like he was being passed through an industrial cooler. In just a moment, pulses of intense light- charged ions, would shoot towards him from all angles.

The scanning machine could detect non-physical problems that other tests would not. It did not help pinpoint cognitive errors or psychological ailments exactly. But for humans, it could come as close to that as possible. It detected metaphysical discrepancies the body itself could not identify. This field was commonly known in the spirit realm. But not to humans or Cybrinthians. The tagnometer could also locate problems at the sub-atomic level. The physicians hoped that this time something conclusive could be gained from the test- so did JT.

He had been in the infirmary at least a week but had little to show for it. He still had two fiber optic rods providing traction for both legs and could not sleep. His insomnia of late was becoming the more serious problem. He could not close his eyes for any good length of time without becoming nauseous and then waking up. His seemingly un-treatable insomnia challenged the doctors. Ordinarily one drug or another could fix this problem. But JT's body rejected all of the medications they tried. His white blood cells saw the medication and its effects like a foreign infection. They broke the chemicals down into harmless and ineffectual sub-atomic compounds. Those pieces not destroyed by his blood cells were literally ignored by his neurons. JT's body could be just as stubborn as his head.

His final experiences aboard the Vissad during its destruction left him with two broken femurs. Fortunately, his legs were close to fully healed. With the fiber optic traction set he now wore, JT could walk on them already. The impressive advantage to fiber optic splinting was that it allowed the arm or leg to bend while healing. So the patient was not restricted to the confines required of casting from centuries before. It also allowed bone mending to take a fraction of previously needed time. The only side effects were occasional but acute pain and temporary loss of sensation. Neither of these were a problem for JT. In fact, if not for the insomnia, he felt physically almost back to normal.

"Alright Sergeant Wayne, breathe normally and try to clear your mind. We need you to relax as much as you can," the technician instructed. "About eight minutes once we start the sequence." JT was not thrilled. This was about to be his third "eight-minute sequence." And so far, the only real information gained from the other sessions was that doctors had obtained no real information. He sighed as he had already convinced himself this session too would not make any difference. The platform stopped moving, now fully encased by the machine's domed sensor chamber. Glass doors clamped and he took a deep breath. Fans humming, it began the reading process. All the internal lights powered up and a low vibration could be felt. Then a faint high-pitched electric whir began. JT closed his eyes and breathed deeply trying to relax as the technician had advised.

In another part of the infirmary, far from the drone of medical machines, a small group met. Isolated from the medics and computers plying their healing power, the room was quiet. It was a windowless conference room well secluded from the other parts of the facility. Some who had worked for years in the facility knew nothing of its existence. There was an unmistakable sanitized feeling about the small space. There were no computers or decorations. No speakers or microphones. Nothing except a plain forged plastic oval table and a dozen matching chairs. The floor was hard carbon-fiber polymer and it matched the walls and ceiling. Apart from a laser pen, two cups and an electronic tablet, there was nothing on the table. Each of those present wore the grey-blue medical suit of a physician. Each seemed bent on maintaining his or her ominous and serious temperament.

"What is his recollection of the moment of impact?" asked a bald-headed doctor named Alfus Simons. Though he would not have stated this or bragged about it, Dr. Simons considered himself the senior and most important among them. While the senior status was not arguable, not everyone present would have agreed about the relative importance. There were some who wanted his job and felt they could be doing it better. Some felt his care and involvement had strayed askew of the greater fleet and Federation needs. They said he made care policy too personal and forgot there was a war on and there were times that efficient and effective triage required cutting loose the lost causes. This was not the time or place for that particular discussion. But it was on a few minds nonetheless. It stayed quiet for a moment more. Aurelle looked around and realized that of all the doctors, she was likely to be the only one who knew the answer to his question. "Does he recall the impact at all?" Simons stated again, semi-rhetorically by now.

"Not much doctor" she quipped in. "He only remembers being outside his platoon's embarkation craft and then the strange sense of the red all-encompassing force." She looked around at the senior physicians. There were three men and two women. She was the only one who was not fully human or at least she was the only one who could have appeared to be not 100 percent human. If there was anyone else in the group of mixed blood, a casual observer could not tell. For Aurelle Gifford, they might not have been able to tell were it not for her reddish-auburn hair and bluish skin. There were plenty of mixed-race physicians, just not any on the senior staff.

Aurelle thought it was odd enough for her to be included in this meeting at all. She would not ordinarily have been part of this group; she was far junior to any of these doctors. But she was the physician assigned as JT's primary care giver; his doctor and his doctrette. In earlier centuries she might have been called a nurse-practitioner, but now doctrette was the title for that role. She knew his case better than any in the medical community. Certainly, better than anyone on St. Demetrius. She was also not afraid to speak her mind and make frank and considered assessments of JT's condition. Consequently, she was asked to confer with the seniors about his case. This gathering had been called by the unofficial lead, the *top doc* for St. Demetrius, not always a physician, but in this case, it was: Dr. Simons. He suspected that officials would soon be asking for access to JT in order to discuss the neutrino gun. Simons was concerned with finding out all he and the staff could before JT was forcibly removed from their care. He expected that could happen any day as the Marine's health was rapidly improving. Simons wanted to know everything possible about the bodily effects of the neutrino gun and JT was so far the only person who had survived such a blast at such close and direct range. And more remarkably, apart from his insomnia, he was getting better, not sicker. The medical command teams needed to learn all they possibly could to help discover what could be the key to saving countless lives. Countless futures of untold numbers of Federation service members and their kin. Without their help and expertise, Simons surmised millions could die unnecessarily.

The infirmary and its parent hospital were seeing an increasing number of neutrino radiation sickness cases. So far, no remedy had presented itself. Unbeknownst to Simons, the deputy military commander of the entire fleet had already contacted the hospital's chain of authority, down to Simons' direct supervisor, the regional top-doc about the problem. It was becoming an overnight concern. Since JT's arrival 10 days prior, many inhabitants of the planets affected by fallout from the neutrino gun began experiencing the same symptoms. But these were less advanced indicators of sleeplessness. However, their broken bodies were not mending. Despite the best medical care, skin burns did not heal, bones did not re-grow, severed nerves could not be re-joined; the list went on. It was as if medicine regressed 3,000 years for these victims. The ones who had managed to survive so far.

"Do we know where the neural activity is worst affected? In which quadrant are the disturbances measured highest?" asked one of the other doctors, a short man named Barnes Quimby.

"Tests from the tagnometer have been inconclusive, but we are running a third series today to get a final rule out of... various... energies," Aurelle responded. She knew that she had avoided the question and answered in such a way that might lead the conversation in a different safer direction. If she was asked to give her opinion on quadrant activity and if she was to be honest, then that would mean that she had to comment on a half-formed prognosis. One that did not look favorable.

"And that may well be, but if you can't or won't, then I'll speak plainly," Quimby interjected. "It doesn't rule out spirit energy activity at the sub-neural and atomic levels. Especially so early on in the condition. Would you not agree Dr. Gifford?" said Dr. Quimby in an almost mocking manner; but really in his mind, this was Quimby's most professional, dignified, and complimentary tone possible. At least as much as he could muster. *Good.* He had taken the bait and let Aurelle off the hook. *Did anyone else sense that?*

Quimby and a few of the others in the infirmary did believe in spirit energies. They, as did a handful of others in the universes, felt spirits played a great role in everything seen and unseen. While none of them thought active spirits still existed in day-to-day life, they all agreed there was a possibility they once did. And if spirits had existed as described, it was likely these entities may have left energy signatures all around the spaces they had inhabited.

"You are quite right doctor, but I also don't want to rule out the possibility of post-traumatic stress, and frankly, the tagnometer is the best machine for that job without question." Aurelle knew this would fire at least one or two of them up. However, she did think that there was something to the theory of post-traumatic stress resurgence.

The problem had been a once misunderstood medical diagnosis. Post-traumatic stress disorder; long called PTSD, had plagued armies for thousands of years in many different cultures and races. Especially for humans. However, after Cybrinthian medicine and culture was mixed with that of mankind, the problem all but vanished. Cybrinthians had a highly developed ability to screen out the disposition for mental disorders. They also had achieved near full success at isolating brain functions. With this capability, if a patient developed problems directly from and following traumatic events, doctors had a ready fix. They could target the processing portion of the brain that initiated and propagated the undesired responses. Then, essentially, they could reprogram or shut it down altogether. Within a very small amount of time, the surrounding neural pathways would take over any functions necessary that the affected area could no longer process. Voila. Battlefield stress reactions and their delayed life impacts all but disappeared.

In time, the technology progressed enough so that doctors no longer needed to isolate individual brain activity and reprogram. They only needed to target the thought processes themselves and give brief treatments. By the new age, soldiers and sailors were screened for any trace of a genetic predisposition for mental instabilities. If found, it would be preemptively treated and the service member sent on his way. There was rarely a need even to separate the member from the service with the advanced screening and treatment capability. And so it was that PTSD became something studied but rarely seen, and then it became an anomaly of the past.

"Come now doctor; don't tell me you really think that ancient ailment is a possibility?" Quimby had now assumed an air of superiority. Aurelle knew that tone. She had heard it many times before from senior doctors and even junior male doctors. Some resented the fact that she was a pretty woman and could get her way more often than them with certain people because of that fact. Or maybe it was the fact that she was smarter and better at her craft than they were. No matter. Some did resent her. Some physicians assumed the holier-than-thou attitude because she was not fully of their race. At least those who suspected she was not all human. Probably more doctors than she cared to admit held these prejudices due to her race, her gender, or both.

"I am not closing my mind to any possibilities sir." She became very serious and looked him straight in the eye. His gaze met hers head on. "We do not understand this new weapon we face doctor. We do not understand the effects it is having on our soldiers and sailors. The 'ancient ailment' about which you speak plagued civilizations for eons. I have considered the possibility that this new weapon might affect dormant traits that our predecessors thought eradicated and controlled." She paused. "Is it not true that in our history, militaries had branches of service dedicated specifically to the psychological sciences?" Her counterpoint was very cool and calculated. Just the right tone and emphasis to get the attention of each expert present.

"She has a valid point Barnes," stated Doctor Simons as he shifted his gaze back and forth between Quimby and Aurelle. "Even though I agree with you, it is highly unlikely." He looked at Quimby and then around the room, "I don't feel we can afford to discount any possibility prematurely." Simons was a greatly respected scientist and doctor in this region. Aurelle knew she was fortunate to be able to work under his tutelage. He was a kind soul and always seemed to know just the right amount of latitude to give his subordinates. He allowed mistakes but only ones that could be learned from and would not do permanent damage. He had a good sense of the line between an acceptable margin of error and the irreversible or inexcusable. Simons was almost a fatherly figure in the infirmary and commanded a great deal of loyalty from his staff. Even the ones who would have liked to have his position. Aurelle was grateful he respected her judgment and looked beyond her skin and sex. Without his support, her ideas and any research she hoped to do stemming from them would probably meet or already would have met a quick dead end.

One of the other female doctors, Doctor J. Natal was nodding her head in agreement. She made an open-handed gesture with her left hand towards Aurelle.

"She may indeed be right, and I agree with you Doctor Simons. But I believe we will be wise to spend some increased efforts cultivating the accelerated growth cell colonies," said Doctor Natal forcefully. She was the taller and prettier of the two other women. Aurelle did not know much about her. "They are our best bet, and we have the resources to do so at the moment," continued Natal with an increasingly urgent tremble in her tone. "In the wake of Quai-14 at least," she added.

The Quai-14 battle was immense. It left a hundred thousand dead, tens of thousands wounded (mostly who subsequently died shortly thereafter) and destroyed hundreds of ships and landing craft of various sizes. In addition, the battle obliterated 14 or so large federal capital vessels of war. There was effectively no noteworthy loss for the Confederation. The triage required by it meant that the regional medical command was forced to request immediate emergency support from all available vessels- even some civilian and commercially operated. The Federation's joint military council on war saw to the need quickly and approved the entire support package as requested. Within five days of the battle, hospital and infirmary staffs doubled in size and supplies were rushed in faster than any of the resident staffs could have imagined. Still, they were swamped, but with the extra help it was tolerable.

Saint Demetrius' infirmary became a miniature town with its temporary wings set up. There were several large transports permanently docked alongside the facility to accommodate the extra personnel. Two of the ships were semi-permanently attached to the massive structure itself and served as expansion pods. Dr. Simons was in his element despite wishing that all this was not necessary at the same time. As the wounded situation had stabilized, the staff was able to keep pace with treatments and even work on some research. This was how Aurelle fit into the picture. Her assigned patient, JT, was the very first survivor to come into the infirmary who was experiencing neutrino cannon sickness.

"Doctor Natal is right about the resources my distinguished friends," commented the third man who so far had only listened. He also wore the same medical attire of the other men. "I have a friend with connections to the joint military council. And while they have just approved much funding to support the additional staff and resources for us, it is only for the moment." He looked slowly around the room at each of them, "but as soon as another battle, another crisis or… the deity forbid," he paused, "another disaster- happens, all this attention and the extra help will go elsewhere." He finished with a very grave and desperate expression. "And we all know that until the Federation figures out how to combat the new enemy weapon, the tide of things is… not good."

The last woman sitting at the table, Doctor George, now spoke up, "we must we give Doctor Gifford full latitude to pursue the various theories which have already been proposed. Perhaps assign her a permanent intern to work on the Wayne case and any others that she thinks fit to test." Doctor George was a middle-aged dark-haired woman originally from one of the lower Quai planets. She had a son serving aboard a Federation starship somewhere in the Far Universe. She was normally quiet, but when she did have something to say it was declarative, opinionated, and to the point.

Natal looked at George and then to Simons.

"That's not a bad idea, but I still propose we continue to pursue further development with the growth colonies. We could make that extra staff member responsible for them and to report to Doctor Gifford but publish a daily update for the executive infirmary council. We need both measures pursued if we are going to keep the research up with the Wayne case," said Natal for them all to hear. She was not ready to concede her efforts to get more research into the accelerated growth colonies. That was fine with Aurelle. She would rather find out something from them before finding it out with JT as the live experiment. Plus, accelerated growth cell colonies were a fairly reliable means of research so long as the work was done carefully. If they were to be overseen by her, she would definitely want an assistant. Even if it was only an intern, a second pair of eyes watching her work was always welcome. Duties taking care of the patients took up most of her time and she did not particularly want to trade that for time in the laboratory.

"I tend to agree with each of you, and want to remind everyone that Doctors Natal and Haaus have the most pertinent observations for our immediate consideration. Our incredible surge of funding and resources will only be here for a limited time. There is no telling what this war keeps in store for us in the near or distant future," stated Doctor Simons and he shifted his focus to the digital clock display over the conference room's door.

He was good at very subtly maintaining command of a group once opinions had been shared and the conversation had made its rounds.

"I am very inclined to support Doctor George's suggestion of assigning an intern to Doctor Gifford. However, I want that intern to come from Doctor Quimby's staff. He has the most experience with spirit affected patients and I trust that he will be able to provide you, Aurelle, with a top notch and dedicated helper." His use of her first name was slightly out of character, but no one seemed to notice.

Perhaps he was trying to impart the personal nature of work with spirit ailments or perhaps he just wanted to ensure she was paying close attention. Whatever the reason, he was clearly starting to wrap things up. Making the point that the decisions were now being made. This was his way of telling the others if there was any other input, now was the time to bring it up.

"I'd be happy to support that, and I've got just the fellow in mind. I'll speak with you later about him Doctor Gifford," commented Quimby. He looked at her with an expression that denoted respect and admiration. Something she had not sensed from him before. *We'll see if this lasts,* she thought to herself.

"Alright then, any objections?" asked Simons. Silence. "Good. We've all got places to be and things to be doing I am certain." Simons was gathering up a few papers into a briefcase he had brought and laid beside the conference table. "I want us to huddle again early tomorrow morning. Oh-seven-hundred. That gives us just over twelve hours to see some patients, digest things, get that intern sliced over to Doctor Gifford, and… with some luck, have a good night's rest." He paused. "And Doctor Quimby, I do want to speak with you before any final decision is made about the intern you select," he said. A very subtle and cool way of reminding Quimby this was his hospital and he was the final decision-maker. Aurelle smiled to herself. That was why Simons was such a good leader and administrator. He did take charge but never in a way to rub other staff members the wrong way. Quimby might not have even seen the unstated hint. Simons had paused again.

Here it comes. Aurelle had witnessed this many times before in other settings. Simons would don the expression of genuine care, give them all a brief grandfatherly I-am-concerned-about-you observation, followed by a quick pep-talk and dismiss them with a well-worn ra-ra statement. She would have bet money on it if she could have. Here he went:

"You all know how much I depend on you. How much the entire staff- much less the patients- depend on you. I know you all give 100 percent 24 hours a day, and I know that you never tell me, or complain about it, but you frequently skip rest. Well, I don't want to see any of you get burned out and I've started to see it in some of the junior staff. Watch your people and watch yourselves. I need you all at your best and these next few weeks are going to be bad. I sense it. Get some good rest tonight. I'm proud of all of you and all you've done in the past week. No team I've ever worked with has accomplished so much in the face of such an emergency. Ok, people, back to work – Go Team Saint D!" And Simons closed his briefcase. *How silly,* thought Aurelle. But that's what he did and they knew it and it amused them. The other doctors found it a funny but idiosyncratic thing. As Simons shut the archaic device, his briefcase, the others followed suit and gathered up their things.

Before Aurelle left the table, Quimby caught her by the arm, "Doctor Gifford, would you be able to meet me on level 2 in my office in fifteen?"

"Sure thing. I'll have the results of this afternoon's tagnometer readings from Sergeant Wayne by then. I'll bring them with me," Aurelle told him. The conference room cleared out. Aurelle stayed behind for a few moments to think uninterrupted. She knew if the accelerated growth colonies could not shed light on what was happening with the enemy's new weapon then it would fall to her and her findings to hazard the medical community's best guess. The colonies simply created a synthetic environment where the weapon's effects on laboratory tissue, humanoid and Cybrinthian engineered clones could be sped up. The time rate of acceleration allowed observation at and experimentation at a rate of more than 1,000 times that of actual maturation. In theory, in one day, the colonies would reveal what would happen in nearly three years of real time. But they were not fast enough. Medical scientists needed to know what would be the effects upon children and grandchildren of those exposed to the weapon. They also needed to know before the next employment killed or maimed thousands or millions more. The clock was ticking fast. Aurelle hoped her work with JT might provide additional insight or augment what was learned with the growth colonies. She knew her work was important. She just didn't know it would have more to do with her quick wit than her medical expertise. Fortunately, Doctor Aurelle Gifford was quite gifted in both of those areas.

Chapter 11
Note

Back in the screening room the light pulses slowed and went dark. The monitor made a series of humming tones and clicked. "All done Sergeant," said the technician. The bed and rails moved back in unison slowly out of the glass enclosed chamber. JT started to feel a bit of a spinning sensation across his whole body but it quickly dissipated as he exited the chamber proper. He opened his eyes and everything was blurry. The sterile room for a while was all a haze to him.

"Why can't I see? This didn't happen last time," JT asked loudly to the technician but was facing a wall instead of the man himself.

"Well, that happens sometimes with people who've had corrective eye surgery if they're not used to the machine and are sensitive to light."

"This is my third time in five days. I've never had corrective surgery. And do I look sensitive to light to you?" JT immediately retorted. JT was not fair skinned. He was actually rather dark for someone of his ancestry.

"Ehh, no Sir. I guess not," said the technician weakly. "I will let my boss know right now," he added. He was glad that JT couldn't see him well since he was already intimidated by the Marine and he could only imagine what the sergeant's piercing gaze would be like.

"Right. Now don't hold back on me either- I want to know anything that may have come up. Even if you think you've got nothing. I need to know if my farts are going to come out my pecker in a purple dust haze from my wee breech before I make it to age 40; you better give it to me straight."

"That would be unfortunate," managed the frail younger man. JT was tired of getting results from these readings long after his chain of command already knew. He was willing to throw his weight around to a junior technician if it could help him get some early warning. JT reflected as he bolstered his less than subtle bullying. After all, these were tests for his body and so why should he not have first access to the results.

"Aye, sir. I will see to it," responded the man. The bed finished its lateral movement then angled upwards as all of the rails turned and automatically flipped themselves over, folding away underneath the bed top. This allowed JT to slowly lean forward and stand.

"Am I done here?" he asked.

"Yes sir, I'll have a runner notify you if the doctor finds anything significant." The technician whirled himself around and faced back towards his screen. JT stood up and walked laboriously around a glass wall to the small table he previously had laid his clothes upon. They were there in a neat pile folded squarely. His vision was starting to return to normal. He tried hard to focus and then picked up his hospital-issued garments. As he unfolded them, he turned to note that the technician was beginning to wrap things up at the monitor station. JT then walked to a corner of the room with a little area for changing and removed the paper-like covering he had worn into the tagnometer. Slowly and painfully, he began to put his pocket-less light gray loose pants and over-sized buttoned shirt back on. He had stopped taking pain killing medication the day prior and the accelerated healing of his legs was taking its toll on their nerve endings.

It was JT's choice to go without taking pain killers or muscle relaxants. He read in one of the better-known medical publications that some doctors held disapproving attitudes towards what they deemed far flung spirit theories. These prevailing opinions held that spirit-influenced maladies were affected poorly by drugs. Subscribing to the use of pain medicine or not, JT deduced that he was being evaluated and researched. Mainly this was because of his continual subjugation to testing but also because he could pick up hints from Aurelle. She seemed to be on his side. Her demeanor was formal and medically astute but mildly flirtatious and genuinely kind. Despite not wanting to be direct and tell him why he was undergoing such extensive care, Aurelle dropped less than subtle clues to the importance of his being there. One morning she told him frankly the medical community would learn from him and his recovery, and so would others; others in untold numbers and ways.

He still did not fathom that he was the first known patient to be affected by the neutrino weapon who was returning to full health. Had he known this, he would have been sure of the reasons for his extensive testing. But then there was the possibility that JT was wrong, Aurelle was just making him feel better about himself, there was nothing special about his case and that he would be on his way as soon as possible. JT feared his gut was wrong and this was the case; and he didn't like to be wrong. He was a Marine. Even when Marines were dead wrong, they rarely admitted it. Or at least admitted this embarrassment to themselves. But then again, JT was not the average Marine. JT was not the average anything.

So shortly after he woke the first time following major treatments and tagnometer sessions, he had asked Aurelle if the pain drugs would affect his case or their study in any way. She tried well to avoid giving an answer, but he pressed her. Finally, she had replied that they could not know but it would be insignificant regardless. But JT told himself he was better than needing added physical comfort. He saw through this answer. He saw into Aurelle's genuine care for him and his feelings; his comfort. But the need for him to feel above that need was greater. He then asked her plainly if she was telling him the truth. Then, caught in the moral quandary, she could not lie to him anymore.

"Fine, since you must know," she had responded almost angrily. "I was not totally forward with you just now. Yes, the pain medicine may affect the evaluation, but what I said was true: we cannot know for sure. When I said it would be insignificant, I implied we knew that for certain. We do not. However, as a scientist," she smiled at him, blinked several times innocently and then continued, "something that I know for sure is that if you insist on stopping pain medication," another pause and smile, "you will be in pain."

JT laughed at this declaration, and was about to reply when she cut him off. This time she did not smile flirtatiously.

"And if you are in pain, then that fact could as well affect the outcome. Given that either scenario could bear an impact upon what we find out, wouldn't you rather not be in agony?" She had a logical point. JT conceded she was level headed and logical. More so even, she was difficult to disagree with. Her cuteness only made it more difficult for him.

In the end though, JT decided that he had a significant enough tolerance for pain that the lesser affect upon the research would be achieved if he ceased the medication. And so the day prior to his third and most recent tagnometer session, he took his last anti-pain drug. He was now feeling the aftermath of that decision. He was strong-willed and determined though. He would not let on that anything was bothering him no matter how badly he felt.

One morning after another tagnometer session he was thinking about that decision very acutely. Every muscle and bone in his body seemed to be screaming for him to yield. JT was good at ignoring them. After waking up and partaking in the now familiar mechanized morning assessment routine, this particular day he decided his routine needed to change. JT decided he would get himself going without aid and maybe even try being completely autonomous for the rest of the day. So, at this thought, he began to dress before any technician arrived to help. He gritted his teeth through the taxing movements that required a contortion of his lower extremities. JT had his pants on, one shoe partly on, and then his task was abruptly interrupted:

ALL PATIENTS REPORT TO BEDSIDE. ALL STAFF TO GENERAL QUARTERS AND DUTY POSITIONS. THIS IS A DRILL. The infirmary intercom blared from everywhere.

JT looked for anyone. He spotted a technician who had been observing him from across the hall through an open door a few beds away. The man was now already halfway to the door. "Can you manage the rest?" the man called through the doorway into the room to JT.

"Yes I'm fine, go see to whatever you need. I'll get myself finished and back," responded JT quickly to the eager and now starting to be flustered technician.

"Right, this could delay your results a little, but probably not long; I'll be back on this to check on you whenever this drill is done." The technician spun around instantly and then without saying anything else, he was gone. JT continued with his dressing. His other shoe was now on too. Any second, he would be ready to head back to his bed. He was not overly concerned. The staff seemed to be taking it seriously. JT was glad of that. He had not yet experienced a drill in the infirmary but he certainly had aboard his ship. He could not imagine that here it would be more difficult than aboard a battle or star cruiser. Those drills were taxing and very stressful. He rather looked forward to seeing what a hospital outpost battle drill would be like compared with his own fleet experiences. He thought little else of it as he got to his feet and headed towards the door. When he stepped to within a foot or so of the two metallic halves of the passageway, they automatically parted with the faint whoosh of a hydraulic pulse. He continued on his way down the passage.

As soon as he stepped out from his treatment area, JT discovered there was a frantic scramble going on in the main corridor. This was outside the tagnometer zone so there were life forms and medical personnel of all types moving in every direction. He saw medics, doctors, doctrettes and nurses, even patients, all moving at high velocities on various paths with seemingly important intents. Most were running and some were at near dead sprints. He would not normally have been surprised to see everyone in a hurry. But this was something else. He was impressed already. During a drill aboard the Vissad there would have been a great sense of urgency as well. But the Vissad was a battle cruiser. This was an infirmary. He took three steps to the left once into the hall and stayed close to the wall.

There were several blinking and whirling orange and red lights attached to the ceiling and upper hallway walls in receded housings. They all seemed to be going off to their own rhythms. The lights threw a weirdly oscillating or intermittently flashing glow in all directions, which, bouncing off the moving forms below created an even greater illusion of a panicked club of some sort. The vicinity just beyond the tagnometer wing door contained a busy hall intersection. JT crossed it quickly to avoid anyone's way. He easily tuned them out and focused on moving back to the ward where he had promised to go. He looked down and imagined himself elsewhere. The hallway travelers were very loud and JT had trouble for a moment getting his bearings. He paused, managed to regain them and then started towards one of the transport elevators. Then the intercom harshly interrupted his concentration once again:

ALL KEY STAFF AND LEVEL FIVE PHYSICIANS MOVE TO COMMAND CENTER. ALL OTHERS REPORT TO GENERAL QUARTERS AND DUTY STATIONS.

This would not affect JT and so he kept moving as he had been towards his own ward. As a seed of an afterthought, he vaguely felt it was strange to have a second alert not minutes after the first. Another alert with additional directions for senior staff and leaders. *Why would these directions not have been announced initially with the first?* Maybe it was nothing at all. A simple follow-on order not considered before in its entirety. Again he thought to himself this didn't matter. JT wasn't sure what the rest of the so-called "drill" would consist of, but he hoped it would get quieter soon. Less commotion and loud energy meant more chance once he got back to his bed that he could actually get some rest. JT had a vague intention of sleeping through the rest of or whatever else this exercise had in store.

After another three minutes, a couple of levels, and a few turns, JT was back near his ward. He made a note to himself: *get out and explore more of the infirmary.* He had been out several times but only close to his ward and usually escorted by a physician or two or some staff member. If he were feeling more like himself: without pain; not so edgy, not so exhausted, he would already have explored the entire facility. He would have had a detailed mental map in his head if he were feeling normal. It was not so large that he could not have accomplished that task within a couple of hours. He plodded along and finally after countless passers-by rushing this way and that, and seemingly countless lights and alarm sounds, he came to his own ward. He got to his bed. If JT could get some decent rest, then he would make that exploratory trip sometime soon. He vowed it to himself to do something productive and get out and around for reasons other than his constant medical and testing needs. After the drill. Or at least as soon as he woke up after the drill, is what he decided. JT made up his mind. No matter how lethargic, pain-laden, or down he felt, he would do it anyway, regardless.

JT eased onto the bed and kicked off his shoes. He flipped back the sheet working his way underneath it. His legs hurt after the trip back, but that would subside shortly. The ward was quieter than the hallways. He was glad for that. He lay slowly back into the small pristine hospital white oasis sinking comfortably as he went. JT moved his arms behind his head arranging the automatic contouring pillow a little more comfortably. He could have used the auto comfort feature on the bed controls, but he found that it never worked as well as doing it himself. He thought about the absurdity of letting a machine decide what felt best. Though he thought at some point he would, he never argued with the doctors who told him it was better to let the computer do it for him. They said it would not make any adjustments that were bad for the body. But a patient doing it himself could do something that might contort or hinder his healing. Hogwash thought JT.

He didn't care what they said. For thousands of years people who were hurt healed in beds that didn't have computers to do fancy things for them. And everyday citizens didn't have computerized sleeping conditions. Marines frequently slept in places far less comfortable and made do just fine. JT generally liked to do things himself anyway. He was never comfortable relying on computers even though at times they were necessary. So much depended upon them that even for the most basic jobs and tasks it was impossible to get by without one. But now in his hospital bed he made himself comfortable like people had done for many millennia. He reached behind his head under the pillow to adjust it. But as he did so he felt something out of place.

His right fingers grasped what seemed like a piece of paper. JT caught hold of a corner, lifted his head just a bit and brought the small sheet of paper around to his front. It appeared torn from a notepad; he looked at it closely. It was a hastily scratched note. The handwriting was a bit hard to read as it was written so quickly. The letters blended together as in semi-script writing. The words had smeared in a few spots as the author had rubbed a hand over the paper before the ink was fully dry. He could just make out what it said. He blinked several times in surprise and baffled comprehension. Then he began reading it twice more. He looked around his bed area quickly for any other clues; not sure what to make of it at all. The note said:

GO TO 1ST LEVEL STAFF LOUNGE LOCK YOURSELF INSIDE

He decided without second thought he trusted her more than the automated voice from the infirmary intercom. He also now realized his suspicion of the second intercom announcement was indeed warranted. Doctor Gifford's bizarre note also served to reinforce that notion. Something important was not right and he didn't have much time to analyze it. He folded the note and put it in his shirt; he had no pockets. He tossed off the sheet cover and turned to let his legs thrust as well as they could over the side of the bed. They pained him. He ignored the sensation. JT grabbed his shoes and put them on in seconds. He had done this kind of heart pounding drill before. Just not in an infirmary -only aboard warships and in training simulations.

He was already out of the ward moving towards the first deck. His leg pain was no longer there; at least he didn't notice it. He blocked out the chaos everywhere around him. But at the same time, he heard it all. He seemed to hear everything yet nothing simultaneously. JT's intuition allowed him to scan any and every conversation within earshot for key words or phrases. Any clues the Marine would pick up. He was on autopilot searching for abnormalities amidst the commotion. He was focused. In the zone. The fact that he was in Saint Demetrius' halls and not the Vissad's corridors made little difference; his training and instincts were operating in full force. His mission was now to follow Aurelle's instructions and he would accomplish it. As he ran he tried to look inconspicuous but it didn't really matter. No one around would have noticed a patient moving about the halls. There were plenty of them. As he rounded a corner, he scanned a directory keying in on the bottom of the deck listings:

Level 1:

-Intake,

-Administration

-Emergency Care

-Case Management

-Staff / Visitor Lounges

Chapter 12
Meeting

The young spirit trusted what the tree told him. The men were not dangerous to him and they needed help. He sensed they would be grateful for anything he could do or offer. He also sensed an opportunity to do something important for his people. This encounter with the seemingly human and possibly neighboring inhabitants of Apequia might prove a perfect opportunity for that purpose. Faeruthan was less than ten yards from the closest of the humans, the knight-like man, Farhale. The knight spoke,

"The key my lady is to be sure we are heading towards a friendly people who will not deceive us in case we are discovered." The lady was turning to walk towards the knight but paused to step over a large fallen limb. The clearing they occupied was strewn with large rocks and branches buried all throughout its high grass. The young spirit decided this was the moment to act.

"You are in welcoming country my friends," pronounced Fae loudly enough for all to hear.

"Who speaks to us? Show yourself now lest we be forced to consider you a foe," said Farhale thunderously and commandingly. At the same time, he drew his sword. The second knight spoke immediately drawing his sword as well.

"Who is there? Beware for we are warriors and are so armed! I command you to come now to a place where we may see you!" he shouted. Fae had not turned himself opaque or moved out from the cover of shadow. He was about to respond when Lady Shera spoke.

"Calm thyselves my faithful soldiers. We will be gracious to anyone unless shown reason otherwise. Stay thy blades." She scanned the area around Fae looking for exactly where the voice had come from. Farhale sheathed his blade bowing his head. Valcor looked around suspiciously but did the same. And, he kept his palm on the hilt.

"I mean no harm," began Fae. "I should like to offer you my help if you wish. I am unarmed and was simply passing through this way when I heard you."

"We are not here on any ill-purpose," said Lady Shera. "We are on a journey to find someone who may live near here. Our travel which brings us to this part of Apequia is of grave importance." Valcor could not believe she had volunteered this much to someone they could not even see. Farhale thought the same thing. The young servant-like girl looked nervous. She had moved up against the side of her horse. And, like Lady Shera, was scanning the area around Fae.

"I believe you. But I do see you are well armed and I do not recognize you or your people. Perhaps you might show me some sign you would not harm a young spirit," said Fae. He estimated they would appreciate this gesture as an increasing exchange of information. He thought that he could offer them more details about himself bit by bit as they did the same for him; he would see how that went. Lady Shera seemed to understand this.

"So, you are a spirit," she said.

"Yes. Are you of the human race?" asked Fae in the most mature sounding, serious but friendly spirit tone he could muster.

"We are menca. The near cousins of humans. We are far woodland people who have been here for ages but share a common ancestor with mankind. We were created from one and the same creator, humans and us. We share much though many would not expect it."

"I understand, you are from the far side of Flarhom then," said Fae, "if that is so, I know some history of your ancestors."

"We are, and we would be in your debt if you might accompany us to the nearest town or place that your elders gather so that we might ask aide of your people," said Lady Shera. "I am Lady Shera Augustus of the realm of Hanoveria. These are my traveling party, Sirs Valcor and Farhale, and Miss Jeanaviere." She had been considering her earlier reluctance to seek help and of her knights' pleas for her to do the opposite. Pride is a foolish thing at times and the more she spoke with this young spirit, the more she felt that swallowing her own pride would be wise.

She hoped he would reveal himself soon so that she and her

traveling party might continue on their quest. And of course, it would be nice to see this spirit who seemed tentatively but graciously offering help. It would ease the minds of her knights. She and her people rarely saw spirits. Lady Shera was shrewd and smart. She calculated that offering the spirit the truth as to who she and her companions were early on in their developing exchange would do good. She hoped it might be recognized as a display of good faith and trust between them. Her knights had not helped the delicate situation. But then, that was their nature. They were protectors sworn to her. Diplomacy was not their strong suit. She was trying hard to come up with another apt way she might show this spirit she trusted him.

Just then Faeruthan stepped out of the shadows and allowed some light to reflect from his transparent body. He did not change from his cat-like form. The horses each stepped backwards keeping watch on him with suspicion.

"I am Faeruthan of Flarhom and I offer you my services," he said. He let shades of blue and white reflect alternately from his clear crystal body. He knew that others of his village were impressed with this rendering. Not many spirits were as clear as Fae and even fewer were able to bend light in such a way. He knew the humans would likely also be impressed even if they did not say so directly. He looked around at each of them. If he was scared in any way, it did not show. He eyed Sir Valcor's hand on his sword handle. As Fae looked from his hand to his face, the knight immediately let it go bringing both palms facing forward as if to show the spirit he was empty handed and not in any way threatening. Fae understood the gesture.

"We appreciate your kindness and readily accept your offer," said Lady Shera. Her horse gave a short whinny and shook her head back and forth. "My steed Zabeth accepts your offer as well," she added with a smile. The party continued to speak for a brief time before it became apparent to Fae that Lady Shera wished to move on with the quest but out of protocol was not rushing the conversation. She was a noble in her land; and, although used to getting her way, her culture taught her sometimes to defer. She knew well how to appreciate letting the pace of discussion be dictated by events rather than attempt to bend it to her party's or her own will. Fae perceived this and comprehended her leadership, her importance and stature in the group. He decided to now make good on his promise. He moved forward and in so doing indicated the direction they should head with a sidestep towards that wooded path. The way was not clear cut but strewn with overgrown but pretty vegetation. Easy to make out for a spirit but near imperceptible for humans, menca or their kin.

"It seems as you are on an important mission, perhaps we should make haste," said Fae. "The day moves on; it will not wait for us," he quoted one of his father's sayings.

"Thank you young master," said Farhale. His horse moved towards him and knelt slowly. The animal acted as if it knew what Farhale wanted him to do without prompting. Valcor nodded to the young girl Jeanaviere then beckoned to his horse. The animal stepped forward and did just as Farhale's had done.

"I echo my comrades and offer apologies if my earlier talk was offensive in any way," said Valcor. He looked at Fae first and then to Lady Shera who nodded her head and blinked slowly. Her look eased as her already soft features grew quickly softer; all the while she smiled gently- as if to say all was well to the knight. During the brief exchange, the girl also turned to mount her steed. They started to move from the clearing. Fae made sure he moved slowly and kept a bit of color in his form so that it would be easier for his new friends to follow him. He beamed a brighter translucence for a short bit so they could adjust to the silhouette they would follow through the woods. Fae had already decided to temper his visibility so the people could follow him but the group would not be terribly visible from too far. There was no need to invite inquiry. The trees themselves would do enough of that. And, they would be talking to each other as the forest always did.

As Fae stepped silently forward despite remaining a colorful opaque, he became slightly more difficult for the humans to see. They were now under tree cover in the fading ambient light. But since they knew his form or at least how it distorted the light reflecting from him, they were still able to follow Fae. At least against the darker backdrop of the woods with relative ease. The humans moved out of the light of the first clearing and trailed behind the spirit in single file atop their mounts. It was much louder than Fae alone would have been for certain, but they kept close and there was not much to fear in these woods anyway. They passed several more clearings similar to the first. No one spoke as they went.

Fae led his new guests through an old familiar but little-used wooded path home. He did not take the direct route. The trail he normally used would have been faster but there was a greater chance of meeting somebody. Now there would be other young spirits out playing since the lessons were done for the year. There were also travelers who occasionally used the other way. It was on the maps. The route he was using was not. This way would add some time to the trip but he estimated it would be worth the difference. He did not bother to say anything about the other available options to his traveling party. Lady Shera indicated to him that they should avoid the well-traveled paths so he simply told them to follow as he led.

"Young friend- How did you come across us but keep thyself so quiet?" asked the burly swordsman Valcor. Fae shrugged and looked back at the big man.

"I didn't have to do much. It is not hard to listen to the woods and hear what they tell you. Besides you were all very intent on your, uhm, talk. It wouldn't have been hard for a herd of elk to trot past unnoticed by you." Fae hadn't thought before speaking and realized his last comment might have been offensive. But there was no taking it back now and for him it was true. "Also I had help from the tree spirits," he added, as if to try and make up for the earlier statement's rudeness. "They were listening to you for a good bit and told me that you were not threatening and needed help." He continued gliding through the forest path leading the mencas. All the while sensing for other spirits within his range.

"Well, young lad, whoever the tree-folks were, they told you right," said Valcor plainly. He did not seem offended by Fae's elk remark. The group continued along for a time until they came to yet another clearing. The four travelers had dismounted before each clearing and were now once again already walking alongside their horses. Fae did not understand the habit but imagined it had something to do with safety, lessening their silhouette, or feeling more secure during the crossing in so doing. The group had not ridden very long before they discovered Fae's chosen path was strewn with low hanging branches and vines. After dismounting they walked easily with their steeds gladly obeying.

None needed to have their reigns held. The animals each walked besides, slightly behind and somewhat in step with his or her master. At the clearing Lady Shera placed her palm against Zabeth's left front side, her horse halted and she took the reins loosely. The group followed her lead.

"How far are we from your home my young guide?" the lady asked. Fae told her they had two choices. They could stick inside the wood line keeping it to their east. In this way shortly they would be at his home which lay seven more kilometers ahead. Or they could move farther inside the forest heading directly west which was a faster route. But this would take them by the old hermit Quildevar's home and Fae didn't care to pass by it. He had never been comfortable around the hermit's house. His dwelling was not more than a modest furrow but it was dark and menacing. And Quildevar didn't care for visitors. Much less foreign visitors. But the way past Quildevar's also led past the nearest village center, another three or four kilometers. And that could be exactly what the group needed in looking for the help they sought during their visit.

"Is this Quildevar a spirit-person?" the lady asked clearly for Fae to answer but loud enough for it to be clear she meant the knights and girl should be included in their talk.

"Yes, and so are all the inhabitants of these woods," Fae replied. "There aren't human or menca people for a thousand kilometers from here to my knowledge." He thought about how long this group must have been traveling to arrive in his homeland on the border of Flarhom Woods. The woods and surrounding country were not overly expansive, but it was still a far distance to reach its borders. It would take a week for men traveling on horseback to get across it and reach the nearest settlement. Unless perhaps they had arrived via some other means and were not from this home world as they claimed.

Elves were known to journey through these lands on their pilgrimages. But it was very infrequent to hear of men or their cousins traversing through Flarhom. Elgamine, the greatest elf city in the world of Apequia lay far to the north of Flarhom Woods. Hundreds of kilometers to the south was Hanoveria, a growing colony of spirits. Elf or spirit families would make the trip across Flarhom's expanse to visit relatives, venture to the new colony or conduct business. Elf horses were very fast and could travel the great woods' distance in only two days while spirits could move at incredible speeds in their nearly non-physical forms. Since the nearest human-like settlements were more than 1,000 kilometers away and their horses were not fast, spirits never saw humans or mencas in the land of Flarhom. Faeruthan did not ask the details of their journey but he wondered about their quest. Perhaps if they elected to continue on with him, he would learn more.

"Is he trustworthy do you think?" asked Farhale to Valcor quietly so that he thought Fae couldn't hear. He did not know that spirit senses were much more acute than those of men-cousins. Fae heard him without any effort.

"Faeruthan has always been completely honest as far as I know," said Fae laughingly.

"I say my humblest apologies young master," said Farhale in complete surprise upon immediate realization that Fae had picked up every word of what he had said. Lady Shera smiled to herself. She was more familiar with the abilities of spirits than her companions. She knew that an advanced spirit would be able to tell what they were thinking. In her own estimation and considering the circumstances, that might not be a bad thing. In this way the spirits would see their cause was just and noble. Fae wanted to keep an awkward silence from developing so he continued:

"My grandfather always raised us to believe dishonesty would lead to hardship and hurt," he said without trying to sound offensive or condescending.

"A wise spirit was he, master Faeruthan," said Farhale. "Is he still among the living?"

"Oh yes, but he is a very solitary spirit. He is full of stories and funny tales from many generations, but he does not share with many," said Fae, this time loud enough for all to hear.

"I should hope we might be able to meet him," said Farhale.

"He keeps to himself except for our family. Also, you should know my family and friends call me Fae. You may as well if it suits you." said Fae.

"Thank you, young spirit. You are kind and we see that," Lady Shera interjected, as if speaking for the knights and herself in one voice.

Fae continued, "I don't think a soul in Apequia, save the old hermit Quildevar, or maybe I, could tell you many of his stories or convince him to share them with outsiders. No offense intended to present company." He said this adding the last part in as kind and gentle a manner as possible. But it still sounded like an afterthought.

"Would your grandfather take kindly to a visit?" asked Valcor.

"He is not as much of a loner as Quildevar, but he does keep to himself. He does not often entertain guests," Fae said. "You see, since he fought in the Grand War fifty years ago, he has never spoken much about any of his experiences." Fae sensed that Lady Shera wanted to continue moving but had not yet made up her mind as to what to think of the discussion. Fae saw an opportunity. "Maybe to aid in your quest is just what he needs. I think serving in some small way to help you could be a great help to him- offer him a sense of a larger purpose once again," he said.

Lady Shera saw he was angling at gaining some more information about their quest, but she also saw he was grasping. It was Valcor who spoke up now:

"How was it thy grandfather fought in the Grand War? That was a fight between men, mencas and elves."

"There were spirits involved in it too even though our nations did not condone the conflict between your people and the elves," replied Fae. He was a good student of history and he knew well of the wars between people and elves. And although his entire education and apprenticeship had been with spirit elders, he had read books translated from the elf-tongue and others written by men. He had a well-rounded and unbiased education. His opinions of the history of all the major races of Apequia was impressive by any standards.

"The boy is right," said Farhale in agreement. "My own father knew of several spirits that came to the aid of mencas during the war. Stories are told of spirits who served openly among our ranks even though it meant for them that they would not be allowed to return to their homelands." Farhale continued, "not to return for violation of the neutrality." Fae looked across the woods. He had the feeling that Sir Farhale also knew a good deal of his people's history.

"And then there were spirits who served the elves," continued Farhale. "It depended mostly on which spirit nation they hailed from. Flarhom had many who supported the elf cause."

Fae did not feel qualified to speak intelligently about the politics of the day or causes of the war. He did not want to discuss with one of the warring factions, mencas or humans- which side was right or wrong. He knew the spirit nations' policy of neutrality was considered right by his people. The wars between elves and men had gone on for ages and the last one- the Grand War, was considered the most violent and destructive by all of those combatant races.

The Grand War's main catalyst had been the right to regulate magic. While the spirits were generally neutral, many had supported the elves. But that is another story altogether. Fae now sensed a question developing in his new companions' minds. *Did Faeruthan's grandfather and family support the elves or mencas and men?* He decided he was not going to volunteer the information unless asked directly. They could either ask him or wait until, and if, they met his grandfather to find out. In the meantime, he would say nothing more.

"Who did your granddaddy fight for then master Faeruthan?" belted out Valcor. *Well that addresses that unspoken question and possibly a problem,* thought Fae. Sir Valcor was apparently not one to bite his tongue. Fae looked at Valcor and then at Lady Shera who told him in a motherly tone that he was under no obligation to talk about it or answer the question if he so chose not so to do. But Fae did not mind, he was proud that his grandfather had fought. Even if he himself did not know whether the cause warranted a stand.

"He was a spy and translator for men up in the north." Fae looked at the servant woman who had pulled out a little piece of parchment and was jotting something on it. She had not yet said a word. He wondered if there was a strong caste system in the nations of men or in those of mencas. Then he added, "But I think he regretted that he did not help to try and broker the peace accords more. He did mention he was asked once to join a group of translators that was working with politicians and diplomats on both sides. But he declined it."

"Well we would not have held it against him either way. That war was long ago. The hatchet between all of our races is buried," Lady Shera said with declarative authority.

"Yes and anyway I don't think you'd find him hostile or bitter even if he had fought for the elves. He is a very calm and peaceful spirit," stated Fae very matter-of-factly.

"I think we shall continue with you master Faeruthan. And we should like to visit your grandfather. If you have no objections of course. We must be glad for any aid that is offered to us." Lady Shera was diplomatic and polite. She was a noble who knew the best ways to get what she desired. Fae thought to himself that he would have had a difficult time refusing her help. She was graceful, stately, and very pretty. "I will try to ensure that my companions show their best manners and do not ill-represent our people," she declared. She eyed Valcor giving him a glance as if to say that he would be under close watch and on a short chain with her for the rest of their journey. "Some of us mean well, but don't always give that impression when we open our mouths."

"No offense taken madam," said Fae. "Well, since we will head to my home and visit my grandfather, let us turn to the left in this direction. We may skirt the clearing and we shall be at his home in two quarters of an hour and mine in only another quarter after that."

The group moved on for a short time after leaving the clearing area where Fae had offered them the option to fork towards Quildevar's dwelling and town but instead they veered towards Fae's grandfather's and Fae's home. The forest was pretty and the humans thought it quiet. Fae's perception was very much the opposite, at least from how it normally seemed when he passed through this area. Fae mentioned another pass as they moved up to it and then beyond it. This was a fork intersection they would take when coming back this way later or the next day. He made a point to show it so they could see how they would find the town Fae had mentioned. Fae was unsure if he would be joining them or not for that portion of their search and guessed they would by then again be on their own. The narrow path was similar to the one they were on. It bisected the route from their south and behind. Something which could easily be missed from the direction in which they were facing. Fae stopped.

"This path will take you to the village of Flarhom," Fae gestured behind them and to his left. "It bears the woods' namesake. Or rather the woods bear its." He paused to let them see and contemplate it a moment. "You may want to return this way if you decide to seek out help in Flarhom for your quest. Its outskirts lie only a few kilometers along this path to the south. It is not much. A few shops, some places to eat and rest and several huddles of homes nestled among the trees. But you may find the help you want and it is the closest place that aid might be other than at my grandfather's." Fae then turned and began moving again along the main path upon which they had been traveling.

Not long after they had picked back up and Fae had told them they were just about there, there was a rumble in the forest. They were actually close enough to his grandfather's that Fae thought the sound at first might have been something upon which his spirit elder grandfather was working. Fae knew he would see his elder's home after just one more bend in the path anyway. But the rumble was not something of the woods or of Spiruthean creation. It grew louder. The mencas heard it too.

"What is that?" said Valcor to the group but mainly towards Fae and Lady Shera. Neither had an inkling. The noise grew and grew until the ground began trembling. Then a terrible cracking whoosh made every tree around them vibrate and bend. Leaves flew about everywhere. It seemed the ground could open up any second and swallow the entire party. Then a crash louder than anything Fae had ever heard or witnessed accompanied a giant display of fire and light. An area of the woods just to their front right lit up like a sun had just exploded and rained down in front of them. The fireball consumed a half-acre of woods and then quickly began to die down. No doubt Fae thought the trees are quelling this from spreading. The scene was only a few hundred meters in front of them and it was bright enough even through the trees that the group did not look straight at it.

"I am not sure what has just happened," said Fae.

"Is everyone alright?" asked Lady Shera. Apart from a small ringing in a few ears, no one was harmed by the event. They responded as such.

"Should we explore this?" said Farhale as more of a declaration than a question.

"I don't see how we cannot," responded Valcor. "But it is for the Lady and our guide to decide is it not thus?" The knights looked towards their leaders. Jeanaviere remained silent as had been her custom, but her eyes gave away she wanted to see what had just happened.

"We are very close to my grandfather's," said Fae. "In fact, I am certain he will have heard it too and is probably already enroute to explore it himself."

"Well, in that case, let us go see for ourselves," said Lady Shera. "And everyone is sure they are not hurt? My ears are a bit numbed and I should think others' hearing might have been as well."

"Yes my lady, mine too," said Farhale. Valcor and Jeanaviere nodded in agreement. "But nothing permanent and it is fading as we speak," the knight added.

The group turned off the path and followed Fae's lead to see what had just shaken the entire woods, perhaps the entire planet. The glow led them there easily. It took only a few minutes until they could see exactly what caused the massive disruption. There in the woods just through a few rows of very shaken trees lay what appeared to be a huge chunk of a spaceship. It was a thruster. A giant turbine like fission converter that would have helped to power a large warship. Maybe four or six of these would power a ship such as a Federation attack class frigate. What the group did not know is this was just one of many component remnants of the Vissad. It was perhaps one of the biggest single pieces. And it was several Astronomical Units (AUs, or the distance from earth to the sun) from the battle itself and a half of a star system from where other pieces of the ship had been blown to. It was nearly unrecognizable as a portion of a once great Federation vessel. It looked like a giant mangled metal grain silo to Fae. The mencas knew instantly what it was.

"This is bad," managed Lady Shera. "Something very bad has happened." The others said nothing. But they all thought she was quite right. "I fear many lives may have been lost," she added. And at that fact, she was indeed very correct.

Chapter 13
Escape

Aurelle hoped JT made it back from the screening and had the chance to find what she had left for him under his bed pillow. She did not dare chance leaving something like that out in the open. Nor did she have the time to wait for him to arrive back or go chasing him down herself. No, she had to trust to chance or fate that he would find it and he would trust her enough to follow its instructions. Aurelle had observed him enough during the time she had cared for him to know that he tended to prefer not to use the computer's automatic comfort setting feature. She began to picture him tossing himself about on the sheets making things just perfect for his form. It was a cute throw-back-esq routine as she recalled it. She dismissed the line of thinking anymore. She had data to retrieve, her thoughts to gather, and Dr. Quimby to meet with. *How much did Quimby know,* she wondered.

Retrieving individual medical records and test data as recent as JT's should not have taken long, but she did not anticipate the drill announcement nor the ensuing commotion. Upon the intercom's announcement she did not even attempt to retrieve them from the central management office. She went to her own office files and pulled them herself. She would have gone directly to Quimby's and used the central system to do it from his work area but she knew they would be incomplete that way. Hers would be more thorough and more up to date. Plus, she did not trust the security of doing it any other way. With the alert, she did not look at all out of place running to and from her office. Her memory drive port was hanging on a locket around her neck. As such, it was so much more quickly accessible anywhere; and, she pulled it out as she approached her hall door. Without even waiting for the motion sensing illumination to engage she flew through the doorway and as if by muscle memory found her workstation data port with the drive. Her fingers typed a few keystrokes and she whirred around the desk for the required retinal security scan. Powered up by a slight hum of electronic sounds and beeps the machine blinked to life. She perused a few screens quickly locating the updated data she desired. As she loaded it onto the drive, she opened the most recent input and began scanning for anomalies or anything noteworthy. Nothing at first. Then, ...there it was.

The latest scan from only the last fifteen minutes had detected a new anomaly. JT's concentration of immune-building neurons was higher than any previous. It seemed his brain's chemistry was in overdrive protecting his body from the toxins no one in the Federation understood. This infection was not attacking the body directly. It was using the host's own brain activity to play a cruel trick and cause the host to attack itself. It was a physical manifestation of a psychological weapon. At least this is what Aurelle's first glimpse of the new data was telling her. Wow. This could be a historically monumental break through. This should be the missing piece of the puzzle behind the Confederation's mystery weapon that had so far stumped every scientist and military mind the Federation had assigned to the problem. Could it be Aurelle was truly on the verge of a break through? Maybe Quimby would be able to help her in the finite diagnostics.

Barnabus Quimby, known as "Barnes" to his colleagues and superiors, or just Dr. Quimby, was a very short fat middle aged human. He was a general practitioner who had been at St. Demetrius, it felt like forever. It was no secret he wanted Dr. Simons' job. He made little effort to hide the fact he felt he could do it better himself anyway. Those details were rather insignificant during the present crisis, but they were still noted facts of the dynamic of St. Demetrius' upper-level politics. Aurelle put it on her mental back burner as she collected the few other things that she thought would prove useful and threw them all into her semblance of a medical backpack. And with that, she was half way out the door enroute to Dr. Quimby's by way of JT's cache pointe in the lounge.

JT had been hiding for what seemed an eternity when he heard the footfalls for which he was waiting. Really, he'd only been in the staff lounge restroom a matter of some minutes. One's mind plays games with them during times of duress. For reasons not yet clear to JT, duress for him and everyone in the infirmary was underway. The soft rhythmic footfall of Aurelle's determined steps approached the doorway. JT's ear was hugging it like sticky tape. The Marine readied himself for something increasingly jarring to this already tense situation. His heart paused. Then it beat twice. Silence. *What if this was not Aurelle?* JT did not have time to answer or think through any alternate plan of action. Eight fast knocks ensued. Two short, four longer but in rapid succession, followed by two more short. That had to be her. It was now or never.

"John Thomas, it's me. Open up and hurry if you're in there," came Aurelle's voice quelling any doubt as the handle lurched a bit and the doctor tried to open the door from her side.

"Alright, are you alone? And how did I find out about Quai-14?" JT trusted her but still had to verify and be sure.

"Yes. And you learned when I told you. We've got no time to waste JT," came the response. He unlocked the door and peered out the crack it just created. She was alone.

"Let me in; I'll explain but we can't stay long. We've got a doctor to meet and possibly an escape off this station to make."

"Now this is inter-stellar excitement," said JT as he opened the door all the way.

"I don't know how much time we have to figure this all out," Aurelle continued once inside. JT had maneuvered himself out of the opening as asked but remained alert keeping a good Marine eye on the lounge and hallway door just in case the unexpected came about. Aurelle closed the bathroom door behind her as she completed her move through the breach. The door was more of a hatch than a door and she felt safer once through it. Maybe that was because she was now adjacent to JT and she knew no one, least of all him, was judging her next actions or words.

"You may be the solitary key to how this war turns out John Thomas," she said mustering all courage and serenity possible. JT furled his brow donning a look of surprise. Maybe inquisitiveness was more the emotion portrayed by his features.

"I… I don't understand…" he managed.

"The short version, is that no one on your ship… No… No one at Quai-14. No… No one in the entire war, to this day, has survived an attack from the Confederation's new weapon. They're calling it a neutrino cannon. Or an N-cannon. Nobody has survived its effects until you did. And not only did you survive it, but you're recovering from it. If the Federation is to have any sort of hope, JT, it may be within you," she whispered the last part directly into his left ear. His hearing did not fail.

Then Aurelle did something her colleagues would have been appalled at her for: she angled her face down a few inches, leaned forward, and lightly kissed JT on the jaw just below his ear. In her mind this was simply to demonstrate that she believed and trusted his health and recovery progress. Trusted it enough to action her own response upon it. Her logical mind said she was simply fooling herself; letting her irrational emotional heart lead. *Trust him,* she told herself. If it helped convince JT to trust and follow her, and that could save the entire cause, then it didn't matter. She needed to do whatever it took to gain his trust and confidence as fast as possible.

"Oh, ok," JT mustered just covering a quick flurry of imperceptible blush.

"You see sergeant, we don't know yet why, or, how powerful this weapon is in the long term. It is possible the Confederation allowed you and your survival here on purpose with some sort of prepositioned contact to be made. We know they have spies. We know it is unlikely that you should have survived. We also know that we have been ordered to turn you over to a new federal agency. A turn over which was ordered before any satisfactory medical testing could be completed at this or any other known federated location."

"So it sounds like we're shooting blanks against a monster," JT paraphrased.

"Worse. We must know how to best work to counter the neutrino gun if we want a hope. And we don't have a clue. Only I and a few others on the station are suspicious enough to question this order. And bold enough to delay or act accordingly without sanctioned authority. We're out on a limb here. I have two doctors helping. Fortunately, one runs this entire station. He is the one who called this alarm-evacuation drill," Aurelle spat out in one seemingly grave semi-sentence.

"Whatever you need from me, I'll do it. You have my word," said JT without hesitation.

"First thing is to use the drill's confusion to inconspicuously get up to level 9 and make contact with Doctor Quimby. He'll help us from there. Follow me as well as you can. If we get split up, go to level 9's control room or physician admin's room if the control room proves too hectic. I'll reestablish contact with you there. Besides Quimby, you should be aware of another I believe we can trust: Doctor Simmons. He is the station head. Now, we need to go."

And with that, Aurelle and JT were off through the halls and corridors of St. Demetrius. They took the emergency stairs rather than the elevators or powered transport services. Aurelle feared either as part of the automated portion of the drill or a real-world event leading to a break-down, the stairs and regular service halls would be best. Even if it added a few minutes to their arrival, there would be greater chance of their movement unnoticed. All of the automatic systems had closed circuit monitoring; the hallways and stairs were only about half-covered. Better odds. The halls were crowded on the staff lounge level but they moved quickly through the maze of passages and people towards the stairwell in the facility's most central wing. Aurelle thought it good fortune that in this central location both the control room for administration and Doctor Quimby's office would then be almost directly above them. Seven levels up, but still nearly at the stairwell exit 35 meters over their heads. Their path would be short once up to level 9.

The jaunt took them maybe five minutes; half of which was used during the stairway climb. Only one time, just after reaching level 9 was Aurelle stopped. It was in the last fifty meters and within sight of both the administrative control room and Quimby's office. A tall technician dressed in black security looking clothes appeared to know Doctor Gifford. He asked her if she had seen a doctor named Smitherson or a nurse named Cratchener. They were "both *needed* at Doctor Quimby's," according to the security person. Aurelle responded quickly in the negative and did not wait to see if there was more to discuss. JT was happy for that fact. They proceeded along the corridor to Quimby's office. As they got close there was an exceedingly noticeable upturn in activity. Especially at the doorway-hatch itself.

Quimby was dead. The scene was a disaster. There were several guards and many of the hospital's top officials all crammed in and around the small space. Aurelle knew immediately they could not stay. Someone knew that Doctor Quimby knew something was not right about the order to extradite JT off St. Demetrius. In her mind they had a matter of seconds to decide what next action to take.

The office looked as it normally did except for at least 12 people jammed into it, a small red stain on the floor which led back behind Quimby's desk. Neither Aurelle nor JT needed to imagine what lay on the other side of the desk. They could already see the physician's arm, torso, and pool of blood streaming from it caking the floor. An officer from special investigations branch of the hospital's security police immediately approached Aurelle and JT. They had not even completed adjusting their mindset to the scene. JT looked quickly to Aurelle whose eyes told him to play cool. She also shot a glance towards a corner of the room. There a shorter gentleman, JT would later learn to be Doctor Simmons, glanced sideways at both of them. The security police officer cut off this unspoken communication by moving into their line of sight. He addressed Aurelle quickly,

"Doctor, may I ask you some questions?"

"Of course, but I must see Doctor Simmons briefly first and I am not prepared to leave my work idle for long."

"That is just it," said the officer. "This entire mess may be impacting and about your work."

Aurelle was unsure now if she would be better to help this security officer or let him flounder. He looked young. She decided that it would have been ill-advised for the Confederation to attempt to infiltrate a hospital through use of young security forces. Plus, he appeared relatively innocent and baby-faced to her. No, definitely not a spy.

"Just a moment," she said to the officer. And she approached Doctor Simmons as well as beckoned JT to join them. He did so. The young security guard watched the three intently. After a moment or two, it became clear: they were on the same side.

"Doctor Gifford, you can see we have a bad situation requiring action now," stated Dr. Simmons plainly. "I want you and Sergeant Wayne to leave aboard an emergency escape shuttle for fleet command or the nearest friendly vessel, preferably a cruiser size or larger. The infirmary is not safe and I don't trust folks here."

"The security officer over there wants to talk with me," said Aurelle. The officer was eyeing the three of them intently.

"He's been with the infirmary a few months," said Dr. Simmons. "But he's been with fleet command several years and he came to us with good credentials and was very well recommended. His name is Lieutenant Higgins. Were I you, I'd give him a few minutes but be on your way shortly."

"Just so you know, I don't have anything definitive from the tagnometer yet nor would I expect it before we get going. My best guess is that we won't know what's going on for certain until the machine has compounded readings and crunched the data for another week. I would also guess that Sergeant Wayne was blessed with a natural immunity to the neutrino weapon because of his experiences as a constantly deployed Marine used to working around radiation debris."

"Right, whatever you say doc," was all Quimby could muster as he smiled with a sinister smirk.

But in truth, Aurelle had learned from JT about some of his extensive radiation training regimes. It could potentially have proved invaluable although JT never would have fathomed learning to activate or deactivate mini-nuclear devices might favorably acclimate his outer epidermal layers. An acclimation to what they might one day experience under attack. The military war machine of the Confederation would deal many varieties of blows, but the neutrino was by far the most revolutionary. It destroyed not only equipment via traditional explosive power but also live cells simultaneously and painfully from forcing quick atomic decomposition. Cells like JT's had a boost to their natural resistance to nuclear decay. A few other specially trained Marines, those with questionable lineage and family history, would have this same natural increased immunity. Just none had been exposed directly yet to a neutrino cannon attack.

With the quick information exchange between Doctors Simmons and Gifford, Aurelle relayed to JT they would make a short stop to meet with Lieutenant Higgins and then make a quiet disappearance from the infirmary. He concurred with Aurelle's plan generally no matter what it entailed. But effectively he agreed that staying around an uncomfortable murder scene too long would be ill-advised.

Lieutenant Higgins was a stocky, young, serious officer. He had been taking notes about the scene while the others talked. There were two other security officers present, but Higgins seemed to be the one dedicated to questioning Aurelle. She approached him cautiously and confidently. JT remained at her side but slightly behind and without saying anything. Officer Higgins said security had been notified when a nurse entered the office looking for Dr. Quimby to weigh-in with a prognosis on a patient status. His first question was what Aurelle and JT were visiting Quimby's office for? Aurelle decided not to confuse the issue or conceal the truth, but she did elect to inform Officer Higgins that the topic was sensitive and not one for public knowledge. She told him quite frankly they intended to visit with Dr. Quimby to discuss research related to the Confederation's major new mass-destructive weapon; that Sergeant Wayne was a survivor of an attack by it; and that this information could not be let out or risk leaking back to any Confederation ties. Lieutenant Higgins was understanding and promised he would ensure it did not and that if he learned anything that could help in the medical research aspect from the investigation that he would be at liberty to discuss he would pass it on.

"Thank you. There are huge ramifications and possible impacts on everyone, not to mention the very war outcome, depending on what we can learn," said Aurelle succinctly.

"Did you know of anything Dr. Quimby may have been involved in which could have put his life at risk? That is of course besides what we have just been discussing," replied Lt. Higgins.

"Nothing remotely, unless one counts the war in general as a hazard," said Aurelle. "He was a very caring and genuine care-giver. Ask anyone who worked alongside or was a primary patient of his.

Nothing but respect. But I can't stay here indefinitely to continue this inquiry. We have significant work to do in continuing what Dr. Quimby had started. Dr. Simmons will know how to reach us and I can promise you more. Just not much more right now." Lt. Higgins seemed surprisingly supportive of this notion-request. He agreed to keep the details between them or the appropriate authorities who had a need to know. They included the head security police agent and Dr. Simmons. Aurelle looked to JT in an effort to bring him into the discussion directly. He nodded in concurrence.

The police turned their attention to crime scene details. The murder was committed heinously with a blunt force stabbing object which had been removed from the area. Dr. Quimby kept a neat office. Searching it for clues was not difficult. Nor did it reveal much for the investigators. Whoever did this covered their tracks well. There was no evidence of a struggle or sloppy overlooked signs or prints. The only suspicious trinket which had been uncovered by the end of the first half hour at the scene was a piece of blank lined paper with a faint hint of red on it. The red mark likely had been from Quimby's blood pool. Weather he had purposefully grabbed the sheet for a reason or it just chanced onto a spot the blood had collected was speculation. It could even have been something as remote as a paper cut he had received well before the incident. Time might reveal more.

Aurelle and JT made their way quickly out of the office, down the hall to a stairwell. Avoiding prolonged contact or continued discussions with anyone they chanced past or encountered was atop Aurelle's priorities. JT's priorities followed suit. Most others were busy hustling in their own directions on their own missions related to the drill anyway. The two most concerning events would be another police or security stopping- one done by an officer less cordial than Lt. Higgins, or, a full lock-down and freeze of any escape means. The stairs were not blocked or even crowded. Passing only a few workers scurrying the other direction, JT and Aurelle made it down to the third level without being accosted. Here Aurelle led them to a small emergency shuttle escape bay. She had the credentials and means to use one of them without much trouble.

The only pause came when she had to recall programming

procedures for navigation to the nearest fleet asset. Luckily JT had a rough knowledge of general whereabouts of most major Federation assets. He recognized the names of several vessels from the shuttle display and offered that the *Crimera* was the head of the Federation's 7th Fleet. A modernized, well-armed and escorted 180,000-ton battleship. It was close enough to make within a few hours of neo drive. So that was the easily made decision. They were off with little fanfare and minimal preparations. Jettisoning themselves in a tiny two-seater escape shuttle, 7th Fleet-bound became the doctor and the sergeant. Observing St. Demetrius Hospital as it began to draw farther away before neo kicked in was humbling for Aurelle. It felt a bit like giving up on her place of dedication. She had worked there predominantly since the beginning of the war. It was her home away from home… if she considered herself to have one. JT was not so much in that same mind set. Yet he did understand how it could feel this way for her. He imagined as if it would have been like this for him to have been leaving the Vissad voluntarily. The infirmary grew small in the window. Then the warp to neo and S-neo kicked in.

Aurelle was prepared to bring her ideas and medical findings to others but she had not planned on feelings of anything but a purely professional nature. JT was also not previously planning on anything but military-esq professionalism and a whole-hearted attempt to return to duty in whatever way his condition would allow. The shuttle was cramped but allowed all the essentials of short duration emergency travel. Plus it had a small stash of sustenance. St. Demetrius was known for its excellent food and its shuttle-craft supply was no exception. The S-neo speed voyage to the Crimera should have taken very little time. However, there was a slight delay caused by rounding the fleet's outer rim of scout posts and vessels. This added twenty minutes but made the route more clandestine and better guarded. When JT and Aurelle's craft came within a few parsecs of the Crimera's sentries, they were hailed and offered safe passage to come in close to the fleet's command ship. Docking alongside a fleet command vessel was no small feat. Only the most important of missions warranted it.

Chapter 14
Gone

Down on the surface of planet 104, the commander of the Suclesahe, Captain Ganjin Majak, watched in absolute helpless horror, as his ship was violently destroyed. He had gone to the planet's surface ostensibly as a diplomatic emissary and taken only three crew members in support of that mission. In reality, he was researching the planet's suitability as a staging base or more than likely, an emergency landing location for Gnorac vessels. The three crew members he took were far from trained diplomats. They knew Gnorac fleet technical requirements and logistics, but not much to accommodate the unfolding situation. They too now watched in shock and horror as their ticket home, their life support system in every capacity, their very and only real survival means, the Suclesahe, was painfully and slowly obliterated. Gnoracs are usually cold and calculating: not easily thrown by even the most surprising and damaging of events. The destruction of their ship pushed that norm.

The four Suclesahe crew members were to have gained contact and trust with 104 inhabitants and then used what they could gather in an assessment for the Gnoracs to acquire the world in their network of remote bases and staging locations. Captain Majak was a career sailor who had made his way up the ranks of the Confederation's fleet officer corps through steadfast dependability and determination. He was not as reckless as many younger Gnorac leaders. In fact he was much more calculating and careful than his own second-in-command, Chief Kgnauld. The captain was a man of some routine and he was accustomed to checking in with his deputy every twenty minutes when he was away from the ship on missions such as this. His internal clock had warned him that this recurring communication was about due when he gazed up to see the unexpected shoot-out between his ship and the two Federation warships. By the time he had brought his transponder to bear and was ready to signal his bridge it was well beyond his, or anyone's, ability to influence or change the course of unfolding events.

By the time the Suclesahe was critically damaged and listing out of her fighting orbit, Captain Majak had already decided he needed to quickly develop a makeshift strategy for survival. For his own survival. The Gnorac higher organizational leaders were not known for leniency or understanding. He knew more than likely he would be held directly responsible for the destruction of his ship. Never mind the salient fact that he was not aboard the craft when it was hit. Never mind that he had given orders to avoid engagement. Orders he felt were unmistakably clear. Never mind he played no current part in what was going on up around the orbit of planet 104. Gnorac culture and general mindset would hold Captain Majak responsible.

Majak had a transient and latent self-sacrificing notion: the option to take his own life. He also had the ability to defend himself and fight for a fair hearing. But neither of these seemed worthwhile options that could result in a favorable outcome. No, Majak came to the conclusion so many leaders in no-win situations hated and tried to avoid: his best chance for survival was to go into hiding. It would be to look for opportunities with private enterprises or even sell his status and try to wait out the greater conflict.

As a senior Gnorac reconnaissance attack cruiser commander, Majak held position and power which would be highly sought after by certain Federation-friendly organizations. For sure there were hosts of characters willing to pay… and willing to pay handsomely for what he knew. He considered himself honorable, but his honor was only good to a point of self-preservation. And at this juncture, he was certain the loyalty between him and his own fleet's highers was not a two-way street. It was a one-way route, and a fairly narrow path at that. And narrowing.

Majak's main goal now became determining where and on what side of the issue his three ship-mates fell. It would be no secret to them that the captain was finished. The question was, did they believe they too would be finished by what was occurring up above them in space? They were all officers. One senior, the others mid-career. Majak could not inquire or make an assessment without raising their suspicions and potentially turning them against him. So, he did what a seasoned opportunist, who did not want to raise suspicions, but who saw himself out of opportunities would do. He set out to break off contact and make his own way as best he could on this unfamiliar planet.

"Comrades, our transportation home is in… uhm, peril. And, there is no hope to salvage the situation up there," Captain Majak began. "I will take responsibility for this no matter what has occurred to cause it. But I do not wish for you to follow in my ill-fated but seemingly predestined footsteps. You have careers which still have promising futures. You have families and loved ones to consider. I cannot say that first part at least anymore for myself." The others heard his declaration clearly and understood what it meant. They interpreted it to mean their captain would be departing this life and he was wishing them well on their own respective journeys. Their understanding was partly correct. At least ostensibly, that is how Majak would have had his situation viewed.

"Sir, it has been an honor and a privilege to serve with you," stated the senior officer among them, Lieutenant Commander Giova Krigsbie. The others offered similar words of support, encouragement, and appreciation. The conversation continued a few more minutes as the warships above them in orbit of planet 104 destroyed each other. When the Suclesahe actually did break apart and her major hull pieces tumbled out of space into the atmosphere above them, the four Gnorac officers went in two different directions. Captain Majak seemingly to end his own life. But, in reality, it was to go into as deep a hiding as he could muster. The other three went in search of sanctuary among the planet's native inhabitants. They found their way among the nearest urban surroundings. Their surface craft could shuttle them with haste, but their ability to dismount and blend on foot was worth its weight more than could be expressed. Soon this would be each man's chosen way.

Majak had already descended the craft and was now on foot heading towards the closest civilian transportation hub they had passed by only some minutes prior. He knew he would at least be able to make his way out of the built-up area and into a rural community that might offer some semblance of hiding for him. If he could find a friendly local vehicle owner willing to give him a ride somewhere, anywhere, outside of the city's limits, then he felt he would be in good standing. So he trekked the few kilometers needed to make it to the transport center. It was not much. But it would suffice. He found a few local farmers and miners willing to let him ride along and they would even bring him to a specific location if he had one in mind. Fortunately, they did not recognize his rank or uniform stature. Therefore, they did not appear suspicious or ask him any questions which might have led to invariably inevitable and uncomfortable conversations.

After a twenty-minute ride, Majak was comfortable with the distance and feeling of his surroundings. He thanked his benefactor, a generous and kind farmer of about age 50. He then prepared to embark upon the impending mystery future leg of his journey. And with the next brief stop, he offered a hearty farewell and dismounted the craft. He was intending to walk towards the closest establishment for anyone or thing which would allow him to remain under any radar. Although Majak was now ship and crew-less, his journey continued. In his own mind he was fast approaching the status of country-less as well. The surrounding company seemed innocent enough. No one was directly eyeing or sizing him up. This was good. The alternative would mean he needed to disappear quickly and quietly. Not a pleasant exit strategy given the situation.

Captain Majak would advertise his new status for hire to the right party in underground circles which he could fathom were safer to trust than the general populace. He began searching for the seediest of establishments containing the most sinister of characters. The more questionable the better, for the greater the likelihood Majak would find those of a nature looking for war secrets and information for sale. As soon as a place with an appropriate private area presented itself, Majak discarded most of his uniform identifications. The plain gray polyester would not stand out once it no longer was highlighted by badges, name plates, stripes, and accoutrements. This way he felt more at ease among the surroundings.

At least he did not feel like the senior level traitor for which a younger nobler version of his blood would have taken him for. It could have boiled the blood of a younger more ideal version of himself. No, this older, fed up and agitated former leader would not suffer those moral conundrums. In his gray sterilized garments, he poked around and sensed what circles might support his information barter. In a pub-casino called the Unlucky Duckling located near the periphery of planet 104's largest population center, Jakarta, Majak found that for which he was searching. A motley band of Federation-friendly businessmen who seemed to possess an entire corner of the main lobby stood out like eager creatures.

There were a dozen or so relatively nicely attired men or near human creatures occupying the general expanse of the main entryway and they were intently engaged in hushed dialogs. Majak entered the establishment carefully with an eye cast towards his rear. He made glancing eye contact with one of the seedy yet nicely dressed businessmen and picked up quickly that they were the overpowering force in this region of the city. Perhaps this region of the planet. He moved towards a corner of the pub but maintained a glance and locked visual contact with the central occupiers. He would wait this out and determine after casual observation for some time how likely they were to be ideal candidates to approach. Ones at least to approach for information exchange.

Majak was a careerist who previously had a family at one time. They had become victims and casualties of the war. Specifically, they had become casualties of the Confederation's non appeasement policy and hardline stance on negotiating civilian-occupied border dispute planet systems. The Callegonus System was originally Federation controlled but occupied and controlled with fairly little resistance by the Confederation early on in the conflict. This meant that seven planets with civilian populations changed masters. Most remained in their homes but some families and many native Federation loyalists desired to evacuate for places more directly dominated by their political beliefs. The Confederation's policy allowed no sanctioned post-occupation evacuations.

Essentially, wherever one found themselves during the initial take-over, was where they would end up riding out the remainder of the conflict. When bombing runs and mistaken covert missions drew the planets back into the fray and civilian casualties began to mount, many held it against the Confederation politicians. Then a year into the worst of hostilities, the Federation launched an aggressive campaign to re-take the lost system. Entire states were cut off from normal supply and resupply routes. People and inhabitants starved and died. Majak's wife and two children were among those presumed lost during this difficult and trying period. Their entire city was bombed beyond recognition and most did not have any opportunity to even attempt to escape.

Captain Majak never criticized any superiors or political higher-ups publicly. He knew better than to speak his mind on something beyond his control and as dangerous as that. But his heart and mind from then onward marched to a different drum beat. This one was not a beat which the Confederation embraced. The change was not something others could see or sense for he continued his command and rededicated himself to his ship and his crew. But in truth, it marked the point at which his soul no longer belonged to the Confederation. It made the decision he made upon viewing the loss of the Suclesahe that much easier. In fact, it was a decision predestined and made already in his heart. It just needed the external ship destruction event to launch it into action.

After an hour of observation, a drink and small talk with a few gambling locals, Majak decided it was about time to test his theory. The theory that the dozen or so businessmen controlling the entryway to the foyer and seemingly the Unlucky Duckling's main passage were open to contact. He ordered a second drink, a bloody-dustoff, and regained eye contact with the first gentleman who had looked him over an hour prior. The gaze was unmistakable. It said without saying, yes, we have things to discuss. Majak sauntered up to the group and inquired how things in the city and in general were faring. The response was not unexpected, but it was favorable.

"Yes my friend we are in business here to serve those who need help. And there are many who desire changes. If you know of ways to alleviate suffering then who are we to stand in that way?" said the well-dressed man who then introduced himself as Fico.

"I am formerly of a group which I am not proud and I know has caused much suffering. I would do what I can to help end that constant tragedy and overbearing dictation," said Majak. The two men lifted their glasses and toasted an end to suffering.

Chapter 15
Debris

Fae knew that it would be best to defer to the mencas and Lady Shera for how to proceed in exploring this piece of unknown hardware. It was foreign to him and would be unfamiliar to any spirit. But the mencas; however, seemed to be well acquainted with what it was; or at least they sensed the meaning of its arrival here in Flarhom Woods.

"Young master Fae, if you and we have the time I think it would benefit all of us to get a closer look at this space hardware descended from above," said Lady Shera. "When components of ships this massive fall from orbit it means war is near and a battle or some similar conflict like event has transpired. Any ship which loses an engine or entire propulsion source like this is doomed. The question begs, is this just the start, or, is this the farthest-reaching debris and already the most of what we may experience?" The lady's question was somewhat rhetorical. But nonetheless, it was an important consideration. Were they in danger or would exploration of the thruster cause them any sort of further possible harm?

"We have time my friends; I am in no hurry. But haste is to be considered for your own timely needs and that of your quest," said Fae. "I believe the site will be as safe as it can be for the woods will do what they can to shield and protect us from a greater harm." The knights and lady Jeanaviere seemed to be in concurrence with the notion to explore the hardware remnant. The knights spoke in agreement, stating their opinions openly. And surprisingly, Jeanaviere spoke too. For the first time since Fae had come upon and joined the group, he heard her voice.

"Yes my lady and my sires, I think we should learn what we can of the descended thing. I would also offer to step forward if there are any spatially challenging or hazardous places to be explored." So it would seem that her role in the group was some sort of subservient but not disincluded place. Fae took note and decided that it was indeed a group decision and all parties from this menca band were being actively included in that decision. No exclusion here.

The woods were thick but not opaque in the region the group had been occupying and continued to inhabit. It was enough to be able to see the full body and outline of the booster. The form was oval-cylindrical and the size of a couple of 21st century earth tractor-trailer combos. The metal was irregularly shiny but still dirty and caked with turbine plaster, booster bits, other pieces of debris and appeared torn in most joining places violently. As if the piece's removal was a great unplanned catastrophic explosion result. Which, it was. As the massive propulsion provider careened through the planet's atmosphere and broke into the wooded surroundings, it left charred remnants across its path. There was a flame-encrusted path blazed several hundred kilometers long beginning far out of sight and sound range of Flarhom Woods.

Up above and beyond any atmospheric interference from Spiruthean, the elements of a once great war ship, of several great ships, spiraled and jettisoned themselves careening in all different directions. Quai-14 would send elements of large and powerful vessels somersaulting and spearing all over the quadrant. Spiruthean was but one receiver of some of these war bits.

Apequia, in particular, was rotated to face the direction of Quai-14's vicinity when the bulk of the destruction occurred. The most devastating portion of the battle resulted in seven cruiser or larger sized Federation vessels becoming total losses. There were twice as many ships which would still become and count as true casualties. Their fate from Quai-14: to be removed from deployed status and scrapped for the near-term. But the worst off from the fight were the lead elements of the 8th Fleet. They effectively lost all of the unit's forward deployed combat power.

The Vissad's largest single component which remained in one piece was this presently crashed thruster that landed so close to the group in Flarhom Woods. There would have been six equivalent sized boosters that powered a ship like the Vissad. Most battle cruisers of its class or similar design had that many. The other five thrusters in the Vissad's case were obliterated into average household chair sized chunks or smaller. The portion before the travelers here ended up being blown into Apequia by some odd luck and technical factors.

Its bulk was composed of predominately the number four thruster. This entire ship component element had been replaced very recently on the Vissad. It was subsequently housed in a brand-new casing. The new housing, which was composed of newly designed and tested structural components and only the strongest metals, was designed to withstand a greater barrage than any other older component on the Federation cruiser. In fact, had the entire ship been re-cased in similar fashion, it is possible the Vissad might have been the sole survivor of Quai-14. Even had the ship not survived, portions of it would most likely have been salvageable. As it stood, nothing was reusable. But the number four thruster was indeed recognizable as a battle cruiser booster engine.

Lady Shera directed her knights to take over-watching positions on the outskirts of the path of travel. She was effectively having them protect the group's perimeter while she, Jeanaviere and Fae closed in on the ship component for a better look. They agreed begrudgingly. Valcor specifically said he was happy to ensure their safety but that he was also perhaps ideally qualified to assess the structural soundness of the element. After all, he noted, he was an amateur builder with several hundred designs under his belt. Farhale readily and quickly pointed out every design of Valcor's was for some form of furniture or home wood project. Nothing like a space ship component or anything even close to it would count among the first knight's resume for assessing soundness. Farhale followed his observation up with a good long hearty laugh.

"You two will have your chance and I won't deny you that opportunity, but I want you looking out for our surroundings first. Yes, I am calling on you to do your duty before you become distracted by great big fallen objects from space ships. We already assess that they are themselves sadly fallen from the sky." Lady Shera was not one to sugar coat her observation and desires. The knights held their mounts loosely and walked them outside the apparent path into the less wooded clearing edge to their immediate north and south. Lady Shera waited for Jeanaviere to bring her mount alongside the lady's and she then addressed Fae directly, "Let's keep a small distance and avoid any inflamed vegetation or still smoldering sub components. It probably won't happen, but I want to make sure we are not in harm's way if something here were yet to blow up."

"Yes. But I am also not affected by temperature differentials in the same way I believe you and your race may be," declared Fae in response. "I can exist in flame or ice and nearly any matter form derived in between the two." And as if to highlight this ability, he immediately turned bright fiery red and then solid blue clear. All the while emanating first red-hot gas vapor and then frozen gasses. Lady Shera may have been keenly impressed but she did and said nothing to betray this fact to her new companion.

"Just be careful," is what she mustered instead. "Let's learn what we can and ensure none of us loses anything we came with." With that declaration, she gave her reigns to Jeanaviere and asked the quiet woman to ensure their steeds stayed out of trouble's way. The indication was such that the burned path and debris field should not come into play of the horses themselves, any place they occupied or chose to use as grazing areas. Easily accomplished with such well-behaved creatures was Fae's unspoken private thought.

The three of them and the two steeds moved closer in towards the thruster. They had only moved off their travel path less than 50 meters when already some temperature differential became apparent. Lady Shera asked the other two if they felt it. Each did and Fae was able to assess that the heat generated was less than 10 degrees different from outside their initial movement area. He relayed that it would not be dangerous unless there was more than a 50 degree difference and even then, unless there was eminent threat of combustion via components or local vegetation, the issue was not one to concern them. They continued walking until the site was before them and in clear view. The thruster was fairly well preserved, considering what it had been through and how far it had come. It had destroyed quite a bit of the woods immediately surrounding it. But other than the debris and blazed trail, there was not much else that it had done to impact the woods.

"This thing was part of quite something was it not?" asked Fae, as if to confirm what he already knew: that it served some sort of greater purpose as a component of a larger entity in the space craft.

"Yes. It would have been one of at least four or six in total like it on a massive battle cruiser or attack vessel. It was one that belonged to the Federation. One can tell by the remnants of color scheme at these points here." And Lady Shera pointed out a few spots on the hull attachment links. They were worn and barely any one clear color, but nevertheless the gray and blue portions were perceptible. The case itself was several centimeters thick and although battered, it was intact. The shell of a hull which formed the outer-most case was scratched and burned in many places but not penetrated. The open far end which had been most connected to an attachment point on the ship's main hull itself was viewable once they had walked half-way around the large structure. And here one could see partially inside the casing to understand the massive size and complexity of the thruster itself. It was an engine the size of a small house encased in its own protective sheath meant to stay directly connected to the ship it was designed to propel.

Lady Shera noted this was a very new looking form for an engine. She had studied mechanics and seen many human designs of war ships before. Her studies were not reserved for what one might think based upon her home world and its embracing of ancient ways and simple forms. Her status and leadership qualities were enhanced by her constant and aggressive pursuit of knowledge outside of expected menca circles. She observed that the portions which had attached this element to its parent components were severed fairly cleanly. She estimated that this indicated the structure they were looking at was not original to the spaceship. Her guess was that this thruster and its housing was a late addition or modification to the vessel which enhanced the craft's base capabilities and contributed to the reason they found it in such an intact state.

Durability was a trait not easily observed from elements in an idle state. Or prior to attempts at total destruction such as witnessed at Quai-14, one might only guess at the longevity and soundness of sub-components of large-scale hardware. Here though, it could be surmised clearly from leftover evidence.

Lady Shera showed Fae and Jeanaviere how a component this size blown apart from its base attachments and main frame, should often itself be stressed and damaged beyond recognition as a clear single sub-component. This was not. It would be easily seen by any trained eye for what it was. She judged that its size and from what was viewable inside the open gashes, that it alone could provide enough power to keep a medium sized cruiser along a designated travel path. Perhaps, if alone, not at a desired neo or ES-neo speed, but at a given trajectory nonetheless.

"We should note above in the atmosphere for any evidence of additional pieces of debris," Lady Shera continued her observation. "If this is what I am sure it is, then there would likely be others and large quantities of them. I fear our world has become witness to only a portion of some great destruction." Fae could not help but wonder how many lives this piece of hardware landing here in his homeland meant had been sacrificed.

"My lady I do sense that this means many have suffered and many have perished," he began. "I wonder if we will begin to chance upon them and find more evidence of this likely 'great' conflict you have sensed already." The young spirit thought this might be a sound time for him to reach out to the forest itself. He could ask the trees to provide their own observations and input to help guide him and the mencas in some direction. To be able to assist if it was warranted.

"Ladies," Fae elected now to address both of his immediate companions rather than continue in sharing his thoughts with primarily and only Lady Shera, "I have a good mind to be able to address my fellow creatures of the woods themselves. The trees may know of more that could mean something to us. They may already be fighting fires and paths of destruction and fallen debris. I will be able to address it directly with them, but it means my mind may seem distant for a bit while I speak with them. Would you be able to excuse me for a bit?"

Both ladies eagerly wished Fae well and encouraged him to learn what he could from other creatures of the woods. They also took the opportunity to speak again with their designated observing protectors, the knights. Both male mencas were brought closer in to the path of the thruster's fallen debris trail and informed what had been learned. They were allowed time to see and explore for themselves what they could and it pleased them both. It made them feel as mencas often so desired: to be a part of the forward most deciding element. Mencas liked to be at the heart of what was being brought to bear for the group. Any group. Even an ad-hoc unlikely group such as this.

Chapter 16
7th Fleet

Aurelle and JT hailed the sentry ships before even getting within firing range of the main fleet body's gun batteries. They were friendly but one could never be too sure of anything when on the run and under duress. The sentry vessels recognized them in their small shuttlecraft as federal and therefore did not give them too much trouble beyond standard code recognition and on-screen clearances. Aurelle did most of the talking and knew what to say to ease any concern the sentries might have had. She was a federal medical officer and JT knew he was the patient and just a "grunt" to them. Marines and naval fleet guards, in this case a pair of warrant sergeants, were on the same team. But they experienced a typical inter-service rivalry and were known to give each other grief just because.

"All clear ma'am," said the one warrant sergeant after consulting with his superior and that superior notifying his ship's command team. "You are destined for docking in bay four along the outer wall of the main hanger of the fleet carrier *Amorhe*."

"Ah the Amorhe," thought JT, "a good flag ship to be on." He decided he would share what he knew of it with Aurelle. He also decided she looked busy and a bit flustered so he would wait. He had already made up his mind she looked pretty when she was flustered. He thought of her as pretty all the time but especially now so with a small bead of sweat across her brow and a very concentrated serious expression. This, as she focused upon the task of getting them to their new destination at the heart of the flagship of the federal 7th Fleet.

The 7th Fleet was the spearhead group of vessels for one of sixteen battle groups the Federation had patrolling the Near and Far Universes. It was composed of 28 ships of which two were carriers, three were battle cruisers and eight were class 1 fast attack cruisers.

The rest were various support ships and frigates. The battle cruisers were each as powerful and well-armed as a battleship; only they were faster and lighter with less armor. The class 1's were the kind of attack cruiser the Federation had been using with such success against the Confederation. They were of the same type against which the Suclesahe had just recently made a first kill using the neutrino cannon. But at this time, no news of that Confederation victory had yet reached the 7th Fleet. None of that news had yet reached any of the fleet as it had just occurred and would only be released once operational security and the censors deemed it appropriate. In a day or two when all communication from more than 4,000 sailors and Marines instantly ceased, the public would begin to be aware.

JT's assessment was that he and Aurelle were certainly going to be much safer at the heart of the 7th Fleet than they would have been in St. Demetrius or certainly could have been aboard the Vissad. But he would wait to pass final judgement upon their level of safety. He helped steer the craft along a guided path of light markers and towards the Amorhe. Along with its sister carrier, the *Flannigan*, the Amorhe could be seen right smack in the middle of a protective ring of five attack cruisers and a battle cruiser. Certainly, *there were fewer safer places to be across the entire Federation,* thought JT. The guide path was smooth and easy to follow. Aurelle did the brunt of the work until tractor beams took over and guided the small craft into the hanger. JT was amazed at how updated and protected the Amorhe seemed. It was indeed the flagship, but this vessel was covered like no other from every angle. Turrets and weapons stations bristled from everywhere. And they were already inside the ring of cruisers and attack ships that protected the carriers.

When their craft arrived at its docking station in bay four of the Amorhe, there was a pause while the docking crew hooked up appropriate sensors and security platforms to the shuttlecraft. JT relayed now to Aurelle what he had known about the Amorhe. "This carrier is the best our fleet has to offer; I remember when it was christened only two years ago. My unit was put on duty to guard the maiden embarkation ceremony. I remember getting a tour of the vessel and thinking it was something else. The best that there is. I think we will be safe here for sure," JT remarked as they waited.

"I wish I had your confidence," said Aurelle. "Unfortunately, nothing in this war is proving safe and sound." Her comment was well taken for it was truthful and spoke of the horror they had all experienced perpetuated by this 4th I-S War.

"Right you are," JT responded. "I just thought of all the places we could have ended up; this is not a bad one... The Amorhe is a good ship."

"Ok. I will not argue with that sentiment. Perhaps we are lucky to be here after all," she said. And at that moment the hatch decompressed and the docking team came onto the viewer again.

"Please exit your craft and prepare to be inspected," was the warrant sergeant's polite demand phrased as a request from on screen.

"Here we go," Aurelle said as she unbelted herself, passed a glance to JT's harness and implied it was time for JT to do the same. The next few minutes were not as stressful as JT or Aurelle imagined they might have been. The docking team was polite and kind and never implied there was anything suspicious about JT and Aurelle's arrival although they certainly could have.

As soon as the initial inspection was complete and the two newcomers had been scanned for explosives or contraband items, they were offered something to eat and drink. JT gladly accepted a tea. Aurelle took water only. Aurelle also indicated that she had information that needed to be shared with the highest levels of command. She said flat out if the commander of the Amorhe, him or herself, was available, this would be for him or her only. Otherwise, immediate members of the command team were the only persons with whom Aurelle said she was authorized to speak. She took some liberty with that declaration but considering the circumstances, it was well warranted. JT understood exactly why she said what she did.

"Admiral Vander is not on the bridge presently, but Commodore Theelson is. She commands the Amorhe and is the ranking officer in the Admiral's absence," said the nearest warrant sergeant in response to Aurelle's request.

"Ok then, Commodore Theelson it must be then," said Aurelle. "This is of the greatest importance to the Federation and really cannot wait," she added. The warrant sergeant indicated that to get the command team to talk with their two guests, he would need to speak with some higher-level authorities. At least for authorization to hail the Amorhe's command team. He said it would just be a moment for this clearance to be obtained. It did not take long.

Soon JT and Aurelle found themselves being brought to a distinguished visitor quarters waiting area.

"Wow. We are being treated well," said JT. "I am not sure I ever would have expected a distinguished visitor suite for just a grunt Marine. The distinguished guest clearly must be you," he added. As if it was a second thought he noted, "You know something about all this don't you?" She gave him a side eye glance as if to say yes, but only said it with her eyes instead.

The journey had not been long, but it was playing out just how Aurelle would have hoped. It appeared they were going to get to speak to the highest level of command available on the ship. Maybe even in the 7th Fleet. JT made himself comfortable on the plush couch and looked around. The room was well decorated with artificial plant life and hologram artwork on two walls. The floor was synthetic brushed metal covered by a nice simulated rug that looked Cybrinthian in its weaving pattern. There was a drink station and a computer screen in one corner. JT asked Aurelle, "sure you would not like something else?"

"I am fine with my water," she responded. JT looked around and then decided it was time to ask his travel companion some questions.

"Do I just follow your lead when we meet the commodore?" he said half to himself.

"I would appreciate it if it is clear, we are on the same team," was Aurelle's reply. Though it was clear she was already concerned since JT had asked the question.

"I didn't mean anything alarming to you by that. Sorry. I was half speaking my thoughts out loud," he said.

"No worries. It's just we are on the same side here my Marine friend. And I don't want anyone to sense anything other than that." Her tone was more relaxed and less defensive now. "Listen, I like you more than I care to admit. But we need to be sure we can trust whoever we get to talk to. That is all I'm saying. Dr. Quimby's death; I don't want it to have been in vain."

"I understand. Please do not worry about me saying anything unnecessarily. I will keep things hush hush until we know we can trust who we are talking with," JT said and then added as an afterthought, "you know we are probably being monitored right now." Aurelle looked at him and indicated with her eyes and a tiny nearly imperceptible nod of her head that she concurred with him.

"We have nothing to hide," she said loud enough that any monitoring microphone could not have missed it. The room's door then swung slowly open and an aide-de-camp ushered himself and a young officer into the room.

"Hello Dr. Gifford and Sergeant Wayne," said the Marine aide. "Welcome to the Amorhe. We are pleased to have you with us. I am Lieutenant Simonds and this is Captain Johanaston of ship security. We will take you to meet with the commadore." Pleasantries were exchanged by all. Then the lieutenant asked point blank, "Do you mind if I or Captain Johanaston read your thoughts for a moment as a security precaution?"

JT immediately felt a little uneasy. But Aurelle was prepared for this and told them it would be no issue except that certain details of their trip were reserved for the highest command levels only. She said they were welcome to probe but that parts relating to the recent drill on St. Demetrius would be reserved for the commadore. Lieutenant Simonds said that would not be a problem and Captain Johanaston concurred and said that he could only probe what they allowed him access to but that if there was deceit or trickery hidden in their thoughts he would know. JT then added there was not, nor would there be, anything like that to find. He also thought, *How bad could it be to allow a fellow Marine to probe his thoughts?* He really didn't have anything to hide.

Johanaston then touched the side of JT's head lightly with a few fingers holding a cord with an electrode on it. He did this for just a second or two as he held a small computer-chip sized device in his other hand. Simonds did the same to Aurelle. In a manner of three seconds or less the two officers consulted the tiny screens on the device and nodded to each other. They seemed satisfied with what they found and indicated to JT and Aurelle all was well.

"Thank you for allowing us into your minds," Johanaston said. "You would be surprised how many people resist that process and it only makes it more difficult for them in the end."

"I would think only people with things to hide would resist such a process," said JT. He had been a bit apprehensive, but his fears were waylaid as soon as he saw how Aurelle had been ok with it. And he was eager to meet the ship's commander.

"You two may leave your drinks here or take them with you as you like," said Simonds.

"We'll leave them and have them again on the way out if that's ok," replied Aurelle. She really wanted to see if the aide would have minded them bringing them or anything with them into the meeting, but he didn't seem to care. They were then brought by the lieutenant through the distinguished visitor passageway and doors. Then up a level and down another short hallway.

"OK, this is where we leave you. This doorway takes you straight into Commadore Theelson's private meeting area. She should be in there already," and then, "Thank you, we'll see you in a bit," Simonds and Johanaston each said as they indicated to the hatchway in front of them all. Aurelle stepped in first immediately followed by JT. The hatchway was very much like a full-sized door and it opened automatically before Aurelle could even search for or find a button. JT noted this area of the ship too was well decorated and very posh. As soon as JT came through the door, he found it opened to a medium sized room with a round table and off to one side of it a set of couches and chairs around a small coffee-like table. Commadore Theelson was already sitting at this table and stood up to meet them immediately.

"Hello my friends," she said and moved around the table to offer them each a seat in the cozy space around the coffee table. The three of them all sat down and Commadore Theelson offered them refreshments, "Can I offer you some food or something to drink?"

"Nothing for me," said Aurelle as she turned to JT. "Your aide Lt. Simonds already gave us some drinks outside." JT noticed that the commadore already had some fruit on the table and a hologram food producer was right next to the bowl of fruit.

"If you are having some of that fruit I will join you ma'am," said JT as if to say to Aurelle, "suit yourself," but of course nothing like that came out of his mouth. He only smiled just a tiny bit and it was not apparent to anyone except JT that he had even smiled in the first place.

"Of course," said Cdre. Theelson. "The machine can make you anything you would like if you have any bit more of an appetite than one for just some fruit."

"Thank you kindly, but just some grapes and maybe a slice of apple will hit the spot," said JT, "and some cheese if you might have some." The commadore smiled. Then she turned to Aurelle.

"I never met a Marine who didn't have an appetite or refused food that was offered to him or her," she said this clearly enough for the three of them all to hear. They each chuckled a little bit.

"Ma'am, I know you haven't offered us an audience to sit and exchange pleasantries about food," Aurelle started to get to the point. "But I also know how busy you must be and this is taking important time from your duties." Aurelle was not one to purposefully take or waste a high-ranking individual's time.

"I appreciate that young doctor," said the ship's commander. But her tone was not that of one that insisted on getting right down to business. "We are not in a rush at present and my quite capable deputy has command of the vessel while I am here with you." But the fact of the matter was that time was of the essence. Aurelle wanted to find out why her friend and mentor Dr. Quimby was dead and why JT was seemingly at the center of the conspiracy that had racked St. Demetrius Hospital. So, the urgency was not so much for Cdre. Theelson as it was for Aurelle and JT and the Federation.

The next fifteen minutes were telling. Aurelle, JT and Cdre. Theelson talked at length about the events that had unfolded on St. Demetrius. JT talked to them as best he could about his experience on the Vissad. Aurelle got the sense specifically that Cdre. Theelson was there to help and would do anything she could within her power to see to it that Aurelle and JT got all the support they needed. She admitted her power to contact fleet higher ups was not limited, but she felt it wise that they not be broadcasting outside of the 7th Fleet that JT and Aurelle were there.

This, she said simply was as a security measure since they could not be sure their external communications were not being monitored. In fact, the fleet had conducted a bit of an experiment with communication traffic sending some false messages and seeing if the Confederation would react to that false information. Without fail, they had. Therefore, Cdre. Theelson felt it best to keep it within the fleet that they were there. Aurelle tended to agree. JT was not convinced at first, but became more so the more they talked.

While Aurelle had hoped there would be some glimmering light and moment of clarity for answers to some of her more pointed questions, there was not. The commadore was able to give them both reassurances but nothing that said yes, we can help you get to the bottom of who killed your friend. Nor were there ready answers as to why JT was being hunted and forced to evacuate on a moment's notice from St. Demetrius. These things Aurelle and JT hoped would come in time. Cdre. Theelson hoped she could help in getting those answers too. But presently, she made no promises.

The conversation was just getting intricate about details from the escape when a buzz at the hatchway interrupted the group. "Pardon the intrusion ma'am," came Lt. Simonds' voice, "but there is a hail on screen on the bridge from Admiral Haverston requesting you."

"Ah Admiral Haverston, I have been expecting his call," Cdre. Theelson said. "If you two don't mind I can take this in here. But I would ask that you wait for a moment outside until I can introduce you both and seek permission from the admiral to include you in our discussion. Admiral Haverston is currently with the fleet and this is a great opportunity."

Wowsers thought Aurelle. *We are being included in a discussion with a group admiral.* JT had heard of Admiral Haverston, but never thought he might make the man's acquaintance. Even if, only on a video or hologram call. Admiral Haverston was Admiral Vander's boss. Admiral Vander commanded 7th Fleet and Haverston commanded 2nd Group which was composed of five fleets. The 2nd Group command answered only to the Federation chief of staff or secretary who answered only to the chancellor. JT was about to have a conversation with the highest-ranking four-star admiral he had ever met. He was actually not really nervous at the idea. He looked forward to it. It was Aurelle who was a bit more nervous than she would have liked.

Cdre. Theelson excused JT and Aurelle and said this would just be a minute or two before she asked them back in. They thought little of this and understood the gesture and still appreciated being included in the four-star conversation at all. As the hatch closed between the waiting conference area and the commadore's private office Aurelle turned to JT and asked if he was ok with this.

"Me? I'm fine. I think it is you who might be a tad uncomfortable," he said matter-of-factly. While Aurelle did not want to admit it, he was right. The commadore was truthful in that it was only a minute or two before the hatch opened back up and she directed the conversation and hologram of Admiral Haverston into the waiting area. All of a sudden, the center of the coffee table transformed into a holographic representation of the admiral. He was sitting at a desk which was also broadcast in the hologram. He was dressed in Federation formal uniform and his medals were clear on his left chest.

"I apologize for intruding upon you all," he began. "But it has become clear that there is a danger afoot and we cannot hide from it anymore." The three in the room leaned in and grasped what the admiral was saying. He had not even bothered to wait for formal or informal introductions. "I welcome you two, Dr. Gifford, is it? And Sergeant Wayne I presume?"

"Yes sir, it is our pleasure," said Aurelle.

"I echo that sentiment," said JT. "We are honored to make your acquaintance." JT wondered how the admiral knew both his and Aurelle's names so readily. Clearly the man had been briefed.

"Well yes, the pleasure is all mine," said the admiral. "If no one minds, Commadore Theelson, would you mind if we included Admiral Vander in this discussion?"

"Of course not, just give me a moment and I will hail him," replied Cdre. Theelson. And with that, Theelson quickly paged Lieutenant Simonds and asked him to bring Adm. Vander into the hologram conversation. In about ten seconds there was a buzz and Adm. Vander's name popped up in the hologram text window. A few seconds later, he was on the table in holographic form as well.

"Thank you," said Adm. Haverston. "Now that I have the three of you and Adm. Vander on the line, it is important we all understand what is said in here does not leave this group." JT and Aurelle exchanged a brief glance. It was the kind of look that said, *here we go, what have we gotten ourselves into?* But that was the end of the look and immediately everyone verbally acknowledged what the admiral was requesting.

"Sergeant Wayne, you are the key to defeating the neutrino cannon. You are the only survivor of a neutrino attack who is actually recovering and has gotten better every day since that attack. We believe you have genealogy which is resistant to this neutrino sickness. And we think the Confederation has learned this and therefore will stop at nothing to find and study if not kill you." The admiral relayed this in a very matter of fact way. There. It was said. It was on the table both visually and literally in the form of facts stated from the table hologram of their very respected admiral.

JT had sort of sensed this information already from Aurelle. But he did not know he was the subject of a universal man-hunt. A man-hunt to the death. But was he really being hunted by the Confederation? How was that even possible. There were millions of soldiers and sailors or Marines fighting. He was just one tiny little piece of that massive machine. How could he have become that chosen one? However it happened, it seemed to be the case that he was the lucky Marine left holding the bag. The question on JT's mind, and probably that of Aurelle as well, was, what were they to do next? They (and he) didn't need to end up assassinated in cold blood like Dr. Quimby. But how could they avoid such a fate?

"Commadore Theelson, we can't thank you enough for your hospitality in taking us in but do you feel we are safe on the Amorhe? Is this the type of ship that can truly guard against clandestine attacks and spies?" Asked Aurelle.

"Our networks may not be perfect but they are the best the Federation has to offer," was Theelson's response.

"I can vouch for that as the ship's ranking officer," said Admiral Vander. "There is no better place you could be. I would swear it with my military experience on dozens of ships across the Federation. Moreover, we will give you your own dedicated armed security team led by Capt. Johanaston and Lt. Simonds... if you would like it." JT thought about the offer and decided it was a good idea. Aurelle considered the same thing but she was a bit more reluctant to accept the help.

"Would it not be best perhaps to maintain a lower profile onboard the ship? If indeed there are Confed spies or sympathizers, would an armed team of security not alert them to a presence of interest?" She added as if to counter her own point, "but I would readily accept any help you are willing to give... so long as it is indeed decided to be in everyone's best interest."

"We can assure that," stated Adm. Haverston. "We will make this decision together." Command decisions were what the admiral was most used to making on his own but in this case, he felt weighing everyone's opinion was a sign of strong leadership and more prudent decision-making. After a few more minutes of discussion. The merits of both sides weighed; it was decided by Haverston to defer to Commadore Theelson's security decision. After all, it was her ship. Theelson heard all input and decided they would allow a two-sailor security detail to shadow Aurelle and JT at all times at least for the time being. They would review the procedure and consider eliminating it if the situation warranted and there was less risk as assessed by the security force and this group. Aurelle reluctantly accepted the decision. What else could she do? She was a guest on the Amorhe and at its command decision making mercy. At least she was not separated from JT.

The holographic display figures expressed gratitude and bid farewell and signed out to return to their admiraling duties across the fleet and the group. Cdre. Theelson offered a tour of the ship via Capt. Johanaston. Meanwhile, Lt. Simonds was directed to prepare the guests' quarters which he went smartly off to do.

Capt. Johanaston pressed the communicator in his ear and ordered a team warrant sergeant or officer to meet him at distinguished guest quarters three and four in 12th wing. The three of them were there in 12th wing within a five minute walk, a few turns and down a couple levels. JT had committed to memory the ship he had experienced up to this point. It was not difficult so far, but there was a space ton of ship left to explore.

The guard who met them at distinguished quarters three and four was a young lieutenant named Shamus. She was about 6 feet tall and stockier than any fleet officer JT had ever seen. Her short haircut seemed to say *don't mess with me or I'll break your face.* But of course, she was professional and knew her stuff. At least so it seemed. She spoke in short spurts and appeared to be more Cybrinthian than human. There was no way of telling for sure, but her look was definitely not fully human. There also seemed to be an immediate understanding and connection psychologically between Aurelle and Lt. Shamus.

"Dr. Gifford, Sergeant Wayne: I'll be caring for your safety. I'm Lieutenant Shamus," she said as a seemingly required matter of fact.

"Glad to have you on the team LT," said JT. Technically, "Ma'am" would have been a more appropriate title, but JT was a senior non-commissioned officer and little did he know he would one day be on the brink of a battlefield commission. But for now it was enough that he had more years in service than either Lt. Shamus or probably Capt. Johanaston. His seniority and accolades earned him the right to call a lieutenant, *LT.* Or a captain, *Cap'n.*

So, JT greeted his new guard team in this familiar fashion. Lt. Shamus squirmed a little in her britches. It was nearly imperceptible, but Aurelle noticed the slight head jerk and barely noticeable shoulder shrug. If JT noticed it, he didn't give it any credence. He was who he was: the best Marine in his outfit, perhaps in his whole fleet, commander of a platoon, acting commander of a lot more than that and now the sole survivor of the neutrino canon and perhaps the Federation's greatest hope to win this war. All this and only a touch more than five years of active federal service. Not that any of that had gone to his head… but well… it is possible he was acting the part accordingly. "LT," he said, "you look like you have done some good time with the federal corps, are you sure you aren't a Marine in disguise?" Crickets for a response from the lieutenant. *Oh well*, thought JT, *so much for some humor.*

"We will be with you but stay out of sight and not in your immediate area," said Capt. Johanaston. "We will be on your six o'clock at most times and trying to blend in with any of your surroundings. This is part of our mandate to protect but remain quiet and in the shadows."

"Works for me and sounds good. Let's get on with this tour of the ship," said JT.

"Yes but can we settle in to the quarters for a moment," asked Aurelle. "We've been traveling and or on conferences for hours and nature is calling this girl." No one could argue with that. JT decided he would like to see his room and also take advantage of the little Marine's facility these accommodations had to offer. The captain and lieutenant showed them quarters three (Aurelle) and four (JT) and gave them a few minutes to use the quarters' private lavatories and then some more to acquaint themselves with the rooms. JT was pleased there was an adjoining door between the rooms. Not that this meant he intended to use it for any purpose other than official communication and ease of coordination. But, well, he did appreciate the fact that he could see Aurelle without having to go outside and alert the security detail which would undoubtedly be monitoring the hallways and have watch over the chambers' external doors. *Thank goodness for small favors,* thought JT.

After acclimating to their new rooms and using the facilities the two newest guests aboard the Amorhe came outside their quarters and linked up with Lt. Simonds and Capt. Johanaston. Now was the time for their official tour of the carrier. The *boat* was the newest and biggest fleet carrier the Federation had in service. Therefore the tour would consist of the highlights only, but JT welcomed it just the same. He had previously served aboard the *Valiant*, an earlier class 2 federal carrier. But it was much smaller and more antiquated than the Amorhe. The Valiant was 30 years old when JT served on it and now it would be nearing 35 or 36. It was capable still, but it was two thirds the size of the Amorhe with a crew complement several thousand smaller. Its weapons had all been updated, but the vessel still had the feel of being old and outdated. JT was happy when his transfer orders came to move on to a planetary assignment and then later to an attack cruiser, even though it turned out to be the cursed Vissad. No, the Amorhe was something else altogether.

Less than two years old, you could still smell fresh paint in some areas. Though this was normal standard operating procedure as something aboard a federal vessel was always being painted somewhere. The Amorhe had 15 main decks and 7 engineering sub-decks. There were four hanger bays. Her weaponry included photon torpedoes, anti-fighter and anti-air flak guns, ballistic nuclear missiles, and extended range trajectory booster cannons. Her complement of single and dual seat fighters amounted to 140 and could carry 180 in a surge emergency although they could not conduct launch and recovery operations simultaneously for all when loaded to that surge capacity. The Amorhe was a sight to see. She was the flagship of the 7th Fleet and while Cdre. Theelson commanded the ship, Admiral Vander commanded the fleet and hung his hat on the Amorhe. His bridge was just below that of Cdre. Theelson's.

There was another Captain promotable to one star admiral aboard the Amorhe too. It was odd but just worked out that the air wing commander, normally equal or junior in rank to the commodore of the ship in this case was senior to Cdre. Theelson. It was no problem as the two women had been friends for a long time and served as cadets together at the Federation Fleet Academy. They had been only one class apart and the more senior, Capt. (promotable) Djaimo had been a friend and mentor to Theelson throughout their whole careers. Being stationed together as ship commander and wing detachment commander on the same flag ship and pearl of the fleet was a dream come true for both women. And, if things continued to go well, everyone expected Cdre. Theelson to be picked up for rear admiral soon anyway. She would most likely follow in the footsteps of her friend and senior colleague.

On their tour, JT and Aurelle were introduced to Capt. (promotable) Djaimo and numerous other senior officers, warrant sergeants and non-commissioned officers. As well they met a host of lower enlisted sailors all hard at work making their ship go while undertaking various tasks and jobs. The carrier kept a crew of approximately 12,000 including its wing complement and a small host of onboard Marines. The Marines manned a few of the guns and pulled mainly security duties but they were trained for embarkation and close quarters combat. All the ship's quick reaction forces and most of the security elements like Capt. Johanaston and Lt. Simonds were composed of Marines. JT was proud to see his brethren doing their part aboard the mighty Amorhe. After about 30 minutes on the main decks, Capt. Johanaston offered to take the group to the engineering decks or return them to their quarters, JT was not ready for the walk to be over. He was busy taking it all in,

"I would love to see engineering, but even more so I'd like to see the other hangers and some weapons platforms," JT said almost apologetically as an eager child might ask for another piece of candy. "Could we maybe see the photon torpedoes and booster cannons or flak guns?"

"That's not really necessary but we appreciate anything else you think might be welcome to know," interjected Aurelle.

"Hell, it may not be necessary, but if I could, I'd like to see any and every weapon system you've got that is manned by a fellow Federal Marine." JT wasn't about to back down from this request. After all, he had fellow leathernecks aboard this ship and he wanted to see them in action doing what they did best.

"Sure, we can look at some weapons platforms and maybe catch a quick reaction force drilling or chat with one for a moment," was the captain's response. JT gave a brief glance to Aurelle and stuck his tongue out of the corner of his mouth. Just a tad. Enough though so that she would see it and either be aggravated at his childishness or laugh at him. JT didn't really care which response it elicited. Luckily it got a smile and a chuckle under her breath.

So, they headed first down several levels to see the engineering decks. Of the seven, they visited four. The senior engineering officer greeted them on the engineering bridge and personally pointed out some of the finer workings of the well-oiled machine. He noted the reactors and all the safety mechanisms in place that would prevent radiation accidents. This was in place in the event of all sorts and different kinds of damage from routine maintenance problems to major battle damage and hull breeches. He pointed out the neo drive systems and shield power generators and finally the transporter and tractor beam capability. Finally, he gave them a tour of the control systems for emergency evacuation and auxiliary power units. Yes, there was a lot to do and understand from an engineering standpoint of a fleet carrier. JT was impressed. Aurelle was impressed. Even though they didn't show it, Capt. Johanaston and Lt. Simonds were impressed.

Next their tour took them to the first hanger. This bay was similar to the number four bay that JT and Aurelle had arrived in except it was about one and one-half times as large. That and it was filled with 30 or so X02 fighter bombers. These dual seat, side-by-side, gull wing shaped small attack ships were recently brought to the Amorhe. They had only been in the fleet a year or so and they were one of the latest small attack crafts the Federation possessed. Some were fully armed and others were in various states of re-arming and bomb uploading.

"Can an X02 fly with one pilot," asked JT as he peered out into the small hall full of fighters and noted their cockpit configuration.

"Oh yes," said Lt Simonds. "The X02 flight controls are completely redundant. One pilot is the flight engineer and bombardier while the other is the pilot and front gunner but either position has complete flight control capability."

"Is this bay dedicated to fighter bombers and just the X02 or can the bays change up what they house?" came the follow-on question again from JT.

This time Capt. Johanaston spoke up, "Any bay can handle any plane." He gestured to the other open individual stalls, one of them housed an X99. "As you can see, but it is more efficient and makes more logistical sense to group them together. That and the training and crew brief facilitation make it so." They continued on with a few more questions coming both from JT and Aurelle. Johanaston and Simonds took turns in answering them as appropriate. They continued to bay two. It was similar in setup to the first hanger, being about the same size and layout. Except it had a flight contingent of X99 fighters. These were stacked two-seater fighter interceptors. Not designed for heavy bomb loads they were designed for attack and pursuit of enemy fighters. They could carry missiles and modifications could be made to the missile mount points to attach small bombs but rarely was this done. The X99 was not as modern as the X02, but being procured in 1499AN it was fairly new itself. JT and Aurelle asked fewer questions this time and were content to see the wing's detachment hard at work conducting rearmament drills.

When they got to bay three, JT finally asked the question he had wanted to know about the wing contingency, "of the 140 planes or so you carry, how many are flown by Marines?" Bay three and four were smaller than one and two but now that he had seen all of the bays (including the fourth bay he and Aurelle landed in and entered through) he had not noticed any attack ships or fighters with Marine markings. Nor had he seen any tell-tale signs of Marine activity.

"Well, I hate to be the bearer of some sad news for you Sergeant Wayne but Marines don't fly off the Amorhe," Capt. Johanaston said reluctantly.

"Sonofa dagum confounded confed!" was all JT could muster.

"While they don't fly on the Amorhe, they do fly on our sister ship, the Flannigan. There is a flight of six fighters flown by Marines based on the Flannigan," Johanaston said and then added, "and if the Flannigan's trial experiment with that flight goes well, they may well bring a Marine flight to the Amorhe and all Amorhe class carriers… time will tell."

"Hmmmf," mumbled JT, seemingly as if his pride was hurt and this small upbeat news would not be able to make up for it.

"We do have several Marine gun crews including one that mans the trajectory booster cannon and several that man our various flak guns," said Johanaston as if it was some sort of consolation prize.

"How about the photon torpedoes? Any Marines on those?" JT was grasping at a straw here. A photon torpedo specialist was a special weapon classification reserved for navy personnel.

"Not a crew in its entirety but I know of several Marines who have taken over for ballistic computational duties and one who is on the gunnery sighting team for the torpedoes," Capt. Johanaston was able to report with an air of confidence.

"Ok, I guess that's better than nothing," said JT morbidly.

"I just don't understand this silliness," interjected Aurelle. "One team, one fight. Who cares what color your uniform is and if you say 'hooah' or 'Aye-Aye' at the end of a sentence?"

"The doctor has a point," added Lt. Simonds. "And with that, perhaps we should continue the tour up to the top deck and see some weapons stations?" But first, they descended a few levels to see the base of the ballistic missile silos, torpedo rooms and the bottom level of the flak and other gun stations. Then after 30 minutes wandering around the lower depths they came up top to see the protruding turrets first hand. JT was impressed. The ship's firepower was immense even though it was designed to launch and recover fighters and small craft. The carrier was designed to be protected by the rest of the fleet, but this ship, the Amorhe, was armed to the teeth. It could handle itself without thinking twice to call for backup. JT thought to himself, despite not enough Marines manning the fighters or guns, there was not anywhere else he felt that might have been safer for him and Aurelle.

With the tour now nearing its end, Capt. Johanaston and Lt. Simonds brought their guests back to the distinguished guest quarters. They reminded them of the way to the mess hall and the commadore's mess, to which they were welcome and always invited. The commadore's mess could make them anything at all at any hour of the day or night. Capt. Johanaston then relieved Lt. Simonds and called for Lt. Shamus.

"We will be down the hall and around if you need us, don't hesitate to call on communicator channel 1. We will be your first point of contact for everything you might need," Johanaston added. With that the captain and the lieutenant bid farewell to JT and Aurelle and allowed the quarters three and four hatches to close behind them. JT was relieved to finally get a break. He wondered if Aurelle was relieved too.

"So what did you think?" JT asked her when they were alone in the passageway between their two rooms. She leaned in close to his face. *Smack!* She slapped him lightly. Not hard enough to hurt but hard enough that he felt it. JT reeled back in shock.

"*That,* was for sticking your tongue out at me earlier," Aurelle remarked as she leaned in just a little bit closer. Then she gently grabbed his shirt collar and pulled him in very close to her. She inched closer and closer to his face until their lips met just for a moment. She kissed him softly but passionately. Just briefly though. A matter of seconds only. "And *that,* was for making me wait since leaving St. Demetrius to plant one of those on your pretty little lips Sergeant." And with that she pulled away and smiled. A little bit sinister. But a smile just the same.

Chapter 17
Fico

Captain Majak was happy to have found a warm and seemingly friendly place to hang his hat and unlace his boots. His newfound friend, Mr. Fico, or just Fico, (he wasn't sure if that was the man's first or last name) seemed nice enough. In seedy places like this, sometimes small details like a surname or family name didn't really matter. Fico was tall. He wore a dark trench type coat and had on a hat that only could have been described as somewhat like a fedora of ancient earth. Fico appeared somewhat human but in truth he was part Cybrinthian and part spirit. He even thought it was possible he had a bit of Gnorac blood in his veins. Whatever Fico was, it was questionable.

His colleagues around the same drinking table were not much better from an outward appearance. Their collective aura spoke an unspoken *don't mess with us*. From Majak's standpoint that was all for the good. He didn't want to be messed with himself and therefore in his mind, the company he planned to keep should espouse the same outlook. They all had on dark clothes. They all smelled of space alcohol and smoke vapor.

"Well friend, what brings you to these parts?" opened Fico. "We don't rightfully see Gnoracs much around here."

"I come out of necessity to preserve peace and dignity of the alliances on both sides of this conflict," said Majak. Where and how he would and could go with this, he was not even sure. The creature known as Fico eyed him hard. A near stare down of sorts. It was as if Fico was trying to ascertain the truth or validity of the words Majak had spoken.

"I go by Kajam," said Majak. "And I appreciate your candor Mr... F..." Fico filled in the pause: "Fico." Majak spoke to Fico in the friendliest of tones he could muster.

"Sure you do," retorted Fico. "Let's get this off to an honest start, *friend*," Fico said with an air of condescension. "You may indeed appreciate my candor. But I doubt if you are called Kajam. If you don't want to share your name then don't. But don't make up a moniker that doesn't suit you and pass it off as your given call-sign. No, that won't do for an introduction."

Majak was a bit taken off guard. He knew if he wanted to befriend this outlander it was now or never. His next words would make or break their potential association.

"Sorry friend, no offense intended. And you are correct, I don't care to share my true name just yet. It might be recognizable to some and there are those that might be looking for me to do some harm."

"Now that I would believe," said Fico. "But I will tell you honestly my name is indeed Fico, though it was not the name my parents gave me. That is too hard to pronounce in the common tongue. But I am just Fico. Not Mr. Fico. Not Sir Fico. Not his highness the count of Fico. Not Doctor Fico. Not Commander or Admiral Fico." With the words *commander or admiral,* he seemed to smile with his eyes just a bit as he spoke and looked Majak in the eye. Majak smiled a bit back offering a hint of deference and recognition that indeed Fico was a smart man. Majak would not purposefully again insult Fico's intelligence. Nor, however, would he give away all he knew without some trade-offs and assurances. That, would come in time.

"Well Fico, if there was a place we could talk more privately, I might be willing to share a little more of my story. It is just in this open bar and with so many ears around I must stay a little guarded," said Majak as a plain offering that he was willing to talk more directly but not here like this. Or, just yet.

"I keep few secrets from my closest friends here," said Fico. "We are all on the same team and want the same thing."

"What exactly is it that everyone here wants?" asked Majak.

"Just like you, we want peace," was Fico's reply. "We are here to see that there is a balance in the forces of the universes and that no one side becomes too powerful for the detriment of the whole." This was an ominous statement. It could have meant many things. But Majak took it to mean that Fico's group did not align with one side but rather saw themselves as opportunists.

"Do you see any harm in profiting from the sale of information and trading in commodities which that information may lead one to get?" Majak was fairly direct in his question. He saw no reason not to be. What else did he have to lose?

"Now the sale of information can be tricky," said Fico. "It depends where it came from and how it was obtained to determine if it is a welcome asset or a liability."

Majak's line of thinking was that this talk was guarded but could be beneficial if they could get past the initial pleasantries and just speak plainly. He would give it one more go and see how the man called Fico reacted.

"Fico, I can tell you things that would make your hair curl," said Majak. Fico smiled and raised his hat. He was completely bald.

"I chuckle at your analogy Mr… Kajam," started Fico. "You see I am part spirit, part Cybrinthian, part Dwarf, and part Gnorac. My genes do not allow me to grow any hair at all. I once had a single chest hair but it turned out to be a biproduct of too much spinach eggs in my diet. Now I am like a true sphynx. There are others like me but not many."

"Ah well please excuse my poor choice for the expression," said Majak. "I can tell you things that would make you surprised and grateful to learn them." The two sat there enjoying their drink for a moment longer and Fico then decided to break the silence.

"One thing I would like to know is a name or at least a term or something with some truth to it that you would like me to call you," Fico said and he meant it.

"That is fair," conceded Majak. "But if I tell you my name, I would like a reassurance that it will not leave this table." Fico looked around. His companions did not seem to be paying attention. In fact, several were talking to other people and creatures not even seated at the table. Fico leaned in to Majak and whispered to him that the bar was being watched but that the back patio was not and they could speak there more privately if he wished. Majak indicated his thankfulness and agreed to follow Fico's lead out to the back.

Once the two had excused themselves, ostensibly for some space alcohol refills and smoke vapor and air on the patio, they met at a corner back patio table. This seemed to be out of all prying eye gazes. Fico assured Majak they were alone and would not be watched out there. He said also that they were not specifically being watched inside the bar, but that there were prying eyes all about. So, it was best not to take any chances. Majak thanked him and thought it would be best to cut right to the chase.

"Fico, how do I know that I can trust you? There are so many spies about and I am not exactly inclined to trust anyone I have recently met at a place like the Unlucky Duckling," Majak said as directly as he could but donned an expression of genuine concern.

"Well, whether or not you trust me is up to you," said Fico. "I don't know if I would trust anyone in this town or this dive either. But I can demonstrate to you what side I am on and you can make your decision from there. Fair enough?" Fico began to roll up one of his sleeves.

"That is fair. I appreciate the honesty and forthrightness as I'm sure you would appreciate mine," said Majak. Once Fico had pulled his left arm sleeve up enough over his elbow, Majak could see the marks clearly. There were several scars on his forearms reaching from midway down Fico's forearm up to the elbow itself. Just above the elbow there was a numeric tattoo inside the Confederation crest. This was the mark of a Confederation slave. One could have them removed if granted their freedom or they knew a talented tattoo removal artist. But some people, like Fico, chose to leave theirs in place as a reminder; a mark of commemoration; a mark of honor.

"Make no mistake, I earned my freedom. Or rather I bought my freedom, but I will never forget what I endured." Fico began rolling up his other sleeve and there was the Federation mark of freedom and the tattoo of a federal soldier. So, Fico, the space bandit, part Gnorac, and back-room peddler was a former slave turned Federation trooper. Who knew? Certainly not Majak.

"Ok, I'll give you some credit and would ask that you offer some asylum for I am certain we are on the same side now," said Majak. "My name is Majak and I am or was a captain in the Confederation. My ship was recently destroyed and the Confederation administration wants me for dead. They expect that since I left my ship to come explore this planet and my deputy was in command that I am responsible for its destruction. I am a wanted man.”

The revelation sank in and Fico gave Majak a look of great ponderance. “Was your vessel the Suclesahe?” asked Fico.

“Yes.” Majak looked down as if it was a mark of shame to have been associated with such a warship of the Confederation.

“She was only destroyed last night or this morning, wasn’t she?” asked Fico.

“Yes, again,” said Majak. *How did Fico know that already?* thought the ship’s former commander.

“Well, she fought valiantly, went out in a blaze of glory, and met a true sailor’s demise,” offered Fico.

“How do you know this?” asked Majak. “There are those with the highest of credentials on both sides of the war who would have no idea yet what you just told me.” Most would have no inkling that the Suclesahe and the federal cruiser class 1 attack ship it destroyed were both space debris.

“I know things,” said Fico a little bit cryptically. “Remember I share blood with all races including spirits. So it is therefore hard to pass things by me.”

“Ah, things like Kajam not being my name,” said Majak, half a question, and half a statement.

“Precisely,” came Fico’s response. “How is your ale? This particular brand is a 104 special and locally produced.”

“It is excellent. I would not have guessed it came from here,” said Majak. “But then again, I know very little about these parts…actually I know very little about this entire world.”

“Oh?” Fico seemed genuinely surprised by this revelation.

“This is true,” continued Majak. “I was here on a diplomatic mission to try and find friendly port facilities. Or at least people sympathetic to the cause. And truthfully the mission was to ultimately find a spot which could serve as a port; a resupply and docking facility for the Confederation.”

“How well did that go for you?” said Fico with a bit of a smile.

“Yeah well…” Majak was proud of his service but not proud of the cause nor of the Confederation.

"So not to keep beating around the bush, but if there is information you have and would like to share, perhaps we should explore that a little more," said Fico.

"I think I may need another ale for that conversation to proceed," joked Majak. "But seriously, this is good stuff. I should like to see if I can get it wherever I end up."

"Where do you see yourself ending up?" asked Fico. It was a fair question. A question that Majak was not sure he had a ready answer for. So, he decided to give an honest one.

"I see myself reunited with my family or in Valhalla, the warrior's paradise. I do not see myself growing old on some remote planet in some remote star system under the thumb of the Confederation. No, no. That will certainly not be my fate." The former commander of the Suclesahe saw himself with his lost crew and his lost family in the great beyond. He saw himself hopefully dying a warrior's death, but that would remain to be seen. "You see my crew is now all dead. My former allegiance was to an entity that was responsible for my family's death and now hunts me and blames me for the loss of my ship." Majak was getting misty eyed as he spoke. "There is no more allegiance for me. I just want this war to end as fast as possible."

"Do you think selling my side your information can bring the war to an end more quickly?" asked Fico.

"Well, I don't rightfully know. But I do know the weapon the Confederation now possesses will make the war go on longer or at least cause hundreds of millions of deaths and much suffering. We, or, They, I should say. They, call it…"

"The neutrino cannon," Fico cut him off. "Yes I know," he continued. "We have been watching its development and we were close to stealing its technology but now the Confeds have tested it and found it is more than even they had hoped for."

"You know? But how?" Majak was amazed at his new companion's understanding and demeanor in speaking so nonchalantly about the universe's most game changing anomaly: The N-canon.

"I have my sources and for now they need to remain mine," Fico casually remarked. "But I can tell you that our spy network runs deep and you came to the right place. The Unlucky Duckling is watched mostly by the Federation. This is true despite my suspicion that there may be a Confed informant who has started coming here periodically. As of late at least."

The two conversed some more and finished their ales and ordered another apiece. Finally, towards the end of the second or third ale Majak admitted to Fico that he was no ordinary sailor aboard the Suclesahe. Although he was not in command when she broke apart and was lost forever, he was her commander. He relayed why he was here on planet 104. He said that his deputy chief was the acting commander and had apparently fired the neutrino cannon without authorization. This would mean even more scrutiny for Majak. He surmised that he would be found guilty of dereliction of duty for having been on planet 104 when the engagement took place. It was just the way of the Confederation. Another reason he could no longer support its cause. He saw too much blame and evil in the ways of the Confederation high command. The fact that the organization allowed slavery still to exist was a clear piece of evidence against their intentions. Majak apologized to Fico for what the old spy had been through and assured him they would work together to help establish a new order.

"Well, I will gladly drink to that," said Fico. And he raised his glass in toast to Majak and their newfound partnership. Majak did the same.

"I should warn you there were three other officers with me on Planet 104 but we split up after the Suclesahe was destroyed. They assume I have committed suicide." This was all true Majak continued, "Lt. Cmdr. Giova Krigsbie was senior ranking among them and I assume they have sought out reconnection with the fleet."

"Nevermind them, we will take care of them. Leave that to me," said Fico. And he did do just that- with a quick call from his communicator to his spy networks Fico took care of the rogue Gnorac officers stranded from the Suclesahe. Majak didn't ask questions.

"Now what I have to share with you I should hope can buy me some peace and quiet and an ability to live as such. Either here on 104 or on some nearby planet without prying eyes and trouble from officials of any kind." Majak was directly asking for asylum for his information. Fico understood this and he knew the Gnorac was not asking for too much.

"I think my networks and my hierarchy can support what you are asking for my friend. Particularly if your information proves as valuable as you seem to indicate it could be," Fico added.

The two discussed the general understanding of the neutrino cannon and Majak passed on some small bits of information that indicated he was indeed who he claimed to be. He did not; however, give away major bits of valuable knowledge that would have shown his hand completely. He knew how this had to work. He would give some tidbits of information and Fico would make good on some of his promises. Then Majak would give some more and Fico would do the same. This trade of ideas and information for safety and asylum would take days and weeks even longer perhaps. It all depended on how well the "network higher ups" of Fico's found the information's value to be. Hopefully it was greatly needed and sought after and was worth immediate returns. One could hope.

It was not as if Majak was giving away tactical or strategic fleet positions. He was telling his Federation spy friend how the neutrino cannon was employed and how it could be countered. His knowledge would actually explain why JT was able to survive the attack. In practical application, spirits would be unaffected by the blast of the weapon because their form could transcend physical manifestation. Any person with a significant trace of spirit energy and genealogy had the ability, if in tune with that energy, to morph out of physical space and return to it as desired.

JT had never done this but when the neutrino cannon went off, it was like he went into involuntary reflex or an instinctual mode. His body transcended space and went into the spirit realm during the actual blast and then returned only minutes later when the fallout was occurring. So, his injuries were from fallout of neutrino effects, not the actual blast itself. This was touched upon briefly by Majak but it was not in his repertoire of understanding nor did he know about spirits per se.

Majak talked about the weapon's weakness as it related to non-physical forms. A person retreated into their own mind or sleeping would not be as affected as one who was wide awake and conscious and aware of the blast of the weapon. This was not to say anyone asleep was unaffected. On the contrary: every single sleeping sailor or Marine aboard the Vissad or the class 1 cruiser the Suclesahe had destroyed were all dead. They just died differently. And, had they been able, like JT, to transport themselves to the spirit realm out of the physical world, then they too might have lived. For the time being though no other federal fleet members had spirit blood or if any did, none knew how to activate the vestigial ability to morph into the other realm. The physical world was all that humans, Cybrinthians, Gnoracs, and Dwarfs knew.

While Majak did not know intricacies of the spirit realm and those who could occupy it, he did know some valuable facts. He could tell what and which ships in the Confederation fleet had been outfitted with the weapon. He also knew that a ship entering or exiting a warp from neo or S or ES neo would be less susceptible to the cannon's effects. So, in effect, fast movement was a way to counter the cannon's potency.

"Keep moving and its effects won't be able to get a bead on the target as well," Majak had heard said of the weapon. The counterpoint of course was that if the weapon had been fired and its fallout effects were across a specific area, that area remained contaminated. If a ship used neo to warp through that affected area then that ship itself might receive fallout effects. Even to a lesser degree but still noteworthy. It was like driving through the scene of an accident and noticing small pieces of debris of the wrecked vehicles strewn about the road. Driving over them didn't mean the late coming driver's vehicle was in the accident itself, but their car might receive blowback from the pieces and small parts as they are flipped up and about and into the undercarriage of his vehicle. It was like neo-ing through a small star system quadrant that had received the effects of a neutrino cannon attack.

Majak knew this and relayed it to Fico who took mental notes on everything the Gnorac commander said. He wrote nothing down. There would and could be no evidence of this discussion. Both men understood that without saying it.

"I would like to know how I might contact you again," said Majak as their conversation seemed to wind down to a close.

"Oh that would be easy," said Fico. "I am usually at the Duckling most evenings. I find it a most welcome place for meetings and dinner." He smiled a bit and picked a piece of something from his teeth. "But in the meantime, here is my communicator information," and he held out his earpiece device to sync with that of Majak's.

"Is there a welcome place to stay associated with this establishment?" asked Majak. "Or perhaps something nearby until I can establish my own network in time."

"Oh, I would say you already have a network. You are now here as my guest and let us consider it just that," responded Fico. "The accommodations you will find across the street and they are owned by the same fine folks who own the Duckling. Consider them friends. I will say all that is needed to be said to keep you here safely."

"I don't know what to say or how to thank you," started Majak when he was quickly interrupted.

"No, it is I who owe you the thanks on behalf of all those who wish to end this war as soon as possible," said Fico. He was careful not to pepper his talk with too many references to the Federation or the Confederation. After all, if there were spies and listening devices about, these would be words to look out for and would certainly give the nature of their talk away.

"Alright then in that case I'll just say thanks, and here is to a new future and an end to hostilities as we know them," declared Majak.

"Well put. Well put indeed my new friend," and with that Fico rose and began to leave. "Just one more thing," he added. "You'll want some new clothes. Even without the rank or insignia, that polyester transmits 'Confederation officer' to anyone who doesn't know any better."

"Duly noted. Thank you for the tip and everything so far," said Majak. And with that he as well rose to leave the table. Fico waived his communicator over the glasses and covered the bill. It was a small and welcome gesture Majak appreciated.

Chapter 18
Thruster

Fae reached out to the trees in the forest surrounding the area the gigantic booster engine had fallen. They were all busily discussing what had occurred. Of course, the trees were speaking in spirited forest fashion that Fae could only partly understand. He broke in directly.

"My friends, I am Fae the spirit coming home to see my family and grandfather, Papa Fae who lives near here. I have travelers, mencas, with me and they too seek something in the land of Flarhom. We know nothing about this engine that has fallen. Can you help us learn about it?" said Fae in one quick breath as if he needed to get it all off his chest before something else unforeseen occurred.

"Yes…" came the reply. "We can tell you things and we can help you." The trees seemed to speak as one. "Any relative or friend of Papa Fae is a friend of ours." This was a good sign. Fae had stumbled across a woodland grove of trees which knew his grandfather. Fae wanted to ask more and immediate questions but he thought better and knew it was best with the trees to let them speak in their own time. Instead of speaking or broadcasting his thoughts, Fae simply allowed a peaceful aura to come about him and he let this calming sense encompass both himself and his traveling party of mencas. He thought the trees would appreciate knowing that Lady Shera, Farhale, Valcor and Jeanaviere were not a threat to any of them. The knights in particular did look a little menacing but Fae reassured the trees that they all were friends.

The trees were able to relate to Fae a little bit more than he could have surmised but not much. The booster engine had crashed here in Flarhom Woods in Apequia on Spiruthean as part of a result of a great battle. This fight was indeed a contest between the Federation and the Confederation. There were many ships destroyed, most of them federal. The trees were able to sense that this engine came from a large cruiser which was the home ship of a single solitary survivor and the mencas would be seeking out relatives of that survivor. Other than this, the information the trees provided was solely technical in nature and spoke of the details of the technology the engine and its associated ship possessed. The trees knew that a massive new weapon had been employed but they could tell little about the neutrino cannon or how it worked. Fae was grateful for what the trees were able to provide. He asked them if they knew if his grandfather was home or if his grandfather had witnessed the massive crashing in the forest.

"We do not know Papa Fae's whereabouts for he has gone into non-physical form and we have not seen him for some time," was the trees' response.

"Well thank you just the same. I will find him and tell him of your kindness," said the young spirit. "Do not hesitate if there is anything I or my grandfather can do for you."

"The spirit is well-mannered," said one tree to the tree leader.

"Indeed he is. He gets that from his grandfather no doubt," was the tree leader's reply. Fae returned to his more physical form and addressed his menca companions. He told them what the trees had passed on about the great battle and the new weapon and the survivor who they might be seeking contact with. The mencas were grateful and intrigued at how well Fae had gotten along and how much he could find out quickly from the trees.

"The trees have always been friends to the spirit people," Fae remarked. "We are kindred races with a symbiotic relationship."

"The question remains, should we explore more or try to meet your grandfather? Maybe he can shed some light on all of this?" said Farhale.

"We will wait to see if our young guide can contact his elder and go from there," said Lady Shera to the group and specifically addressing Farhale's comment. Fae was already expecting this would be the group's desire so he had prepared to seek out Papa Fae as they spoke. Fae shifted back into his spirit non-physical form and sped through the immediate area searching out his grandfather. He found him sitting near his back porch in the spirit realm. He was nearly imperceptible to anyone. Fae had a unique talent though for finding spirits in the realm, especially his own family members. He didn't want to disturb his grandfather too much but he also didn't want to let things get too late and so he spoke softly with his mind.

"Papa, can you hear me? It is Fae. I have come to say hello and bring you news and ask your advice," Fae transmitted into the realm of thoughts that only his grandfather might hear.

"My boy, hello. Please forgive me a minute I am deep in thought trying to ascertain knowledge of this thing that has crashed here in our world," thought and transmitted Papa Fae. *Excellent,* thought Fae, *he knows about the engine already.* This would make at least part of their discussion that much easier. Fae was not sure what his grandfather would think about the mencas whom Fae had brought with him. Typically, Papa Fae kept to himself. Maybe he would be receptive when he learned of their origins or their leanings in the Grand War. Fae could only hope.

"Papa, that thing that has crashed here, it is in part what I want to talk to you about," said Fae. "That and a few other things."

"I know you have travelers with you and you are probably wondering how I might react to them," Papa Fae said after a long pause.

"Well, er, yes. I do and I beg your forgiveness if it offends you?" managed Fae.

"Not at all my boy. No offense taken. Remember I too listen to the trees and heed their counsel. Even if I do not actively participate in their conversations and reveal myself. I am often listening. They tell me much," he said in a way explaining how he knew so much already. Fae was relieved at this. He felt now he could be rather up front both with his grandfather and his menca companions.

"Papa, the crashed spaceship part is an engine from a Federation cruiser. It is only one of many destroyed ships from a great battle that has happened near Quai-14. There are a hundred thousand souls dead or displaced from this event is my sense. One of the survivors is now sought after by both sides. And the mencas I have with me now are seeking out kin of that survivor. I don't exactly understand it all but somehow it fits together and our world is at the epicenter of these events," said Fae in one or two breaths before his grandfather could even stop him to get a word in. When he had finished, Papa Fae looked at Fae inquisitively and said he would do what he could. He then indicated they should return to the physical world and Fae should escort his guests to meet Papa Fae at his house.

"Thank you, grandfather. I will do as you say immediately. I will meet you at your home in the physical world with them," Fae said as he began to transform into his clear bluish cat-like form the mencas would be able to see and follow.

Fae bounded through the woods the half a kilometer or so to the edge of the small clearing where he had left Lady Shera and her company. For Fae it seemed like ages he had been gone, but in reality, it was only a matter of minutes. Time always seemed to pass more quickly in the non-physical spirit realm than in the physical world. An adept trained spirit could accomplish twice as much non physically as they could in the world. When he arrived back with the group, he found them nearly exactly where he had left them. He saw they were engaged in a deep conversation about the kindliness of spirits and trust of them verses elves. Fae wanted to listen in before revealing himself but decided that would be rude. So, he therefore announced his presence from a bit of a distance.

"Hark, and hello again my friends," he opened. "I have come from my grandfather's. He is called Papa Fae or just Papa and he wishes you well and wants to invite you all to his home just over the clearing and a bit more down this road."

"That is very kind and we welcome this news young master," stated Lady Shera. "We will gladly accept his invitation." And so, the group continued around the clearing and down the wooded road that led past the home which looked like a woodland cabin. Papa Fae's house was a humble four room cabin deep in the woods but it was grand enough for an elderly spirit. It had all the warmness of a spirit-home and it was very neatly laid out. It was made of logs and mortar surrounded by stone at the base and had a straw or thatch roof. It was just one level but it also had an extensive basement which Papa Fae used mostly for storage and some extra sleeping quarters when he had large gatherings.

Pappa Fae lived alone. Mami Satine his wife had passed away years ago and he had no mind to remarry. So this was the way that Fae knew him most of his days. A bit of a kind old hermit with many good stories to tell. Some of his late wife. Some of the Grand War. Many of family and times that had passed. Papa Fae was obviously the donor of Fae's namesake. He too was born Faeruthanamereson, but of course he too went by Fae. He was relatively short in stature for his form was that of a pony. He was actually quite large for a pony but very small for a horse. He was fairly translucent like Fae but could color himself reddish-orange when he so chose. He was out in front of his door when the group arrived.

"Greetings travelers and friends of my young grandson," he said loudly to the group as it came within earshot. "Welcome to Flarhom. Welcome to my home." The group returned the pleasantries in kind with Lady Shera speaking up first.

"Hello kind sir. Fae tells us you are Papa Fae and he speaks very highly of you and all you have done, all your great accomplishments," she said.

"I don't know much about accomplishments," he replied. "I have lived a life as best I could and it has been well lived, I should think." Papa Fae then bowed low from his front legs and indicated they should be welcome to enter his home. When the group had come inside, he offered them all seats around his hearth in what was his living room and dining area. He morphed from his oversized pony form into that of an elderly bearded gentleman and pulled some tea off the fireplace.

"It makes it easier to boil and pour refreshments with hands than it does with hooves," he said with a smile through the thick grey beard. "I hope I can help you on your quest for… information?" he said as if it were also a question.

"Well, we are actually here on a great mission and journey to find out what or who among the spirits may have crossed lineage with humans in recent centuries," Lady Shera cut right to the chase and did not waste time with more pleasantries after they had exchanged a few more and tea had been poured for all who wanted it. Fae and Jeanaviere took only water. The rest enjoyed some of Flarhom Woods' finest freshly brewed apricot plant tea. Which, happened to be Papa Fae's favorite.

"I can tell you stories of what I know of my own ancestry but I cannot speak definitively or for other families in the enclave, Flarhom or even Apequia," Papa Fae said disappointedly. "I wish I could give you facts, but the genealogy charts and trees that I have are a little fuzzy around the time a hundred years ago when some of the Thanameresons went to seek their way off of Spiruthean."

"Anything you can give us might help us find the heir we seek," said Lady Shera. "You see, we believe a rightful heir that is of mixed human, menca and spirit blood may exist. We further believe that calling him or her home to the Kingdom of Mencalia would give credence to quelling old quarrels. Some such as the Grand War in which we understand you played a part. More importantly, we believe it could lead to brokering a peace accord and maybe… just maybe… ending the present Inter-Stellar War."

"I don't know if my records will help you or not," Papa Fae said as he rose from his chair and headed to an old six-drawered chest in the corner of the room. He pulled out some parchment rolled up and tied with bands and pawed through a stack of other old papers in the corner of the bottom drawer. For a future modern race of beings, spirits were very traditional in their record keeping. Papa Fae had a house computer and knew how to use it readily. But he preferred to look at charts and maps printed on old paper. Had he lived in the 21st or 22nd century AD, he probably would have listened to vinyl records rather than anything digitally recorded. So, after a bit he came to what he was looking for. "Here we go," he said as he pulled a family tree chart and a few other documents from the stacks.

"Wow, these are something," said Valcor. "I don't know if I've seen records kept as such."

"Nor will you again most likely," interjected Fae. "My grandfather is one of a kind." Papa Fae brought the largest of the sheets around to the central table for the group to see. He unrolled it and laid it across the flat surface tacking the corners down with coasters or tea cups.

"Now if you look here to this side of my own grandfathers' line, you'll see seven generations before me, nine before my grandson here, there is a line that seems to end. This would have been my great to the fifth-degree uncle. Well, the story in our family is told of great-great-great-great-great Uncle Barnab Thanamereson." Papa Fae went on, "the rumor of great Uncle Barnab is that he left Spiruthean and made his way to Angola on Europa. The family scuttlebutt goes that he chose to take physical form like a human or Cybrinthian and stayed that way. He was already nearing a hundred years old when he left as you can see here from his date of birth on the tree. But in human form he was still young enough to father children. They say he met a Cybrinthian woman and fell in love and they had offspring who intermarried with humans but there is no record as you can see here. We don't know if any of this is true or if it is just family tall tales that have grown over time."

"My my. All of that seems so… unlikely," managed Farhale. "I have never heard of a human-spirit-Cybrinthian hybrid."

"All that's missing is a menca, a dwarf, and elf and a Gnorac," joked Valcor.

"This is a serious matter," interjected Lady Shera. Not to put a downcast mood on the group. But she did want them to realize what serious implications there were if it was true and if they could find some of the line of this long-lost Uncle Barnab. She wanted to know, did he have a single line of descendants, multiple? How many relations now a hundred and fifty years later could trace their blood to this spirit in disguise as a human or Cybrinthian. Did his spouse even know? Could they prove what was claimed? It was certainly an interesting story.

As the afternoon wore on Papa Fae became more acquainted with the mencas. He was invited by them to share some of his war stories from the Grand War. He was happy to do so. In a way it warmed his spirit heart to have someone other than his grandson or the trees listen to his tales. He did have some good ones. Like for example the time he had to transform into an armadillo like creature to hide from Elvish spies who were hot on his trail. He still had some marks from laser blasts taken during a shoot-out at a place not unlike the Unlucky Duckling.

He went on for hours and the group was all too happy to oblige his tale telling. When it got late and stomachs were grumbling at least from the knights, Papa Fae offered some of the best roots and vegetables he had in the pantry. Spirits as a general rule do not eat meat or game but they do make certain vegetarian dishes which are close approximations to meat and were able to satiate the hunger of even Farhale and Valcor. There was one bean and rice casserole dish with cheese and some sort of fruit like an avocado that Farhale found particularly tasty.

As the afternoon turned to evening Papa Fae offered the group some mead which was also readily appreciated and accepted. Some more discussion about Uncle Barnab ensued and the travelers eventually shared some of their own tales from great wars and battles of the past. Papa Fae realized that the closest inn or anywhere that the mencas would find acceptable was many leagues away so he offered the space he had in his extra room and basement.

"Ordinarily I would offer the best room for our lady guests but I feel it might be safer for Lady Shera and Jeanaviere to take the basement and for Sirs Farhale and Valcor to take the extra room on this floor. That way they can act as a guard of sorts. There is plenty of bedding and space to sleep for all," Papa Fae remarked. "Generally, spirits sleep in their own form, which for me is that of a pony but I have enough guests who take near human or menca like form or that of smaller animals that prefer some bedding or a mattress. Therefor I have two mattresses downstairs and a couple of cots in the extra room up here. You are each welcome to whatever accommodations strike you best."

With that declaration, the group decided it was best to get some rest for the night. The mencas would continue their quest tomorrow and would be seeking out other members of Fae's family to try and locate whereabouts of descendants of Uncle Barnab. The night was still young but everyone was tired from a long day of traveling and Fae had a short sprint back to his own home before the evening got too late. He promised to come back over at first light and continue to help the group. After all that had happened, Fae had completely forgotten to share the news of his end of year exams and how well he had done. It seemed small in comparison to the great quest on which were his newfound companions.

Chapter 19
Delle

Delle was surprised by the bright lights and crashing sound in the woods but it did not deter her from getting home to her family. Delle had already sensed that Fae was on some sort of mission and was totally tuned out from all beings around him. Normally Delle could easily get his attention and the two would have headed toward their homes together. But not today. Today it seemed that whatever had crashed down in Flarhom Woods had Fae's complete attention; or maybe his attention was already taken up before that crashing item. Either way, Delle could not signal Fae and so she headed home on her own as fast as her quickest winged form, a Dragoness, could take her. She had no idea there were others in the woods and she had no idea they were mencas and that they were traveling with Fae. No, Delle knew very little about what was going on today in Flarhom Woods.

She had decided to go straight home when she was unsuccessful in hailing Fae. So, when the great crashing and bursting across the woods took hold of the land, she was well on her way already. When Delle got home a few leagues later she wanted to share the news of the end of year studies. But the predominant talk in her home was centered around the great calamity of the woods. Everyone apparently had heard it. Therefore, when Delle was questioned about where she was when the crash occurred, she could only honestly reply she was headed home. She made good time and was speeded along by the fact that she knew something big had come down and landed in the woods. She was afraid that Fae had somehow played some part in whatever had occurred. This was her sense simply because Fae had been out of touch and unreachable.

Delle's family was a close-knit unit. Her mother and father and surviving grandparents all lived together in a large woodland cottage of seven rooms. It remained hidden to most who did not know of its existence. Occasionally the family would have gatherings with cousins or friends and neighbors such as Fae's family. But tonight was not one of those nights. Tonight, Delle's family was concentrating on the strange noises and strange occurrence in their woods.

"I am back," Delle transmitted as she arrived outside her house.

"Are you alright?" asked her mother. "We heard the calamity in the forest."

"I am fine. It was nowhere near me or my path of travel," the young spirit responded. This, of course, was only partially true.

"Young lady don't tell us falsities," said her father. "We know how you come home and we know that great fallout in the woods had to have been rather close to you."

"Oh Papa, I didn't want to alarm you. Yes, it was somewhat close but I didn't stop for it and it didn't impact my way home at all. And that is the truth," said Delle to her parents.

"Alright child," said her mother. "Come in and get ready for supper. We will figure out if there is anything to know about the crash in time." And Delle did as she was bidden. She came inside and washed up and then listened to her parents and grandparents talking about the strange crash. They had heard it from the house and were naturally curious. Delle wanted to talk about how she had seen Fae but could not contact him at all, but she feared that might only make her family more concerned. After a bit she decided that it did not matter.

"Momma and Papa, can I tell you something about the strangeness in the woods?" she asked. "Something at least that I think may have something to do with the crash," she added.

"Of course, my girl," her mother replied. "What is it?"

"Well, I am not sure if it is anything or not but I saw Fae on the way home," she started. "And I tried to contact him to say hello and talk about the end of the year," Delle continued. "But I could not reach him at all. He was moving fast and had turned away from all his sense abilities. I could not tell why. Fae is always able to sense me when I reach out to him. But not today. It was strange. And then, a little later, the crashing thing occurred."

"Thanks for sharing that my girl. I don't know what it means but it might be important," Delle's mother added. Her father concurred and then spoke with her grandparents at length about the events described by Delle.

"This could be a sign," he said.

"And it might not be," replied Delle's grandfather: her father's father. Both spirits were correct. "But we should be on our guard for anything that might come our way," her grandfather added.

"We can go out there or make some calls to others to figure this out," her father said.

"We should do that," her grandfather added. Delle's father decided to reach out to some of their neighbors and find out what he could. He went into the small closet of thought projection their house had and cleared his mind. Then after a bit of time he had sent and received thought communications from several neighbors, some up to 20 leagues away.

He was able to determine the general situation from the reports of the others. He knew it was a giant engine from a space ship that had crashed. Probably Federation. He knew it had come down to Flarhom Woods from a large battle far away. He was able to get some information from the trees of the woods as well. They were always helpful. He found out that Delle was completely safe and had not been in danger by it. He also found out that Fae had been close to it. He learned that Fae had made friends with some mencas who were also in the woods prior to and after the crash.

Fae's new friends, the mencas, were the most unique part of the information Delle's father uncovered. Delle's father, Damon, had learned a lot of valuable things over the years from his talks with neighbors and trees. But one thing he hadn't learned this time was what a band of mencas was doing in Flarhom Woods and why they would befriend a small spirit boy. Damon also wanted to know if the engine crash was in any way related to the mencas or if that was just a coincidence. His thought projections and receipts indicated the events were unrelated. But he had no proof.

"Delle, I am going to reach out to Fae's family and find out what they know about all this," Damon said to his daughter.

"Sure, please ask about Fae for me," she said in response.

"I will," said Damon. "Do you want me to include you when I speak to them?"

"If you think it would be helpful father. If not, I am fine eating dinner here with mom now," Delle replied. Damon nodded in approval and then moved back to his seat in the thought projection room. He contacted the Thanamereson family and was able to reach Fae who was pleased but surprised to hear from Delle's family. Damon passed on that he had gotten from Delle the particulars in the woods. Fae readily admitted he was distracted by both his new guests, whom he did not seem to want to talk about. He also admitted that he was distracted by the crashed engine. He relayed what he could but also finally said plainly that he was not really authorized to speak about the mencas. Just yet. Fae was happy to get his parents or speak to his grandfather, neither of which Damon felt was needed.

"Thank you for offering, but the hour gets late and I don't want to be a bother to anyone unnecessarily," Damon replied to Fae when the young spirit offered to get additional family members to speak with him about the events.

"Perhaps tomorrow then when I go back to my grandfather's," said Fae, "you or Delle may want to come with me and meet some of these amazing folks for yourselves?"

"OK, that sounds fair. I think Delle would like that and I know she would like to see you," said Damon.

"And I would like to see her," said Fae. "Please tell her I am so very sorry to have alarmed her inadvertently earlier."

"You can tell her yourself right now. She is just outside the thought projection room," Damon said, as he paused a minute and opened the door to the tiny room.

"Darling," he called to Delle. "Would you like to say hi to Fae?"

"Yes, please," she said. And Delle squeezed past the door and her father moved out of the room to allow her in.

"Hello, Fae?" she said.

"Hi Delle," Fae said. "Listen, I am sorry I was out of touch earlier."

"It's no problem," said Delle. "I was just worried about you with everything that was going on."

"Yeah, that was my fault for being so focused I missed all that was happening not immediately around me. I am sorry," Fae responded. The two talked for a while longer and then agreed to meet the next morning at Fae's grandfather's house. Fae told Delle that the mencas had been looking for a hybrid race person. Some sort of a spirit and human, menca or Cybrinthian. Fae relayed that it was possible that his grandfather knew of family history that might mean they indeed could have had this spirit in their lineage. Or at least they might have had a long-lost relative who qualified. By this part of the conversation, Delle's father Damon, was back listening in and was part of the talk. Damon was now very curious about the mencas' quest.

Damon and Delle's family shared a bloodline with Fae's. This shared ancestry, went back about seven generations. Just about to the time of Fae's ancestor Barnab. In fact, though there was not a record or a piece of paper to prove it, Barnab had been very close with Damon's great-great-great-great-great grandmother. The two had even had a relationship on Spiruthean which resulted in the birth of a child. They then took this child across the galaxies and landed on Angola. Barnab and Damon's ancestor, Gailena, chose to take on human form and discard their spirit realm cover. In human form, they were able to blend into their surroundings. They never aroused suspicion because they stayed hidden.

Barnab was able to find meaningful work and provide for his clandestine spirit family. Delle's ancestor, Gailena, had been Barnab's companion and mate, but never his wife. As their relationship on Angola was mysterious, they simply told everyone there they were already married. This was a plausible tale as they had arrived together and their previous spirit life was known to no one in Angola or anywhere on Europa. They had children there and blended in with the population amicably.

However, before they could grow old together on Angola, Barnab grew sick and eventually died. Gailena, distraught from grief elected to return to Spiruthean. Her children, already grown into young adults stayed behind for they knew none of their ancestry on Spiruthean. So here is where the family lines split. Part of the ancestry staying on Angola and the other coming back to Spiruthean with Gailena.

She was still young by spirit standards and was able to remarry and begin a new family on Spiruthean. Thus, Delle's ancestors were born. Fae and Delle's families had only bits and pieces of the story of Barnab and Gailena. No one had put it all together and learned the truth that there was an entire branch of these families born and inhabiting Angola.

At the end of the thought projection call Delle and Damon both thanked Fae and wished him well with his guests. And they promised to come to Papa Fae's early in the morning so they could coordinate in person what they had already discussed through thought projection.

When the morning came, Delle was excited to meet the guests Fae had told her and her father about. Damon told Fae's mother the story and invited her to join them but she declined in favor of letting this be a father-daughter activity.

"You two have fun stirring up the spirits and don't get into too much trouble," her mother said. Then Damon and Delle transformed into their best traveling spirit forms, a leopard and a horse-like creature and headed out to conquer the eight leagues to Papa Fae's house. They took the most direct route and did not stop for a break but they did not travel at sprint or near sprint speed. Rather they took up a brisk but adequate pace.

When Delle and Damon came within viewing distance of Papa Fae's cottage, Damon transmitted greetings to all inhabitants. Fae had already arrived earlier in the morning. Papa Fae and all the mencas were awake and enjoying some breakfast when Delle and her father sent their greetings. They then arrived at the front door and transformed into human spirit form. Delle's form was that of a school aged girl and her father Damon's was that of a bearded man about age 50. They knocked at the door in the traditional fashion just as Papa Fae was going to open it and invite them in.

"Ah a knock at the front door, how I have missed that sound my friends and neighbors," declared Papa Fae. "We have lost touch with the old ways as a general rule. But I am glad to see you two have not. Welcome, welcome. Do come in," he added cheerfully.

"It is good to see you Papa Faeruthan," said Damon as he greeted the elder at his door.

"Hello Papa Fae, it is good to see you again," declared Delle.

"Hello my dear friends Delle and Mr. Lastalle," said Fae as soon as the new guests had come in. "Allow me to introduce my new friends. Delle and Mr. Lastalle, this is Lady Shera, Sir Farhale, Sir Valcor, and Miss Jeanaviere of Mencalia. Ladies and good sirs, this is Miss Delle and Mister Damon Lastalle of Flarhom Woods." Damon insisted on being called "Damon" rather than "Mr. Lastalle." Once the appropriate "hellos" and "how do you dos" had been exchanged, Papa Fae offered Delle and her father some breakfast and tea which the two accepted.

After some tea had been poured and some toasted bread and jam had been passed around, the group got to conversing. The mencas were straight forward. Lady Shera shared with their hosts and new guests that they were seeking the family of a spirit who had travelled far abroad and intermixed with humans or Cybrinthians and had descendants today both here in Spiruthean and on Europa. She shared that they were seeking this bloodline because they felt it would be the key to combatting the newest horrific weapon introduced to the war. If somehow the mencas could find the descendants of this spirit-human hybrid they just might be able to find the DNA sequence that showed resistance to the new weapon's potency. If nothing else, they would find out who came from Spiruthean blood lines and where there might be mixed spirit blood in humanity.

Delle, Damon, Fae, Papa Fae and the mencas enjoyed a leisurely rest of their morning discussing the Barnab blood line and Gailena story. They determined there was enough credence to give the tale a likelihood of being true. Moreover, if it was true, it would mean there was a line of humans with spirit blood from Angola or somewhere out there in the Near Universe which was related to all of them. It was a strange and unlikely, but seemingly, likely, tale.

After the morning together, the group decided to venture out to explore the piece of space ship which had crashed the preceding day. The engine. They would take a little bit of time at the mencas pace to get there but it was not far: only several leagues. They all left together and although Lady Shera offered that the spirits take off without them and the mencas catch up, the elder spirits refused this offer and preferred to stay together.

When they had traveled half the distance Papa Fae suggested a rest stop at least for the mencas' horses but again Lady Shera and the group refused and preferred to keep on pressing. Then they arrived at the site. It was recognizable from a distance as there were bits and pieces of burnt foliage and trails cut into the trees from pieces of flaming debris that had landed. The group slowed to a crawl when they got near and examined the evidence and looked for signs that betrayed this was a Federation ship. There were many.

From the color scheme on the engine's paint to the way it was built and the markings on bits and pieces of paneling, it was clearly Federation. The group touched very little but observed very much. Papa Fae made some notes and created a sketch of how things lay on the ground. The group stayed on the site for maybe an hour and took their time as it seemed no one else was chomping at the bit to get to the site or examine the engine.

After that hour or so they seemed content with their findings and spoke among themselves. They decided they had enough to confirm what was already suspected: that their presumption was correct: No Federation officials were coming out to retrieve pieces for evidence or other purposes. And with that, the spirits and mencas headed back to Papa Fae's.

Chapter 20
Screen

JT and Aurelle were settling in to their quarters. Each of them was thinking about getting some rest in the form of a brief nap or maybe an early to bed evening when those plans were derailed. Maybe fifteen minutes after Capt. Johanaston had left the two of them in the capable hands of Lt. Shamus, the lieutenant called them each on their ear communicators.

"I am sorry to bother you two but I have been advised that the fleet is going to be moving to ES-neo and conducting a screening movement around the Confederation 12th Fleet," Lt. Shamus said to them both. "There is nothing required of you but to be aware it could get a little choppy once we are out of neo. With that said, you may feel safer somewhere such as the commadore's mess or the security bridge for the jump and once we near coming out of it."

"Thank you," responded JT first. "I'll discuss our location with Dr. Gifford and we'll come out to see you in a moment."

"I am just outside your doors down the corridor about 10 feet," added the lieutenant.

"Roger. Out for now," JT responded.

"I am not sure I want to be anywhere around any bridge or mess hall during a screening attack," said Aurelle once JT had joined her in her quarters. "I mean, shouldn't we just stay out of the way? After all *you* are the precious cargo that we are trying to protect. And in truth, this screening action is probably all in support of throwing the Confederation off as to your correct whereabouts, don't you think?" JT was not sure he agreed with Aurelle but he decided he would defer to her good judgement. He was used to being in the middle of many types of fights and so that was where he was most comfortable. But he was also not used to being the high value target himself.

"They did say it was just a screening action or movement," said JT to Aurelle. "There may not be any attack for us to be concerned about."

"That may be, but you know how these things start out and how they end up," she said.

"Point taken," JT conceded. "Well, if you ask me, we go to where the LT indicated we might be best positioned to observe yet stay out of the way."

"Ok," she said. "I don't guess there would be anywhere better than the security bridge for that." And with that they had decided the unspoken: to go with Lt. Shamus to the security bridge during this screening action. They took a moment to gather and tidy a few things and joined the lieutenant outside their rooms in the corridor.

"Security bridge it will be," Lt. Shamus said as she indicated the direction and told them they would be going up a few levels. "If you would follow me, we will be there in a few minutes at most. The neo travel distance will take several hours at least and maybe a half day to get there," said the lieutenant. The Amorhe valued guests did as they were told and followed Lt. Shamus down their hall up several flights and down two more halls towards the front of the ship. When they arrived, they found several sailors and officers hard at work processing orders and issuing commands.

"You can stay right here for a moment while I check you in and have passes issued," said Lt. Shamus. JT and Aurelle took seats in a waiting area just beside the main security bridge. They watched as Lt. Shamus seemed to know her way around and returned quickly with some badges for them.

"Just wear these while you are in this area and no one will have any questions," she said as she handed them the badges which easily clipped onto their shirts.

"Please be patient as we process securing the ship for the jump to ES-neo and run computations for associated risks," said a warrant sergeant who had just entered the bridge area through the main hatch which Aurelle and JT had also entered through. There were some standard procedures that ran like a drill on the security bridge and some others that were being processed individually as if for a first time. The warrant sergeant called over an officer who told him standard procedure for warp to ES-neo was in effect. The warrant sergeant repeated the command over a closed-circuit intercom system. This meant all hatches would be checked, security teams would be placed on alert, and items not secured would be stowed or checked where they would not be a hazard. Additionally, all screening checks underway or those about to take place would be frozen and set to pick up once the move to neo was underway.

The ship would be traveling nine million light years at nearly 10 billion times light speed so this trip would take a matter of less than a day. The whole fleet would be accompanying the Amorhe on this mission and coordinating nearly thirty ships to all make the same space and time for this trip was no small feat. If too many calculations were out of synch the arrival points could be dispersed across an entire star system.

Computers did the brunt of the heavy calculations but human/Cybrinthian checks and oversight gave the final go ahead or not. In this case all fleet assets, the carriers, the battle cruisers, the attack and reconnaissance cruisers, the frigates and corvettes and support ships all were cleared by their engineering teams to make the coordinated jump to ES-neo. The Amorhe's security bridge reviewed its piece of the equation and approved and issued its respective orders. Then the jump began. Other than a small rumble as hyperdrives and neo drives worked together, there was not much to be felt or distinguished from regular propulsion.

The key was when the magnetic plow diverters kicked in at the ship's front there was a noticeable hum and the ship's artificial gravity seemed to get momentarily weaker. This happened because the diverters took some of the energy ordinarily used for artificial gravity and used it for creating a field in front of the ship. This field would repel any minute physical particles of size enough to cause damage to the ship if smashed into at ES-neo speeds. The course computations would avoid planets, stars and anything of magnitude like asteroids and matter that would show up in the computer. But the computers could not account for minutia and particles not pre-charted. This is where the plow diverter kicked in. It was a simple but essential component of neo or faster travel. After the diverter power turned on and the hum subsided, the ship and all others in the fleet synched into ES-neo and the vast distance to the Cigar Galaxy was covered in eight hours or so.

JT and Aurelle did not stay on the security bridge the entire time, but rather checked back in to it and moved about the ship and their cabins. Lt. Shamus had simply suggested they check in and get acquainted with the bridge for security and that during the screening itself, they might want to be there instead of elsewhere on the ship. Once badged and checked in to security and briefed that there would be a seven-to-nine-hour travel time, they were freed to wander back about the ship or their cabins. They both got some needed sleep in their cabins. At about seven and a half hours of ES-neo time a broadcast was announced they would be coming out of neo in 30 minutes. All fighters and bombers in both hanger 1 and 2 were to be ready for screening action. The carrier would be launching two waves of the small star-craft as soon as no longer traveling at ES-neo. It would not wait for the rest of the fleet to pull up or screen themselves to launch the first waves. Ideally, the other ships would be in place already or at the same time and the launch would be simultaneous with the other ships being set to screen the carrier. This was an ideal arrival scenario. It was a fifty-fifty chance scenario the arrival would go exactly like that as planned.

At seven hours and 55 minutes the five-minute warning was sounded and the ship began its power down sequence to jump back from ES-neo. There was not a noticeable hum this time but there was some shuddering as the regular drive engines kicked on. The Amorhe was powered by eight thrusters in four two-pod nacelles. It had a single neo drive which worked in tandem with the power core when at neo, S or ES-neo and the regular thrusters shut down except for two remaining at idle. These functioned sort of like a pilot light on a gas oven or furnace and could be immediately powered up to full capacity if something went wrong with the neo drive. A standard thruster alone could not maintain neo speeds but it could provide a steady deceleration and safely take the ship out of neo if needed.

Before the jump to ES-neo, Aurelle and JT decided after some talk they both needed to sleep more than discuss anything. Discussions might have included their expected locations during travel moving to neo or screening actions, or more pertinently, their developing feelings for one another. Neither thought this later topic warranted much discussion. It was just understood.

Aurelle's playful slap and brief kiss earlier had spoken volumes for what JT might have thought she was feeling towards him. He did indeed return the kiss which itself spoke enough without words for him to betray his own feelings for her. But what was this after all? Was it a lustful attraction born in the heat of dire circumstance? Was it something which could amount to much more given an opportunity? Did it matter at this point? If JT had met Aurelle during peacetime during a routine visit for some regular medical check, would he have felt the same attraction? JT could answer none of these questions. He wondered if Aurelle could either.

For her part Aurelle had already decided there were no coincidences in life. JT was put before her for care for cosmic and spiritual meanings they might not understand, but clearly for now their paths had crossed for the better. Yes, she liked him. No, she didn't care to delve more into why or how. She was riding the feeling for what it was worth and was living in the moment. Circumstance was just that, the circumstance she found before them. She would continue to live in the moment and make smart decisions based upon both logic and her feelings. Yes she had kissed JT. He seemed to like it and returned the passion. She would not delve more into the what or why of that action. She needed sleep now and she meant to get it.

Then after several hours for both of them the jump from neo warnings came and they roused themselves from respective slumbers. The trip had taken less than a half-day but in space, 24-hour cycles were arbitrary creations to keep crews on 12-hour on or off shifts. Effectively, they traveled what would have been overnight. When JT and Aurelle roused, Lt. Shamus was off duty and Lt. Simonds was back. He greeted them on the speaker system in their rooms as their ear pieces were out.

"Hello Doctor, Sergeant," Lt. Simonds began. "This is Lieutenant Simonds again outside your quarters. I will be escorting you as we come out of ES-neo and begin the screening action in a little bit."

Simonds was very plain spoken. "We have about five minutes," he added. It did not take JT and Aurelle three minutes to get up and ready and they then headed with Lt. Simonds, who was now in tow behind them, to the security bridge. They arrived with their badges visible just as the move out of neo was being completed. The screen was immediately set up. Fighters and bombers were launched and thousands of orders and actions were taking place simultaneously abord the Amorhe.

The same was occurring on 27 other vessels across the 7th Fleet. The move from neo and the deceleration of all these ships was timed impeccably. One corvette only which consisted of 2,000 sailors missed the target system but only by less than a single light year; and it was able to be back with the rest within a few minutes once the error was corrected. The ships were able to provide a protective covering screen and weapons field of fire for one another as if laid out by fleet textbook. The ships were spread across the new star system's quadrant and were several thousand Astronomical Units (AU) from the Confederation outposts which had yet to detect them. If all continued as planned, they would remain undetected but provide an accurate picture of the Confederation's 12th Fleet which was conducting its own screen in force. So far, no leader or staff officer in any Federation ship had any reason to complain about the movement or screen setup. Confidence abounded but overconfidence was also a risk.

"Things are too perfect," said Commadore Theelson. "I don't like how easy this was," she said to Admiral Vander, who had returned to the Amorhe for the movement and screening. They were on their respective bridges but communicating via earpiece and had been as such since the initial jump to ES-neo.

"I concur but let's not over or underestimate our adversary," Adm. Vander added. "Maybe we did simply catch them asleep at the wheel." The first two waves of fighters had already been launched and were setting their own micro screen only a few AUs from Confederation ships. The fighters were all camouflaged by ship individual masking devices. For some reason, the Confederation screening outposts were not using their own masking devices and were plain for the 7th Fleet observers to see. This was another reason Theelson and Vander were both hesitant to accept how easily the movement and screen setting had been. They expected the Confederation sentries to have been masked and other masked ships to be hidden. But, here they all were set up in what seemed like a textbook tactical screen line with observation post sentries set all along the perimeter.

The Federation fighters were given strict non-engagement orders unless fired upon first. If fortune continued to favor them, none would be discovered and thus none would be engaged or doing any engaging back. The range of a tactical fighter's main weapon system: either laser cannons, or fusion missiles, was only a few AUs anyway. Their own screen line was set at the limit of their weapons' ranges. Even right now if nearly a hundred pilots and flight engineers had their fingers on their respective triggers, no one was ready to pull them. There was also seemingly no reason to pull those triggers, for the time being. If the Confed outposts knew the Federation fighters or fleet ships were there, they gave absolutely no indication. So, in effect, each screen was doing what it was meant to do: allow vision across the mesh and make reports of what was observed while allowing some things to pass and deterring others. Nothing currently needed to be deterred. What the Federation 7th Fleet didn't know was that the Confederation 12th Fleet was only the tip of the iceberg. Indeed the 12th Fleet had no idea the 7th was there. But the 7th also had no idea the 12th was supported by the entire Confed 3rd Battle Group. Four more undetected enemy fleets were in the area.

The 12th confederate Fleet was a few ships smaller than the federal 7th Fleet. But the 3rd Battle Group was more than a hundred ships larger. The combined forces of all fleets within the 3rd Battle Group could easily have obliterated the federal 7th Fleet… if it had known of the fleet's position and existence. The fighters' presence would have given away the fact that there was a fleet carrier nearby but no fighter had unmasked and none had been discovered. This was a blessing but it worried the federal admirals and commadores.

"Well, that was something," JT said to Aurelle and Lt. Simonds after the fighter waves had been launched. "I feel like I should be on an embarkation shuttle and getting ready to board some Confederation vessel or offload onto some new world." Simonds agreed but said nothing. As a Marine he liked to be in the thick of things and was not particularly fond of security or "babysitting" duty as he thought of it. But his duty was important and served the good of the Amorhe, his fleet, and the entire Federation. He accepted that truth.

The federal fighter screen was set up in a wide arc around the external perimeter of the confederate center point. The 7th Fleet remained out of range of small ship like fighter or bomber weapons ranges, but close enough to be able to support its own fighter screen easily. This was a delicate balance for the leadership. *How close was close enough yet not too close?* Admirals Vander and Haverston had decided on a screen several star system lengths away from the fighter screen which was a few AUs from the known enemy positions. The known forward most outposts. This was proving sufficient but it was only a matter of time before some ship or some fighter somewhere got discovered. At least that was the biggest fear for Cdre. Theelson. It was not a concern for JT or Aurelle. But had they been apprised of the risk and the situation with the enemy fleet and battle group, it might have been a concern for them too.

"I wish I could be out there with them," said JT as he watched on an overhead monitor a sequence of the last group of fighters departing the bay.

"I'm glad you're here with us," replied Aurelle. "For reasons I should say are only due to our cause and finding the answer to this weapon's mystery I should add," she said quietly with a side-eye and smile. JT himself chuckled and wished they were alone so that he might poke her in the ribs or show some indication he caught her unspoken meaning. As it was though, with Simonds and others around, he bit his tongue and made no gestures other than the returned smile.

With all fighters establishing their screen and the fleet's ships now in place, there was nothing to do but wait. Either for contact or intelligence. Unfortunately, this was exactly what the confederate 12th Fleet and 3rd Battle Group was waiting for as well. The fleets were like two animals stalking each other in the night: one not fully aware of the other's presence, and the other completely unaware.

The first contact to be made was about to happen. But neither side realized how it would occur. It was not going to be a fighter or bomber or screening outpost sensing an enemy vessel. It was going to occur due to an overflow of dark matter in an accident aboard a spirit vessel which happened to be traveling in the vicinity of the two fleets' screen lines. The wayward reconnaissance exploration ship, the *Valuable*, was coming out of S-neo near the edge of the 12th Fleet's screen and suffered a cataclysmic failure of its front hull shield. The shield failure caused it to break from neo dangerously quickly and also caused a ripple effect across the star system in question. The 12th fleet outposts misidentified the Valuable as a Federation vessel and called a general alarm and began to open fire. The 7th fleet observed this action and chose to respond accordingly.

When a neutral peaceful vessel is fired upon, the belligerent has only one choice: to act like it was defending itself. And that is precisely how the Confederation behaved. Forward outposts reported hostile movement and failure to heed their hailing. In truth, there was no hail to the Valuable. Just an open barrage and an unprovoked attack upon the foundering spirit ship when it could not protest the action much less defend itself.

The Valuable was not a warship. It was a science observation vessel. It could have been violating occupied space neutralities but amidst a crisis like a failing dark matter front hull shield, there really was no validity to claim any space neutrality violation. The Confederation would later claim in international and inter-planetary tribunals that the Valuable attacked its outpost without any reason. But the inter-planetary courts would see through this claim and find in favor of the spirit vessel. But that would be years down the road. In the meantime, the Valuable was destroyed and the 7th Fleet's positions relative to the 12th Fleet outposts were just about given away. Just. About.

When the Valuable was lasered and torpedoed it lit up the surrounding area and caused the closest federal fighter to react and de-mask momentarily to arm its weapons and prepare to engage. When the commanding fighter pilot realized he was not, in fact, under attack, it was nearly too late but he was able to divert his laser cannon's laze. And no weapon was actually fired at the outpost or in the direction of the exploding Valuable or its assailant.

It was mainly good fortune and perfect timing that allowed the de-masking to go unnoticed. The federal fighter was visible for nearly ten seconds while the pilot gathered coordinate information and targeted the offending Confederate outpost. The post itself was nothing more than a permanently moored frigate overseeing its section of the screen line which was the better part of the solar quadrant. It just so happened that in the ten seconds in question, all observers were preoccupied with the Valuable's appearance and subsequent quick destruction.

While computerized scanners could have spotted the anomaly in space time resultant from the de-masking, the ship's observation settings were all temporarily set to manual. This was a precaution against overflow of data during weapons engagement by the small ship. Anything or any ship larger would have had computerized scans still in operation but the tiny confederate frigate, was simply too old and too small. Therefore, the federal fighter got away with being visible yet remaining unnoticed. It was simple chance.

When the federal pilot realized no one was engaging him and he had little reason to think they would upon this epiphany, he re-masked. He did so as quickly as possible and stayed as still against his backdrop as possible to remain masked. There was no neo or warping of any speed. He just sat. His immediate radio traffic spoke volumes.

"Salty Dog 6 this is Pepper Cat 1, we have multiple shots fired at unknown vessel from bandit outpost," the pilot transmitted before he had even re-masked. "Unknown vessel is in flames and breaking up fast. I have de-masked and armed weapons for engagement." Then the pilot, Pepper Cat 1, realized he was not in jeopardy. "Re-masking now and not engaging. This is Pepper Cat 1, I say again, I am re-masking and am not now engaging."

The rest of the radio traffic described the Valuable's disintegration and how events had unfolded. No other pilot on the screen line de-masked or got close to going hot with his or her weapons. There was a brief discussion, which was quickly quelled at higher levels, about a rescue operation for victims of the Valuable. Federation command at fleet level decided protecting the concealment of the screen line was a higher priority. A higher priority than saving lives of unknown spirits or other neutral third parties who happened to fly into the wrong place at the wrong time.

So, the screen of fighters observed the sad fate of the spirit science vessel, the now not so aptly named, Valuable. They did and could do little else other than to take note and record its destruction. The confed 12th Fleet did not send out search and rescue parties either. Not only was that often impractical in deep space but it was generally the Confederacy's policy not to rescue survivors of any ships other than its own. The Federation's policy was kinder but in practicality it rarely worked out that rescue missions even by their standards were largely successful.

Survivors had to have found an escape capsule or have been in a space suit prior to free floating into space. If by chance they were able to find an air-tight section of the ship in question it often would not last long. Cases were rare of anyone outside of a full powered suit or ejection capsule being rescued after more than a few hours of needing it. And therefore, if there were any survivors of the Valuable, they were destined to meet their maker. As spirits, they believed in a very rare form of deity which had created them and they wholly embraced that opportunity.

Aurelle and JT were kept up to date as to the near catastrophe on the federal screen line and the demise of the spirit ship. But there was nothing they could do or say that would impact these events. So, they simply listened and observed.

When Aurelle asked JT, "Would you have engaged the Confederation forces if you had witnessed them doing what they did to the research vessel?" she thought she knew the answer already.

"Hell yes," was his only response.

"Good thing you aren't in charge out there," she joked.

"Yeah, probably so," JT concurred. "Marines tend to like to break things. Reconnaissance is not exactly our forte."

"But you're good at other things," Aurelle said with one eyebrow lightly raised and a slightly sinister look in her eyes.

JT made a prrrrrrr sound under his breath.

"At ease there Marine you might get me purring too if you keep that up," Aurelle whispered in JT's ear.

"You two are making me ill, what are you now in middle school?" JT's old buddy Raffordy was saying in JT's mind. Raffordy had always been one to tell JT the honest truth and now was one of those times. Even in death and only in JT's head, Raffordy's hard truths were coming through to JT's conscience. JT only paid it a modest amount of attention.

"Thanks, old pal. Good to hear from you too," JT thought back to the imaginary battle buddy in his mind.

"You ok? Something going on up in there," asked Aurelle as she tapped lightly with one finger on the side of JT's skull just above his left ear.

"Just thinking of old friends now turned to space dust and sharing a laugh I might have once had with one of them is all," said JT in response.

The screen lines settled back in. 7th Fleet was able to provide accurate and up to date intelligence on the movement and actions of the confederate 12th Fleet. The Valuable was no more. At least the several hundred lives lost with its destruction did not suffer long. Though it was not the neutrino cannon that had vaporized them, it was a powerful enough bombardment that life was snubbed out rather quickly. Those who did not die from the immediate explosion were killed by the vacuum of space within tens of seconds. As the screen lines settled, JT and Aurelle walked steadily back into the security bridge and prepared for whatever might be next on tap in their adventure.

"Well done," said Raffordy in JT's head.

Chapter 21
Majak

Capt. Majak worked hard that night to erase his steps and any evidence of his existing. His officers who had been with him on the planetary exploration team would be a slight risk if Fico didn't take care of them quickly. But he felt most likely they were convinced that Majak would have committed suicide already anyway. For what it was worth, Majak wondered if maybe that option was still his best way out of this mess. He was taking a count of the few things he had with him: his communicator, a small phaser, the clothes on his back- which was a Confederation officer's uniform without his rank or insignia- his ID card, and that was about it. He did not need any credits since it seemed that for the time being his Unlucky Duckling patrons would have his immediate needs covered. But at some point, he would need some credits.

"What are you going to do Remmy?" Majak asked himself. He could indeed do the unthinkable and end his own life. But then that was not what he was setting out to do with Fico. That would be the cowardly (but honorable by Confederation standards) way out he thought. What was the odd truth was that the Confederation, and his superiors in particular, would have seen this as the noble and honor-bound way to end things. Two very different perspectives for the same act. No. He could not do that at this point. He had come too far and promised and been promised too much.

He decided that the best thing he could do was to take Fico's advice and get some sleep. He had had a few local brews to drink at the Duckling and he was tired already. Yes. Sleep was his best option. He would think clearer in the morning.

Majak's eyes were closed practically as soon as he hit the pillow. His dreams were relatively somber considering all he had been through. He dreamed of his actions abord the Suclesahe. He dreamed of his next command and the fleet and his family. Fortunately, he did not recall most of his dreams nor did he desire to. If he did it was the dreams of his family he would have cherished the most. Yet he would have been saddened the most by them as well. So he slept for about six hours and woke up before first light. This was the warrior within him. Whenever there was danger nearby, he could not get a full night's sleep. His body knew and sensed that he needed to be alert. And so, he was. After six hours it was near dawn but not yet actually light out and so Majak tried to go back to sleep. No luck there. He got up and went to the restroom. This was normally a shared accommodation with neighboring rooms. But Majak had his own private bathroom. That was a small nicety Fico was able to secure for him.

Majak found the bathroom was adequate but a little small. Most guests on planet 104 were menca or dwarf or elven therefore the accommodations were built for their smaller stature. The bed was large enough for Majak since the inn did have the occasional human or Cybrinthian or Gnorac. It was just the sink height was low as was the toilet. It was nothing he could not easily overlook. And that he did. So, he freshened himself up and splashed some water on his face.

Majak was not one to easily give in. He was going to figure this out and overcome it. He found some toiletries stashed underneath the sink and was able to brush his teeth and decided he would have a shower. It was probably 0500 or 5 am. He was not sure what time system this planet was on but he knew it was early and no one else seemed to be stirring yet. Majak would enjoy his shower as hot as he could get it and see if that cleared his thoughts. He found a towel and some cleansing gel and turned on the faucet. It did not take long for the water to heat. The warm water was a small blessing. Majak hopped in and closed the glass door behind him. The water felt good. It was a cleansing purge. This was a cleanse he needed.

After a while, he turned off the shower and stepped out to dry himself. This was strange. The towel he knew he left next to the sink was hanging on the towel rack. No matter. Maybe his mind was playing tricks on him. So, he grabbed it off the rack and toweled off. Meanwhile he had a strange feeling like he was being watched. Majak had had this feeling before and it never turned out good. He decided to dry off a little faster. Then he went to get his clothes and found they were where he left them. Phew. Maybe the towel was just his imagination. He put on his old stripped of rank uniform and decided he would go out to try and get some new clothes. He could not be going around in an ex-Confederation officer's uniform even if it was one that no longer sported its badges and rank. Majak looked around the room giving it a mental note. What things were where. A small mental exercise in acuity. Then he stepped outside and went to the main front desk. From there he asked where he could find some clothing. The desk attendant was helpful.

Majak took note of what the attendant told him and decided he would ask if anything had been left for him. The clerk checked in the room mail slots and noted there was an envelope for Majak's room. He handed Majak the envelope. Majak took the time to sit down at a small table in the inn's waiting area beside the front desk. Inside the envelope was a note and a memory card. The card was small enough to fit into the extension slot on his earpiece. The note said:

"On the enclosed you will find 200 credits. Please use as you see fit. Regards, JM Liang, proprietor." So, this was who Majak had to thank for the hospitality: a Mr. or Ms. Liang. Majak made a mental note to remember the name and handed the note and envelope to the attendant to shred them. He attached the memory card to his earpiece and checked it. Indeed, as described it did have 200 credits on it. So, the first question Majak had, *how would he pay for new clothes,* was now answered. His second question, *where would he get new clothes,* had already been answered by the attendant. His third question he would look up on his own, *when did the clothing store open?* Indeed, it was not open yet. Were this a larger town it might have been a 24-hour store, but this store appeared to be a small-time operation and would be far from keeping big city hours. Majak found it was to be open in about three hours. So, he went back up to his room to wait.

Finally, when the time came, he decided he would walk the distance rather than call for a transport. It was only a kilometer or two away and he decided the walk would be good for him. It was not exactly the best way to keep a low profile. But he decided that the exercise benefits and the benefit of not calling attention to himself hailing a transport or leaving evidence of his travels outweighed the risks. Majak gathered his few belongings and set out down the town's main street. He was at his destination in less than 15 minutes. He walked into the cozy shop and eyed its merchandise. He asked the employee or maybe the shop's owner where he could find outerwear for exploring and everyday general-purpose use. The elderly gentleman pointed to a wall off to one side and offered there were changing areas in the rear if he wanted to try anything on first. He also offered a hologram projector if he just wanted to try clothes on digitally to see how they looked.

"Thanks, this will do perfectly," Majak said of some pants with pockets and a couple of shirts he found. He would keep his boots but needed some socks and undergarments. He found these readily along a wall on the other side of the store.

"If you need anything like these in different colors, I can have the computer generate it for you in no time before you leave the store," remarked the elderly gentleman as he noticed Majak was buying a few sets of certain things.

"No, I don't think that will be necessary but thank you for offering," said Majak. He then collected up all the items he had selected and decided that he would try them on holographically.

"Do you mind if I use the hologram generator after all?" Majak asked the gentleman.

"That is no problem. Here you are," and the gentleman handed Majak a bottle sized device with two camera ports. Majak took it gratefully. The device had two buttons only: one for turning it on and the other for projecting the item on the wearer. The user placed the item to be projected in front of the lower camera eye. The upper one projected its likeness on the user. It was simple enough to use. Majak had used similar ones before. He projected each of the shirts and the set of pants he had selected. They all appeared to be good fits. There was no setting to project underwear or socks, these did not concern Majak. They would fit.

"Thank you. I'll take them all," he declared to the elderly gentleman. When Majak went to take out his memory card with the credits on it the elderly gentleman waived him off.

"Your money is no good here," he said.

"I only have these credits though; I can't pay you any other way," Majak protested.

"You misunderstand me," said the old man. "Your money is no good here because these items have already been paid for."

"Well, thank you but I don't know what else to say," offered Majak.

"Any friend of Mr. Liang's is a friend of ours. You can thank him when you see him next," said the man.

"I will do that. But I also want to thank you now," said Majak. And with that the elderly gentleman offered to put Majak's new clothing items in a bag but Majak interjected.

"If it's alright I would like to change into some of these here before I leave."

"Of course, I understand," said the gentleman. "You may change in the back as you like."

"Thank you," said Majak. He then went and changed into some of his new attire then and there. He took the rest of his things in a bag. He did not plan to leave the old uniform as evidence there even if he felt it was a safe place.

The shop proprietor was kind enough but Majak was not going to blindly trust anyone just yet. It was hard enough for him to trust Fico. Majak finished changing and got on his way. It was still early morning and not many people were about. Majak thought that was a good thing. His walk back to the inn was uninterrupted. When he got past the front desk, the attendant asked him if he found the shop ok and he replied yes. The attendant also asked if he would be needing anything else. Majak thought for a moment and said nothing that he could think of but he would call down if he came up with anything.

"Very good sir," was the attendant's response.

Majak decided that there was nothing suspicious about his walk to the clothing shop or his walk back and that he could relax just a bit. No sooner had he decided this than he got a call from Fico,

"My friend, we need to move you as soon as possible," said Fico over the communicator. "The Duckling and its inn are no longer safe," he continued.

"What do you mean?" interjected Majak, who was just settling down to the idea of spending some time in his new quarters.

"I mean, there is no time to explain but we believe you are at risk the longer you stay there," Fico pleaded. "The sooner we move you to a new safe house, the better."

"Ok, ok. But I just received a couple of hundred credits from JM Liang," Majak added.

Fico responded, "That is fine. The credits are fine. It is the location we are concerned about." Fico continued, "You remember that I told you the Duckling was being watched by both sides?"

"Yes,"

"Well, it is. And we have reason to believe that the Confederation has an active spy watching both the Duckling and the inn," Fico said in a disappointed manner. "I am sorry we didn't know this for certain earlier. But it is pretty much confirmed now."

"That is unwelcome news," said Majak. "I will gather my things and be ready in a matter of minutes."

"Excellent. Be aware: do not indicate to anyone there that you are leaving."

"Uhm, ok." Majak was starting to become alarmed.

"I will personally be by in ten minutes to see you out and we'll get you to your new location; it is not too far," said Fico.

"I'll be ready in three," said Majak. "See you soon."

"Roger. Out here," ended Fico's call. Majak quickly got to work gathering his few belongings from around the room. He thought he might take some of the toiletries just in case wherever he was going didn't have any. He was not sure of what to expect. Therefore, he felt it best to be prepared for anything.

It did not take long at all for Majak to be completely ready to go. Fortunately, with so few belongings it would not seem like he was leaving the inn. He could place his worldly possessions in his pockets and one small store bag. He quickly began sanitizing the room: making traces of his staying there disappear. Majak knew he could not completely clear the place. But he could make it more difficult to the common observer to determine that he had been there. This started with the bathroom. He wiped down the sink, toilet, and shower to remove and flush any traces of his hair. Next was his bed: he shook out the pillow cases and sheets to remove any traces of hair or skin cells. After a bit, he decided that he had made enough progress in thwarting a casual glance from determining he had been there. This was just in time for Fico to arrive.

"Ah, my friend, I see you have made some efforts to conceal your presence," said Fico upon his arrival. "You know that is nearly pointless."

"I know. But it gave me something to do," responded Majak. "And moreover, even if it only slows them down, is it not better than nothing?"

"Good point," Fico conceded. "Now we must be going. We are going across town to a place I will tell you about later."

"I will follow your lead," Majak said. "Lead away." And so, the two men picked up the few things Majak had in the room and headed out. They went out a back door entrance rather than going by the front desk. The back door led to an alley behind the inn. As soon as they came out into the alley Fico turned to Majak and said they needed to be extra careful because he believed that the Confederation spy network was active right here near the inn. He was not even sure that they could trust the inn workers such as the attendant at the front desk.

"Not so good," said Majak. "I asked him about places to buy clothing this morning and he directed me to a store nearby."

"I don't know for sure if the inn workers are a risk, but we can't be too safe," said Fico. "Until I confirm our status, we must treat everyone as if they are a threat."

"Well, if that is the case, then so be it," said Majak. "I just don't want to be a risk to you and your network."

"This is what we do," said Fico. "I am used to taking risks and this is little different." And with that declaration, Fico led the way to a waiting cab on the back side street from the inn. They both got in and the cab took the two men across town to a safe location Fico had picked out an hour before.

"This place is one we can trust. At least for now," said Fico as the cab pulled up to a hotel-type place on the far side of the small city. The men stayed inside the cab for a bit.

"What was so wrong with the inn near the Unlucky Duckling?" asked Majak.

"It was not so much the location of the inn as it was its location near the Duckling," declared Fico. "You see the Duckling was definitely being watched," he went on. "And if it was being watched, that meant the inn was probably being watched as well. We cannot be too cautious."

"You know what these parts are like and what is best. So I am completely in deference to you," said Majak. "But I would like to keep moving on with our plan to talk about things." Majak, looked in the rear-view monitor to see if the computerized driver was paying attention. The automaton did not seem to be. Majak looked around the cab. There did not seem to be any evidence of listening devices or tampering with the vehicle.

"I know what you are looking for. Our enemies are too smart for that to leave any evidence of their actions," stated Fico.

"Well, again, it can't hurt, and we can't be too cautious," said Majak.

"True, true," Fico replied. The two men stayed in the cab a minute longer and after looking around the exterior of the vehicle, Fico decided it was safe enough, and it was time to exit. He paid the machine with a wave of his communicator and indicated Majak should follow him out of the cab. With that, they were on the streets. Fico was an astute observer. He had noticed in the cab that the automated driver had not looked around or expected payment promptly. This made Fico suspicious.

"Did you notice the bot driving the cab didn't ask for credits right away when we stopped?" Fico asked. "Not even the least bit worried we weren't going to pay…"

"Yes but I didn't think anything of it?" replied Majak. "After all, he had us on video probably."

"That may be, but it concerns me nonetheless," Fico went on. "Any cabby you ask me that doesn't expect to get paid the second his tally is up, is trouble."

"I hope you are wrong about that since he knows where he let us off," Majak added.

Fico had thought of that, "Which is why we are not at the place where you are staying."

"Smart man," Majak mumbled half to himself and half so that Fico could hear it.

"We'll see if it is smart enough," said Fico. "Our enemies are quite cunning and think through things like this with ease. At least I fear they do." The two men went into the hotel in a conspicuous enough way so that the cabby would see it if it was watching. But then they doubled back around and came out another door on the building's back side.

"This way about four blocks," said Fico.

"I'm right with you," replied Majak. Then the two of them continued on a rather winding route through some seedy alleys to get to the actual hotel where Majak would be staying.

"This may seem overly cautious but I would rather it be overly cautious than the opposite and we find you dead in the morning," Fico was rather blunt.

"My living self, appreciates that," Majak said. Capt. Majak thought for a moment about his consideration of suicide and quickly dismissed the thought. No, indeed he had committed himself to this cause and he would not be going back on that now.

After a walk of about nine or ten blocks to go a total of four, the two men got to the new accommodations. It was an inn-type hotel called the Second Chance. It looked not much better than its name implied. But, as Fico surmised, it would be out of the prying eyes of the Confederation. There was a tavern across the street and a bar in the lobby of the hotel. It just so happened that JM Liang was a part owner of this establishment as well. So therefore, the hotel bill and credit supply would last from the previous place to this one. This fact made Fico a tad bit nervous that the new place might be watched as well. But he had been assured by Liang himself that they would know if there were any eyes on the Second Chance.

Majak quickly checked in and brought his few things up to the second-floor room. There was an egress route available through the room's window onto the first-floor roof and out the back. Majak took note of the quickest ways out in all directions. Then he remarked to Fico that the day was still young, if Fico had no plans, perhaps they could meet his contact to discuss *the* topic. Fico reassured Majak to not get ahead of himself. That would all come in time. But for now, and the time being, he needed to sit tight and wait it out. Fico said he would be advised at least two days before any contact with his handler was made. Majak understood.

Majak knew that he needed to be patient. But this was difficult when he knew his information was time-sensitive. He wanted to trade it as quickly as he could and get it off of his mind. He also wanted to be safe and sound; and off planet 104 as soon as humanly possible.

Fico understood this desire but knew better than to act too quickly.

"We will act in time and it will be the right time," he assured Majak. The two conversed for a bit more in the dark hotel room and then Fico took his leave to go do whatever it was that Fico did. Majak didn't ask too many questions. He settled in for a wait of some time. He knew the contact would come. It might just not be on his desired timeline.

Chapter 22
Family Tales

The trip back to Papa Fae's did not take long. It seemed that the trip out to the engine was more drawn out. But perhaps that was because the group did not know what to expect or what they were going to encounter. After some time traveling but not yet at his house, Papa Fae said to the group that they would be best off if they ensured that there was no one following them. Damon and Delle did not sense anyone was but they also understood the wealth of caution that Papa Fae wished to exhibit. Spiruthean was a safe world, but there were evil doers about even in Flarhom Woods. So Papa Fae suggested they double back on their trail and the group did just that.

About a half a league before Papa Fae's house they all made a great circle and came back on their own trail a league away from his house. There were not any noticeable indications of their being followed. This was a good sign thought Delle. She half expected they would encounter some indication that the group had been followed.

"We cannot be too careful," said Papa Fae. "There are spies in the least expected of places."

"My grandfather knows these things," said Fae. "His instinct is to be trusted."

"I would have it no other way," added Damon. "My old friend is the most respected and revered forest ranger of these woods." And so, the group: Delle, Damon, Fae, Papa Fae, Lady Shera, Valcor, Farhale, and Jeanaviere all came back to Papa Fae's satisfied that they were not followed and that they had seen all that the engine had to show them.

"What shall we say regarding the story of Barnab and Gailena?" asked Lady Shera. "Can we find out more about their travels and whereabouts?"

"I should like to think so," said Papa Fae. "After all, we suspect they have children who inhabit now, or at one time inhabited, Angola."

"The more we can find out about them the better," added Damon.

"Maybe we can go see the old hermit you spoke of earlier Master Fae?" said Lady Shera. The old hermit about which she spoke was Quildevar. He was an old spirit who inhabited Flarhom Woods not too far from Papa Fae's. Fae had mentioned him and his peculiarities earlier in the trip the day prior. He was impressed that Lady Shera had picked up on it and remembered it.

"Yes, maybe we could do just that and visit Quildevar?" stated Fae but as more of a question statement than an actual declaration. This interrogative statement was directed towards the senior group member, Papa Fae.

"That is not a bad idea. He may be able to help us and shed some light on things," said Papa Fae. "First I think after our morning's journey we may want to get some refreshments at my house." The group consensus seemed to agree as several in the assembly, especially Valcor and Farhale, perked up at that notion. So, Papa Fae led the way, after the group's doubling back on its own path, back to his house. He readily brought out a light lunch and some refreshments when they got to his home. Everyone was rather hungry at that point so the food was quite welcome. The mencas' horses grazed outside Papa Fae's in his nearby pasture. He had running water in a small stream that bordered his property so the equines were satiated both with food and drink.

"So now we should plan this trip to see Quildevar," said Papa Fae. "He is a crusty old hermit of a spirit and generally would not take kindly to strangers."

"Sounds perfect," joked Farhale. "Just the kind of codger we are looking to meet!"

"He will not find any of us welcome unless I prepare him accordingly," said Papa Fae. "Leave that to me. I have known him many years and know how to deal with his idiosyncrasies."

"Thank goodness for that," said Damon. "I don't think I've ever had a pleasant encounter with the old git."

"You just don't know how to massage his ego," said Papa Fae. "I have much practice." And so Papa Fae excused himself while he prepared his thought projection chamber. After a bit, he returned to the group and said it was ready. He was going to project to Quildevar that they needed his help and would be arriving within the hour if it was to the elder spirit's liking.

Papa Fae invited the group to listen in to his projection which they did. Quildevar seemed open enough to the visit and even Papa Fae remarked that he seemed in extremely good spirits.

"Bring the group and bring yourselves in good cheer!" Quildevar said at one point.

"It almost makes me suspicious," added Papa Fae after the call. "But I sensed no mark of deception or anything to be alarming."

"That is a good thing, no?" replied Fae.

"Yes, my boy, it is," said Papa Fae. "Just a bit of caution is always recommended. Kind of like why we doubled back on our trail to ensure no one was following us earlier."

"But Papa Fae, have you ever sensed deception from Quildevar before?" asked Delle.

"No, I can't say that I have," replied Papa Fae. "But that doesn't mean I am not going to be cautious and that there is not a first time for everything."

"Well put," said Damon. "Perhaps we can go over to Quildevar's en echelon, and arrive at staggered intervals with someone at the rear to guard our movements and act as a security force?"

"Excellent idea," said Valcor. "I would not have suggested anything less."

"I can provide that rear guard," interjected Farhale. "I and Miss Jeanaviere can serve as the guard and ensure the group is safe."

"Terrific. Then it is settled. We will head off momentarily. It should not take us but a half-hour to travel the distance to Quildevar's," said Papa Fae.

"Ok then, let's gather up our steeds and be ready to travel," said Lady Shera. The group then finished the small lunch that Papa Fae had provided and made ready to head out again.

The way to Quildevar's was an easy one. It was about 135 degrees off from the engine's direction. So, it made the stop over at Papa Fae's not much out of the way. The group was able to make the time quickly. When they were a few minutes out from the old hermit's house, Papa Fae contacted Quildevar and advised him they were near. The hermit was actually looking forward to the visit. He did not receive many guests and this was a sort of a rare treat for him.

"Don't expect to be getting too much from me," said Quildevar to Papa Fae. "I am old and my memory is not what it once was," he declared.

"We will be indebted to you no matter how big or small your contribution might be," assured Papa Fae. "And I can promise you no one of our group keeps expectations." Then the group arrived at Quildevar's and the mencas all dismounted leaving their horses grazing in the vicinity of Quildevar's yard. They met for a moment outside Quildevar's main front door. After the introductions were complete, Quildevar invited everyone inside his humble cottage. It was not much more than a two-room woodland home. But it was homey and quaint.

"Can I offer anyone something to drink?" Quildevar started to say. But he was interrupted by a commotion outside. The horses were whinnying as if something was amiss. "Excuse me, I am not sure what the problem is out there," he said.

"I will check on them," said Lady Shera. And she turned to head back outside and to see if she could see Farhale or Jeanaveirre. Neither one was in viewing distance but they must have heard the horse's commotion since they arrived running along the fence line within a minute of Lady Shera's walking outside.

"My Lady, what is the trouble with our steeds?" asked Farhale as soon as he was within earshot of the lady.

"I don't know," she admitted. "They just started screeching so all of a sudden."

"Well, something has caused this. And we should figure it out lest it become a problem," stated Farhale.

Farhale began to reach out and sense the horses with his intuitive thoughts.

"There my boy, what is the trouble?" he projected toward the first horse. Mencas were excellent with animals. But at times like this when there was a stressing event, even mencas could have trouble communicating with other species. The horse, which had been Lady Shera's mount sent a clear message back to Farhale that there was another being in the woods which was foreign to them but would not be so to the spirits or maybe even to the mencas.

"Ok, that is alright, tell me about this sense in the woods that you have," projected Farhale. The horse relayed that the foreign being came from the trees and it seemed to be in the trees. The other horses concurred. The sense was that the trees were trying to talk to them and the horses didn't know what to do about this.

"Well, that is a relief potentially," said Farhale. "The trees are alive and communicate with the spirit people regularly we have learned."

Farhale brought this information to Lady Shera who in turn, brought it back inside Quildevar's house to share with the rest of the group.

"That is a welcome bit of news," said Quildevar. "Our tree spirits apparently are comfortable enough to try and speak to your horses."

"Well the comfort level is not reciprocated," said Lady Shera. "We sense our horses are alarmed and do not know what to do."

"Simple. Calm them and reassure them the trees mean no harm," said Quildevar. "It should not be difficult to steady their fears I shouldn't think."

So, Lady Shera did just that and told Farhale to do the same. They spoke to the steeds through their senses one at a time. The horses did seem to calm themselves. The trees meanwhile, had lessened their attempts at communication but were able to reach out to the spirits of the group directly. Delle volunteered to speak with them to gather the gist of the commotion. Fae went with her. They stepped out onto Quildevar's deck and cleared their thoughts completely to allow themselves to receive. They gathered that the trees wanted to warn them about the engine that had crashed and to be aware others might come looking for it. Delle thanked the trees profusely and took the news to Quildevar, her father Damon, Papa Fae and the rest. They all concluded this was a welcome warning but nothing to be alarmed about. They had already explored the engine and determined what they needed from it.

After the discussion about the engine and the trees' warning to the group, they all got down to business with Quildevar. The travelers sat around his foyer-living space in the home's main room. Papa Fae began the discussion.

"My old friend, we seek information about both the family history of our ancestor, and perhaps that of our friend Mr. Lastalle and young Delle here. Fae and I know the story of Barnab and the family of Thanameresons and we have recently learned the story of Gailena. We don't know what truth you could maybe tell of these family stories. Or perhaps of any information you might be able to lend about the recent crash in the woods. But we would appreciate any light you can shed upon these things," said Pappa Fae, getting right to the point.

"I have been around many years, but not as many as one could say to tell you first hand about Barnab or Gailena. My insights for those two are second-hand as are yours. But sometimes enough second-hand knowledge when combined together, can tell a tale just as well," said Quildevar. "I will tell you gladly what I have heard. But please take it for what it is: tales passed down from generation to generation of my ancestors from these parts."

So Quildevar began to confirm what Damon and Papa Fae had suspected and discussed. He affirmed that his family had told stories about the generational ancestor of the Thanameresons running away to Angola along with the Lastalle ancestor. His understanding of the story was the two had fled Spiruthean to avoid persecution. The part of the tale none had known was that their love was forbidden simply because their parents had not sanctioned it. Therefore, it was taboo and they faced ridicule and ostracization. They chose to escape and live their lives freely on Angola rather than face estrangement.

Quildevar knew nothing about ancestral lines from the two's time on Angola onward. He presumed there might have been children, but none of his family stories indicated there were or were not Angolan, seemingly human, offspring. Quildevar indicated he was a keeper of this information but it was not talked about much since recounting the bloodlines of spirits generally stopped when they could not be traced any longer.

As for the woodland crash and the Federation starship engine,

Quildevar was not very versed. He had heard the crash himself, but not bothered to seek it out or explore the site. He had heard through the trees just now in the message they had delivered to Delle and Fae that a great ship thruster of some kind had crash landed and others might be looking for it. Had he been alone and received this news, he might have let it go at that. He would have figured someone would come about who could tell him more than this. He was right. As he had heard the crash originally, Quildevar was thinking of sending out his own projected thoughts to gain more information about it when Papa Fae had reached out to him earlier that morning. He was happy to learn what he could about the crashed piece of spaceship hardware from his guests and the trees. His new guests though had provided more for him than the trees had been able to do so far.

As for Papa Fae, Fae, Damon and Delle, they were happy to learn what they could from Quildevar about their ancestors. As for the mencas, they were gracious towards their host but hungry for more information about the spirit ancestral stories. Lady Shera for one, was anxious to gain more clues to where they could find the supposed lineage today of Barnab and Gailena.

"Do you know where in Angola the story line stops?" asked Lady Shera of Quildevar.

"I have told you most of what I know," said the old hermit. "But I do know that if there were children of the two we have spoken about, those would have had the ability to possess full blooded spirit traits." He went on, "it is not like the generations would have suddenly become fully human and lost their spirit abilities."

"Well, I wasn't suggesting they would," Lady Shera continued. "But indeed, might some things have subsided like spirit skills and traits after several generations? No?"

"The skills of spirits are both inherited and learned so without formal training, you are correct."

Lady Shera went on, "So subsided and become dormant or subsided and awaiting for a reawakening?"

"Neither," said Quildevar. "Subsided, and become… something else." Lady Shera decided that she might not want to push the point.

"Thank you. I think I understand," is all Lady Shera said softly.

"I am not sure I do," interjected Farhale. Lady Shera gave him a look as if to say "hush."

"Nor I," said Valcor. Lady Shera turned towards him and frowned as if to tell him the same thing. It was no matter though since Quildevar did not seem to mind.

"What I mean to say is their skills would wane, but the ability would still have been there. And over generations yes, the spirit in their blood would diminish but they could still access the abilities if properly evoked. You could call it a dormant trait I think, but it is more something that the mind would be able to understand had one experienced it firsthand." Quildevar was doing his best to explain something he felt was just not explainable to a non-spirit. "I think if we knew of heirs to this day, we would see spirit like abilities but that being would have no understanding of how to harness their latent powers."

There was a bit of a collective light bulb turning on for the mencas.

"If there were heirs today, I think we might see a resistance to diseases or sicknesses that might affect non-spirits. Something like an immunity to fusion sicknesses or radiation resistance is possible. An unparalleled ability to intuit others' thoughts. Something like what we see with certain Gnoracs. But nothing that person would understand how to control," Quildevar explained.

"So, we need to look for outliers? People who don't understand their own abilities. And those with overly active and effective immune systems?" asked Lady Shera.

"I would say that is probably correct," said Quildevar after a brief pause.

"Sounds like nails in hayfields," muttered Farhale.

"It may be just that," said Quildevar who had heard the knight's comment despite it being muttered quietly and quite under his breath.

"But we must keep up the faith. I swear by the good gods that we will succeed," said Valcor.

"We will. We must," added Lady Shera. "The fate of many races and future generations may depend upon it."

"I am not sure I want to know how important this is," projected Fae to Delle. But his grandfather, ever astute, Papa Fae, caught most of the projected thought and intercepted it before Delle could respond.

"You are wise to wish to lessen how important this may be, but foolish to try and keep the importance from all of us and you know that you and I and Delle and Damon will be critical in helping these mencas on their quest," Papa Fae interjected so that both Delle and Fae knew he was listening. "Also, don't think you can keep your private conversations that private when we are all in this close proximity."

"Ok, sorry Papa," said Fae.

"No need to apologize to me, just be mindful in the future," responded Papa Fae. "There are many out there in the worlds and the universe who would and could do many of us harm by intercepting seemingly innocent thoughts." Papa Fae was full of wise isms and knew how to express things so all could understand. Even those of a young age or those of other races.

The group conversed with Quildevar some more and discussed more details about the history and likelihood of existence of heirs of Barnab Thanamereson and Gailena Lastalle. The conversation could have gone on long and late into the afternoon but Quildevar was growing tired towards the late afternoon and the group had a bit of a journey ahead of them to get back to Papa Fae's and to plan their next actions. Fae for one, was excited to recount the things he felt he could to his family. He knew of course that much of what was discussed had to remain private. But there were some things he felt he could relay to his parents and those things that he could, he was anxious so to do. Delle as well felt she wanted to share some of what she had learned with her mother but of course she would first consult with Damon, her father. She would gain his blessing before she decided what could or could not be said.

The rest of the group, the mencas were eager to continue on their mission of finding the chosen heir whether he resided in the human, menca, Cybrinthian or other worlds. They were fairly certain, at least Lady Shera was fairly certain, they would find the heir among humans. But she had to confirm that there was no possibility there were heirs among elves, Cybrinthians, dwarves, mencas, even Gnoracs. No races were ruled out as a possibility for harboring the spirit mixed race heir.

After another hour or two the conversation naturally started to wind to an ending point. Quildevar was thankful for it since he was becoming tired. He was older than any of his guests including Papa Fae by at least a generation. He appreciated the break from his routine and his guests, especially the spirits, were happy to find him much more pleasant than any of the others would have guessed him to be. There were many stories about the old hermit and not many of them were kind. The spirits in Quildevar's sitting room were pleased to learn not many of those stories proved true. Maybe they had simply caught him on a good day. Maybe not. Maybe it was more than just that. Whatever it was, Quildevar proved very helpful in the budding quest.

Perhaps the most useful information that he was able to provide was the old family tale of where in Angola it was rumored that Barnab and Gailena had settled. According to the stories that Quildevar knew, they went to Anglen which was a city not far from Arlgon in Angola. They then supposedly moved to the west end of the city of Arlgon. It was here in west Arlgon that the trail went cold for Quildevar's knowledge ended at this point. But it gave the group something to work with.

"We must go to Arlgon with all haste," said Valcor later as the group was departing and was again enroute back to Papa Fae's.

"I tend to agree," said Farhale. "But should, perhaps, we do some more research here on Spiruthean?" The group paused in thought to consider the options. Lady Shera was for one in favor of moving as quickly as possible but leaving no local stones unturned. This meant that for all intents and purposes she felt they should do some more digging in Spiruthean first. Farhale and Valcor were both openly in favor of moving on to Europa and to the city of Arlgon in Angola as soon as practical. Jeanaviere was as usual reserved with her judgement but she tended to think in line with Lady Shera's logic. In effect: while they were in Flarhom Woods on Spiruthean they might as well make use of that fact and gain all the information locally that they could.

The spirits were less opinionated as it was not their quest, but Papa Fae did recognize that it would make things much easier for the mencas if they had a spirit accompanying them. Fae could already read what Papa Fae was thinking. The old spirit's thoughts were so in tuned with those of his grandson that he could rarely get much past the young spirit. The question was, would Papa Fae and Fae's parents let him go on the quest? The answer would be found out soon enough since the group could make it back to Papa Fae's fairly quickly. Damon could already speak for Delle's mother and himself. The journey across the galaxies was out of the question. Delle was a school girl and he was her father. He knew the answer from her mother would be not only a no but a resounding no. He did not even need to check. So, he communicated that to Delle quietly before it even came up in open discussion.

The group had wished Quildevar well and bid him adieu but before leaving he had given them all some food for the road and something to drink. He also gave the mencas' horses some treats to supplement the grass and field hay they had been scrounging upon. The group traveled quickly back to first Damon and Delle's house and then discussed some more details there. They then ensured there was an open communication line between everyone which could traverse the great distances they planned to travel.

The need to communicate across star systems was more complex than a simple thought projection chamber could ordinarily muster. However, Damon had been a communications engineer earlier in his life and his chamber was no ordinary thought projection chamber. He had rigged it to be able to project audio communications at 100 times ES-neo speeds. The science of it is more complex than he had time to explain to anyone else in the group. But rest assured, if Delle or Damon had anything important to tell the others from Spiruthean, they had the means to get the messages to where they needed to be… no matter where that was.

After Damon and Delle bid the group farewell, Papa Fae led the rest back to his place and they decided their next move. Lady Shera heard the desires of Farhale and Valcor. Then she listened to Jeanaviere's opinion and weighed the merits of each. She asked Papa Fae and Fae what they thought about the group's next move. Papa Fae said rightly so that they could continue the quest for information in Flarhom

Woods through Damon and Delle who would be here and able to continue helping them as needed. With that logic, why not go ahead and begin planning the long trip to Europa? No one could argue with that thinking.

The next task once and if it was decided was how they would travel to Europa. The Jupiterian moon was nearly 80 million light years away. Even if they could find a ship that could achieve 10 times ES-neo it would still take three days to get there. But finding a ship capable of that speed would be the tricky part. They started planning how to contact the best spirit pilots and find out if there were any ships making that trip for hire. The task was a tough one at best and an impossible one at worst. But if there was anyone up to this task, it was the four mencas supported by a spirit.

Chapter 23
Amorhe

urelle and JT were conversing with Lt. Simonds on the security bridge when the screen lines settled back in to place and neither the 7th nor the 12th fleet had fired a shot at one another. This was the best outcome possible despite the complete destruction of the spirit ship, Valuable. The fighter screen line had remained undiscovered and all elements – all 28 ships - of the federal 7th Fleet were safely conducting their reconnaissance and screen missions. Things had gone well considering the close call with Pepper Cat 1 at the front end of the federal fighter screen.

This was how things remained for the next few hours. Some fighters began rotating line duty and trading out with other ships when it happened. It was what Cdre. Theelson feared most. One of the fighters at the center of the screen line was debriefing a relieving fighter and accidentally hailed the new fighter with its masking device only half charged. The hail was broadcast on open channels and the nearest screening confederate outpost, a moored frigate, picked up the hail. It was a simple mistake. An easy overlook of protocol and truly a rookie thing to do. But it cost the entire federal screen line its clandestine cover.

The confederate frigate moored on the enemy line in its outpost position immediately triangulated the broadcast. It sought clearance and received go ahead orders to fire upon the location from where the broadcast originated. Simultaneously the confederate battle cruisers went on alert and carriers began readying and launching waves of small attack ships and fighters. All these ships began to scramble and triangulate on the broadcast location of the soon to be stricken federal fighters. This meant both the one who broadcast the hail and the receiving fighter intended to be the first fighter's relief were bombarded by confederate lasers, missiles, and cannon fire.

And so, the screen lines began collapsing and the hunt was on. Each side began evasive maneuvers and multiple wing coordinations to seek and destroy each other as fast as possible. The fighter lines began intermixing and the few AUs between both sides were quickly closed as fighters, bombers, and various attack gunships all began maneuvering. They commenced conducting technical and tactical pursuits of one another immediately.

Lt. Simonds called for Capt. Johanaston and Lt. Shamus; all three came together for a debriefing in the security bridge command room. JT and Aurelle were told immediately following this huddle that they needed to brace themselves and gather anything they might need or want from their quarters. They were directed to proceed to an escape vessel staging area near bay four just in case the Amorhe came under attack. At this point the action was purely precautionary since there was no reason to think that the carrier would be anywhere near the direct action. But one never knew. The Confederation was tricky and had been known to try frontal assaults on capital vessels deep in friendly territory before. And this was far from friendly territory. If there was one, the Cigar Galaxy's remote screen lines were indeed truly the front of the war.

JT and Aurelle did as instructed and gathered what few items they had in their quarters and linked up with Capt. Johanaston outside in their hatchway. He led them first to the main bridge where they quickly saw that things were in an organized chaos. It was here that all the flight operations for fighters and attack ships were being coordinated. The carrier would not maneuver much especially during flight operations. But it did sit as the flagship of the 7th Fleet so there was a lot of coordination going on across the bridge with other vessels and the higher echelons of command. Cdre. Theelson greeted them quickly then excused herself while she issued orders and spoke with several officers at once and attended to a hologram call from Adm. Vander who was on his own bridge a deck above them. There was not much for them to do but be in the way so JT and Aurelle mutually decided off to the hanger bay it would be.

Just before they were out the hatch into the main corridor there came a burst across an ensign's monitor. "Incoming bogeys!" yelled the young officer.

A flight of six confederate X1 attack craft in two groups of three suddenly burst into the Amorhe's proximity warning space. Alarms started sounding and red lights began flashing on monitors all over the bridge.

"That doesn't sound good in there," said JT to Aurelle. "We had best be getting to the bay tout de suite!"

"I think I agree with you Mr. Frenchie, 'quickly' is appropriate now," Aurelle laughed a bit but not much. The gravity of the situation did not really warrant humor.

Back on the bridge the auto cannon command team leadership was directing crews to engage the X1s at furthest possible range. They were simultaneously coordinating close in fighters who were not yet on the screen line to engage the hostile craft. The X1 was the Confederation's most advanced fighter and it was able to engage targets several AUs from itself. This meant it could launch attacks from further distances than the bulk of the Federation's fighter force.

But the autocannon crews could engage from the same or greater distances. And they began to do just that. Six X1s alone would not be much of a threat to a carrier like the Amorhe. But these fighters were closing their distance fast and getting under the safe distance for minimum arming of autocannon fire. It was a tactic used by some of the best pilots of the Confederation.

The first three X1s broke right while the second three broke left and then they spread out individually to prevent a target signature too big from being presented. The first autocannon shots all missed. The X1s were still at too great a distance for the missiles to correctly target and track the small craft. But they were getting too close for the same missiles to arm themselves correctly and safely. Normally the arming process took an AU and these missiles were taking that full amount of distance. The other three bogeys had closed the distance to a half an AU and were circling about from both sides of the Amorhe. Where were the screening fighters and how had these ships slipped past them all? This should not have happened.

"I need all available laser cannon and autocannon crews to target those X1s before they get any closer!" commanded Cdre. Theelson.

"Aye-Aye ma'am," came several replies.

"We know they slipped past the screen but we don't know how they got past our ship's sentries," came a comment from a lieutenant commander at the gun command station.

"We also need to speed up our launch sequence for flights from bays two and three." Cdre. Theelson added for all to hear. The understood implication was to get more fighters and attack craft into the fight now before more X1s or other confederate small craft could breach any sentry guard points.

"One bogey down!" came a report from the observation deck bridge via the hologram communication device. And it was true. An autocannon crew had engaged and destroyed with a fusion missile one of the X1s that had banked a little too close for comfort into one of their missile's paths.

"Great but we have no cause to celebrate. There are five more out there," was the response from Cdre. Theelson's executive officer. Just then one of the Amorhe's X02 fighter bombers swooped down and engaged two of the X1s only a quarter AU from the Amorhe. It fired proton torpedoes and laser cannon shots in a wide arc around the two enemy fighters and managed a direct hit each. Unfortunately, this was not before one of the X1s was able to circle around and lob a barrage of its own laser cannons against the X02 scoring a few glancing shots. The X02 was severely disabled and thus sent crashing towards the nearest asteroid.

Two for one was not a bad trade though and the X1 count was down to three bogies. Just then another wave of X02s joined the fight. These were some of the Amorhe's most skilled pilots. But they were up against some of the Confederation's best themselves. The X1 was the newest attack fighter the Confederation had to offer. It was nearly as modern as the Federation's X02 except it was strictly a fighter whereas the Federation attack craft, the X02 was a fighter bomber. In its dual role the X02 was more versatile but it traded some capabilities for the versatility as a dual-purpose spacecraft. Speed was one of them. It had no neo drive. Neither did the X1, but the X1 was nevertheless a little bit faster. But the X02 was better armored and could take more punishment. It worked better in packs and could bomb fast moving targets as well as shoot with its auto cannons and lasers.

"We are detecting a larger presence on the screen line," came the report from an ensign on the bridge observation deck. And he was right. There was a large attack vessel possibly a destroyer or a battle cruiser closing the distance from behind the screen line of the 12th Fleet. The Confederation fleet had the advantage of having already established its screen and having four more fleets backing it up in the area. But the crew of the Amorhe and the rest of the 7th Fleet had no idea about the rest of the Confederation battle group nearby.

"We have at least a frigate and a destroyer and possibly something larger maneuvering behind the forward most outpost," came the follow up report from the same ensign.

"Let's see what we have before we engage our resources and commit," was Cdre. Theelson's order to the bridge crew. "We don't want to be playing cat and mouse before we know if we are the cat or we are the mouse."

"We can engage in approximately one minute if they maintain their present course and trajectory," said the ensign. Just then Adm. Vander weighed in and made his observations known.

"Cdre. Theelson, I see what you are looking at and I will direct the frigates and battle cruisers on our flank to target the threat," said Vander as Theelson was just about to ask for support from the escort vessels. Her carrier was not meant to be engaging in direct contact at all costs. It was too valuable as a fighter and attack craft platform. It had the weaponry to do so but it was not designed to go toe to toe with battle cruisers, frigates, and destroyers.

"Roger that skipper, we will maintain our distance. But be aware we are able to engage in just a few minutes or less at present course," reported Theelson.

"Duly noted commadore," said Vander. "We'll keep up our attacks from here at this distance from the Amorhe. We will keep you out of trouble unless it's completely necessary."

Cdre. Theelson turned her attention back to the three remaining X1 bogies and got an update from her observation officers. As she was doing this the threat from the enemy destroyer, frigate and what appeared to be a battle cruiser began to materialize faster than anyone on the Amorhe would have liked. The enemy ships came out from behind the screen line and used the small frigate outpost to mask their movement. These ships may have been using masking devices. Or, they may have just been hidden behind asteroids and other space matter, for they had not been readily visible to the federal screen line ships. At least not to the Amorhe.

Meanwhile JT and Aurelle had made it down to the bay near their assigned escape shuttle.

"Where are we going to go if this goes south and we need to pop smoke out of here?" JT wondered out loud.

"Well, honestly I think we should let the commanders here on the Amorhe decide what is the best location for you to remain safe," said Aurelle.

"We thought you might be most safe back behind the front lines and where they have excellent medical care and research capabilities. Plus, somewhere Sergeant Wayne knows well, his home world: Europa," was Capt. Johanaston's response to the discussion.

"Isn't that a terrible idea, since the Confederation would be looking for him there wouldn't they?" was Aurelle's thought in response to Johanaston's statement.

"Well, we have no reason to believe the Confederation has any idea who they are looking for, nor do we think that if they do, they would have any idea where the person they are seeking is from." Johanaston had already briefed his higher command and they concurred that Europa, specifically Angola, was the best place to hide JT. Plus the medical science teams on JT's home world were second to none. They might have the best chance at figuring out just what made JT so immune to the neutrino cannon's effects.

"I am game," said JT. "Just make sure we aren't advertising this and the circle of knowledge about this remains small and need to know only."

"Absolutely," said Johanaston, "But again this is just a precaution in case the Amorhe becomes compromised."

The Amorhe was fast inching closer and closer to becoming just that: "a compromised vessel." It had plenty of protection, but it was clear from the X1 attack and now the battle cruiser, frigate and destroyer moving into her proximity, that the carrier had been spotted. The Confederation knew she was here and they knew they needed to neutralize or destroy her. The small group of capital ships maneuvering out from the confederate outpost was aiming to do just that: destroy the Amorhe.

This confederate group split into two forces. One, the battle cruiser was covered by fighters and X1s already engaged. The other, the destroyer and frigate, managed to screen itself behind a small belt of asteroids just outside the outpost. Then, the second force moved in for its main attack. The destroyer unleashed a fury of laser cannon fire but this was really just a distraction. At a distance of more than two AUs, it was more of a blind "fire and forget" action. But it was able to achieve its objective: distract the Amorhe leadership momentarily.

"We have multiple incoming rounds: appearing to be laser fire," commented a gunnery sergeant on the auto cannon bridge.

"Engage!" shouted the officer in charge of his station.

"Autocannons engaged," said the sergeant. And as this exchange was playing out the autocannons laid a screen of fire like a blanket up in the direction of the incoming rounds. This volley succeeded for the most part. Except for one round exploding dangerously close to the Amorhe. It had penetrated the screen of autocannon fire without exploding but burst just off the bow of the Amorhe. The space equivalent of shrapnel rained down as the ship was jarred and alarms began sounding on all decks and all bridges.

"See to that right now and re-patch all forward energy to proton shields," commanded Cdre. Theelson. "We are going to get out of this mess (*or die trying*)."

"Yes ma'am," responded the executive officer on the bridge. "You heard her! Make it happen already!" he yelled in three directions it seemed at one time.

"Aye sir. Aye ma'am. Roger..." came several responses immediately. But the immediate need it seemed was actually elsewhere: the enemy battle cruiser had just simultaneously begun to launch its main attack. The battle cruiser was initially hidden behind the outpost frigate and not detected until all three confederate ships began to attack. When the battle cruiser was finally spotted, the destroyer's laser cannon fire was already on the way. Already on the way to its near misses and the explosion off the Amorhe's bow. Meanwhile, the battle cruiser approached from the other flank and began launching fusion missiles as soon as it was clear from behind the outpost.

"New incoming missiles!" shouted an ensign on the observation bridge.

"Full energy to proton shields already," came another report.

"Let's get clear of the fallout area," suggested the executive officer to Cdre. Theelson.

"Yes, good idea, make it so…" she responded right away.

And with that the ship's main thrusters were fired in reverse and she began to back out of the engagement area. All the while fighter launching and recovery continued.

Meanwhile, in bay four JT and Aurelle were preparing for their evacuation. Capt. Johanaston had not received clearance to load or launch them yet but he was about to make an executive decision. When the laser cannon round exploded off the Amorhe's bow it shook the ship. He knew that he might have to make the call.

"Ok you two, I'm going to load you guys and say my goodbyes now just in case I don't make it with you and we need to clear you to go," he started to say. Just then the nearby alert sounded and overhead red lights started flashing. Everyone was to be at battle stations. Which right now, for him, this was Johanaston's primary alert station. He was tasked with providing for JT and Aurelle's safety. So, he beckoned them to a waiting escape craft. The coordinates to take them across the galaxies to Europa were already loaded up. All they had to do was sit back and await clearance for the flight.

"You are not coming with us?" asked Aurelle.

"I will if I can, but I am not sure yet if that is going to be allowed to happen," Johanaston responded. Just as he said this, his communicator buzzed in his ear.

"Launch the cargo," said the voice in his ear belonging to the security bridge commander and Capt. Johanaston's immediate boss.

"Roger," was all Johanaston responded. "Ok, it is time for you two to go. I am staying here." And with that Capt. Johanaston gave a last look at JT and Aurelle and said, "Goodbye. Good luck. Godspeed."

"Thank you, best of luck here yourself," said JT.

Johanaston then closed them in to their escape craft. The X7R emergency escape craft is designed for long distance space travel but not for the amount of time it would take JT and Aurelle to make it to Europa. They would be fine, but they would have to improvise ways to use the craft's facilities (there were none), and eat and sleep over the more than 24 hours their flight would take. That would be for them to figure out and right now Johanaston's priority was getting them into space safely without the Confederation discovering they were there or that they had been launched. And he was needing to do this in the middle of a firefight with three major enemy capital ships and several fighters.

Capt. Johanaston could have waited until higher clearance gave him more instructions but luckily, he did not. He did not need to because his lieutenants had done their homework and readied the ship completely for him. So, when it came time and the decision was made, nearly everything was already done. What remained, was finding out the best way to sneak the craft out. That opportunity presented itself every 60 seconds or so when X02 fighters were launched or recovered. Johanaston simply had to time the launch to coincide with a fighter launch and mask the escape vessel behind a launching X02. This is easier said than done amidst a capital ship bombardment. But needless to say, Johanaston performed the task perfectly. Less than 45 seconds after shutting them into the craft and wishing them Godspeed, the X7R containing JT and Aurelle was safely hidden; masked behind an X02 and well on its way into deep space for the long trip ahead.

The Amorhe continued to fight and survived for another 30 minutes before Adm. Vander was forced to transfer his flag and his command. Cdre. Theelson performed admirably but ultimately was unable to keep her carrier from destruction. What happened in the end was the Amorhe ran low on forward shield power and was in the process of diverting reserve neo drive power to those shields when a perfectly timed proton torpedo found its way through her screen and exploded just aft of her third bay. It was a noble but vain effort to save the

Amorhe after that. The torpedo incapacitated the bay and caused secondary explosions amid ships. Adm. Vander had approximately ten minutes before the ship foundered beyond repair and it only took him two to make his decision to transfer flags. Cdre. Theelson chose to stay with her ship. She would later be memorialized by a senior staff school award given in her name and several buildings across the Federation would be renamed in her honor.

Captain Johanaston would be similarly remembered in smaller ways for his role in ensuring that the precious cargo of Sergeant Wayne and his escorting physician, Dr. Gifford, escaped the ship in time. Like Cdre. Theelson, Johanaston never made it off the Amorhe. Lieutenants Simonds and Shamus did make it into escaping discharge pods. While Simonds did not survive the battle (his pod was destroyed in the fight), Shamus did. She was able to make it back to link up with JT and Aurelle before the end of the war. So, in a way, Johanaston's team, or at least his influence, was able to make it full circle, just with only one of the team's three original members.

JT and Aurelle were well on their way before they could learn any of the fate of the Amorhe. They had their hopes and suspicions from what they saw as the escape craft was departing. But neither one would imagine that the Amorhe was doomed. After a few hours into the day-long, almost 12 million light year flight, they decided to rotate to get some rest. There was no external communication while traveling in an X7R at ES-neo and faster speeds. So, without anyone besides each other to talk to, they figured they might as well get some sleep. JT offered to take first watch. Aurelle reluctantly accepted.

He promised to wake her in several hours or if anything changed. Especially so if it was regarding their mission to get to Europa. JT was personally excited about seeing his home nation of Angola again. It had been many years since he had seen his home or his mother and any of his few remaining extended family members. It had been a long time since JT had experienced anything remotely close to his home or family. He was looking forward immensely to the prospect.

Chapter 24
Backroom Meeting

Majak looked around. He had been waiting at the Second Chance Inn for two days and that was about the amount of time that Fico had said he would need to remain on the down low before Fico's handler would meet him. He had been in the same room for most of the 48 hours. Except for an occasional break for some food and to stretch his legs, this was the world he had known. He did have some connection with the outside world via his communicator and Fico. And there was a monitor and computer station in the room. So, Majak was able to watch news and hear reports from both local and international agencies. The Suclesahe's destruction had by now made the news but nothing had been reported about him or any of his senior crew members' demises. He figured it was just a matter of time before it became an issue.

Then he got the call. Fico rung Majak's earpiece mid-morning on his third day in the room at the Second Chance.

"Good day my friend. That thing and the meeting we talked about… it is about ready. Can you be down in the hotel lobby in a half an hour?" asked Fico.

"Of course," replied Majak. "I can be there in a few minutes if you like."

"No that is not necessary. Just 30 minutes. I will make the introduction off site. Use the code words if anything is amiss." Fico hung up. Majak remembered that Fico had told him previously to refer to the weather in the city as turning sour if anything was not right. He then gathered himself up and grew slightly excited about the introduction. Well, after 48 hours of staring at the same walls and furniture, nearly any change of pace would have been moderately exciting for him. As he had 30 minutes, he decided to use the restroom and ready himself a bit.

At 27 minutes past Fico's call, Majak headed downstairs to the lobby. He arrived just as Fico was getting there. The two of them were men of fairly precise timing and so it was not surprising they would arrive exactly when it was specified. Majak's propensity was based upon his military life style and naval background. Fico's was simply because he had learned as a spy to be specific and precise. It usually meant things would go better than when practicing with imprecision.

"Good day," said Fico to lead off the conversation.

"Hello and top of the morning to you," replied Majak. "The weather looks good."

"Excellent. And how is your family?" Fico asked. What a strange question since Fico knew Majak's family was dead. Majak shot him a funny look. Fico immediately shot Majak a look back which seemed to say: *hush.*

"Fine. All fine," Majak said as if it was partly a question instead of a response. The two men left through the lobby in a very inconspicuous manner. Fortunately, there was no attendant at the desk and the lobby was completely empty.

"We are going to walk. It is only a few blocks away from here," said Fico once they were outside.

"Ok," Majak responded. He continued to look over at Fico as if something was amiss.

"I'll explain in time," said Fico. "Well ok, I'll explain it now."

"I had to make sure you were of sane cognizance and had not been tainted or influenced by any mind-altering substances. You see I expected the real and uninfluenced Majak to give me a suspicious look when I asked him about his family. In that regard, you passed my little test with flying colors," said Fico in explanation for the commentary about family.

"I see," said Majak. "Not bad."

"I try. And now we will meet the boss-man. His name is Fin. It is really Finaldo, but he goes by Fin." Fico then explained their next actions. He recounted how they would go a few blocks and duck into a false front restaurant that was really a safe house and make-shift meeting room. Majak was ready to make this happen so he readily agreed to everything Fico explained.

When they got to the restaurant entrance there was a password buzz in to the main door.

"Gildersharks," stated Fico into the voice communication device beside the door.

"Pendleton," came the reply through the device.

"Smidgeon," Fico responded. Click. The door unlocked. Fico held it open and ushered Majak through the entryway. They went into the back and were padded down for weapons by an attendant. Majak had left his phaser in his hotel room as he predicted Fico would cover their security and he did not want to alert or raise any suspicions. After passing the pat down, they went down a flight of stairs into a basement entryway/foyer. There was a small table set with glasses and napkins at the middle of the room.

"Ah, here we are," announced Fico. "This is one of the meeting places of our little resistance group on planet 104."

"Resistance?" asked Majak.

"Well, you know what I mean, resistance against the Gnorac incursion at least." Fico was promptly interrupted by a knock at the door leading down to the basement area.

"That must be Fin and company now," he said. And it was. Finaldo came downstairs leading two henchmen behind him.

"Fico, my man. So good to see you again!" announced Fin.

"And you likewise," responded Fico. "What has it been a month or more?"

"More like two I think," said Fin. "But who is counting?" And the two men laughed.

"Allow me to introduce my associate and friend, Mr. Majak," started Fico.

"You know we are in a safe space," said Fin. "Gentlemen, I can smell a Gnorac officer a mile away. But no offense intended." Fin directed his latter comment to Majak who did not seem to mind. Majak gave the two men a bit of a look but not one that would cause any alarm or concern.

"It's ok, he is right. We are in a safe space," added Fico.

"Well, in that case, yes I was once a Gnorac fleet officer but that is no more for me," said Majak.

"A rather high ranking one I would guess," said Fin. Majak paused, looked at Fico, who gave him a nod as if to say, *it is ok he is a friend.*

"I commanded the Suclesahe," said Majak matter-of-factly. There was a pause.

"Ehm, wow. Not exactly the level of officer I would have expected," said Fin. "But we are happy to have you... no, we are *grateful* to have you on our side." The group settled in.

"We are here to discuss the facts and circumstances surrounding what you have to offer us, but first if you don't mind I would like to know why a career officer and commadore or admiral, I presume, would wish to throw that service by the wayside," commented Fin.

"A fair question, let me explain..." and with that Majak commenced his tale and explained how his family was gone and it would have been expected that he die by suicide taking all blame for the loss of the Suclesahe. The explanation took more than a few minutes but Fin was happy to oblige and Fico was happy to hear the tale again. When it seemed that Fin was satisfied with the reasoning and Majak's background, Majak finished the story and sat back.

"My next question for you is one a bit simpler: what can I provide you with?" Fin asked. "Can I see to any immediate needs? Are you hungry or thirsty; do you have enough credits? Are your accommodations satisfactory?" he asked all in one breath.

"Yes, and I am fine on all accounts. The new room is fine. I have enough credits. Maybe a touch of something to drink for us all and we can toast to this new alliance," Majak responded.

"That sounds good to me," Fico added. Fin waved his hand towards one of the henchmen and said, "three drinks. Make them good. Something regional and strong." The man immediately disappeared upstairs and came back a few minutes later with three brandies.

The three men settled back and toasted one another and their partnership. The conversation switched from verifying Majak's intentions and credentials to that of discussing what he could provide for the Federation. Majak previously had classified access to reports which outlined what ships were being fitted with the neutrino cannon. He also knew in a general sense how the weapon worked. Although he was not a technical expert and he did not recall all the ships, he knew that all attack cruisers and reconnaissance cruisers were being fitted with it. He knew certain frigates and destroyers that had been selected. He knew which fleets were considered priority fills for the weapon. He was willing to share all of this information without any strings attached. Well, without many strings at least. Majak had a few small conditions which included: one) to protect his safety and get him behind front lines as soon as possible and, two) to use the information to bring the war to a swift close… as much as was within their power so to do. Fin and Fico agreed to the simple requests. Though they made it clear that their power to affect the war bringing it to a swift close was severely limited. Majak understood.

What Fin and Fico could not definitively agree to was any sort of a timeline for how long it would take to make these things happen. They also had no idea how long Majak was going to need to stay at his current location. They both presumed that he would be moved and Fin's higher ups in the organization were going to take over the exchange of information at some point. But they did not have a guess as to the timeline that this would encompass. Fico thought that it might be a week while Fin thought it could be sooner than that. Fin took good mental notes on everything that Majak had to report for fleet information. He did so especially when it came to what confederate ships and priority for ships or fleets would have been equipped with the neutrino cannon. Those would be hot pieces of intelligence for his organizational decision makers.

So, the first part of the meeting between Fin and Majak was a success. They seemed to trust one another and Majak was able to provide enough information to keep Fin very interested in his continued help. They agreed to meet again in another two days. Fin would keep Fico and Majak informed if anything changed or if Majak would be needing to move locations.

"Thank you for the audience," said Majak. "It feels good to be making a positive difference in the outcome of things despite losing my old ties."

"And we feel the same way as you it seems," responded Fin. "Thank you for providing all that you have. I am sure there will be much more in the time to come. Meanwhile, I will pass on everything you have given me and we will meet again in a few days. Let me know through Fico if you need anything in the meantime."

"I will, and I look forward to it," said Majak.

"I will see you out if I may," Fico said to Fin and the two men stood up to leave. Majak stood up and lifted his glass for one final swig of brandy from it. He then held it up in the air as if to toast the two departing men.

"Cheers," he said.

"To the Federation," responded Fin. And Fico responded likewise. The henchmen led the way back upstairs and Fico accompanied Fin up the stairs and the two of them conversed for a few moments before Fico came back downstairs and rejoined Majak.

"Now we are going to be in a waiting game again," said Fico. "In the meantime, what would you like to eat? I know of a few places all within walking distance and a couple are quite good."

"Anything without too much spice would be fine for me," said Majak. "I think I am adjusting to this planet 104 cuisine, but not so well. It is quite tangy and I find one must take it in moderation or that person ends up spending some time in the latrine." At this statement Fico laughed audibly.

"Don't worry my friend, I know just the place that won't cause that sort of... uhm, issue." Fico was sure that he did know a good local tavern that would not spice up the fare too much and it was only about five blocks from their current location. "Come along and we'll be there in less than fifteen minutes." And so the two of them left the safe house and took to the streets in the small town and headed to a local tavern where Majak did find some food to suit his palate... and his intestines.

Chapter 25
Travelling

With Fae and Pappa Fae's help, the mencas succeeded in finding a spirit ship which could get them all the way to Angola. Once they reached the planet after three days' travel, they would be on their own to figure out how to find transportation to its more remote locations. Specifically, they would be looking for transportation from the main terminal of Angola City to the lesser known places in the west end of Arlgon. That was the last known location of the Thanameresons' and Lastalles' ancestors Barnab and Gailena. The mencas, especially Lady Shera were eager to learn what they could from the land of Flarhom but also to get on their way to Angola as quickly as possible.

Their stay was not long for the next spirit ship headed to Angola was leaving in two days. It was decided by the Thanameresons that Fae would not be joining in the great voyage. After all, he was a very juvenile spirit and had only recently completed his studies. Pappa Fae, however, decided with familial consent that he could and would join the mencas on their voyage. His age and wisdom could lend itself to help in the quest. Moreover, his spirit status as an heir of Barnab and an actively practicing spirit could only lend credibility to the group's search.

The ensuing 48 hours were a whirlwind for the mencas. Lady Shera, Farhale, Valcor, Jeanaviere and Pappa Fae prepared for the trip quickly. It would be of an unknown duration so they tried to think of any and all contingencies. After consulting with other spirits in Flarhom Woods, the mencas became satisfied that they needed to make the trip to Angola. Several neighbors of the Thanameresons all agreed that the ancestor, Barnab had gone to Angola and some knew of his secret relationship with Gailena. After meeting with enough spirits to confirm the stories they had heard from Pappa Fae and

Quildevar, the group secured their passage aboard the outbound spirit ship, *Dressel*, and said their thanks and goodbyes. The mencas were sad to leave their steeds behind, but they knew they would see them again at some point in the future. And, they were all in good hands with the Thanameresons.

The Dressel was a converted freighter which had adequate but not luxurious accommodations for passengers. The group met the crew and captain the day before the vessel set off for the voyage. There were approximately a hundred other souls on board the space liner. It was carrying cargo as well in some of the holds which had not been converted for passengers or crew. The journey was not terribly long considering the vast distance involved. The Jupiterian moon ordinarily would have been inaccessible in a single voyage if not for the ES-neo drive capability. As it was, the three-day trip passed uneventfully and the mencas and Pappa Fae were thankful for that.

The landing and docking procedures in Angola took a little while but this was to ensure passenger and cargo safety and to ensure no contraband or war-related items had been smuggled aboard the ship. As it was, nothing suspicious was noted and the customs and security agents allowed all to pass without too much of a shakedown. Pappa Fae in particular, was impressed by the efficiency of the agencies involved in the voyage and he made note of the vessel's crew and captain for their hospitality over the 72 hours or so he and the mencas inhabited the ship.

When it came time to get from the port of Angola City to Anglen on the west end of Arlgon, the group was able to secure passage via ground transportation. Specifically, they used monorail trains and hover-vans for hire to get to their end destination, the seediest part of Anglen. Pappa Fae had a contact who was able to show the group around the city and knew of a few places they could stay. He knew all the better places to eat or take care of personal demand items and needs. They arrived mid-week in the late afternoon and made it to Anglen, to Pappa Fae's friend's place, by evening. The old friend of Pappa Fae had been a school mate of the elderly spirit so he too was advanced in years. However, spirit ages are difficult to judge. Their forms lend themselves well to appearing decades younger than they actually are. Pappa Fae's friend was no exception. He went by the name of Gilder.

Gilder provided the group with sustenance that evening and brought them to an inn they could stay at for a fairly inconsequential sum; and, they could stay as long as they liked.

The group decided to venture out the next day. They also decided to split up to do their searching. The knights decided Valcor would go with Lady Shera. Farhale would escort Pappa Fae and Jeanaviere. Ordinarily Jeanaviere would have accompanied her leader. But Lady Shera thought her services would not be needed directly and that she could provide better support for Pappa Fae and lend herself as good company to the other knight. Farhale and Valcor were fine with the arrangements as such. So, on the second day after their arrival, early in the morning the two groups split up. They began scouring the city's west end for signs of the promised heir of Barnab and Gailena. The task was not an easy one considering the number of generations which had passed since the spirits had emigrated to the Jupiterian moon.

The first signs of Barnab's passing came to Pappa Fae when his group decided to visit the city's hall of records. This library-like facility had all the information which was to be gained from the surrounding area. Pappa Fae was methodical in his ways and this mission was no different for him. He viewed it like any other quest for information. He first sent Farhale to ask the record keepers about anyone by the name Barnab or Thanamereson. The records revealed some families by that name had inhabited the furthest reaches of neighborhoods on the very west end of the city. A further search of those families' descendants revealed that there was a tie-in to a family called Wayne. While this seemed arbitrary, Pappa Fae made note of it when Farhale reported it to him. Meanwhile, Jeanaviere was working on a separate task: to find out where the footprint of the Thanameresons would lead. Where did they inhabit and where did their descendants move to?

Jeanaviere was able to uncover that the Waynes were mostly outlanders who had intermixed and married with the Thanameresons not long after the later's arrival in Anglen. Some had stayed in Arlgon, but most had moved to Anglen. This fact made it easier to follow the trail of the settlers. She found there were four main housing areas they had occupied. Each of these was within a few kilometers of the hall of records and therefore would be easy for the group to check out.

Meanwile, Lady Shera and Valcor were not having as much luck. They had run into a road block while tasked with scouting the local leadership: the equivalent of the town's mayor's office. They were met with a skeptical eye from the security police of the public works building and although they were allowed in to look around, no one would readily talk to them. Perhaps it was because they were menca and perhaps it was because Valcor looked rather menacing in his demeanor. Whatever the cause, Lady Shera found it difficult to get any information out of anyone at the city hall. Finally, she elected to give up and check in with the others at the hall of records.

The two groups met in-between city hall and the hall of records at a park which was dedicated to all veterans of all great wars. It was a serene setting and one which worked perfectly for them. Pappa Fae led the discussion by relating what they had found about the Thanameresons. Jeanaviere and Farhale both voiced their opinion that the entire group should scout out the Arlgen corners where the known Thanamereson houses were. For all they knew, a descendant might still live in one of them and be able to direct them more pointedly. After a brief retelling of their difficulties at city hall, Lady Shera and Valcor decidedly concurred with the others and offered that they could stick together but should only approach each house with one or two of the group at a time. They did not want to overwhelm or alarm residents.

So they set off. As it was only a few kilometers to the first house, they walked. The mencas were not so used to walking longer distances without their mounts but they were in excellent shape, all of them, so it was no problem. Upon reaching the first house Lady Shera said it should be her and Pappa Fae to approach the door initially. The others accordingly held back and stayed out of sight. The two tried to look as unassuming as possible and rang the digital bell.

"Hello, you must be here about the sewer problem we've been having," said the elderly gentleman who answered the door. "It has been a real stinker, no pun intended."

"So sorry, we are actually not here for any such purpose," stated Lady Shera. "We are here on a quest to find the heirs of Barnab Thanamereson or Gailena Lastalle."

"Well shiver me down and blow me over," came the gentleman's response. "I haven't heard those names in quite a while. But you are in the right place to unearth their past." Pappa Fae and Lady Shera looked at one another questioningly. "I am Pete. Pete Snodgrass. At your service," said the aged man.

"We are Lady Shera and Pappa Faeru of Spriuthean," responded Lady Shera. "We seek out the heirs of Mr. Barnab Thanamereson and Ms. Gailena Lastalle. You see we believe their descendants hold the key to saving our races and ending the great war now underway."

"You don't say? Are you serious?" was old Mr. Pete's only reply.

"Well yes, of course," said Pappa Fae who had chosen a human like form to represent himself. He wanted to be more fitting and accommodating to the likes of the humans and Cybrinthians in Angola. "We have no reason to make a tale like this up. And, we have traveled a very long way from Spiruthean to be here."

"Spiruthean eh? Isn't that millions of light years away?" asked Pete.

"Yes, but with ES-neo at our disposal we made it in only days," responded Lady Shera. The three looked at one another for a moment before Pete decided to invite them in so he could share what he knew about the heirs of the Thanameresons and Lastalles. Before long he had learned that there were more to Lady Shera's and Pappa Fae's group and, being a good host and kind soul, he invited them all inside his home. As soon as all the mencas and Pappa Fae were comfortably seated and had explained the situation for Mr. Snodgrass, Pete told them they were very much in luck. He believed that he and his own family were descendants of the great spirit emigrees the Thanameresons and Lastalles. He did not possess his family tree in written form but he had oral histories which related back to Barnab and Gailena. He was ready to share with these new-found friends and guests.

"My family has known about the spirit ancestors in our line for generations," he said. "Of course, it wasn't talked openly about and still isn't much. But we know they came over a hundred and fifty years or so ago and settled here in this area." Pete shot each of them a look as if he had just declared a statement of fact that was indisputable.

"Well, what I would like to know," said Lady Shera as Pappa Fae began to open his mouth as well but was cut off by the menca leader, "is how can we find the youngest descendants and determine if they exhibit spirit traits and powers?" It was a straight forward question but one that needed to be asked.

"No one to my knowledge has ever exhibited spirit like traits and attributes," said Pete. "There could be outliers of course for possibilities that are unknown or talked about. But I personally have not ever experienced any telepathic, shape shifting or extra-terrestrial supernatural like experiences."

He went on, "There was once; however, a boy born to the Wayne family not far from here in this corner of Angola. They moved from Arlgen but the family underwent tragedy. The boy's parents were killed in the hostage incident that incited the war and then his adopted uncle died. Last I knew he went off to join the federal service. I only mention it because he was incredibly gifted as a baby and young boy. Learned things quickly and spoke full sentences at like age one or something ridiculous. I don't know about him having any special powers or spirit related abilities but I do know he was very gifted. Like, beyond any normal gifted kid."

The group let this information sink in. They had no idea at that very moment that JT and his escort, Dr Gifford, were headed to Angola after their space disaster aboard the Amorhe. Had they known the details of JTs life, they might just have been confident that this could indeed be the miracle descendent whom they sought. As it was, they were all intrigued, especially Lady Shera and Pappa Fae.

The group was collectively grateful to Mr. Pete for his graciousness, hospitality, and willingness to share what he knew of his family history. He estimated that although he could not remember the boy's name: (James, Jay, Johnathan, Jerry, maybe,) he did know that the youngster was a distant cousin once or twice removed from Pete. As far as Pete thought, the boy's widowed and adoptive mother was still alive. He was happy to direct the group to her if they wanted. They certainly did.

Sarah Wayne was not only still alive but had been living in the same condominium in which JT had grown up for more than two decades. She could not bear to leave after Gus died; and, the place was still a bit of a memorial to Gus and JT: both them and their accomplishments. The mencas and Pappa Fae were able to walk relatively quickly to Sarah's place; it being only a kilometer or so away from old Pete's. They showed up unannounced but were still welcomed by Mrs. Wayne with open arms. Anyone who had traveled as far as they had for her son and for a quest as noble as they said… for saving a race and ending a war… in her book, deserved some hospitality.

As soon as they had settled in, they began to recount their reasons for visiting. Sarah was very interested but held her tongue for she knew JT would not like to have his personal business broadcast to strangers, especially ones coming from across the universe. "I would like to hear more," she said. "But I don't want to pry or intrude too much… I want to know why is your race dying?"

"We are succumbing to a sickness transmitted by radiation we believe is spread by a new vast and horrible weapon being used by the Confederation," said Lady Shera. "It is spreading to mencas where and whenever they are in any proximity to a battle in which this super weapon is employed." Sarah let this sink in. She looked skyward and reflected.

"But how can I or my boy help and how can we play some part in ending this conflict? He is already deployed as you know. He is a Federal Marine and served at Quai-14. I pray he survived," Sarah said, becoming teary-eyed.

"Oh, if he is who we believe he is, then he survived," said Lady Shera. "We just need to locate him and perform some tests and hopefully, learn from his DNA and blood how we can survive and prevent this sickness from spreading. We pray he or one of your relations may be the key to preventing a genocide and putting an end to this war."

"Wow, that is pretty heavy stuff," said Sarah matter of factly. "But I don't know where exactly he is. I haven't heard from him in weeks. I just know his ship was destroyed at Quai-14." Tears welled up more so in her eyes. "I am scared he didn't make it."

Just then, as if by some unforeseen mystical force, a hail came through on Sarah's hologram telemonitor. It was a priority traffic message from the Angola space port. It was a communication for Sarah's eyes only. Top Secret. "Excuse me," she said.

It was a written message from JT and Aurelle. They had just landed and were coming to visit. Immediately.

And like that, fortunes were enmeshed and due to collide for whatever reason. The mencas, Pappa Fae, Sarah, and JT and Aurelle would undoubtedly be meeting. What they could all learn from one another, remained to be unveiled.

Chapter 26
Reunion

JT and Aurelle made little note of the succinctness of their journey. St. Demetrius' Forward Hospital was far from Arlgon but the Amorhe was a bit closer when the signal was given for them to depart. It had been in the vicinity of the Cigar galaxy. This meant their voyage lasted a little more than a day. When they slowed from ES-neo to standard approach vectors they were able to communicate with Angola City flight operations and send priority messages to selected individuals. Despite not having his normal military hardware for succinct or secret communication protocols, JT relayed to flight control that he needed a priority message sent. That message would be to his mother, Sarah Wayne, in Arlgon's suburb of Anglen. His rank and Dr. Gifford's presence made the decision to allow such a message to be sent with priority easy. It was a simple request to let her know he was coming and he would be in touch as soon as they landed: for her to keep her communicator handy.

Aurelle agreed with the decision to contact JT's mother. After all, who else did they (he) know that well in Arlgon? The message was transmitted and received without any fanfare. Sarah was busy hosting the mencas and Pappa Fae when it came through. She answered and tried to withhold her excitement; her baby boy was alive! This was the news she had prayed and hoped for. As she received the text priority message she could not hold back. Tears began to flow and she excused herself but the guests understood completely. Lady Shera had children of her own and relayed to Sarah that there is no love like that of a mother for her progeny. Although Sarah was just an adoptive mother, she had been JT's mother since he was an infant. That little darling boy to whom she might as well have given birth would always be dearest to her.

The conversation was short and to the point and the information needing to be relayed to Sarah was conveyed directly. Their arrival time and place and how long JT and Aurelle imagined it would take to reach her residence. They estimated it would be approximately five hours from when they sent the message. It was a little after dinner hours for Sarah and so they would be on her doorstep around or before midnight. She would not be sleeping a wink before their arrival and likely would not sleep a bit following the homecoming that night. She fondly remembered the last time she had seen JT. It had been nearly three years. Back then he was a young staff sergeant. He had overseen a squad then. But now he was in charge of his own platoon.

He had (past tense) had his own platoon… until they were all killed by the Confederation's neutrino cannon during the Quai-14 disaster aboard the Vissad. Ah those poor lost souls whom JT could do nothing about. But maybe he could avenge their deaths. Make them to not have died in vain. That was his mission now. He and Aurelle had been on this mission since they first met only those few short weeks ago. But intense conflict and intense situations bring people together for causes that otherwise might not have been the case. JT and Aurelle shared a cause now and they were going to see it through to the end no matter what it took.

"So I'll see you later this evening. I can't wait. I love you," was Sarah's recorded voice message response. She sent it right away as soon as she received the communication from JT. She had to encode her reply since these messages were secret traffic marked for priority authentication only. Sarah had to validate through a retinal scan device to even read her message from JT. She was the only one who could open or read it.

JT and Aurelle received the response only ten minutes after they had sent their initial message and this was even before their X7R had begun docking procedures. JT listened to his mother's voice and was briefly hit by a small wave of emotion. It had been many months since he had read anything from her much less heard her voice. Space mail across great distances can take time, and much like the old Pony Express of the American west, it was subject to issues with elements and factors outside of the delivery mechanism's control. Especially during wartime. So, JT had a brief second of pause when he heard his mother's voice and it made him happy. Aurelle let him have the moment uninterrupted.

"We should be able to come in with a good view of Europa and Angola," said JT finally. He had made this trip a few times before when he used to take personal leave every few years and come home to Angola. The X7R had one small space viewing portal. It was crowded in the craft but there was still a live view and it was something to behold. The Jupiterian moon was gorgeous in the light of earth's old solar system. The craft slowed to approach speed and then began subsequent afterburn thrust to align itself with the docking port. The X7R was not large but could fit maybe four people and currently it was shuttling only JT and Aurelle. They each could see out the portal as it came to the dock.

"We should contact your mom again once we are on solid ground," said Aurelle. "She may want to come meet us somewhere instead of at her home, don't you think?"

"I am not so sure. She doesn't like to get out much. Never has. Plus, I have a strange feeling she may be going through something. I do not know why but I think she is distracted. Maybe it was how she said she loved me or the succinctness of her message. I dunno. I just feel like something is going on and therefore we should go to her." JT's intuition had kicked in again.

"Ok, you know her better than me," came Aurelle's response. The two buckled in for the final approach after having strapped down some loose items and punching a few buttons on the holoscreen. This ensured the autopilot had all the parameters of the approach correct. The thrusters fired and aligned the ship into its proper docking angle and slowed it to a near crawl as it got to within ten meters of the port platform. Then it linked up with the docking arm that attached and brought it to the landing strip pad. There were a few bumps and jolts but nothing startling. Within five minutes they had landed and were ready to open the hatch. The port landing area was sealed by a force field and maintained artificial gravity for traveler and station worker ease. JT and Aurelle unstrapped, gathered what few things they had with them and stepped out onto the platform.

The space port was in orbit around Europa approximately 200km above the moon. JT and Aurelle would take another shuttle to the moon's surface into Angola. Angola City had a very bustling surface transportation hub. From there it would only be an hour or so to get to JT's mother's apartment. The shuttle from the orbiting space port left every 15 minutes. JT and Aurelle made their way through the port and customs and declarations facilities with relative ease. One thing the admirals had done for them was front load all security clearance protocols so they could move more freely about the universe. This was one of those times that action came in extremely handy.

When JT and Aurelle made their way through the transportation port and boarded a taxi shuttle for Anglen JT had a sobering thought. He had not seen his mother in three years; he had only known Aurelle a few weeks and he did not know what to say about the status of his relationship to Aurelle. Dire circumstances had brought them together. They clearly had a connection. There was no doubt about the attraction between them. But were they romantic? Was this too early and too complex a situation to think about that? JT decided it was and he should stop discerning about it. But he could not help but think to the last time he had brought a girl home to meet his mom. In short: he hadn't. At least not since joining the military. So now, this would, in a way, be a first of sorts.

"I haven't seen my mom in three years," he said to Aurelle almost as if it was an offhand thought.

"I'm sure she is a lovely person," said Aurelle. "After all, she raised you."

"She is technically my aunt, you maybe should know," JT continued, "My birth parents died when I was a baby. So she and my Uncle Gus adopted me and they are the only parents I have ever known. I have always called her, mom."

"I see. I am sorry that you lost your parents. Say no more. And I won't ask any questions unless you want me to know more."

"That's ok. As I said, I was a baby so Sarah and Gus were the only parents I ever knew. My dad, or uncle technically, Gus, died when I was 19 and then I joined the service and Sarah has been alone ever since. I try to visit her when I can. But as you know, the war often has other plans."

"So if it has been three years since you've seen her, when did you last talk to her?" Aurelle questioned.

"Maybe four or five months ago. We have sent voice messages and video recordings and texts but I haven't had a live conversation with her in a while." JT wished he could have kept up with his mother more but duty was duty and he was a good Marine.

"Have you regretted anything that you have done or not done to stay in touch?" Aurelle asked JT thoughtfully and delicately.

"No not really. Of course, I would like to talk more often but I just can't the way things have worked out," said JT. He knew that Sarah would have tons of questions. But she would hold back to flood him with them. The shuttle ride to Angola City was not long and then the wait for the next shuttle to Arlgon and subsequently Anglen also was not terribly long. The longest leg of the trip was from Angola City to Arlgon. It took maybe an hour and some change. As it was late, there was not a lot of traffic on the roads and skyways so the shuttle moved fairly freely.

It was nearly 2300 local time when JT and Aurelle boarded the small taxi shuttle from Arlgon and programmed the autodriver to take them to JT's mother's place in Anglen. Anglen was not its own city or town but more of an enclave of Arlgon. As it was, this final leg of the trip took them less than 30 minutes.

Meanwhile, Sarah had been entertaining the mencas and Pappa Fae. She had excused herself to change into something more formal when she received the news that her son was paying them a visit. But other than that short interlude, she had kept them busy by explaining how things here on the Jupiterian moon worked. She had also been feeding them snacks and arranging for them to stay nearby as well. She found it amazing how far they had travelled on a hunch that they would be able to find the chosen one they sought. She did not know if her son was indeed that person. But she imagined that he might be. From the day he was born and then adopted by her and Gus, she knew he was special and destined for greatness.

Then it happened. A knock on the front door. It was more a portal than a door, but in old tradition, everyone referred to the main portal as the front door. Even if it wasn't technically a door. Sarah scanned the central monitor and asked it to show video of the front entryway. It did so and there he was: JT looking regal and handsome, just as she remembered him. Aurelle stood just behind him slightly out of frame. Sarah noticed her right away and asked the camera to pan right and back so she could better look at this Cybrinthian-looking stranger who was escorting her son home.

The camera did as instructed and Sarah decided instantly that she would trust this strange woman if her son did.

"Hello son," said Sarah to the monitor. "I can't believe it's really you. Come in, please right away!"

"Hi mom," JT managed in return. "I have missed you. You want to let us in?"

"Oh, yes. Geeze, I'm sorry." Sarah had forgotten to unlock the security system and as they spoke, JT and Aurelle remained locked outside. She looked into her screen for it to scan her eye for the retinal protocol password unlock code and the door unlocked immediately. There was an audible thud as the tumblers moved and the mechanism unlatched itself. JT smiled at Aurelle and remarked under his breath, "here we go."

Aurelle liked meeting people's parents. As a former doctrette and now a doctor she had enjoyed being able to make connections to people and their traits. She was always amused to see from where someone got their characteristics. She knew that Sarah was truly JT's aunt, but she did not recall if JT had informed her if she was his blood aunt or an aunt by marriage. Sarah was JT's aunt by marriage to Gus, but still she could have passed for a distant blood relation. JT and his aunt Sarah both shared a strong jaw line and light brown hair. He did in actuality resemble his Uncle Gus enough to have been his offspring. Sarah, not quite as much. But still it was clear from the look in her eyes, Sarah loved JT dearly.

As soon as the door opened, she stepped outside into the dwelling's foyer and threw her arms around her adopted son planting a gigantic hug around him. JT returned the gesture and kissed her cheeks, one big peck on each side.

"Oh my boy I've missed you so much," Sarah said. "And now introduce me to this young lady friend of yours…"

"Mom, this is Aurelle Gifford,… Doctor Gifford that is," said JT. "She is in charge of… well… she's in charge of my well-being."

"It is a pleasure to meet you Doctor Gifford," said Sarah as she leaned in to offer Aurelle a friendly mom-type hug. "Thank you for looking after my not-so-little guy here." With this statement she looked back over her shoulder and up towards JT. The women shared a moment for this genuine embrace.

"It is my honor and privilege ma'am," said Aurelle. "Please call me Aurelle."

"And I am Sarah… or 'mom' if you like," Sarah said with a smile. "None of this 'ma'am' junk."

She continued, "You Marine types are all the same with your fancy speak."

"Well, I am actually not on active duty," said Aurelle. "I am a civilian general service medical staff doctor who happens to work for the Federated Navy."

"Whatever you say Doc!" said Sarah. "You work for the Navy so you are part of our defense against the Confederation and are responsible for protecting and healing our service members so I think of you like I think of JT here. You're both on the same team in my book."

"That's true and we certainly are on the same team," replied Aurelle as the embrace ended. "We are keeping the Federation's best guarded secret safe." She eyed JT knowingly. He returned the look.

"Please come inside," Sarah gestured them in from the port-way. "We have some guests visiting who just arrived earlier today and I think you will find it more than just a coincidence that they came here on the date you decided to arrive."

The three of them came inside and Sarah introduced the mencas to JT and Aurelle. Sirs Farhale and Valcor rose to their feet in greeting. Lady Shera and Jeanaviere did likewise. Pappa Fae struggled for a moment but eventually rose to his feet as well.

"Please excuse these brittle bones," Pappa Fae said. "The parts don't work as well as they used to," he chuckled.

"This is Lady Shera and her knights and traveling companions, Pappa Fae of Spiruthean, Sir Valcor, Sir Farhale, and Lady

247

Jeanaviere," Sarah introduced the guests in her quaint living room which was quickly filling up with people. "They have traveled from the distant spirit planet to find you my boy. This is JT and Doctor Aurelle Gifford recently arrived from…"

"From a distant ways…" JT cut her off realizing it would not be smart to talk about the Federation's whereabouts in an unknown security environment. They had come from the Amorhe's X7R escape craft after it was destroyed on the screen line outside the Quai-14 battlespace near the Cigar Galaxy. But that was not important now so JT just said, "We came from the Angolan space port while I am on leave for a bit and perhaps a little longer depending on how things with the big fight go."

"We are friends to you and we are not here on any ill-will or sinister mission," said Lady Shera. "We hope to work together and to find out if it is you who can save our race."

"What do you mean?" asked JT.

"Well, we, the mencas are dying and we know that there is a human who has survived the radiation blast of the neutrino cannon. We believe he may be you and that you hold the key to salvaging the health of our race and keeping us alive," said Lady Shera.

"Well I don't know about all that saving the health of a race and such," said JT, "but I am happy to help in whatever way I can."

"What you have heard is true," said Aurelle. "That Sergeant Wayne here has survived a deadly neutrino blast and has for the most part, recovered fully in remarkably quick time." This was correct and the mencas let it sink in that perhaps they had found the one they were looking for.

Farhale spoke up now, "Will you allow us to access the medical records and treatments you have undergone?" He looked longingly at JT, as if the fate of all menca-kind depended upon his answer.

"I am not so sure the answer to that question is up to him or me for that matter," said Aurelle. "You see, the fleet has got to know and bless off before we share anything."

"Right of course," replied Farhale. "A good soldier always knows when he must inform his chain of command."

"And I have to agree with Aurelle," JT added, "the Fleet has got to be ok with sharing medical knowledge and information gained from my recovery.”

“So how do we contact them for their permission?” asked Lady Shera.

“Quite simply, we message Admiral Vander and await his response,” said Aurelle. “He will know what to do and understand the imperative nature of the request.” Aurelle in truth did not have the information the mencas sought anyway. It was stored away in fleet cloud drives. She could access it, but not without permission and clearance from the highers up. Admiral Vander was the logical higher up Aurelle thought of as he was the highest-ranking officer aboard the Amorhe. He would most likely have transferred his flag and command to another capital vessel if the Amorhe was actually destroyed. This was indeed the case for the admiral as the Amorhe was forced into oblivion by the massive waves of small attack ships from the Confederation.

“How soon can we send that message?” asked Farhale. “The sooner the better I should think.” The group was able to send priority traffic at will, but a message across the space and time they needed, with the urgency they needed, would only be able to be sent from a local government mail facility.

“We would need a federal mail synch system,” said JT and Aurelle nodded in agreement. “Wasn’t or isn’t there one a few blocks away towards downtown?” JT asked his mother.

“Yes, it’s still there,” was her reply. “We could go tomorrow… or tonight if you wish. I think it still has a 24 hour self-service kiosk.”

“I agree with Farhale,” said Valcor. “The sooner the better.” The mencas all seemed to nod in agreement.

Lady Shera took charge of their collective fervor. “We will wait until the time is right, and we have explained ourselves to our hosts.”

The mencan desire for haste was for good reason. Their race was indeed dying. But more so, they feared the requisite turn-around time for permission to be granted.

“We believe that Sergeant Wayne’s blood holds the key to survival of the neutrino blast and can offer us clues to help our race survive this war. With a little luck, we might be able to help put the war to an end as well," said Lady Shera.

Pappa Fae now chimed in, "I don't see why we can't find the answers we are looking for together. The mencas, spirits, Cybrinthians and humans all share in a common goal: survival. If we help each other, we can defeat that which the Confederation has created to destroy us all." Defeating the Confederation was surely the goal for the humans and Cybrinthians. But it was by default also a goal for mencas because their livelihood and very being depended upon it. Their bodies were unsuited to survive anything near or close to a neutrino cannon attack. They could not even be in the same solar system as one and hope to survive. Therefore, they needed to figure out how to stop the attacks or end the war or be far away from any future conflict spaces.

"We would be forever in your debt if you could receive the permission you require for us to study Sergeant Wayne. You see we think his survival is the key to our entire race's survival. As of this moment, any menca within several thousand AUs of a neutrino blast does not survive. Anyone who is brought near someone who has been exposed to a blast, cannot survive. In short, any proximity to a neutrino blast is a death sentence for a menca. We are hoping to end that morbid situation as quickly as we can." Lady Shera spelled out her case plainly.

The mencas led by Lady Shera explained their exact case to JT, Aurelle and Sarah. Pappa Fae chimed in as necessary to support what the mencas were saying. They all concluded that after a little rest, a few of the group would go down to the government mail facility and send a flash priority traffic message to Adm. Vander. In the meantime, Sarah showed the mencas to their quarters in places she had earlier arranged for across the condominium complex. JT and Aurelle were to stay in Sarah's extra room which happened to be JTs old room from his childhood. It was much changed from when he was a small boy living in it. But there were vestiges from his younger years that gave away this had been his room. Aurelle found it touching that JT's mother would keep those items in homage to her son.

After Sarah had shown the mencas and Pappa Fae to their quarters, three simple rooms in an unoccupied condominium, she returned to her own abode. There she found JT nuzzled up to Aurelle on the couch in the living room. When Sarah came in, JT pulled away from Aurelle and put some physical space between them on the piece of furniture. Sarah smiled knowingly.

"You two aren't fooling anyone," said Sarah matter-of-factly.

"What?" came JT's response.

"I can tell you care for each other. I am not going to interfere nor am I going to ask questions. Just know that it is obvious something is going on there." Sarah was always a to-the-point type of woman.

"Don't sugar coat it mom, tell us what you're really thinking," JT chuckled. "The truth is we have only known one another a few weeks and it has been a bit of a whirlwind at that."

"That doesn't matter, when you know someone is special, you know," came Sarah's reply. The three of them talked for another hour or so before Sarah pointed out they had experienced a long journey and it was long past midnight and they would have a big day tomorrow. They elected to get some sleep before heading the few blocks to the government mail facility to send a message to Adm. Vander or at least one to his staff. Whether he got the message now or four or five hours later would not make or break the cause for the Federation. And so, the three of them after much catching up for JT and his mom and some in-depth discussion for them all, decided to get some shut-eye. Aurelle fell asleep nearly right away. JT and Sarah each took a bit longer to quiet their minds and relax enough to actually get to sleep.

When they woke up it was early morning and they decided to make the trip to send the message to Adm. Vander before doing anything else. They had promised that much to the mencas, Lady Shera and Pappa Fae. The walk to the government mail building was not long, just a few minutes. They got there in no time and it was not crowded. Sarah suggested she affix her name to the message in case it was intercepted. In that capacity, nothing would incriminate JT or be traceable to him. They would both compose it but she would be the one to sign off on it. So they did write a short note stating both parties were safe and at their planned destination. They asked if the subject's medical records and treatment history could be unsealed so they could be learned and studied from by a Federation ally. Aurelle knew this was well above her pay grade to make this decision so she put in a plug for the mencas. She stated that they were dying at a much greater rate than humans or any distant contact victim from the neutrino cannon. She said that their race was becoming extinct as a result of the N-cannon and they thought the subject could aid in their survival. It was a long shot the admiral would even receive the message much less approve of it and reply.

After the excursion to the mail facility, Sarah suggested they meet up with the mencas and talk about what they knew. So they did. Lady Shera was sure that JTs blood had some form of rare antibody that was resistant to neutrino radiation and if it could be unlocked and replicated, her race would stand a chance. Farhale and Valcor were not as certain but nevertheless they were hopeful. Jeanaviere was content to agree with her lady. Pappa Fae held his opinions to himself. What they all did agree on was that they appeared to be on the right trail by chasing the whereabouts of the descendants of Barnab Thanamereson and Gailena Lastalle.

The group decided that if they were to succeed and Aurelle and JT got permission to receive and pass along his medical files, they would probably need to seek out a medical center. Only there, would they be able to use the machines and devices required to diagnose and assess JT's seeming gift. There was a small center in Anglen, but the more reasonable and likely candidate was the regional center in Angola City. It had thousands of patients and as many staff.

The group would anxiously await the answer from Admiral Vander. JT secretly feared Adm. Vander might not have survived the attack on the Amorhe. If he didn't, surely there would be protocols in place for someone else in the chain of command to step in JT knew. Aurelle had the same thoughts, -that it was possible their message might not reach the admiral. Time might not have been on their side. But only time would tell.

Chapter 27
Another Traveler

Majak was satiated with the cuisine that Fico had chosen. It didn't startle his intestines too much and was actually quite tasty. After the two men had finished their meal and talked about pleasantries of planet 104, Majak posed the pointed question, "How long do you think I'm going to be here until I get to whatever is next?"

"Well that is hard to say," said Fico. "It is really up to the boss and his boss."

"Understood. I just have the feeling that if I don't keep moving, someone or some… thing is going to catch up to me. You know, that sinking feeling."

"I can relate, my friend. I can relate. That is the life of a spy."

There was a piece of information that Fico wasn't sharing that he felt he might in due time, but not yet. He knew that the Federation had located a survivor from Quai-14 who might prove to be the answer to survival of the neutrino cannon. He didn't have much information, but he did know there was a closely guarded knowledge trail as to this survivor. He had the ability to gain more from Fin, but he felt it was a little early to press the matter.

"I will inquire to see if we can keep you moving and ensure your safety the entire time," said Fico. "I would like to see if we can move you far away from planet 104."

Just then Fico got a priority message on his ear communicator. He checked it as he thought it would inform him of how long he had to sit tight with Majak before moving him. The information on the message said two to three days only and then they would move him to the far-reaching old word of Europa, the Jupiterian moon. It did not explain why or how but it gave him a timeline of 48-72 hours until movement. This was news indeed. Fico relayed the information to

Majak. "Does this mean anything to you?" he asked.

"Well, not really, but I do know that this timeline will take us a day of travel even at ES-neo speeds."

"Leave the transportation to me," said Fico. "I don't know what is afoot but for some reason my spy network wants to get you back to the old Alpha Centauri solar system in the heart of the Federation."

"Geeze."

"Obviously they know something important about you and the knowledge you possess to get you somewhere protected and safe."

"Whatever you say, I am no good to you guys dead," said Majak.

"Exactly," Fico replied. "I will get more information about this in time I am sure, but in the meantime, let's keep an extremely low profile."

"Couldn't agree with you more," came Majak's reply.

Fico, as the acting host, paid the bill for dinner with his communicator and bade them to head back to the room. "I am sorry it won't be sooner, but another waiting game until I get instructions. But at least we have an estimate: two to three days," he said. "We should have more info soon."

They walked back to the inn and Majak began his waiting game. It was only approximately 12 hours later that Fico contacted him, "We have a lead," he said. "There is a shuttle headed to Europa in less than two days and we intend to get you on it. It will be a civilian passenger ship taking known safe routes through the galaxies. We will have a light escort but that is just a matter of standard protocol. It should not attract any attention and should be a safe passage. My highers up are working on securing our contacts on Europa now."

"Excellent. So Europa is the home moon and planet for Angola, which is the capital for the Federation. Is that correct as it is my understanding," continued Majak. "Is it really safe to have a high-ranking Confederation imperial defector so close to your cause's leadership? I mean, were it me, I would be overly cautious."

"We have vetted you already and your story has come back reliable. In short, we believe you truly want to support our cause and have no ill-will."

"Thank you for the vote of confidence," stated Majak. "You are a more trusting conglomeration of races than the Gnoracs."

So plans were made for the cross galactic trip to Europa and Majak kept a very low profile for the next two days. When it came time to board the civilian passenger liner, Majak was a little uncomfortable with its lack of defensive weapons. But at least there was an escort destroyer. And the route to Europa was expected to be totally clear of hostile forces. Most of it was within Federation controlled territory. There would be one stop at the AX planets as the ES-neo drive on the civilian liner was rather antiquated and would need a recharge.

So the morning of the voyage came and Fico met with Majak in his room and explained the procedures. He had fake travel paperwork and IDs for Majak and he regretted that Fin could not be joining them but Fin had other pressing matters in this solar system that would keep him here. Majak understood. They took a hover cab to the port and not to be suspicious did pack personal bags even though they were filled for the most part with little of consequence. They intended to keep up their appearances as routine travelers.

The boarding went smoothly and the flight proved to be uneventful. Of course, at the AX planets there was a customs check, but Majak's fabricated paperwork did the trick and no one was suspicious. Fico's made-up paperwork caused more of a scrutiny for him as they had not had him on the list of pre-screened travelers. Though this little hang-up was easily rectified with a few calls and some well-crafted digital relaying to Fico's higher ups who were impersonating customs supervisors and high-level executives. Fortunately, it worked like a charm. Lesson learned for Fico, process both fabricated documents at the same time and ensure they both could get on the pre-screened lists.

After the customs officials cleared both travelers to pass through AX customs, they were on their way again. It was a two-day trip total and apart from the customs delay, they were back on their transport ship with little time lost.

The approach to Europa was also without incident, but Fico was prepared for the customs clearing situation again. He had messaged ahead to Fin and his handlers to ensure he was added to the pre-screening list. It was done relatively easily. Majak was ready to move on to help serve this new cause he had embraced and was eager to feel safe once again. He never truly had felt safe while in the service of the Confederation. Fico led the two men through the customs station and upon completion they both moved into the passenger pickup area to wait for the next departing shuttle craft. Europa was a bustle of activity. It was normally in the throes of expansion and building. This time was no exception. Majak thought that this might help him to blend in to the surroundings. Fico told him to rest assured they would both be safe in this new environment.

Majak was eager to learn who or what was next in store for him. But he was not so eager that he was going to get on his host's nerves.

"Where will I be meeting my next contact?" he asked rather off-handedly.

"We will set that up in the next day or so," came Fico's response. "You must have patience," he added, almost as an after-thought.

The next day went by slowly thought Majak. Almost as slowly as the trip over from Planet 104. But then it occurred. Fico came to fetch Majak without warning. "We must go now," he said. "The next contact is ready to receive you." And with that, the two men were on the move again. Angola was host to a lot of activity and it was easy to feel overwhelmed in the city's crowds. That is how Majak felt at the moment.

Fico led him to a back alley and through a series of switch backs and finally out into a place that Majak felt was going to be the death of them both if they didn't meet the contact soon. As it turned out, the contact happened to be none other than Fico's old mentor and friend, the Count of Angola. The Count was a contact of Sarah's and knew the story of JT. He was ready to make the necessary introductions when the time was right.

"So who are we going to meet?" asked Majak once again to Fico.

"Oh we are going to meet the grand master of the Angolan movement," promised Fico. "He is on call to be linking up with us tonight."

"Excellent. What shall I call him?" asked Majak.

"He just goes by the Count, but his real name is Aribo." Fico was direct and did not seem to have more for Majak.

"Ok, the Count it is then," responded Majak. "When will we be linking up tonight?"

"It will be a last-minute decision," said Fico. "We will have to await his orders."

And so, the waiting game began once again. But this time it did not last long. It was only a few hours until Fico came knocking on Majak's door with the news. They were to be meeting in a half hour at the closest watering hole which reminded Majak of the Unlucky Duckling. Then, when the time came the two men headed out for the short walk to the nearby pub. It was not far. Only a 10- or 15-minute walk. When they came to the door, there was a passcode procedure which Majak was used to by now. Once they were easily passed by the security check both men went inside and headed to the back. The Count was waiting for them there at a table in the corner. Pleasantries were exchanged and the men got down to business. The Count had several redundant questions Majak had already confirmed with Fin and Fico. Perhaps he was checking the validity of his story and to make sure it held water. Things seemed to be going smoothly and then the Count mentioned the elephant in the room.

"What do you know about the chosen one? The Federal Marine who has survived the neutrino cannon?" asked the Count.

"Well, to be honest, not much. Only what I have been told: that he has survived the new weapon and his medical condition is an anomaly. That he could be the key to understanding how to defeat the Confederation's new technology."

"Yes, that is pretty much it," continued the Count. "We don't know what to think yet of the situation but it is most disturbing."

"We intend to figure out what is the secret to this I hope," said Majak. "It could mean an early end to this war… and a favorable outcome for the Federation."

"Yes, you see the gravity of the situation," said the Count. "We intend to have you link up with the Marine in question and see if we can put our best heads together and come up with some solutions."

"He or she is here in Angola?" questioned Majak.

"Indeed, we have traced him here as it is his home world and he is on close watch by his medical team handlers while he visits his mother and some guests."

"Guests?" Majak and Fico asked simultaneously.

"Yes, we have reason to believe they have been paid a visit by spirits and mencas," said the Count. "They were also here searching for the sole survivor of Quai-14. It could be a coincidence but frankly I am not sure I believe in them… coincidences that is… at this point."

The Count told Majak they would be traveling to a remote corner of Anglen where they hoped to meet the parties in question including the young Marine who they believed possessed some sort of medical anomaly that allowed him to survive the neutrino cannon. They would be leaving that day. The trip would not be long but it would also not be direct. There were spies of every type lurking around every corner of the universe and they could not be too careful.

"Well, I'm ready when you are," was Majak's reply. Fico seemed ready to start on the trip as well. And so, the three travelers boarded some local transport shuttles and made a few change overs along the route. The journey took about 12 hours total but it went by fairly quickly. Majak was able to catch up on some sleep and so was Fico. The Count stayed awake and alert the entire journey.

When they arrived at the small apartment complex that Sarah called home, they were worn out from the trip but alert nonetheless. She greeted them at the portal in her typically surprised fashion.

"Hello, can I help you?" she stated through the monitor.

"Yes, we are here looking for JT Wayne and his traveling companions. We are friends and are not with the Federation or any allied force per se." The Count took the lead with the greetings and ensuing discussion. "I don't know if you recall, but we met a few times many years ago Ms. Wayne."

"Uhm, this is rather, uh, surprising," was Sarah's reply. "How do I know you are a friend to my son?" she continued.

"Would this do us justice in proving our intentions?" said the Count and he held up a piece of the Vissad's patch work. It was from a uniform collected via an embarking sailor prior to the ship's doomed last voyage. "We are here on a diplomatic mission from the friends of the Federation," he said. Majak wondered how the Count came by such a Federation memento but did not ask any questions.

Sarah paused. She did not know whether she could trust this old acquaintance and these strangers but her instincts told her to do so.

"OK, hold on a minute." She went back into the apartment and found JT and Aurelle to ask them if they knew anything about this latest development. They of course did not. But JT was used to strange unexpected events happening in his life at this point.

"I don't see why we should not follow this rabbit hole and see where it leads," was JT's initial response. "I agree," said Aurelle. "They might be able to help us make sense of the menca and spirit visit as well," she continued. So, Sarah opened the portal and let the new visitors in. JT initially thought the new situation might be tense but it was not. Majak, Fico and the Count were all cordial and happy to be allowed in as a new audience for JT and his family and their guests and companions. Moreover, Sarah briefly knew the Count already so she was trusting of him and his intentions. She and the Count had met many years prior not long after JT left for federal service. Sarah explained that having all the visitors arrive as they had was alarming. Be they a coincidence or not, she was concerned.

It was uncanny that everyone would come descend upon her in the space of less than a few days. She rarely hosted guests and kept to herself most of the time. And now, she had her son, his doctor handler, four mencas, a spirit, and now two new travelers brought by her acquaintance and contact, the Count of Angola all at her doorstep. Plus, one of these newest travelers (Majak) appeared to be of Gnorac lineage. It was downright distressing. Sarah's only coherent thought was to put all of these beings together in one place, and let them figure out what they needed to know. Her apartment was big enough, but it would be a bit cramped for the eleven of them all to gather there. She determined that a common room downstairs in her building would be the best location for this growing assembly.

Sarah had just the place in mind. Her landlord who also owned the building, had a meeting room out of the way and on the ground floor accessible from either the back stairs or the front of the building. She arranged to occupy this space with him directly within an hour of Majak and company's arrival. So, the meeting was set for the immediately following morning. Sarah was the host but she was not going to be the master of ceremonies of sorts. She left that to JT and

Aurelle to determine who would be fortunate enough to do those honors.

JT quickly determined that Aurelle should lead the gathering. She was ok with that so long as she had a backup in Lady Shera. The two strong willed women would make it happen. The morning came a few hours later and the gathering was set. Sarah collected and brought her new guests to the gathering room and they were able to meet and determine that JT was indeed the sole survivor of Quai-14 and he had in his blood certain antigens that allowed him to survive. They would need to find a medical facility to harvest the needed data from his antibodies to replicate the genes and produce some sort of a vaccine for mencas and any life forms impacted severely by the neutrino cannon. This was more easily said than done since Anglen was not exactly a population center. However, it did have a civilian Federation friendly medical facility in the heart of its downtown. This was where the group determined they needed to go. They concluded that they could make the trip back to Angola City for the larger hospital there if needed once JT was assessed in Anglen.

The medical facility in question in Anglen was not guarded or even secured from the public. Therefore, it was a bit of a risk to send JT there on his own. It was decided by the group that he would be escorted there by Dr. Gifford and one of the mencas, Farhale. Majak's handler, Fico, would provide an additional security element from outside the facility. Farhale was selected to go because as the menca representative he was strongest and bore the closest resemblance to a human. He was happy to do so. JT, Aurelle and Farhale headed to the medical center the next morning. JT was able to meet with some representatives of the Federation and have his body tested for antigens which proved to be resistant to neutrino sickness. The whole process took a few hours. But it was only so fast because JT had been pre-screened by the Federation and all protocols for security were already passed.

The medical center was cold and icy for JT but this was a small price to pay as he knew that his screening was going to be the key to understanding the neutrino sickness. Farhale knew that this was likely the most important mission of his life and so he guarded JT with great care. Aurelle also looked out for JT and ensured that the medical aspects of his treatment and care were attended to. Once JT had his CAT scan and MRI completed and all his vital signs screened, the doctors took him to a spectrometer, then a tagnometer where they ensured that JT's antigen count could be replicated. Fortunately, it could.

JT's body would be able to save the mencas from certain destruction and death via his blood pathogen levels and antigen readings. It was miraculous and overwhelming for JT but it was something that could and would save an entire race. When he completed his screening at the medical center, he was asked to stay in the hospital for safety and security reasons. He reluctantly agreed to do so. He would not be able to return to his mother, Sarah, at her apartment, but she was allowed to come see him.

JT had a private room and was allowed as many visitors as he wished. Lady Shera elected to come see him as soon as was practical and she was ever grateful for JT's role in becoming the savior of the menca race as it turned out. The entire process was surreal for JT but he was proud to do his part to help. The replication process for antigens and for the spectrometer to do its work for JT's pathogen comprehension took about a week. That was a very tense time for both JT and his care-giving group of friends.

Fortunately, during the ensuing week, the requested message from Adm. Vander found its way back to JT and company. Dr. Gifford's clearance and clout in the Federation helped ensure that the admiral, who was alive, did receive their request. He made a fairly quick decision to approve release of records for JT and the process was initiated for his treatment plan to be shared with the Anglen facility medical professionals. Accordingly, they were able to ascertain that JT's antigens and antibody levels could be understood and duplicated. Aurelle was ecstatic to learn that the admiral had survived the attack on the Amorhe. That not only had he survived the attack, but also that he was still in command of the situation and making decisions was a miracle by any account.

The mencas were able to take the replicated antigen and antibody information and pass it along with Pappa Fae to their Spiruthian representatives. The mencas and spirits both were able to benefit from the knowledge gained from JT's medical records and treatment information. While it was not replicable easily for humans, even mankind was able to learn how to reproduce his unique antibody signature and the antigens in question were able to save thousands of lives in the weeks following the wider release of the vaccination created from JTs antibodies.

The Count was intent on using Majak's information for good as well so he was able to pick the former Gnorac commander's brain for all the vessels in the Confederation which were equipped with neutrino cannons. This allowed the Federation to pre-position vaccination distribution points to areas threatened by those vessels. The war was not ended but it was drastically altered by the turn of events related to JT's medically introduced miracle.

Aurelle visited JT and stayed with him several nights at the Anglen medical facility and when JT was transferred to Angola City, she went with him. Her vigilance was that of a valiant protector and a bit mother-like. She was committed to JT not just because she cared about him, but because she cared about all human, Cybrinthian, and universal life-kind.

Aurelle wanted what was best for not only the Federation but all life forms. And that meant ending the war as soon as possible and negating the effects of the neutrino cannon. Of course, she did care for JT personally as well. Deeply. She was beginning to fall for the young Federal Marine. In truth, she could see herself staying with JT long past the end of the 4th I-S War. For certain, that would have to play out in time and there would have to be a lot of steps between now and the end of that war. Aurelle was hopeful but cautious.

The neutrino cannon's effects having been negated set up a near truce between the Federation and the Confederation for the short term. Although the end of the war was months if not years away, things were beginning to look better for peace in the Near and Far Universe and a cessation was talked about in military and political circles. Towards the end of the month after JT was treated and his antibodies replicated, Aurelle asked him if he had thought about the future.

"What do you think you'll do after the war?" she said to him in

Angola City.

"I suppose I will continue on as a Marine and do my duty to the Federation," he replied. "I don't see this war ending soon, but I also don't see it going on forever."

"I hope you are right about that," said Aurelle. And she really did hope JT was.

Chapter 28
Results

The result of the destruction of the reconnaissance-attack cruiser was a tremendous blow to the Gnoracs. The Suclesahe was not the newest or the most technologically advanced ship in the Confederation fleet. But it did carry the most closely guarded secret of the Confederation: the N-cannon. The weapon resulted in a dramatic turn of events in favor of the Gnoracs and the tide of the war… until now.

It was the bane of the Federation's existence. The neutrino cannon worked by harvesting molecular energy and dispersing it. It was an atomic weapon on steroids. Any life form generally succumbed to its awesome powers immediately. Spirits were a little different though. When and if they were able to enter the spirit realm in an alternate dimension and an alternate reality, it was not as effective against them. Especially with some form of preparation and allowed reaction to the weapon.

Group Commander Juselb Yfoar could not believe what he heard in the lieutenant's report.

"Sir the Suclesahe is under attack and has discharged its N-cannon. We believe she is hailing may-day and may be out of shield power or range of support." The lieutenant was sweating as he delivered the news to the admiral and his fleet's group commander.

"What?" is all the group's highest-ranking officer could manage in reply. Time ticked by.

"What are your orders Sir?... Sir?" asked Yfoar's one-star admiral executive officer. The two-star leader snapped out of his reverie. It took him more than thirty seconds.

"Send any available support and attack vessels within ES-neo to the Suclesahe immediately," he quipped.

"There are none Sir," responded a senior chief from the

navigational section of the battlecruiser's bridge. It was true. For the moment the Suclesahe was on its own. In truth it was already doomed. By the end of the thirty seconds or so it took Yfoar to respond with his order, the Suclesahe had already been dealt its crippling blow and acting Commander Gnauld was wishing he had donned his best dress uniform to go down with his ship. It was immaterial by the time Yfoar ordered all available Confederation vessels to speed to the lost ship's immediate aid.

What Yfoar was not planning on dealing with was the extreme loss of intelligence the Suclesahe's destruction would bring. The Federation was able to not only destroy the reconnaissance cruiser around Planet 104 with one of its newest small and fast class 1 attack cruisers, but also to record its break up. The Federation did so in detail and archived the footage. This piece of intelligence would be analyzed by scientists across the Federation. Both military and civilians would work together in learning how the new weapon these enemy reconnaissance cruisers carried worked.

The scientific community would be able to put the pieces of the weapon into enough of a working order, like pieces of a puzzle, to make understanding it a reality. This, in combination with what would ultimately be learned from the sole survivor of the weapon's point-blank use, would turn the tide of the war.

It did not happen immediately. It would take months and the remainder of the year for the results of this learned information to materialize into usable data for the Federation. Yfoar knew none of this as he stood on the bridge of his vessel lost in thought of how to respond. He knew he must act swiftly. He knew he certainly had not ordered or allowed anyone aboard the Suclesahe to fire the N-cannon. That privilege was not even reserved for him. It took authorization at the absolute highest level of command to allow employment of that weapon. It took a fleet admiral's ok. The weapon had only been fired once in combat so far: around Quai-14. It had worked there to the expected elation of the developers and command of the Confederation. But all had been reluctant to allow its use again mostly out of pure fear.

It was a fear of discovery and understanding. The Gnoracs believed the use at Quai-14 would be all that was necessary to bring the Federation to its knees. Much like the two atomic bombs dropped on Japan at Hiroshima and Nagasaki on Earth to end the Second World War thousands of years prior. The Confederation believed one use was all it would take. They were waiting for the Federation to come to its senses and surrender. Their wait was also one born out of fear. The Confederation leadership was afraid that continued employment of the new weapon increased its chances for the Federation to capture its information. This could lead to understanding and development of the Federation's own N-cannon. That could never be allowed to occur. In effect, they feared the Federation might piece together the neutrino's systems. Doing so with its components could balance out the war's recently shifted power dynamic.

This power dynamic had indeed changed hands to the Confederation since the new weapon had been used in its debut battle. There had been no survivors… save JT. Group Commander Yfoar was not thinking about that strategically at this point. His focus was on the present tactical reply needed to hopefully save his foundering reconnaissance cruiser. A mid-grade old cruiser which had fired the N-cannon without permission.

Yfoar feared his own position's safety. The fleet command would hold him responsible for the actions of his ship commander. Yfoar didn't particularly care for Capt. Majak. But he didn't dislike his junior ship captain either. There would have to be repercussions. Majak would probably be demoted. Possibly even fired. Yfoar would do all the damage control he could to save his own career but even that might not be enough.

Little did Yfoar know it was too late. The seeds of the turning of the tide of the war had been planted. His charge, the Suclesahe and its destruction had been the catalyst for that shift. What could or would he do? He would reluctantly do what he had to. What he was duty-bound as a Gnorac officer and senior leader to do. He would report the incident to fleet command and await their decisions. Of course, that too would take time. Unbeknownst to Yfoar, time was something he didn't have.

Chapter 29
All Together

The team of mencas, spirits, Majak and his handlers, in addition to Sarah visited JT and Aurelle regularly. The Angola City hospital staff was also welcoming and supportive of JT and his mission to help the Federation. As for the war's ending, it became a topic which was covered by all the major networks and news outlets.

It kind of became a known theme for discussion like in the waning days of WWII thousands of years prior. Towards the middle and end of 1945, the Allies knew the end was near, but did not want to jinx things so people treaded lightly around the topic. It was like that now in 1506AN almost 3,410 years later. The Federation knew the war would come to an end soon, but no one wanted to say so out of fear of the worst (a losing outcome) coming true.

Aurelle was not one, however, to sugar coat her thoughts.

"I think it will end sooner than we think now that we have your healing powers harnessed," Aurelle remarked to JT after one particularly grueling half-day in the tagnometer. "This can only go on so long."

"I hope you are right about that," said JT. "Although I love my profession, I wish there was no need for it."

"Amen to that." Aurelle was reflective. "While I love my profession as well, I never wish sickness upon people or beings just so that I can practice it."

"That is an apt comparison I had not really thought about," said JT. "I think we see eye to eye in that regard."

"I think we see eye to eye in many regards," and Aurelle came close to JT and held his hand, kissing him softly on the cheek.

"Aye… Aye-Aye doctor, I will second that notion," JT said playfully and he leaned in to kiss Aurelle as well, but he aimed not for her cheek but directly on the lips. The two embraced and held each other for a moment before realizing the door was open to JTs room and anyone could walk in or by at any moment.

"Let me get that," said Aurelle. "Just to give us a hint of privacy even if it is only fleeting." And she got up and went to get the door. At that moment, Sarah and Lady Shera approached the room entering the doorway and offered them some company.

"Mom, so happy to see you guys," said JT. "Lady Shera, it is my honor," he continued, trying to muffle his consternation at their timing's impropriety.

"We are here to tell you some news. And we are very happy to say that you will soon be able to join us back at home," said Sarah. "The doctors appear to be nearly complete with their work."

"That is good news, but won't they need me for continued monitoring and antibody reading?" asked JT.

"Well," said Aurelle, "It actually is a very good sign that they may not need you any longer." She was quiet as she spoke. "It means that they have figured out how to replicate the antigens and we are at or nearly at having a cure which can be distributed."

Only the four of them were in the room when Aurelle revealed this facet of the treatment plan.

Just then an alarm went off in the hospital corridor and most of the medical staff started running to and from all areas of the facility. The personnel seemed to be in a great panic as they would be whenever something drastic was occurring.

Aurelle immediately came to JT's side and told Sarah and Lady Shera to seek shelter under the safe wall against the door frame: a bit of a safety zone each room in the hospital had for emergencies.

"THIS IS NOT A DRILL. TAKE COVER IMMEDIATELY. ANGOLA CITY IS UNDER ATTACK," stated the announcement. But fortunately, the alarm sounding was just a precursor for a routine periodic drill the staff underwent every month. Indeed, despite its initial claim otherwise, it was only a drill. The next announcement was a cancelation for the previous one. The all-clear signal followed suit. The war was indeed winding to an end and people were happy for it. Especially Sergeant Wayne and Doctor Gifford who were perhaps the happiest and newest couple in the Federation. Sarah and Lady Shera elected to give JT and Aurelle some privacy and made up an excuse to leave the room for a bit.

"We'll be back, just going to check on things after that not-a-drill / drill," stated Sarah as she and Lady Shera left the room and headed down the hall. Their departure was certainly calculated thought JT and Aurelle. But of course it was subtly welcome.

"Wow, I guess we can expect more of that in the future?" said JT questioningly.

"More alone time? I hope so!" joked Aurelle.

"You know what I meant," said JT with a smile."

"I would definitely count on it," she replied.

Unfortunately, the winding down of the war came with it not only a sense that the end was near, but also a need to remain even more vigilant. Drills and preparations for last ditch efforts and desperate battles were rampant in the last months of the war.

An ancient history buff, might compare what happened in late 1506 to that of the WWII Battle of the Bulge in Europe when Germany made a last-ditch effort to punch through Allied lines to the coast and win the war with secret weapons like the V2 rocket or ME-262 jet fighter. It could even be compared to Japan's last ditch 1945 kamikaze efforts. No matter what the historical analogy, there was an increased sense of heightened security and preparedness.

Aurelle was counting on many things, both an increase in emergency drills and an increase in personal time with JT. She had a feeling he would be released soon from the prison-like atmosphere of the hospital and she very much looked forward to exploring JT's world, his home, with him. She also had a feeling they might have some trips in store for their futures. She hoped to visit the universes with him, under more favorable conditions than war.

She was lost in this daydream when JT pulled her from it gently.

"Hey, are you ok? What's going on in there?"

With that, Aurelle came close to JT and bent over his bed.

"Just thinking is all," she said. The two of them then embraced, this time for a long time. If anyone came to disturb them, they were completely unaware.

"I would definitely count on seeing more of you in my near future as well," Aurelle said with a smile.

"I definitely hope so," JT said as he leaned forward to kiss her softly but passionately. It was more than just a kiss. It was a bond. A bond between two service members who were growing to love one another and had experienced traumas together that no one should ever have to experience.

The newest and happiest couple in the Federation was off to a wonderful start as the war wound down to its last months and days. And for the first time in more than a month since he was blown off the Vissad and out into space where he nearly died, JT felt a welcoming peaceful sensation.

Although he still had no idea what the future would hold, after many weeks of difficult recovery and being on the run, JT was at peace. While he did not know what was specifically next in store and where it might take him, JT felt a serene calmness. A feeling that things were going to be ok. Were he to pick a word to describe it, only one came to mind. Finally in his life, JT once again felt *hooah*.

ANNEX 1
TIMELINE:

Major	3850 (AD*)	1st I-S War (1830~ years from now) = 0AN (3851=1AN*)
Years and		
Events	1260-1265	2nd I-S War
	1477-1480	3rd I-S War "Federal Alliance" vs Far Univ. and Gnoracs
	1478	JT is born
	1497	JT's father Gus dies
	1498	JT joins military
	1503+	4th I-S War (current event ongoing)
	1505	JT is assigned to Vissad
	1506	JT meets Aurelle / 4th I-S War peace talks begin

*AD – Anno Domini (L. - The year of our Lord)
*AN – After New Age (New sequential year numbering system)

ANNEX 2
CHARACTERS:

List of major selected participants:

Humans – (Those of slightly mixed ancestry)
>Sgt. JT John Thomas Wayne - (Sgt. 1ˢᵗ Class Federal Marine / also chancellor of Federal Alliance -no relation)
>Gus Wayne – (JTs adopted father (deceased)
>Sarah Wayne – (JTs adopted mother)

Cybrinthians/Mixed race – (Formerly at war with, now allied and intermixed with humans)
>Dr. Aurelle Gifford - (Doctor at St. Demitrius, also mixed race)
>Various minor players and military members

Gnoracs – (Alien race intent on destroying the Federation)
>Capt. Ganjin Majak – (Captain of Suclsahe)
>Lt. Cdr. Giova Krigsbie - (Senior officer on away party)
>Exec. Officer Remouln Kgnauld – (Gnorac chief / Acting commander of Suclsahe)
>Various minor military members abord the Suclsahe
>Juselb Yfoar – (Kgnauld's fleet commander)
>Jfandel - Gnorac (Engineer on bridge)
>Ytelfor – (Gnorac bridge officer)
>Clurfg – (Gnorac bridge Lt. & possibly a Federal spy)
>Col. Sjouft - Gnorac dep. exec. chief under Kgnauld on Suclsahe)

Spirit (Forms) – (Mage/telepath species from the planet Spiruthian)
>Delle – (Young spirit girl / friend of Fae)

Damon Lastalle – (Delle's father; a spirit of Flarhom Woods)
Faeruthan "Fae" - (Spirit who discovers human/mencas
in woods)
Quildevar - (old hermit in Flarhom Woods who Fae
mentions
to mencas/humans)
Papa Fae – (Fae's grandfather spirit, leads mencas)
Barnab Thanamereson – (Great ancestor of JT emigrated
from Spiruthean to Angola)

Gailena Lastalle (Thanamereson) – (Ancestor of JT in Angola
returned to Spiruthean)

Mencas – (Human-like old world dwellers of Spiruthian)
Lady Shera - (Lead menca in Flarhom Woods)
Valcor - (Menca warrior in Flarhom Woods)
Farhale - (Menca warrior in Flarhom Woods)
Jeanaviere - (Menca servant in Flarhom Woods)

Humans- (Descendants of old-world Earth after its destruction)
Adm. Haverston - (2nd Group commander)
Adm. Vander - (7th Fleet commander)
Dr. Alfus Simmons - (Head doctor on St. Demetrius)
Dr. Barnabus Quimby - (Doctor assigned to help Aurelle)
Commadore Theelson - (Amorhe commander)
Commadore (P) Djaimo - (Air wing commander of Amorhe)
Capt. Johanaston - (Amorhe security team leader)
Lt. Simonds - (Amorhe security team executive)
Lt. Shamus - (Stout female officer on Amorhe security team)
Pete Snodgrass – (Elderly distant relative of JT in Angola)

Mixed/unknown race -
Fico – (Initial helper and protector for Capt. (Cdre.) Majak)
Fin – (Senior boss in charge of underground helping Cdre.
Majak)
Aribo – (Count of Angola, helps Cdre. Majak)

ANNEX 3
CHAPTER SUMMARIES:

1	All Stop	(infirmary opening)
2	JT	(protagonist history)
3	1503	(storyline & mankind history)
4	Aurelle	(infirmary meeting)
5	War	(universes go to war up to present)
6	Memory	(JT recalls something)
7	Executive Chief	(far universe battle)
8	Spirits	(spirit Faeruthan)
9	Surprise	(spirit world discovery)
	Galaxy chart	(distance measurements to action areas)
10	Discussion	(infirmary –tagnometer, doctor meeting)
11	Note	(drill)
12	Meeting	(spirit world meeting)
13	Escape	(Aurelle and JT encounter bad news)
14	Gone	(Suclesahe commander on planet 104)
15	Debris	(Fae and mencas explore piece of ship)
16	7th Fleet	(Aurelle & JT in new location on the run)
17	Fico	(Majak and Fico meet on planet 104)
18	Thruster	(spirit world update to Debris story line)
19	Delle	(spirit world update, Papa Fae and Delle)
20	Screen	(Aurelle & JT experience Amorhe screen)
21	Majak	(Majak makes contact with Fico's friend)
22	Family Tales	(continue spirit tales and Quildevar visit)
23	Amorhe	(Aurelle & JT see attack launch to Europa)
24	Backroom Mtg.	(Fico introduces Majak to Fin)
25	Travelling	(spirit world travelers go to Angola)
26	Reunion	(Aurelle & JT land and meet mencas)
27	Another Traveler	(Majak goes to Angola)
28	Results	(Suclesahe fleet command assesses loss)
29	All together	(everyone links up)

ANNEX 4
SELECTED RANK/TITLE EXPLANATION

1st Pvt. (First Private) – a low ranking Marine or soldier often
    having been promoted once or twice after basic training.

Sgt. (Sergeant) – a generic title for many mid to high ranks
    of NCO enlisted members; also the lowest rank of NCO.

Staff Sgt. (Staff Sergeant) – one rank above Sergeant.

Sgt. 1st Class (Sergeant First Class) – one rank above Staff Sgt.
    JT's rank during most of the action.

Sgt. Maj. (Sergeant Major) – the highest enlisted rank; two
    ranks above JT's level.

Chief – a generic Naval term for several NCO upper enlisted
    ranks; sometimes used as a term for a ship commander.

Wt. Sgt. (Warrant Sergeant) – formerly called Warrant Officer;
    a rank between enlisted and commissioned officers.

Ens. (Ensign) – the lowest level Naval officer.

Lt. (Lieutenant) – the lowest two officer ranks in most branches of
    service. The second and third officer ranks in the Navy.

Maj./Lt.-Capt. (Major/Lieutenant-Captain) – a rank promotable
    above or below that of Captain; a junior or senior Capt.

Capt. (Captain) – the third officer rank in most branches of
    service; the sixth rank (just below Commodore or
    Admiral) in the Navy; often commands their own ship.

Col. (Colonel) – a high ranking officer in most branches of the
        military; the equivalent to a Capt. in the Navy.

Lt. Cmdr. (Lieutenant Commander) – a middle grade officer
        rank in the Navy just below that of Commander.

Cmdr. (Commander) – the leader of a unit in any branch; also
        a fairly high Naval officer rank.

Cdre. (Commadore) – Naval officer leader of a group of ships.

Adm. (Admiral) – Naval officer ranks (four different levels of
        Adm.) at the highest level of the officer rank structure.

Flt. Adm. (Fleet Admiral) – the highest of Naval officer ranks
        Equivalent to a five-star General in other branches.

Chancellor – The highest-level government official presiding
        over a council or senate of multiple nations.

Dr. (Doctor) – a highly skilled medical professional which
        could be a civilian or military member; if serving in the
        military, a Dr. will concurrently hold a military rank.

Doctrette – a very skilled medical professional just below that
        of Dr.; equivalent to a 21st century nurse-practitioner.

Count – a formal title for a highly regarded civilian; possibly
        a noble or royalty but not necessarily; a Count may, but does
        not often concurrently serve in the military.

Acknowledgements

I am deeply grateful to a host of people and organizations for helping me complete this work. In no particular order, they are: Fred, Liz, Chara, and Melina; the crazy family into which I was born. Tom and Don for joining that family. The Soldiers, civilians, and military family members of various units across the United States Army. The teachers and administration of Leavenworth, KS and Hillsborough County, FL. The Veterans of Foreign Wars. The Dept. of Veterans Affairs. The Boy Scouts of America. Betty Byers for loaning me a place to compose my thoughts. My editors: Charlotte R. Fernee, Esq., Elizabeth (Liz) S. S. Haeussler, M.Div., and Ronald (Ron) B. Kline, Jr. for their invaluable insights. EM Hughes and the great folks at New Book Authors. Finally, as my father used to call Him, the Great Scoutmaster in the Sky.

About the Author

Ricky Hausler has six years of K-12 classroom teaching experience. He owns a property management and refurbishment company. He retired with 20 years of Army military experience in leadership, operational, compliance, staff planning, cavalry/armor and public communication roles. He served as chief executive officer for Army organizations from 16 to 2,000-members. He is an airborne Army Ranger. He is qualified as the spokesperson for high level military executives and 10,000-member organizations. He was a senior level training manager and strategic planner.

Ric is a visual artist/photographer and author/editor with works displayed and printed in various military publications. He is an Eagle Scout, an awarded teacher with public school core curriculum English and special needs teaching experience, and an amateur historian tour guide with experience planning and conducting guided events. He is a multi-state property owner/manager with a registered active LLC. He holds a master's degree in education from Kansas State University and a bachelor's in history from the University of Texas. Ric was born in New Jersey and has lived all over the United States and the world. He enjoys running, motorcycle riding, veterans' events and resides in Tampa, FL.

Find Out More At:

www.rickyhausler.com

<u>Follow Ricky on social media:</u>

Facebook:
www.facebook.com/ric.haeussler

LinkedIn:
www.LinkedIn.com/in/ric-haeussler

X/Twitter:
@HaeusslerRic

Goodreads:
www.goodreads.com/user/ric-haeussler